CALLING ME HOME

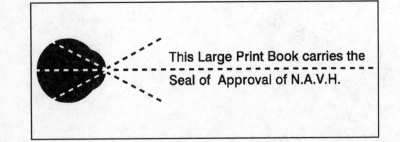

This Large Print Book carries the Seal of Approval of N.A.V.H.

CALLING ME HOME

JULIE KIBLER

WHEELER PUBLISHING
A part of Gale, Cengage Learning

GALE
CENGAGE Learning·

Detroit • New York • San Francisco • New Haven, Conn • Waterville, Maine • London

GALE
CENGAGE Learning®

Wheeler Publishing Large Print Hardcover.
The text of this Large Print edition is unabridged.
Other aspects of the book may vary from the original edition.
Set in 16 pt. Plantin.

LIBRARY OF CONGRESS CATALOGING-IN-PUBLICATION DATA

Kibler, Julie.
    Calling me home / by Julie Kibler. — Large Print edition.
        pages cm. — (Wheeler publishing hardcover)
    ISBN-13: 978-1-4104-5597-0 (hardcover)
    ISBN-10: 1-4104-5597-1 (hardcover)
    1. Interracial dating—Fiction. 2. Female friendship—Fiction.
    3. Self-realization in women—Fiction. I. Title.
    PS3611.I27C35 2013b
    813'.6—dc23   2012043686

Published in 2013 by arrangement with St. Martin's Press, LLC.

Printed in the United States of America
1 2 3 4 5 6 7 17 16 15 14 13

For Grandma, for what might have been

But all lost things are in the angels'
  keeping,
    Love;
No past is dead for us, but only sleeping,
    Love;
The years of Heaven will all earth's little
  pain
    Make good,
Together there we can begin again
    In babyhood.

— from Helen Hunt Jackson's
poem "At Last"

1
MISS ISABELLE, PRESENT DAY

I acted hateful to Dorrie the first time we met, a decade or so ago. A person gets up in years and she forgets to use her filters. Or she's beyond caring. Dorrie thought I didn't care for the color of her skin. No truth to that at all. Yes, I was angry, but only because my beauty operator — hairdresser they call them these days, or *stylist,* which sounds so uppity — left with no notice. I walked all the way into the shop, which is no small effort when you're old, and the girl at the counter told me my regular girl had quit. While I stood there blinking my eyes, fit to be tied, she studied the appointment book. With a funny smile, she said, "Dorrie has an opening. She could do you almost right away."

Presently, Dorrie called me over, and certainly, her looks surprised me — she was the only African-American in the place, as far as I could tell. But here was the real problem: change. I didn't like it. People who didn't know how I liked my hair. People who made the cape too tight around my neck. People who went away without any warning. I needed a minute, and I guess it showed. Even at eighty, I liked my routine, and the older I get, the more it matters. Picture me now at almost ninety.

Ninety. I'm old enough to be Dorrie's white-haired grandmother. And then some. That much is obvious. But Dorrie? She probably doesn't even know she's become like the daughter I never had. For the longest time, I followed her from salon to salon — when she wouldn't settle down and stay put. She's happier now, has her own shop these days, but she comes to me. Like a daughter would.

We always talk when Dorrie comes. At first, when I met her, it was just the regular stuff. The weather. News stories. My soap operas and game shows, her reality TV and sitcoms. Anything to pass the time while she washed and styled my hair. But over time, when you see the same person week after week, year after year, for an hour or more, things can go a bit deeper. Dorrie started talking about her kids, her crazy ex-husband, and how she hoped to open her own shop one day, then all the work that entailed. I'm a good listener.

Sometimes, she'd ask me about things, too. Once she started coming to my house, and we got comfortable in our routine, she asked about the pictures on my walls, the keepsakes I have on display here and there. Those were easy enough to tell about.

It's funny how sometimes you find a friend — in the likely places — and almost immediately, you can talk about anything. But more often than not, after the initial blush, you find you really have nothing in common. With others, you believe you'll never be more than acquaintances. You're so different, after all. But then this thing surprises you, sticking longer than you ever predicted, and you begin to rely on it, and that relationship whittles down your walls, little by little, until you realize you know that one person better than almost anyone. You're really and truly friends.

It's like that with Dorrie and me. Who would have thought ten years later we'd still be doing business together, but so much more, as well. That we'd not only be talking about our shows but sometimes watching them together. That she'd be making excuses to stop by several days a week, asking if I need her to run any errands for me — wanting to know if I'm out of milk or eggs, if I need to go to the bank. That I'd be making sure when I ride the cart around the grocery store, after the Handitran drops me off, I put a six-pack of her favorite soft drink in the basket so she'll have something to wet her whistle before she starts on my hair.

One time, a few years back, she looked embarrassed when she started to ask me a question. She stopped mid-sentence.

"What?" I said. "Cat got your tongue? That's a first."

"Oh, Miss Isabelle, I know you wouldn't be interested. Never mind."

"Okay," I said. I was never one to pick something out of people that they didn't want to tell.

"Well, since you begged me . . ." She grinned. "Stevie's got this concert at school Thursday night. He's got a solo — on the trumpet. You know he plays the trumpet?"

"How could I miss it, Dorrie? You've been telling me about it for three years, since he auditioned."

"I know, Miss Isabelle. I'm kind of over-the-top proud when it comes to the kids. Anyway, would you like to come with me? To see him play?"

I thought about it for a minute. Not because there was any question whether I wanted to go, but because I was a little

12

overcome. It took too long for me to find my voice.

"It's okay, Miss Isabelle. Don't feel like you have to. My feelings won't be hurt and —"

"No! I'd love to. In fact, I can't think of anything I'd rather do Thursday."

She laughed. It's not like I ever went anywhere, and Thursday was a boring night for television that year.

Since then, it hasn't been uncommon for her to take me along when the kids have special events. Heaven knows, their father usually forgets to show up. Dorrie's mother usually comes, too, and we have nice little chats, but I always wonder what she thinks about my being there. She studies me with a shade of curiosity, as though she can't fathom any reason for Dorrie and me to be friends.

But there's still so much Dorrie doesn't know. Things nobody knows. If I were going to tell anyone, it would likely be her. It would definitely be her. And I think it's time. More than anyone, I trust her not to judge me, not to question the way things happened and the way things turned out.

So here I am, asking her to drive me all the way from Texas to Cincinnati, halfway across the country, to help me tend to things. I'm not too proud to admit I can't do this alone. I've done plenty for myself, by myself, as long as I can remember.

But this? No. This I can't do alone. And I don't want to anyway. I want my daughter; I want Dorrie.

2
DORRIE, PRESENT DAY

When I met Miss Isabelle, she acted more like Miss Miserabelle, and that's a fact. But I didn't think she was a racist. God's honest truth, it was the furthest thing from my mind. I may look young, thank you very much, but I've had this gig awhile. Oh, the stories they tell, the lines around my customer's closed eyes, the tension in her scalp when I massage it with shampoo, the condition of the hair I wind around a curler. I knew almost right away Miss Isabelle carried troubles more significant than worrying about the color of my skin. As pretty as she was for an eighty-year-old woman, there was something dark below her surface, and it kept her from being soft. But I was never one to press for all the details — could be that was part of the beauty of the thing. I'd learned that people talk when they're ready. Over the years, she became much more than just a customer. She was good to me. I hadn't ever said so out loud, but in ways, she was more like a mother than the one God gave me. When I thought it, I ducked, waiting for the lightning to strike.

Still, this favor Miss Isabelle asked me, it did come as a surprise. Oh, I helped her out from time to time — running errands or doing easy little fix-it jobs around her house, things too small for a service person, especially when I happened to be there anyway. I never took a dime for it. I did it because I wanted to, but I supposed as long as she was a paying customer — even if she was my "special customer" — there might always be some tiny sentiment it was all an extension of my job.

This? Was big. And different. She hadn't volunteered to pay me. No doubt she would have had I asked, but I didn't have any sense this request was a job — simply someone to get her from point A to point B, with me being the only person she could think of. No. She wanted me. For me. I knew it as clearly as I knew the moon hung in the sky, whether I could see it or not.

When she asked me, I rested my hands on her shoulders. "Miss Isabelle, I don't know. You sure about this? Why me?" I'd been doing her hair at her house going on five years, since she took a bad fall and the doctor said her driving days were over — I'd never have deserted her because she couldn't come to me. I'd become a little attached.

She studied me in the mirror over her old-timey vanity table, where we rigged a temporary station every Monday. Then Miss Isabelle's silver-blue eyes, more silver every year as the blue leeched out along with her youth, did something I'd never seen in all the time I'd been cutting and curling and styling her hair. First, they shimmered. Then they watered up. My hands felt like lumps of clay soaked by those tears, and I could neither move them nor convince myself to grasp her shoulders a little tighter. Not that she'd have wanted me to acknowledge her emotion. She'd always been so strong.

Her focus shifted, and she reached for the tiny silver thimble I'd seen on her vanity as long as I'd been going to her house. I'd never thought it was especially significant — certainly not like the other keepsakes she had around her house. It was a thimble. "As sure as I've been of anything in my life," she said, finally, tucking it into her palm. She didn't address the why of it. And I understood then; small as it was, that thimble held a story. "Now. Time's wasting. Finish my hair so we can make plans, Dorrie."

She might have sounded bossy to someone

else, but she didn't mean it that way. Her voice freed my hands, and I slid them up to wrap a lock of hair around my finger. Her hair matched her eyes. It lay upon my skin like water against earth.

Later, in my shop, I paged through my appointment book. I took inventory, checked what kind of week I had ahead. I found a lot of empty space. Pages so bare, the glare gave me a headache. Between silly seasons, things were quiet. No fancy holiday hairstyles. Prom updos and extensions for family reunions were still a month or two down the road. Just the regular stuff here and there. Men for brush cuts or fades, a few little girls for cute Easter bobs. Women stopping by for complimentary bangs trims — it made my life easier when they left the damn things alone.

I could postpone my guys. They'd drop twenties still crisp from the ATM on the counter like always whenever I could get to them, happy not to explain to strangers how they wanted their haircuts. I could even call a few to see if they'd come by that afternoon — I was usually closed Mondays. The nice thing about leasing my own little shop the last few years was I made the rules, opened on my closed days if I wanted. Even better, nobody stood over my head, ready to yell or, worse, fire me for taking off without notice.

Surely Momma could handle the kids if I went with Miss Isabelle. She owed me — I kept a roof over her head — and anyway, Stevie Junior and Bebe were old enough all she really had to do was watch their steady parade in or out of the house, call 911 in case of a fire on the stove, or send for the plumber if the bathroom flooded. Heaven forbid.

I ran out of excuses. Plus, if I were honest, I needed some time away. I had things weighing on my mind. Things I needed to think about.

And . . . it seemed like Miss Isabelle really needed me.

I started making phone calls.

Three hours later, my customers were squared away and Momma was on board to watch the kids. The way I figured it, I had one more call to make. I reached for my cell phone, but my hand stopped mid-air. This thing with Teague was so new — so *fragile* — I hadn't even mentioned him to Miss Isabelle. I was almost afraid to mention him to myself. Because what was I thinking, giving another man a chance? Had I misplaced my marbles? I tried to scoop

19

them up and dump them back into my stubborn skull.

I failed.

Then the ring of the shop phone yanked me from my thoughts.

"Dorrie? Are you packing?" Miss Isabelle barked, and I snatched the receiver away from my ear, almost flinging it across my tiny shop in the process. What was it with old folks shouting into the phone as if the other person were going deaf, too?

"What's up, Miss Izzy-belle?" I couldn't help myself sometimes, playing with her name. I played with everyone's name. Everyone I liked anyway.

"*Dorrie,* I warned you."

I cracked up. She breathed hard, like she was leaning on her suitcase to zip it closed. "I think maybe I can clear my calendar," I said, "but no, I'm not packing yet. Besides, you called me at the shop. You know I'm not at home." She insisted on calling the shop's landline if she thought I'd be there, though I'd told her a hundred times I didn't mind her calling my cell.

"We don't have much time, Dorrie."

"Okay, now. How far is it to Cincinnati anyway? And tell me what to bring."

"It's almost a thousand miles from Arlington to Cincy. Two good days of driving each way. I hope that doesn't scare you off, but I hate flying."

"No, it's fine. I've never even been on an airplane, Miss Isabelle." And had no plans to change that anytime soon, even though we lived less than ten miles from the Dallas–Fort Worth airport.

"And what you'd wear anywhere else will do, mostly. There's just one thing. Do you even own a dress?"

I chuckled and shook my head. "You think you know me, don't you?"

In truth, she'd rarely seen me in anything besides what I wore for work: plain knit shirts paired with nice jeans, shoes that didn't kill my feet when I stood in them eight hours a day, and a black smock to keep my clothes dry and free of hair clippings. The only difference between my work and not-work clothes was the smock. Her question was valid.

"Surprise, surprise, I do have one or two dresses," I said. "Probably wrapped in cleaner bags and mothballs and stuffed way in the back of my closet, you know, and maybe two sizes too small, but I've got a few. Why do I need a dress? Where are we going? To a wedding?"

There weren't many events these days where a nice pair of slacks and a dressy top wouldn't do. I could only think of two. Then Miss Isabelle's silence brought the foot I was gnawing into the spotlight. I winced. "Oh, gosh, I'm sorry. I had no idea. You never said —"

"Yes. There will be a funeral. If you don't have anything appropriate we can stop along the way. I'll be glad to —"

"Oh, no, Miss Isabelle. I'll find something. I was mostly kidding about the mothballs and such." While her packing noises continued in the background, I tried to remember exactly what I owned that would do for a funeral. Exactly nothing. But I had just enough time to run by JCPenney's on my way home. Miss Isabelle had done plenty for me — big tips every time I did her hair, bonuses whenever she could think up an excuse, greeting me with a pretty sandwich when I didn't have time to eat before her appointment, acting as a sounding board when my kids were making me crazy — but no matter how close we felt, I would never let her pay for this dress. That crossed some kind of line. But why hadn't she mentioned we were going to a *funeral?* That was an important detail. Make that a critical detail. When she said she needed to tend to some things, I'd assumed she meant papers that needed to be signed in person, maybe for property to be sold. Business. Nothing as big as a funeral. And she wanted me to take her. Me. I'd convinced myself I knew her better than any of my other customers — she was my *special* customer, after all. But suddenly, Miss Isabelle seemed a woman of mystery again — the one who'd eased into my hair chair all those years ago carrying burdens so deep inside, I couldn't even speculate about them.

Miss Isabelle and I had spent hours in conversation over the years — more hours than I could count. But it occurred to me now, as much as I cared for her, as much as she trusted me to accompany her on this journey, I knew nothing about her childhood, nothing about where she came from. How had I missed it? I had to admit I was intrigued, though I usually left mystery solving to television personalities — figuring out how to pay my bills was mystery enough for me.

Miss Isabelle apparently got things all zipped up, and she startled me out of 007 mode. "Can we leave tomorrow, then? Ten A.M. sharp?"

"Absolutely, young lady. Ten A.M. it is." It'd be tight, but I could manage it. Not to mention, what'd felt like technicalities before seemed weightier now.

"We'll take my car. I don't know how you young folks tolerate those tin cans you drive these days. Nothing between you and the road at all. Like navigating a ball of aluminum foil."

"Hey, now. Tinfoil bounces. Kind of. But sure thing, I'll relish driving that big boat of yours." Too bad CD players were still mostly options back in 1993, when she'd purchased her fancy Buick. I'd tossed all my cassettes. "And Miss Isabelle? I'm sorry about —"

"I'll see you in the morning, then." She cut me clean off, mid-sentence. She obviously wasn't ready to discuss the details of this funeral yet. And me being me, I wasn't going to dig.

"Fuel?" said Miss Isabelle the next morning as we prepared to pull out.

"Check."

"Oil? Belts? Filters?"

"Check. Check. Check."

"Snacks?"

I whistled. "Capital C-H-E-C-K."

I'd arrived at Miss Isabelle's an hour earlier than we planned to leave, so I could run the car by Jiffy Lube. They gave it a once-over; then I stopped for gas and other necessities. Miss Isabelle's list of road snacks had been well over a mile long.

"Oh, shoot," she said now, snapping her fingers. "I forgot one thing. There's that Walgreens down the road."

What on earth could she need so fast it required a detour before we ever left town? I shifted into reverse and eased the Buick down Miss Isabelle's driveway and into the street. At the corner, I waited an extra long time, patiently allowing cars to pass until I had a long, clear space to enter.

"If you drive like this the whole time, we'll never get there," Miss Isabelle said. She studied me. "You think because you're accompanying an old woman to a funeral, you have to act like an old woman, too?"

I snorted. "I didn't want to get your blood pressure up too early, Miss Isabelle."

"I'll worry about my blood pressure. You worry about getting us to Cincy before Christmas."

"Yes, ma'am." I touched the tips of my fingers to my forehead and pressed down on the accelerator. I was happy to see she was as ornery as ever — death wasn't a happy business, after all. She still hadn't given me all the specifics — just that she'd received a call, and her presence was requested at a funeral near Cincinnati, Ohio. And, of course, she couldn't travel alone.

At Walgreens, she pulled a crisp ten from

25

her pocketbook. "This should be plenty for two crossword puzzle books."

"Really?" I gaped at her. "Crossword puzzles?"

"Yes. Wipe that look off your face. They keep me sane."

"And you plan to work them riding in the car? Do you need Dramamine, too?"

"No, thank you."

Inside, I surveyed the magazine racks and wished I'd asked for more details. To be on the safe side, I chose one puzzle book with large print — "Easy on the eyes" — and one regular. I figured I had things covered either way, and I'd only have to make one trip inside the store. Who'd ever heard of people actually buying those crossword puzzle magazines unless they were sitting around in the hospital? Though come to think of it, I remembered my granny working them when I was a little girl. I guessed it was an old-people kind of thing to do.

I carried them low, against my hip, as if I were toting a giant-size box of feminine products to the lone male checker in a grocery store. But the cashier didn't even look at the magazines as she slid them across the scanner. Or, for that matter, at *me*. I waved away her monotone offer to bag them. It seemed wasteful, in spite of my shame.

Back in the car, Miss Isabelle eyed my purchases at arm's length. "That'll do. Now we'll have something to talk about on the road."

I imagined the topics crossword puzzles might inspire: Four across: "a pink bird." *Flamingo.*

We were going to be on Interstate 30 a long, long time.

We were quiet on the road the first hour or so, though, me trying to navigate mid-morning Dallas traffic without cussing too much, each of us a little awkward in this different environment, each of us still mired in thinking of other things, other places.

My mind was on the night before, right about when things had calmed down. My new dress, tags removed, hung in a clear bag on the door of my closet. Bebe had settled into bed with her book. Stevie Junior was keeping company with a video game, as usual, except when his fingers were busy texting his girlfriend a hundred miles per hour.

And my mind was on Teague — on why I'd felt so nervous about calling him. Maybe, just maybe, it was that little voice chanting in my mind, Teague, Teague, out of your league!

But my phone had gone off, the ringtone I'd assigned him a few weeks after our first real date. *Let's get it on* . . .

Oh, yeah. Corny.

"How's my special lady?"

I know, I know. With anyone else, I'd cringe and head for the hills. What a line. But with Teague? I could hardly explain how it made me feel.

Okay. I'll try.

Special. It made me feel special.

"Doing good, doing good. Yourself? Kids all settled in for the night?" I said. I tried to be all chill whenever he called me, tried to let him know he couldn't melt me with a few words, slurp up whatever he wanted from the puddle, then leave the leftovers for someone else. I'd kept men at arm's length for years now after so many mess-ups — theirs *and* mine. But where other guys took my attitude as a brush-off and my reluctance to get physical as some kind of kinky game, eventually calling me a prude and running the other way, Teague kept hanging in there. And I'd let him see past my cool a few times. The littlest peek at the woman who longed for a real man in her life. Somehow, I felt like he was willing to wait for that woman to make up her mind.

28

When I hung up ten minutes later, I pinched my arms and slapped my cheeks. Was I awake or sleepwalking? "I understand," Teague had said. "You're doing the right thing, helping your Isabelle out this way. I'll miss you, but I'll see you when you get back." And: "Give your mom my number. I'm used to dealing with kid stuff." True! He was a single dad of three! "If she needs help with Stevie or Bebe or anything at all while you're gone, I'm a phone call away."

I wanted to believe he *would* be there if they needed something. I almost could. Almost.

I hadn't known what to expect when I told him I was leaving town out of the blue. I knew exactly how Steve, my ex, would react, even before I dialed his number. I had to let him know, in the event the kids needed something — in which case I wished them good luck. Steve whined. He berated me. Asked how I could up and leave my kids for days. Funny how he never seemed to take a good, hard look in the mirror, right?

And other guys in the past? When I left with the kids for a little visit somewhere, it was always "Oh, baby, I can't survive without you. Don't leave me." But as soon as I passed the city limits, I swear someone fired the starting gun: *Gentlemen* (in the loosest sense of the word), *start your engines!* Then they'd run to the nearest whatever to pick up a substitute girlfriend. When I got back, spied the lipstick on their collars, and smelled the knockoff perfume in their cars, they'd be all "I'm sorry, girl, but what am I supposed to do when you go and leave me? You know it's really you I want, but I just didn't know for sure."

Right.

But Teague had surprised me. Again.

There was something *different* about a man who called after a first date to see how you were doing and to make sure you'd had a good time. Now, not too desperate. It's not like he called five minutes after I turned the dead bolt, all pitiful because I hadn't invited him in, already shooting me signals I'd made Yet Another Bad Choice. No, Teague had waited a respectable twenty-four hours, and then he hadn't even acted like we had to set up another date immediately, though he'd said he wanted to see me again. And now, more than a month and several dates later, whenever I thought of him, a single word still came to mind: *Gentleman.* The real kind.

Well, okay, two more words — Wayne Brady. Because Teague reminded me of the

Let's Make a Deal game-show host with his goofy smile and sense of humor and hot-in-a-geeky-hot-kind-of-way looks.

Other men had held doors for me on first dates. They'd even offered to pay, though I always insisted on splitting the check — me and my independence, we are joined at the hip, the shoulder, and the elbow. But this went beyond the basics. We were well past first-date status, which I'm pretty sure surprised both of us, and the new had worn off some. Yet he still held doors, still picked up the check unless I managed to snatch it first and hold on tight. Still treated me, in every respect, like a lady.

With Teague, I suspected, the gentle went all the way to the bone.

But I wasn't sure I trusted myself. Could I recognize a real man? A trustworthy one? Like they say, Fool me once, shame on you. . . . Fool me ten times and I am plumb stupid.

On the bridge over Lake Ray Hubbard, we were still crawling through heavy traffic, but Miss Isabelle finally piped up. "You met Stevie Senior in your hometown, right?"

He was just plain Steve, but I never bothered to correct her. And I tried to remember what I might have told her. Steve was forever calling me at work, interrupting my appointments, and if I didn't drop everything, next thing I knew, he'd show up in person. How well that went depended on his mood and choice of beverage the night before, so I tried to keep him on the phone and out of the shop. I figured a customer came in for a nice, relaxing getaway along with a hairstyle, even if only for an hour. I made every attempt to keep my personal history and problems low on the radar, but it didn't always work. And, because things with Miss Isabelle were different — she'd listened to me gripe about my kids' dad for years — she had at least a piecemeal picture of him. It seemed she would have picked up all the details in the process, but maybe not. After all, I'd been surprised to realize how little I knew about her childhood, right? But I didn't really want to start over at the beginning.

"Yep. High school sweethearts," I said, hoping my simple answer would refresh her memory.

"And you married right out of high school." She paused expectantly, as though she wanted the whole enchilada all over again. I scraped a fingernail back and forth across a tiny rough spot on the otherwise-cushy armrest.

"What's three down, Miss Isabelle?"

She fumbled to bring her readers back to her nose and peered at the puzzle she'd started. With a triumphant smile, she read the clue. "It's a seven-letter adjective for 'much adored; favorite.' "

"Uncle."

"Uncle? That's only five letters."

"By 'Uncle,' I mean I give up."

"You can't give up. You didn't even try."

"Trying to drive is what I'm trying to do."

"Beloved."

"Beloved?"

"Yes. That's the answer. Used in a sentence — Stevie Senior was your high school beloved."

So much for the crossword puzzle book steering us away from uncomfortable topics.

"Maybe Steve was be-loved at one time. Now he's downright be-noying."

"That's so sad."

"Tell me about it." I sighed, and I felt my resolve to keep it simple weaken. "I always thought he'd be the steady one. A good husband and father. He was our school district's star athlete, racking up touchdowns in the fall and three-pointers all winter. And championships. Everyone figured he'd go off to college on a scholarship and make something big of himself. And I figured after he graduated, we'd get married and ride off into the sunset. House, babies, picket fence. Everything." My voice trailed off, and I listened to the echo of my disappointment.

"Things don't always work out the way we expect, do they?"

"Shoot, Miss Isabelle. You know how it turned out. I got the babies. I have the house. But I figured wrong on the picket fence. And Steve."

A little later, I said, "What about you, Miss Isabelle? Did you have a high school sweetheart? Your husband — was he yours?" I knew folks back in her day usually did marry young and stick with it for decades. I wondered if the men were different back then, or if the women were just more patient with them when they acted like idiots.

Her answer just then was a sigh, and it seemed filled with pain. Rib-cracking, chest-expanding, larger-than-life pain. I felt I'd said the wrong thing, but I couldn't take it back.

She flipped to a new page in the crossword puzzle book and proceeded to fill in answers as though her life depended on it. Presently, she said, "My high school sweetheart . . . that's a story."

It all started and ended with a funeral dress.

3
ISABELLE, 1939

Nell released a lock of sizzling hair from the iron and smoothed it into a wave that dangled in front of my ear. "You might be the prettiest girl at the party," she said, distracting me from scrutinizing my plain black dress. I tilted my head to study her handiwork, then shook it, carefully, so as not to disturb the style she'd struggled more than an hour to perfect. Stubborn and wiry, my dark hair curled on its own in inappropriate patterns. For now, the crimped waves hung around my face like a neat fringe of prisms on a lamp shade, but soon it would resemble fuzzy rickrack instead. I'd have to tuck a ribbon in my pocket to tie it back later.

I snorted. "Nell Prewitt, I'll never be the prettiest girl at any party, but you're a dear for trying." My face had been called intelligent, and my features striking, but never pretty, even as a toddler in short dresses and patent-leather shoes. As I neared my seventeenth birthday, I'd accepted that the boys at the parties my mother forced me to attend would always look beyond me to the softer girls, the ones framed in pastels and ruffles. But I'd have loathed having the word *pastel* associated with me ever, whether applied to my appearance or my personality. I was even halfway pleased with being called serious — what I heard from the other girls more than any other adjective. "Oh, Isabelle, why so serious?" they asked, biting their lips and pinching their cheeks as they studied their reflections, checking the dabs of powder and rouge their mothers allowed them, or peered over their shoulders to ensure the seams of their stockings traveled straight and narrow down their calves.

"Anyway," I said to Nell, "I should start doing my own hair. Women nowadays are independent. They do things for themselves."

Nell flinched as though I'd slapped her. Too late, I realized my statement had been careless and hurtful. She'd helped me dress and primp for parties and special occasions for years — not just as a household employee but also as my friend. We'd never attend a party together, of course, so the preparations became our private rite of passage. But as close as we were — more like dearest confidantes than a privileged girl and her mother's housemaid — she wouldn't feel free to voice her hurt that I would so easily cast her aside.

"Oh, Nell, I'm sorry. It's not you." I sighed and clutched her sleeve, but still, Nell didn't speak. She shifted away ever so slightly and returned to her task. It felt as though a tiny fault line had opened, creating a space between us never there before.

And as close as we were, and in spite of the fact that I'd shared nearly every detail of my life with Nell, I couldn't tell her my plans for the evening. Of course, I'd make my appearance at Earline's party. But then I'd tell my hostess Mother needed me at home. And then I'd escape.

I'd had as much as I could tolerate of the tame game nights the parents threw to keep the kids in our sheltered little clique out of trouble, away from the temptation of the glamorous nightclubs only minutes away in Newport — even creeping up on the outskirts of our little town. When I was younger, I'd watched my aunt prepare to go out in the evenings, her body draped in daring knee-length dresses that flowed loosely around her hips and shoulders like the gowns of a Greek goddess, trimmed with brilliant jet beads or sequined embroidery that glimmered like peacock feathers. Her escorts called for her in dark, close-fitting suits that showed off their broad shoulders. My mother stood by, lips thinned and brows knitted together. She complained her sister's wildness would bring us all down. After all, we had a reputation to uphold as the family of Shalerville's only physician. But Aunt Bertie had her own income, and she reminded my mother she wasn't dependent on the family. Mother had no choice but to let her come and go as she pleased.

Sometimes, when she returned late at night, I stole into her room and begged her for stories about the places she'd been, and Aunt Bertie, her clothing perfumed with cigarette smoke and her breath with something sweet and sharp and vaguely dangerous, would tell me — the abbreviated version, I suspected now. She whispered about the other women's dresses, their escorts, the music, the dancing, the games, the rich food and drink. These glimpses were enough to illuminate the differences between her adventures and the stuffy events my parents attended. They returned home in their somber attire less enthusiastic about life than when they left — which seemed to defeat the purpose of going out. Eventually,

Aunt Bertie left, my mother no longer willing to put up with her disregard for our house rules. Only weeks later, her inebriated escort turned the wrong way and drove his car off the bluff, plunging both of them to instant death. I stood by in shock as Mother claimed it was Auntie's comeuppance for living that way — even as grief sent her to bed for days. We kids were kept away from the funeral. I wept alone in my room while she and Father attended the service, and we never spoke of her sister again.

I still missed Aunt Bertie desperately. And tonight, I hoped to glimpse some of the things she'd whispered about. Early in the week, I'd been assigned to sit with a new girl at school. Trudie had moved into Shalerville from Newport to live with her grandmother. The other girls insulted or ignored her — anyone new to our town was suspect anyway, but someone from Newport was doubly so. She didn't seem to mind. She tossed her head at their slights, at their concerted efforts to cut her out of the lunch line or shift themselves so she had no room to sit at their tables — not that she'd have wanted to. Trudie told me her mother had moved her to get her away from the bad influences of Newport — "Newpert," she called it, running her vowels and consonants together even more than the rest of us did, no clear syllables — and she wasn't thrilled with the change of environment. I asked her what living in town was like, and she seemed amused at my interest, though also surprised, considering how the other girls shunned her. The next day, she drew me aside after class and said she'd be going home for the weekend. She asked if I'd meet her downtown Saturday night. She'd show me around. Perhaps we would even slip into the new nightclub her friends from home had been yammering about — a clean little place with good music and dancing.

My face tingled with some unidentifiable emotion as I considered her offer. I knew, as much as I hated the confines of my own life, I didn't belong in Newport at night, but I was tempted. My parents would never agree, of course, which meant I'd have to sneak away. But I wouldn't be alone once I got there, and I'd have the chance to observe something I'd only heard about before. Nobody else I knew would have had the nerve to go.

Later, I overheard my older brothers gossiping with a friend about the Rendezvous, the newest club down on Monmouth Street — classy, they said, an okay place to take their girls, but they grumbled that they wouldn't make it there Saturday because they'd promised them a movie. Their bad luck — my opportunity. It eased my nerves that they thought the Rendezvous was nice enough to take a date there. Some. The next day at school, I told Trudie I'd go, even while the lining of my stomach clenched in a warning. We planned to meet outside Dixie Chili Saturday at seven-thirty.

Nell gave my hair one last tug as an automobile horn tooted outside the window. "Best I can do. Run on now. Enjoy your party."

Impulsively, I hugged her. "Oh, I will, Nell. You wait and see. I'll have all kinds of stories to tell you tomorrow." She flattened herself against the door. I couldn't tell what flabbergasted her more — my sudden affection or my excitement about a Sunday-school class party, which she knew I'd hated since round two, when I realized they'd all be the same. Same boys and girls. Same dull games. Same bunch of nothing.

"Miss Isabelle?"

I glanced over my shoulder.

"You be careful."

"Oh, Nell. What kind of trouble can I find?"

She pursed her lips and crossed her arms

42

and leaned against the door again. She looked so much like her mother — worry shaping her whole demeanor — it startled me. But I fluttered my hand behind me and clattered down the stairs, slowing at the landing. I knew my own mother waited near the front door to approve my dress and hair and general attitude.

"I heard you," Mother said. "Ladies do not run. And never down stairs." She tapped my shoulder with her eyeglasses.

"Yes, ma'am." I ducked away and hurried past her.

"Why are you wearing *that* dress? It's not at all right for a party." She frowned.

"No reason," I said.

Daddy rounded the corner, his glasses low on his nose as he studied the newspaper he carried. He pushed them up and looked at me. "Hey, ladybug. You look stunning. Have fun at the party."

Mother sniffed. "The Joneses are driving both ways this evening? Home no later than eleven-thirty."

"Of course, Mother. I might turn into a beggar girl if I'm not home before midnight."

"Isabelle, mind your manners." She watched me all the way down the walk. I suspected she would watch until long after

43

the car was out of sight before she closed the door.

I'd deflected her question about my dress, but I couldn't avoid it altogether. Sissy Jones poked her head out of the window from the rear seat of her father's car. "Isabelle. Darling. Whatever are you wearing? You look as though you're dressed for a funeral in that old rag."

She was correct. I'd worn this same plain, dark dress to my grandfather's funeral a few months earlier — but it was the one thing in my wardrobe that didn't scream schoolgirl. I'd sifted through the costume jewelry Aunt Bertie had given me to play pretend with all those years ago until I found a beaded brooch not too battered from my games and hid it in my bag, as well. I'd fancy up my plain old dress by pinning the brooch to its collar, and that would have to do. Surely not every woman who frequented the Newport clubs would be as glamorous as my aunt had been. Ideally, my simple dress wouldn't stand out anyway. My only goal in meeting Trudie, after all, was to see how things were beyond the invisible fence the mothers of Shalerville had erected to keep us kids in line.

"Silly old Cora," I said to Sissy. "She took all my pretty dresses to freshen and press days ago and hasn't returned them. What else could I do?" I crossed my fingers behind my back as I produced the fib. Nell's mother's face would have betrayed her bewilderment at my statement even more than Nell's had when I'd hurt her feelings earlier. Cora often seemed more a mother to me than my own, nearly always the one to clean me up when I fell and scraped my knee, or hug me to her soft, laundry soap and starch–smelling bosom when I ached from my mother's unpredictable rebuffs. But I needed some excuse for my unusual attire, and what Cora didn't know couldn't hurt her.

"Thank you for picking me up, Mr. Jones." I settled myself next to Sissy. "I won't need a ride home. I'm leaving early."

Sissy tilted her chin. The line of her eyebrows judged me. "And how do you propose to return home?" she asked. Everyone knew Mother didn't allow me to walk home alone in the evening.

"Oh. Well. Nell and her brother will come for me."

"So you'll leave before dark? Why bother with the party if you must leave so soon?"

Negroes weren't allowed on the streets of our town after sundown, but I hadn't counted on Sissy's homing in on that so

45

quickly. She was sharp, however, too clever for her own good and never my favorite friend, though our mothers had thrown us together since we were tots. She was one of the girls who'd been so rude to Trudie, and I smiled, imagining her reaction if she knew my real plans.

"I can only stay an hour or so, but you don't think I'd miss Earline's party, do you?" My eyes challenged her. She knew exactly how much I hated these parties, but she also knew I'd never sacrifice an escape from my house on a Saturday evening. "I'll be gone well before dark."

In fact, this was good luck. Now I had the perfect excuse to make my stay at Earline's party short. After all, I wouldn't want to get Nell and Robert in hot water — or worse — by keeping them in town after sunset. They'd need to be on their way home well before the sun threw its last rays upon our monotone little burg.

Mr. Jones dropped us at Earline's, and I tolerated the usual flurry of hugs, squeals, and pecks on the cheek from the other girls. Several gave my dress the same suspicious once-over Mother and Sissy had, but I brushed their comments away. Next time, I'd bring out the jade cigarette holder Aunt Bertie had left behind — the one hidden in my purse tonight along with my contraband makeup. I'd sneak a cigarette from my brothers when they weren't looking, then ask one of the pimple-faced boys at the party to light up my Camel and see how the girls liked that.

I counted the minutes by seconds until I'd fulfilled my obligation. After an hour precisely, I thanked Earline and went to the kitchen to find her mother. "Thank you for inviting me, Mrs. Curry. The party was swell, and Mother says hello."

"Already leaving, hon?" she asked.

"Yes, ma'am. Mother needs help setting up for a special family dinner tomorrow." I told a half-truth. Mother had invited my brothers' sweethearts to eat Sunday dinner with us. She planned to stay home from church to finish her preparations, but Mrs. Curry and Mother rarely spoke except at church. By the time they saw each other again, Earline's mother would have completely forgotten my early departure.

"I didn't hear a car," she said.

"Our housemaid and her brother are walking me home. I'm going to wait out front." Mrs. Curry squeezed my shoulder absently and returned to slicing the tiny bland sandwiches that seemed compulsory at these things. I think some of my friends actually enjoyed them.

"Careful, dear. We'll see you in the morning."

"Night, Mrs. Curry."

I tiptoed back through the main hallway, pausing to glance into the front room, where my peers spun Freddy around and around so he could pin the tail on the donkey. We were far too old for the game, but the girls still became giddy and hopeful when boys they had crushes on tried to pin the donkey tail to their dresses, so they kept it up. Poor Freddy, who was so blind without his specs I never knew why he bothered with the blindfold, stumbled all over. With everyone distracted and laughing at him, I slipped out and pulled the front door nearly closed behind me — not enough to make the click that could alert someone to glance out the window and discover my solo departure. An unescorted young lady on the streets of Shalerville, Kentucky, population fifteen hundred — plus or minus three — was hardly uncommon, but the whole town knew how my mother was. In less than half a mile, though, I'd catch a streetcar and take the short ride to Monmouth Street.

But now my nerves played up. Even by daylight, Newport was worlds away from the cleaner, loftier streets of Shalerville. Fast men and women crowded the sidewalks day and night, and our preacher thundered about the gambling rooms and dens of prostitution.

But I replayed my brothers' words. They might venture into shady businesses when it was just the fellows, but surely not with their girls — nice girls who had no idea what imbeciles Jack and Patrick could be.

I'd stick close to Trudie, and if, in the end, my courage deserted me, I'd turn tail and run.

Trudie arrived at the chili parlor late, fifteen minutes after our agreed-upon time. I gawked, speechless, as she clattered up the sidewalk toward me. She scarcely resembled the plain girl I sat beside at school. She wore a low-cut dress sewn from a print of emerald green diamonds on white. The clingy dress, her lipstick — brighter times four than what I'd applied on the streetcar — and her shiny spectator pumps gave her the appearance of a woman far older than our true ages, even though she'd admitted to me at school that she was a year older than most in our class, having fallen behind at Newport High.

"You came," she squealed, and swung me around in a hug as I fought to keep my balance. "My ma would *never* have let me come out if I hadn't told her I was meeting a nice girl from Shalerville. Just what she hoped for when she shipped me off . . .

"C'mon," she said, and pulled me after her until we arrived at the Rendezvous. I was surprised she was in such a hurry to get there, having assumed we'd stroll Monmouth Street for at least a few moments, making good on her promise to show me the nighttime sights. But I let her drag me along. Inside, I hurried to keep up with her long stride — she was taller by half a foot — as she wove through the crowd, heading toward the bar. No sooner had we found a spot nearby than a young man bought her a drink, which she tossed back quickly, and he swept her onto the dance floor. She gave me a half hearted apology — "Isabelle, you don't mind if I dance, do you, honey?" — then whirled away in the man's arms.

I shrank against the wall at first, out of breath, my jaw slack. Trudie was worldlier than I'd imagined — even knowing her mother had moved her to get her away from trouble. But I hadn't expected to be deserted like this. What was I to do? I almost left then.

Instead, I stood alone against a wall almost thirty minutes while Trudie circled the dance floor. I stole glances at the crowd while I tapped my foot, pretending to be engrossed in the swing music a trio played on a tiny stage elevated half a foot above the rest of the place. Men and women mingled around the room or danced on an oval parquet floor enclosed within a brass rail. Others dined at tiny tables against the rail or at the edges of the room. Everyone smoked and drank cocktails, and the laughter and music and clink of stemware combined in a song I'd heard only in movie theaters.

I'd never felt more out of place in my life. At my classmates' parties, I belonged, more or less, even if I didn't quite fit in from my perspective. And I'd been dead wrong about the black dress. Now I wished I'd worn a print, no matter how juvenile my flowered dresses had seemed. I made a sad little pigeon in this flock of pretty birds. I reached into my handbag for Aunt Bertie's cigarette holder. Maybe if I gave the appearance I smoked, I'd look less like a little girl and more like a woman. Just as I produced the holder, a handsome young man in a navy blue suit headed across the smoky room toward me.

"You need a light, doll?"

I glanced at Trudie on the dance floor. She seemed to be having such a grand time.

In a split second, I made a decision. "I need more than a light," I said. "Got a cigarette on you?" I hoped the way I dropped my voice low and clipped my vowels to speak with a confidence I didn't truly possess gave the appearance I knew what I was doing.

He fished a pack from his pocket and inserted a cigarette into Aunt Bertie's holder. I leaned toward him, the jade tip between my lips, and imitated what I'd seen. I inhaled while the man held a match to the end of the cigarette. The heat rushed toward my throat, more powerful than I'd expected. I held my breath until the urge to cough passed.

"What're you drinking?" the fellow asked.

"Nothing yet."

"What's your pleasure?"

I searched my memory of the movies my friends and I had watched. The leading men and glamorous starlets always had cocktails in hand. "Sidecar?"

"You got it." He snapped his fingers at a passing waiter. In no time, I held a glass of the sweetest and sourest and most delicious thing I'd ever tasted — once I overcame the shock of my first sip. This was working out fine now. Just fine. I emptied the glass quickly. Too quickly? I had no idea. Another appeared in my benefactor's hand, as if by magic, and I accepted it, too.

"First time here?" he asked.

"Is it obvious?" I rushed ahead before he had a chance to answer. "I heard it was a swanky place." The ash at the end of my cigarette curled and stretched like a scorched snake, undulating as though it would drop to the floor any second. I held it away from me, horrified. My companion swept a crystal dish from an alcove. I tapped the ash into the dish.

"Thanks. You might have saved my life, Mr. . . ."

"Name's Louie. Short for Louis, but all my friends call me Louie." He winked. "How's about a dance?"

"Sure, um, Louie." He seemed like a gentleman, his suit starched and spotless, and he certainly was Johnny-on-the-spot with the cigarette and cocktails, not to mention capturing my runaway ash. I pressed the glowing end of my cigarette into the dish and returned the holder to my bag while Louie whisked away my second glass, along with several he'd emptied.

He led me to the dance floor, where he drew me close — closer than I liked. I held my arms stiff to force a little breathing room between our shoulders and hips. My head felt swimmy, and the design of the parquet floor now seemed more detailed than my brain could absorb. I trained my eyes on Louie's chin. When the song ended, I backed away, relieved to see Trudie had left the dance floor and was making her way back to the bar with her partner. And I needed to use the ladies' room. But Louie grabbed my arm and steered me toward a door at the back of the room. "Let's grab some fresh air, sweets. It's stuffy in here."

He pressed his fingers into my arm, and I tried to shake his hand off. He grinned and held on. "Holding you too tight? Sorry — this place is a furnace. I'm in a hurry to get outside, where I can breathe." He loosened his grip but pressed me steadily toward the door. I craned my neck to see if Trudie saw us leaving, waved frantically in her direction, but she stood near the bar, unaware of me or my dilemma, her head thrown back in laughter at something her companion had said, a fresh drink in her hand. Louis pushed me through the door. I hoped to simply chat with him a minute, then escape back into the club and find the ladies' lounge without being rude.

We leaned against a brick wall in the alley. It had grown dark in the short time I'd been inside the club, and the sour aroma of trash made me watch my toes carefully in case of scavengers in the shadows. A couple of fellows and one young woman stood to the side, in hysterics at a story one of the men told. When their laughter dwindled, they turned to go inside.

Louie tapped his cigarette pack on my arm. "Need another cig, doll? Hey, wait. You know my name, but I don't know yours. Not fair."

"Isabelle. And I'm afraid I have to go. I need to find the ladies' room." I turned to follow the others.

"Oh, no, you don't." Louie grabbed my arm again. His grin widened. He must have sensed my discomfort, though, because his face changed. I no longer thought of him as handsome at all. Now his features seemed harshly drawn, not chiseled, and his smile menacing. "Don't rush off, now. I want to have a little talk with you. Isabelle, hmm? Sweet name for a sweet gal."

I peered over my shoulder toward the door, wishing for more patrons of the club to emerge. But the heavy door firmly ignored my silent pleas to open.

"Really, Louie, I have to go inside. My friend will be looking for me. And . . . I think I'm going to be sick." I pressed my hand to my mouth. It wasn't an excuse. My stomach churned, and I truly thought the drinks might come back up. Before, I hadn't felt their effect, other than the buzzy, halfway pleasant feeling in my head. Now I felt positively green, and Louie's aftershave, combined with the stink of rotting trash, overwhelmed me.

"You're fine. Come on. I just want a little something. You know, in exchange for the cigarette and drinks. A little kiss . . ." He pulled me close and pressed his mouth against mine. If I'd thought I might vomit before, now I felt almost certain. His lips, fleshy and clammy, stank of alcohol and tobacco, and his teeth ground against mine when he forced his tongue inside my mouth.

I gagged and tried to shove him away. "Hey! Stop! I'm not like that. I'm not even old enough to be here. Let me go!"

"The only kind of girl who comes here without a date is that kind, dollface. Age don't matter. Don't play games with me, now. Makes me impatient."

He held me even tighter, pressing one hand against my rear and sliding his fingers through the thin silk of my dress toward places I knew he shouldn't be touching. With his other hand, he cupped my bosom and squeezed — hard. I yelped, and now I fought back, scratching whatever I could reach. "Leave me alone! You can't —" He laughed and kept on. I struggled harder, but the alcohol made me clumsy and slow, like a bad dream where I couldn't move fast enough to save myself.

The club was the last building on the block, and a figure in the shadows caught my eye, emerging from around the corner at the end of the alley. "You heard the lady, sir. Let her go." The voice — familiar, low, and full of character — startled me. I tried to place it. I strained to see the man's face as he drew closer. Louie turned his head, relaxing his hold long enough for me to slip from his grasp. I scrambled away, still holding my breath and trying not to vomit. Near the door, I hesitated, thinking that maybe I should run as far away from the place as fast as I could. I owed Trudie nothing at this point — not after how she'd abandoned me the minute we'd gone in the place.

"Hey, who do you think you are, fella? She's my date. You niggers should mind your own business anyway." Louie lurched toward the other man, and I recognized him then — not really a man at all. Close to my age.

"Robert?" I said, and Nell's brother looked over his shoulder at me, giving Louie a clear opportunity to land a punch square on his jaw. Robert staggered backward, and he ended up nearly in my lap as we both fell. He sprang back up, his hands held out in front of him.

"Please. I don't want trouble, sir. I just want to escort Miss Isabelle home. Her daddy's highly respected around here — you don't want trouble, either."

"Aw, go chase yourself. She was asking for it. Besides, why would I listen to a nigger?" Louie drew his fist back again, then glanced at me.

Robert cringed at the insult Louie had thrown so casually, but he squared his shoulders. "She's only a girl, sir. Don't even know what she's doing. Not to mention, Doc McAllister wouldn't be happy to hear about nobody messing with his daughter. And her brothers . . ." Robert shook his head. I was sure Louie had no idea who my father was, but Robert spoke the words with conviction. And my brothers didn't go easy on anyone who offended them. *They* probably *did* have a reputation around Newport.

Louie finally relaxed his stance. "Doc McAllister . . . and the brothers . . . should keep a closer eye on little Isabelle, then, not let her go tramping around places she don't belong. Newport girls have a reputation — public school by day, public service by night. They come around juice joints for their paychecks." He spit, landing a gleaming wad of phlegm on the toe of Robert's shoe, and stumbled toward the club. I realized now that he was probably drunk. I'd been too naive to know the difference — or too affected by drink myself. "I'll be on the lookout for you," he called back to Robert. "If I see you again, you'll regret the day you crossed my path." He slammed inside.

I buried my face in my knees, sobbing now that I no longer believed my virtue — or my life — was in danger. "I'm so stupid," I cried. "What was I thinking, coming here . . . staying here? . . . I should have turned right around when Trudie pulled me inside that place."

Robert pulled his cap from his head and threaded it through one hand with the other. Obviously, he agreed with my self-assessment, but of course he wouldn't say so out loud. I reached toward him. "Help me up, Robert, please."

The thought of touching my hand must have made him nervous. Now he twisted his cap as though he might wring water from it.

"Oh, come on. There's nobody else here. Help me!"

He tugged me to my feet, then dropped my hand like a hot coal. I slapped my palms down my skirt, knocking off the debris of countless fights and drunken assaults that had probably happened in this very spot. I grew more ashamed as I realized how silly I'd been. I'd thought myself so grown-up. Louie had surely recognized me for the inexperienced little girl I was, playing dress up, playing like I knew what to do with a cigarette and a cocktail and a man. Playing right into his trap.

"Miss Isabelle. Why you here? Who's this Trudie you met up with?" Robert slipped awkwardly between the speech patterns I'd heard my whole life from his mother and Nell and the more refined language he'd been learning across the Licking River at Covington's Grant High — the only one in his family to go that far in school. Nell had quit after the seventh grade to work full time for my family, and Cora, wise as anyone I knew, had never even attended.

"I told you. It was dumb. I thought I'd be smart and find something more exciting than the silly parties my parents send me to every Saturday. The way my brothers talked about this place, it seemed like a good idea. Trudie's my friend from school." I almost choked now on the word friend, angry at myself for my own naïveté. "She ditched me. And the rest was more than I could handle." Robert snorted, and I pictured my brothers, too, my foolishness clear now that I wasn't kidding myself. Jack and Patrick were lazy, and they could be rough. I'd be wise to disregard 90 percent of everything they said. And now I wondered about Trudie, and the things Louie had said about Newport girls. Her mother had sent her away for a reason — maybe the reason he'd named. I shuddered at my gullibility.

"I'm going to have to walk you home now, Miss Isabelle. Can't leave you here alone. Your daddy would have my hide if I did."

I stared at him. If standing up for me here in this alley was risky, Robert's crossing into Shalerville after dark was downright danger-ous. "Oh, no. You can't do that. If anyone saw you —"

"It'll be fine," he said. "I'll think of something by the time we get there. We'd best get away from this place, though, before that idiot comes looking for you. Or me." He shook his head and gestured down the alley. "C'mon, Miss Isabelle. Let's go now."

I fell into step beside him, though I sensed the instant he dropped slightly behind me when we crossed into open territory at the end of the alley. I slowed my pace to match his again, but he slowed, too, until I sighed and resigned myself to the superior position. We'd both had a lifetime of practice.

The irony of my situation struck me again — my earlier lie to my friends had come partially true. Here was Robert to escort me home, though Nell was probably snug in bed by now. "How did you find me?" I asked.

"Your momma, she sent me to Lemke's for extra eggs for your Sunday dinner." I pictured Danny Lemke looking down his nose at Robert. Danny's family had been in the States only a few generations, yet Danny acted more entitled than anyone I knew. "When I left your house again to head home, I saw you walking out of town like you knew where you was going. I thought to myself, This ain't good, so I followed after you. I was afraid you'd end up in a mess."

"Boy, were you right." I sighed.

"I waited there at the corner, hoping before long you'd come back out with your friend and go on home, but then I heard you fussing with that crumb, so I peeked around, and I saw you struggling."

"Oh, Robert, I'm so glad you followed me. I'm afraid to think what might have happened." I sighed, shaking my head at the predicament I'd brought upon both of us.

"You're okay now, Miss Isabelle. But what will your momma say if I show back up with

62

you? And at nighttime? Both of us'll be in hot water for sure. And we'd best hope to God Mr. Jack and Mr. Patrick ain't around. That Louie guy would fare better than me with those two."

"No way I'm letting you take me all the way home." He was right. The gates of hell would flood open if Jack and Patrick saw me alone with Robert. They were always harping about honor, about protecting the white woman — even when they treated their own girls like playthings, discarding them when they grew bored.

"We'll see."

I knew he wouldn't argue with me, not out loud, but he seemed resolute in his plan to escort me all the way to my doorstep.

We waited at the streetcar stop, mainly silent, but starting and stopping conversations in awkward fits when others passed. Generally, people were going into town instead of away from it; it was still early for a Saturday evening in Newport. We had the stop to ourselves.

Robert had functioned as a vague fixture in my life, the son of the woman who'd always cared for me, the brother of my childhood playmate, until she began to work for my family, as well. Once we were beyond childhood, Robert ran errands for my mother at times, assisted my father with odd jobs around our home, or stopped in to eat with Cora or Nell in the kitchen on occasion when he wasn't in school. He was just a boy to me — a more or less insignificant one.

I knew he was patient and kind — even when we were small and Nell snubbed him, told him he couldn't join in as we played in the gardens behind the house, he shrugged good-naturedly and returned to his own quiet games of creating entire worlds, drawing borders in the dirt, then populating his countries with pebbles and twigs. I knew he was responsible and respectful — he followed his mother's directives without complaining, carried out the tasks set him with little need for correction. I knew he was intelligent — Daddy often tutored him in math or science at his desk in his office on Shalerville's Main Street, sometimes alongside me, whereas he'd thrown up his hands in frustration over my brothers' inattention to their schoolwork and seeming inability to make more than average marks in school.

And somehow, even in my indifference, I knew Robert was special. He had an aura that set him apart — not just from the few colored boys I'd encountered here and there but from the white boys, too. An intensity smoldered in his eyes, contradicting the steadiness that, in any other young man, might have been a sign of a lack of complexity.

Yet I had never once intentionally contemplated his dreams and goals.

That night, I did. I wanted to know them in detail. But before I could ask, the trolley arrived, its squealing brakes interrupting our conversation.

I sat alone at the front of the car, scrubbing away rouge and eye kohl — which seemed more childish than grown-up now — with a handkerchief damp from my tears, while Robert sat at the rear, watching me like a hawk guarding its nest from a distance. We descended separately, one stop early, not quite to Shalerville, then fell into step again outside. The driver hesitated, eyed me with concern when only Robert and I alighted from the trolley, but I smiled reassuringly and he released the brake. I could have taken the streetcar all the way back into Shalerville, but, of course, being with Robert changed everything. The driver wouldn't let him off the car there.

In a valley between the Licking River and the bluff we walked along toward town, South Newport's steel mills worked around the clock. From this height, the bright lights, belching smoke, and machinery's rhythmic clamor appeared independent of human manipulation. I hadn't viewed their eerie, almost fantastical nighttime facade so close in years. I hesitated, my previous desire to return home as quickly as possible taking a new shape — a desire to suspend the moment. Robert's mood seemed to match mine, and we gazed at that distant, alien world together; our attempts at conversation now seemed extraneous.

At the edge of town, I slowed even more. This, I'd seen my whole life, every time we'd crossed in or out of Shalerville. It was more or less wallpaper, no different from the trees by the side of the road. But tonight, my chest tightened with a painful sense of shame. Robert had saved me from something I could scarcely imagine, yet he was forbidden from seeing me home by virtue of this rule I'd never questioned before. I read the sign as if for the first time: NIGGER, DON'T LET THE SUN SET ON YOU HERE IN SHALERVILLE.

4
DORRIE, PRESENT DAY

We were officially away from Dallas traffic, and before long, pine trees bordered the sides of the road, taller and thicker and closer together with each mile. I began to feel crowded, trapped in my own body, like I always had growing up in East Texas.

Miss Isabelle's inevitable sadness, however — I'd been expecting it, waiting for it — seemed strangely soothed by her memories of her Newport adventure. And I won't lie. The story of Robert, her unlikely savior, surprised me, and the thought of this sequestered little town both angered and intrigued me. I wanted to know more. But wouldn't you know, the exit for *my* home-town rose from the pavement, and damn, if that wasn't right when Miss Isabelle decided it was time to stop for lunch.

"Here?" I gawked at her.

"What's wrong with here? It's your home-town. And look, there's a Pitt Grill on the other side of the overpass. I always wanted to eat in a Pitt Grill."

I groaned, with a sneaking suspicion that stopping here had been her plan all along. I'd lived in this three-light and a Wal-Mart bump in the road my whole life until Steve and I moved to Arlington to make a fresh start — that is, so I could work somewhere that paid more than minimum wage and build my clientele until I could set up my own shop while Steve continued his shining career of not having a career. But I'd never once considered eating at the Pitt, not even when I lived nearby. And after all the time I'd been away, I suspected not much had changed in East Texas. I'd had no reason to visit for years, and wasn't sure I wanted to experience that part of my life again. Unfortunately, the Pitt was the only restaurant near the highway.

"Oh, come on. It'll be an adventure," Miss Isabelle said. Now, if it was even possible, she looked excited about the Pitt, while I, in turn, squirmed. But I shrugged, pleased she was back to herself — and knowing the argument was futile anyway.

"Whatever you say, Miss Isabelle." I exited and pulled across the bridge and into the dinky parking lot. Logging trucks idled on the gravel in an open space between the restaurant and a cheap motel. "Looks like Paul Bunyan eats here, too," I observed. Miss Isabelle rolled her eyes and hobbled her way into the greasy spoon — the only way to describe our first view of the place. I followed patiently, holding my breath and praying she wouldn't stumble on anything. I knew she'd slap me if I offered my arm. A waitress in a pink polyester zip-up uniform dress stuffed an order pad in her pocket and a pen behind her ear and hurried toward us. She grabbed a menu from a stack at the counter and greeted Miss Isabelle.

"One, hon? Nonsmoking?"

Miss Isabelle's jaw fell slack inside her mouth, causing her chin to droop unattractively low against her neck. She glared at the waitress. The woman's assumption that we weren't together — even though we were standing close enough to kiss! — came as no surprise to me.

In the meantime, the waitress hardly glanced my way, but about that time, I recognized her. By golly, if it wasn't Susan Willis, queen of the homecoming court the year Steve and I graduated. Steve had been king and escorted her across the field, to the dismay of her redneck daddy and nearly the whole town. I could tell she didn't recognize me back, though. I almost felt embarrassed for her, so I hoped maybe her amnesia would hold. I couldn't imagine being the most popular girl in school, only to end up waitressing at the Pitt Grill nearly two decades later. I'd always thought she had pretty hair in high school, but good heavens, if she didn't need to take the eighties bangs down a notch or three now to bring her into the new century and get a few lowlights to tone down that piss yellow.

Miss Isabelle tsked with her tongue and said, "Table for two. If that's a problem, we'll sit at the counter."

"Two?" Susan's head shook just enough for me to detect it, but she pulled herself together. "Oh, yes, ma'am, we have a table. Of course we do. Right this way."

As we followed, I wondered, What would she think of my life? Sure, I owned my own business, but I lived month to month, constantly worrying about whether I'd be able to pay the bills and feed and clothe my kids. How was that any better than slaving away for tips at the Pitt, probably trying to support a couple of kids because your no-good husband had run off? Maybe we had more in common than I'd ever dreamed we would in high school.

Or maybe not. Maybe her husband owned the Pitt Grill.

Susan kept glancing curiously — and not especially covertly — at us the whole time we ate. I couldn't decide if it was because she was nosy, trying to figure out the relationship between Miss Isabelle and me, or if she was trying to place me. I actually preferred the first. But I knew my luck had run out and Susan had recovered her memory when I heard, right as Miss Isabelle and I were about to exit the Pitt, "Why, Dorrie Mae Curtis, is that *you*?"

I cringed and made a quarter turn, still hoping for mercy. But Susan had stopped halfway through sliding the five-dollar tip Miss Isabelle had left at our table into her zip-up polyester pocket. The look on her face confirmed our reunion was unavoidable.

"Hi, Susan. You're right. It's me, Dorrie. How're you doing?" I crossed my fingers, hoping she'd give an easy answer, something standard, like "You're looking great! Can you believe it's been almost twenty years?" and let me go on.

But my luck was all out of whack by then.

"Oh, Dorrie, you wouldn't believe me if I told you the half of it. Me and Big Jim bought this place back in '98" — so my backup prediction was correct: Hubby owned the Pitt! — "and then Big Jim got too fat for his britches, as if that's a surprise. A gen-u-wine redneck real estate tycoon. He left me for some young thing he met over to the new roller rink we built. He got custody of the rink and I got the Pitt, and it's all I can do to keep it running and chase after our boys. All four — who are following right in their daddy's footsteps, far as I can tell when I can hog-tie them for a minute."

So, prediction number one was correct, too. I wasn't sure how to feel about that. "Uh-huh, well, I'm sorry to hear — gosh, good to see you landed feetfirst." I shrugged. No response could do that story justice.

"What about you, Dorrie Mae? What's been happening with you all these years? I bet you and Steve have a whole football team by now. Y'all moved away, right?"

Like she could have missed us if we were still in that little town. And I wished she'd stop calling me Dorrie Mae. I'd had to move nearly two hundred miles to lose the name I'd hated all through school. I glanced over at Miss Isabelle, who clutched her handbag tight against her waist, her lips twitching. If she called me Dorrie Mae when we got to the car, I'd screech.

"Sounds like you got the football team. I only have two — a boy and a girl. We're down the road in Arlington, in DFW. Steve and I, we're divorced, too."

"Aw, that's too bad," Susan said, screwing her face into something resembling sympathy — *as if she hadn't just told me her equally, if not more, pitiful tale!* "You and Steve. Me and Big Jim." She sighed loudly. "Remember when me and Steve were homecoming queen and king? Just goes to show all those yearbook predictions don't mean a thing, huh? I always thought the four of us would be the ones with fairy-tale endings."

"You and me both, Susan. Well, listen, my friend and I need to get back on the road. We've got a long trip ahead."

"Oh, well, where ya headed? Who's this nice lady?"

Susan was obviously desperate for conversation with anyone over the age of eighteen who didn't wear a trucker's cap and have syrup stains on his elbows. I felt bad for her, I did, but not enough to keep this surreal reunion going much longer. I glanced at Miss Isabelle.

"Dorrie and I are traveling to the Cincinnati area for a family funeral," she said. Her politely icy tone dared Susan to say more. She obviously hadn't completely forgiven Susan for assuming we were separate parties.

"Oh, I'm so sorry to hear." Susan's gaze

toggled — me, Miss Isabelle, me, Miss Isabelle. She looked more bewildered than ever about how the two of us fit together. "Well," she said. "I won't keep you, Dorrie Mae. Now you be sure and stop in again next time you come through. If I'd recognized you earlier, your tab would have been on the house. Both of yours, of course. Can I at least send you ladies with drinks to go? Coffee? Cokes?"

"No, we're good. Thanks anyway. You take care, Susan."

I turned and headed deliberately toward the door. This time, I let Miss Isabelle follow.

"How exactly does one go from homecoming king to someone who mooches off his ex-wife?"

Ouch. Miss Isabelle never minced words, but that stung. I'd figured she'd have all kinds of nosy questions for me after Susan let that particular cat out of the bag, but we hadn't even been back on the interstate for two miles, heading for the state line. "Oh, Miss Isabelle, it's such a long story. You don't want to hear about it. Hey, what's twenty-three across?"

Miss Isabelle sniffed and tugged her crossword book out of the console, folded back on itself to a half-completed puzzle. "Twenty-three across: 'a rodent with a case of stage fright.' "

"That's a cinch. *Possum.*"

"Seven letters. *O-possum.*" She marked the letters while I did my best to miss bumps in the road. It wasn't too hard. We weren't to Arkansas yet. After we crossed Stateline Avenue in Texarkana, I couldn't be responsible for letters crawling over into wrong boxes. "Mmm hmm," she said. *"Opossum."*

The word lingered in the air like a challenge. I felt the urge to roll over and play dead.

"You know, Miss Isabelle," I said, "my momma and I, we're nothing alike."

"Were we talking about your mother?" She contemplated me across the car.

"Well, if we're talking about Steve and why I let him take advantage of me, I guess we'll have to talk about my momma first."

"Go on." She said it calmly, as if she were some kind of shrink, me reclining on her couch. *Tell me how you really feel about your mother. . . .*

"Momma has always needed someone to rescue her. First, a man, and now me. I swore up and down I'd never do that. Early on, I made up my mind to be self-sufficient.

I'd make damn sure I had the resources to take good care of my kids — with or without a man by my side.

"Of course, I hoped Steve and I would marry and start a family, but I took cosmetology courses my senior year of high school as a backup plan. I was lucky I did, because I came up pregnant two weeks before graduation, and Steve dropped out of college after one semester. He said he needed to be home when his baby arrived so he could take care of things." I snorted. "His idea of taking care of things was literally being *home,* watching Stevie Junior all day while I worked my butt off — pardon my French — at the Stop 'n Chop, then going out with his loser friends and drinking beer all night."

Miss Isabelle clucked her tongue.

"I mean, the complimentary child care was something, but come on, really? I also worried that Stevie Junior had stayed strapped in the baby seat all day, because that's where he usually was when I got home. Steve always claimed he'd only put him there for a minute to keep him safe while he showered or started dinner — that is, took the hamburger out of the freezer and set it on the counter for me to thaw and cook.

"And you're right. I let him get away with

it, I guess. But I kept my promise to myself. My kids are healthy and happy . . . more or less. Most of the time." I reached to turn up the radio and fiddled with the stations. There wasn't anything but country music, and I doubted that would change between now and Memphis. I twisted the volume knob back down and decided to risk another nosy question I hoped would eventually bring us back to the subject of Robert. "Tell me more about your mother, Miss Isabelle."

Miss Isabelle turned her face to the window. "After all these years, why do you still call me that? You could just call me Isabelle. But I guess it doesn't matter as long as you don't call me any of those other silly names you come up with."

"Hey, now, silly names — that's my trademark. But you know, 'Miss Isabelle' just flows. It's cute. Plus, one thing my momma did teach me was to respect my elders." I waited. She didn't let me down. She twisted around and whacked my elbow with the crossword puzzle book. I pretended to duck — not easy while driving. "I call all my little old ladies Miss Whatever. Don't you think for a minute I'm singling you out for special treatment." Miss Isabelle rolled her eyes. "But you changed the subject."

"It's such a long story," she said, echoing

my own words.

"Well, it's, what, nearly a thousand miles from home to Cincinnati? And we're less than two hundred in. I'd like to hear more."

"I think . . ." Miss Isabelle paused and gazed out the window again. A cover of clouds had sneaked up on us as we left my hometown and headed for the Arkansas border, and now a slow drizzle began to fall, creating a teal-and-chocolate blur of the tall pines we barreled past at the side of the road, like some kind of painting — like, you know, that guy Monet. Thunder rumbled in the distance. "I think my mother was terrified."

5
Isabelle, 1939

After we stole past the sign leading into Shalerville that night, we ducked into the shadows the few times we saw anyone. Robert walked me as far as the end of my street, then watched from that distance until I reached my house. I turned in time to see him slip away from the shelter of a huge old oak he'd hidden behind until I reached my front steps.

I sent up a prayer for his safety, too. I hoped it reached a God who protected both the whites and the Negroes. I suspected our town worshiped one who wouldn't honor such a request. In the purple dusk beside the porch, I waited until an automobile roared nearby, then clattered through the front door. I called out I was home, breathing easier when Mother didn't come to tell me good night or quiz me about Earline's party. As I drifted to sleep, I realized I'd been wrong about so much — not the least, my ability to handle myself in an adult world. But something else, too: I'd been wrong about Robert. That his existence had no bearing on mine.

This intrigued me. Beyond simple gratitude for his being in the right place at the right time, for his intervention in what might have been disastrous, I began to entertain thoughts it had been more than coincidence. It seemed almost mad, but I couldn't banish the notion that something bigger than both of us had steered the situation, bringing us both to a place where we couldn't avoid each other.

I saw my prayers had reached the appropriate God when Robert returned to our house the next week safe and sound, his jaw nicely healed from the imprint of Louie's fist. I was in the kitchen, sent by my mother to inquire whether Cora was ready to serve lunch, when a rap at the back door startled me. I turned. The window framed Robert's face and close-cropped head. Heat rushed to my face. I ducked my chin against my chest as Cora hurried to the door.

"Excuse me, Miss Isabelle, while I let my son in. Tell your momma luncheon will be served right on the nose at noon — like I told her this morning." She smirked. We had an unspoken arrangement: We both agreed

Mother was fussy, and Cora trusted me to keep her facetiousness to myself. When she waved Robert in, I knew he hadn't seen me through the window. His neck seemed to flush to a deeper shade of brown, and his prominent cheekbones turned even darker. I remained motionless, like a waiting chess piece on our kitchen's checkered tiles. Cora studied each of us with puzzled eyes, and I knew then Robert had kept my misadventure and his subsequent rescue a secret. Her voice, full of quiet authority, jolted me into motion. "You run along now, Miss Isabelle. Your momma will worry herself if you don't tell her what I said."

"Thank you, Cora. I'll tell Mother," I said, then turned to Robert. "Hello, Robert," I said, but I stumbled over the easy syllables. He bobbed his head, looking everywhere but at me. I turned and fled, suddenly conscious of how I walked — my awkward gait surely exposed my jangled nerves.

"What was that about?" I heard Cora mutter as I slunk down the hall toward the parlor.

I slowed to a tiptoe and heard only a low mumble, but my best guess was that Robert said, "Nothing, Momma." Cora harrumphed, and flatware clattered against china and the oven door creaked. I pictured her bewilderment as she transferred hot dishes to a serving tray.

Later, while she was doing the clearing up, I excused myself from the table and ducked into the kitchen again, knowing I had only a moment before she'd return with the tray. My heart raced when I found Robert still at the table, engrossed in a schoolbook splayed next to the plate Cora would have filled between trips to the dining room. He looked up, his expression changing as he discovered me in the doorway instead of his mother. His puzzled eyes questioned me, but he didn't speak.

"You made it home without any problems?" There he sat, in obvious good health, but I didn't know what else to say, and we couldn't just gaze at each other indefinitely.

"It was fine. Nobody even noticed me being late —" he began.

"I was lucky. Mother never even came to check on me —"

Our words intersected, and we laughed nervously.

"I said thank you before, but Robert, I can't tell you . . . I've replayed the possibilities time and again. . . ." I took a deep breath and plunged on. "You being there that night, seeing me leave town, following me — I believe it was kismet."

After I said the word, I felt my face flush. It was a word I'd discovered in Sunday's crossword puzzle, after I'd lain awake so long the night before. It seemed a sign my thoughts weren't ridiculous. But I'd never heard the word uttered in everyday conversation, and now I just knew Robert would find me silly and dramatic — if he even knew what it meant. Especially if he knew what it meant.

The amusement in his eyes confirmed two things: He knew the word's meaning, or could discern it from the context, and I was dramatic. Yet, he didn't deny my statement, and his amusement verged on another emotion I couldn't name, although I wanted to.

That spring, I tracked Robert's comings and goings from our house, at first subconsciously, then on purpose. Before long, I realized my interest had altered into something more, and I didn't completely comprehend it. I caught myself primping in the mirror when I thought he might be around, then scolded myself for caring. What reason could I have to make myself attractive for a colored boy?

I was embarrassed on the one hand.

I was terrified on the other.

I knew if my mother ever learned about

the night Robert had seen me home or if she discovered me patting my hair or biting my lips to make them brighter just as he climbed the steep driveway to our back door, she'd come unglued.

One day, I overheard her argument with a neighbor about the sundown signs. I was sitting on the stairs, sorting decks of playing cards that had been jumbled together, when their voices floated from the sitting room at the front of the house.

"What could it hurt to take down those signs, Marg?" the neighbor said. "Colored people have worked for nearly every one of us over the years. How much easier would it be if they didn't have to hurry away before sundown? Or if we didn't have to transport them across the city limit like we were running the Underground Railroad because we worked them late?"

My mother harrumphed. "Imagine this town if coloreds were allowed here after dark, Harriet, or — heaven forbid — permitted to live here again. Goodness, they'd probably want to go to our school. Next thing you know, their children would be mingling with ours, their boys trying to sully our girls." I detected the shudder in her voice. She'd started out as not entirely certain but had picked up steam as she neared the end of her speech.

Nell had been sent to the kitchen for iced tea, and she emerged, carrying a tray heavy with a crystal pitcher and glasses of ice. My brother Patrick passed through the hallway as she headed toward the sitting room. He bumped up against her, causing her tray to tilt at a precarious angle, setting the iced tea to sloshing and the glasses clinking into each other. Patrick reached to steady the tray, and as he released it again, he brushed his hand against her aproned breast, leaving it there a moment as her eyes widened. His eyes dared her to react as he slowly squeezed. She flinched but didn't make a sound.

"Nell, is that you?" my mother called. "We'd like our tea now."

"Yes, ma'am," Nell said. "Coming, ma'am." She pushed past Patrick, her eyes averted. He spied me on the staircase, my hands frozen, clutching the aces from three different decks, and he grinned, as though I'd be amused by what I'd witnessed. I felt nauseous. Mother worried their boys would sully ours? She hadn't seen the combined effect of terror and resignation on Nell's face. After hearing what she'd said to the neighbor, I guessed she'd view this differently, maybe even accuse Nell of enticing Patrick.

My father would have harshly reprimanded him — except it seemed as if he'd given up trying to influence my brothers now that they were supposed to be men. As far back as I could remember, for reasons that were never quite clear to me, Jack and Patrick had emulated the other boys and men who surrounded them in our town instead of Daddy, and Mother's lack of intervention hadn't helped. I was the one who'd imitated my father's behavior since I was a tiny girl, and he had always modeled respect for our household help and any colored folks with whom he interacted — for all the good it did with my brothers.

Patrick lumbered up the stairs, thwacking me on the forehead with his fingers as he passed me and kicking the cards I'd already arranged, jumbling the decks again.

But at that moment, the interest that had begun to possess me since the night Robert had walked me home became clear — an interest that might even confound my father. If my mother could read my thoughts, she'd believe an evil spirit had taken up residence in my heart — not unlike her vision of Negroes living in our small town, with all its implications.

My thoughts, not entirely platonic, gave me shivers.

One late spring afternoon, I was reading in the backyard, propped up against a tree, when Robert ambled up the drive. He lifted his hand when he saw me but continued walking toward the back door. My eyes began tracking the same lines of text over and over as I wondered what had brought him to our house that day. Moments later, he came out of the house and went to the garage, where my father stored his prized 1936 Buick Special. Robert backed the crimson car into the driveway. He shut off the engine, then returned to the garage, eventually emerging again with a bucket and rags.

He'd washed my father's car plenty of times before. Daddy was proud of it and liked to keep it in top shape. He no longer trusted Jack or Patrick to do it — the few times he had, they'd done a sloppy job and damaged the immaculate surface by leaving soap spots in their hurry to move on to less menial preoccupations. Mother claimed their carelessness was only because Daddy wouldn't allow them to drive his precious Buick, especially considering he rarely drove it himself. Shalerville was so tiny, he visited most of his patients on foot unless the weather prevented it or they lived out of town; only rarely did he take appointments in his office, which was a few blocks from home. He took turns chauffeuring my friends and me to our parties, and occasionally we'd drive across the Ohio for dinner in Cincy or take the car on a family holiday out of town, but mostly it stayed right there in the garage, shiny and awaiting its rare adventure. The boys made do driving Daddy's old Model T, the first car he'd owned, which only ran part of the time — the reason he'd abandoned it.

But I'd begged my father to teach me to drive the Buick, and he'd actually agreed to it, claiming he'd teach me in the summer, when I sometimes accompanied him on out-of-town calls. Mother intervened. "Now, John, don't put ideas in Isabelle's head," she'd said. She wouldn't dream of getting behind the wheel, and wouldn't hear of my doing it, either. It was unladylike. Daddy shrugged his hands, an unspoken apology, and I stomped off to sulk. But even though I'd been thrilled that Daddy almost taught me, I'd felt troubled, too. He wouldn't allow my brothers to drive his car, but he was willing to teach me to do it; Mother wouldn't dream of letting me drive, yet she didn't understand my father's adamant refusal to let the boys near his car. It seemed, sometimes, we were pawns in an unacknowledged battle between our parents. Was Mother's permissiveness with the boys a way to get back at my father in some way for a fault I couldn't see? I found myself studying him after that, trying to discern what he might have done to disappoint my mother. He seemed perfect to me.

Now I watched enviously while Robert walked to the outside spigot, jingling the keys in his pocket. I glanced at the back windows of the house, though I knew my mother rested every afternoon about that time. Satisfied nobody was watching, I carried my book to a lawn chair nearer the car, where I pretended to immerse myself in my story again. "Too shady over there," I said. "I was getting a chill."

"Yes, ma'am, it's a nice day out, but I can see how it might be cool in the shade." Robert filled the bucket with suds and carried it to the car, then stopped short. I recognized his dilemma almost as soon as he set the bucket on the ground. I'd glimpsed him from inside the house in the past — he usually wore only his sleeveless undershirt when he washed the car.

But usually I wasn't there.

I could have jumped up to go inside so he could follow his usual protocol, but something inside me rebelled. I buried my nose deeper in my book, shifting away slightly so my line of vision wasn't so direct. But instead of removing his shirt, Robert rolled his long sleeves as high as they'd go and plunged his arms into the suds. He couldn't avoid soaking the sun-bleached fabric in the process. He wrung out the sponge and dragged it over the hood of the car, grimacing at the water stains on his sleeves.

I couldn't help it. A giggle sneaked past my lips. I slapped my hand against my mouth.

"You were me, you wouldn't be laughing," Robert said quietly, his back to me.

"I'm sorry," I said, but my giggles turned into uncontrolled laughter. "I hope you don't have to wear that shirt anywhere else today."

Robert glanced at the house, then before I knew it, he dipped the sponge in the bucket and flung a stream of water my way. I gasped as it made perfect landfall, drenching my book and skirt, and my laughter increased to a shriek.

"Oh, pardon me, Miss Isabelle. I didn't realize you were so close behind me. Get you wet?" He made full eye contact with me. A grin split his face like a sunrise, and for a moment, we were simply young people enjoying a mutual prank, neither well-off nor poor, white nor Negro.

Until the screen door slapped closed. I turned. My mother stood on the back stoop. She frowned and squinted, her hand shading her eyes from the sharp afternoon sun. "Isabelle? Is that you out there? I thought I heard a commotion. You've been in the sun too long, dear. Your skin has become unattractively dark. Come inside, now."

"Coming, Mother," I called dutifully, but my singsong voice betrayed my impertinence.

She waited while I shook out my skirt and scooped my book from the chair. I wiped at the cover, hoping she wouldn't notice the dark spots on it or smell the telltale scent of soapsuds mixed with road dust on my clothing. When she was satisfied I was doing as she asked, she turned to go inside. I glanced at Robert, and then, though I knew it was childish, I stuck out my tongue at my mother's receding backside, jammed my thumbs into my ears, and wagged my fingers. Now it was his turn to cover his mouth. He was more successful than I'd been in covering the chuckle that tried to escape. He shook a finger at me, then returned to his task.

I took my time entering the house, but Mother was right inside the door, a look on her face I could have sworn was sheer terror. But then she pursed her lips like she used to purse them at Aunt Bertie. "Isabelle, you're too friendly with the Prewitts," she said. "You must remember your place. And they must remember theirs."

"Mother —" I protested, but she'd already turned away.

School let out for the summer, and my days alternated between lethargy and tasks Mother assigned to keep me busy — learning to arrange peonies or daylilies from the garden, selecting ripe cucumbers or prickly okra for Cora to pickle, and any number of things that seemed pointless to me, as though we still lived in the nineteenth century. I'd much rather have read or wandered, but I was no longer allowed the freedom I'd had when I was younger. On rare occasions, though, Mother's watchful eye relaxed.

On an early afternoon in July, when the heat had given its most impressive performance of the season so far, bearing down on us like a steaming iron, she complained of a headache and retired early for her afternoon rest. She asked Cora to send Nell to my father for a powder to relieve her pain, but Nell was in the middle of laundering linens. Though I suspected Nell would have favored a break from her task, doubly oppressive in the heat and humidity, I jumped at the chance.

"Oh, no, Miss Isabelle," Cora said. "Nell can finish it up later. That laundry's not going anywhere."

"I don't mind. I'd like to say hello to Daddy, and besides, I can't bear this stifling house a minute longer." I clutched my hands over my heart. "Pretty please?"

Cora laughed. "You win." But then she shook her finger at me. "You hurry back with that powder, now, or your momma will be all over us."

I promised I'd rush both directions. I called the office first, and Daddy's nurse assured me they'd have the medicine waiting even if Daddy was called away.

My father sat at his desk, eating a cold lunch. He waved me into his consulting room. "Sit, honey. Visit for a minute; then you can take my lunch box back with you." When I was younger, I'd often kept him company over his lunch in the summer. I think we both missed our chats. I suspected my mother's plan to turn me into a ready-made bride wasn't any easier on my father than it was on me.

"I better hurry, sir. Mother will be upset if she doesn't have her medicine right away — especially since she's expecting Nell."

"Oh, well, go on, then. We don't want Nell or Cora in trouble with the boss."

"No, sir. We don't." I tucked the medicine in my pocket. "Daddy?"

He grinned. "Thought you were in a hurry."

"I am. But I was wondering . . ." I ran my fingers across the thin fabric of my dress, around the outline of the envelope, and swiveled my sandaled toe against a dark fleck in the linoleum. I shook my head. "Never mind."

"What is it, honey?" My father's hand was halfway to his mouth, but he put down his sandwich and leaned back in his chair, his fingers clasped over his vest.

I didn't answer immediately. I'd suddenly been swept from the present to the past, in a memory I'd never revisited until this moment, probably six years gone. Robert and I sat in two straight chairs, which flanked my father's desk, one on either side, instead of facing it as they did for patient consultations. My math book was in the middle of Daddy's desk, where we could all view it, and Daddy was helping me with my assigned work — the first year I'd struggled with it — while Robert copied the same problems onto sheets of paper. It wasn't our first session of this kind, and I hadn't understood at first why Robert was doing the same work I'd been assigned — he was a year older than I was, after all. I was also puzzled because Robert hadn't brought his own book. Why did he need to use mine? Daddy explained on our walk home that Robert's school received cast-off textbooks from the white schools in the area, and those were so battered, they rarely left the classroom — they were too precious and few for the teachers to chance damage or loss. The school never had enough teachers, and so it was easy for even the smartest students to fall behind. Robert's classmates were often doing work my class had mastered several years before, and Daddy helped him work ahead to ensure he'd be ready for college. I was ashamed to recall how I sometimes flung my schoolbooks across my bedroom in frustration, sick to death of all the busywork that rarely challenged my mind. I pictured the student who might use it next, cracked spine and all, and began handling my books with care, understanding it was a privilege to carry them back and forth from home to school each day. I fussed at the boys in my classes who carelessly dropped their books in the dirt after school when they formed spontaneous ball games, and they rolled their eyes and ignored me.

That day, I fidgeted while Daddy dissected a problem with Robert. Robert generally caught on faster than I did, which annoyed me. But I noticed he was fidgety, too. Daddy was always patient with both of us, and he simply plodded through the work until Robert looked up at him with nervous eyes. "Sir?" he said.

"Yes, Robert? What is it? Don't you understand?"

"Yes, sir, I understand fine. It's just . . ." Robert glanced at the window. "It's almost dark, sir."

My father's head swung toward the window, and he seemed startled, as though he hadn't noticed how quickly sunset arrived after school was dismissed now that it was late fall. Rare impatience flashed across his face — no, something stronger than impatience; it was anger — but he composed himself and gathered Robert's papers together, quickly pointing out what he should complete before we met again. "You better run along now, Robert; we don't want you in trouble with the boss."

I wasn't sure whom he meant. It seemed he should be referring to Cora, as he often referred to my mother as "the boss" in our household, but I'd never heard him label Cora that way. Robert stuffed the papers into his worn knapsack, a hand-me-down from Patrick, and rushed from Daddy's office. My father returned his attention to me, though he never appeared fully invested in the remainder of our lesson that day.

"What is it?" Daddy's voice echoed my memory now. "Honey?"

I said, "Those signs . . ."

"Signs?"

"The ones when you go in and out of town — not the ones that say Shalerville and the population . . . but the other ones."

Daddy frowned. "What about them?"

"Have they always been there?"

"Always?" He lifted his fingers now, studying one nail, scratching as though something was caught at the crescent. "No, I don't suppose they have." He straightened. "You'd better get going now, Isabelle. Cora will wonder what kept you."

"Yes, sir." I turned to leave, but his voice, unnaturally bright, stopped me again.

"Why don't you run that medicine home, then give yourself an afternoon off? Your mother has set you many tasks this summer, sweetheart, but if she's not feeling well, having you underfoot will only make things worse, don't you think?" He winked, and my spirits lifted. He hadn't exactly answered my other question, and I still wanted to know — but a whole afternoon where I could do anything I desired? With my father's blessing? It was an excellent distraction.

"If your mother complains later, I'll assure her it was my idea, but run along while you can. That powder might work faster if she knows you have permission to flee."

"Oh, yes, sir!" I almost slammed the door behind me, then reminded myself to slow down as long as it took to pass by Daddy's nurse, who was busy straightening the supply cabinet in the examining room. She always smelled painfully sterile, as though she'd never actually touched one of Daddy's patients. She and Mother collaborated regarding his tendency to give away medical care for less compensation than was strictly good business, even though times were especially hard for others compared to us, but Daddy tolerated her complicity because she was an excellent nurse. She'd report any of my infractions directly to Mother, as well.

"Afternoon, Isabelle," she called. I thanked her, but as soon as I was through the entry and beyond her window view, I broke into a half jog, slowing only when I was going uphill or when I passed folks on Shalerville's short Main Street — not many that day; the heat had made everyone lazy and inclined to stay anywhere they could catch a cool breeze.

Back home, I found Nell pegging the last cumbersome tablecloth to the line. I held the corner tight while she slid a wooden pin over it. She dragged her fingers across her glistening forehead. "Would you ask your mother to give this to mine?" I said, withdrawing the medicine envelope from my pocket.

She wiped her hand down her apron and took it. "What you up to now?" she asked. I struggled to keep a blank face. Though a fissure had remained between us since the night I'd hurt her feelings, she knew me. I knew we both regretted being too old now to escape into the hiding places of the garden and backyard as we had when we were younger. We'd hardly noticed the heat then, playing with my jacks or jump rope, dolls or tea set, giggling and whispering about important things, such as what we'd name our firstborn children. Occasionally, we'd allowed Robert into our exclusive club when we needed a heavy lifter or someone to play the male roles in imaginary scenarios we'd concocted.

Mother hadn't cared so much about my interaction with Cora's family then. Jack was a year older than Patrick, and both were several years older than I. They kept each other busy or in trouble, and I'm sure she was simply relieved I had a convenient playmate, too — though in my case, Nell served to keep me occupied and deterred me from running all over town, whereas my brothers were given free rein as boys. Mother was always excessively concerned I might mingle with the wrong people, but at that time, Nell was exempt. Mother probably already considered her an employee of sorts at age six or eight. And at the right price — free.

"Daddy's given me permission to roam," I said to Nell. "I believe I'll take my book down to the creek." A gentle stream ran near our property, half a mile or so from the house if you left through the back gate. Close enough to be considered a safe spot, but sufficiently distant to deliver a temporary sense of freedom. As children, we'd played there, too.

Her eyes flashed with uncertainty, but she

carried the packet to the house. I wondered if she'd notice I wasn't carrying a book — and didn't follow her inside to fetch one.

I wasn't allowed to wear trousers. Most times now, when I visited friends' homes during the day, they lounged in fashionable slim pants that hit right at the ankle, which didn't look mannish to me at all, or divided skirts, as feminine as any dress I'd seen. But Mother's campaign to wind back the decades was comprehensive. For once, I was thankful I was wearing a loose cotton dress I could tie shorter at the sides. Perfect for wading.

The creek bed was studded with limestone, molded and smoothed by the flow, and I loved to step from stone to stone in the cool, rushing water, seeing how far I could travel the creek before I reached a spot too deep to negotiate without full-on swimming. My bathing suit, alas, saw daylight only when my family picnicked at the lake or took a driving trip to North Carolina to swim in the ocean. I'd never have been permitted to wear it for playing in the creek. I'd grown a few inches since the last time I'd worn it anyway, though I suspected it would still fit my skinny hips and flat chest well enough. I figured I was stuck with my boyish figure until I married and bore children.

Near the creek, I slipped the ribbon from my hair and sawed it in two against a broken tree limb. I'd hardly miss it — I was never short of ribbon to keep my frizzy waves in line. I gathered my skirt into bunches at the sides and secured them. I surely looked ridiculous, but I didn't care. I wouldn't sacrifice a free afternoon to vanity.

I dropped my sandals at the edge of the creek and leaped onto the first stone, pausing there for a moment to glory in my liberty, gulping the air fanned and cooled by the rushing water, so alive compared to the stagnant stuff I'd breathed all morning.

Soon, though, I hopped from one visible stone to the next, stretching my arms like a soaring osprey to keep my balance. I stopped, finally, when I reached the last one I could without crossing back to the bank. The stone's surface was large and flat, and I squatted close to the water, resting against my heels with my skirt pulled over my knees.

I gazed into the familiar creek, and melancholy surprised me. I longed for the time when I'd had more space, the summers I'd been allowed to play without the burden of someone else's expectations — ones I wanted no part of. I was too smart, said my mother. She wrinkled her nose when I claimed Father's newspapers after he'd read them at breakfast. She complained when I returned from Shalerville's tiny library lugging another teetering stack of books, believing I should show more interest in womanly skills. But needlework and learning to be a hostess bored me silly. I'd entertained the notion I might attend college, and it seemed my father had even encouraged it. He never discouraged it, at any rate. But Mother said, "You? College?" laughing — not unkindly, yet her derision festered. "The only instruction you need to be a wife and mother is right here, under your own roof." So, I foresaw a future where instead of going away to a university — something I'd always dreamed of, somewhere far away from this godforsaken place — I'd be expected to marry the first acceptable suitor who happened along, likely without love or common interests guiding our dull courtship, probably someone like Jack or Patrick, who would work and spend his leisure time at whatever he wished while I shelved my own dreams in order to keep house and bear children. I felt a flash of anger toward my mother, who would surely have her way in this, and I rose quickly and lunged for the creek bank, where I pounded the dirt with my fists, the aroma of its dry, dusty cloud both comforting and infuriating me. I was privileged, wealthy, even, in comparison to so many girls, but I railed against my fate, my cries unintelligible, as though I were an out-of-control toddler. When I'd run out of steam, I dropped my head against my arms, then turned my gaze sideways.

It landed on a pair of worn work boots.

"You all right, Miss Isabelle?"

I scrambled to my feet. "Where did you come from?" I pressed my fingers against my cheeks — on fire, I was so embarrassed.

"Been here the whole time. You didn't see me, I guess, or I imagine you'd have kept that all up inside." He chuckled. "I was way down the creek when you got here. Just . . . minding my own business." A smirk filled his eyes with humor.

I had to be honest with myself then: The chances of his being there had been good. My whole life nearly, in the summer, if Robert wasn't doing small jobs for Daddy, he was hanging around by the creek. But today, after my apparently not-thorough-enough surveillance, I'd determined I was alone. The thought that he had witnessed my tantrum — yes, caused in part by his absence — hurt my pride.

So I changed the subject. "Fishing?"

"Catching bait. Looking for minnows. If I can get a mess of them, I'll head over to the river. Nothing running here except little bitty things not worth keeping."

"Show me," I said impulsively. "How you catch the minnows." I'd tried before, for fun, but the tiny fish had eluded me. I'd attempted to scoop them up with a bucket or my hands, but they'd raced away as soon as I'd touched the water. I'd never managed to capture more than a few.

Robert regarded me, wary, bemused, and amused all at once. But he turned and hooked his fingers, beckoning me to follow. This time, I noticed, he wasn't careful to drop behind after I brushed the dirt from my dress and fell into step beside him. In fact, in spots where the creek bank narrowed to a space only wide enough for one of us, he went ahead. He paused and gallantly held rushes and hanging branches away from me where they crowded the path.

He led me to a wide spot in the creek where the minnows tended to congregate. Here, the creek drifted lazily, pausing to swirl in shelters created by larger rocks and hollows in the bank. He grunted and pointed, gesturing for me to sit on the bank, a finger over his lips warning me to stay quiet and still.

He placed his pail next to me, then pulled a Nehi soda bottle from his baggy pants pocket. He held the bottle up to show me how he'd dropped a chunk of bread, squeezed and molded like a ball, inside. It rolled around the bottom like a marble, though he'd also dropped porous scraps of bread inside with it. He'd tied a long string around the nose of the bottle, and now he removed his boots and stepped into the creek bed, silent as an Indian, scarcely ruffling the surface of the water. He moved carefully, bent over, eyeing the small pools up close. Finally, he stopped. He dunked the bottle into the water, then lowered it into the stream on its side, the opening facing the same way as the flow, and pressed it into the creek bed until it stayed planted. He pulled a small stone from his pocket and trapped the end of the string on top of a river rock, then climbed back over to the bank and dropped beside me. It seemed an awfully long, complicated process to catch a few minnows, but I was curious to see how well it worked.

"Now what?" I whispered.

"We wait," he said in a normal voice.

"Why did you tell me to be quiet and you're talking?"

"I saw how loud you can be," he said, and looked off down the creek, his lips pursed. I could tell he was trying not to laugh.

I exhaled, shaking my head. "How long do we wait?"

"Long enough. Not too long."

That clarified things.

While we waited, we struggled to make small talk. I could finally speak to Robert alone again — what I'd longed for all summer — yet I could think of nothing to say. Time both stood still and gathered speed while I berated myself for not having paid more attention to the girls I'd mocked, for not noting how they talked to boys so effortlessly. Robert seemed comfortable in the silence, though, content to wait for me to initiate a topic. Finally, I said, "You like to fish?"

"It passes the time. And makes it so Momma doesn't have to buy meat for our supper or do without."

I frowned, feeling chastised, though not by Robert himself. I'd never considered Cora might struggle to find meat to feed her family. Food had always been plentiful for mine, even through the worst years of the Great Depression. Patients often paid my father in kind, with produce or home-canned fruits or vegetables, and sometimes with fresh or cured meats. I knew Mother shared with Cora when we had more than we could use before it went bad, but I'd always assumed it was more a bonus than a need. Jack and Patrick often shot small game in the woods for pure sport. I was sure they simply left it to spoil.

After ten or fifteen minutes, Robert eased back over and gently tugged the bottle back up by the string. He held it toward me, displaying a dozen or so little minnows squirming frantically inside. The bread ball had been reduced by only a fraction, though the other scraps were gone. He dumped the minnows and water into his pail and waded out again. He reached inside a pocket and added new bread crusts to the bottle.

"How many minnows do you need?" I asked.

"Oh, fifty or so ought to do. I'll keep what I don't use for tomorrow."

I did the calculations in my head. We'd be sitting there for the next hour or more while he gathered his crop of bait. I'd been gone from home less than an hour, so I'd be fine. Nobody would come looking for me unless I stayed away until it was nearly suppertime.

"You're starting college in the fall?" I hoped he wouldn't find my erratic subject changes odd.

"That's the plan, Miss Isabelle."

"Wish I were, too. Robert," I said, impulsively, before I could snatch the thought back. "You don't have to call me *Miss* Isabelle. At least not out here. It makes me feel . . . Well, I don't know how it makes me feel, but I'm not sure I like it. Would you call me Isabelle?"

"Oh, I could never. My momma — your momma," he mumbled, shaking his head, his eyelids lowered uncomfortably.

"They'd never know. Please?" I pleaded with him. It seemed as important as anything I'd ever wanted, as inconsequential as it might have been.

"Isabelle," he said. "Okay, then. Isabelle." He rolled the sounds around in his mouth as though he were sampling a new recipe his mother wanted to test. He looked at me tentatively and grinned. "You don't want to get me in trouble, now, do you?"

"No! I'd never —" The back of my neck prickled. I supposed some of the girls I knew — and the boys, too — might be that ruthless, willing to do something to get one of the few Negro boys we knew into trouble on purpose. The ugliness made me cringe.

"Oh, I know you'd never, Miss — Isabelle." He shook his head. "That'll be a hard habit to lose. But if you say so, I'll try."

We sat in silence again. As the moments passed, I felt increasingly awkward. I became aware of myself — my skin, my hands, my bare feet, the downy hair on my shins and calves. My mother shaved the hair from her legs, but I'd never bothered. Mine were covered with stockings when it mattered. Now they appeared childlike, and I wanted to tuck them under my skirt again.

Then I grew more aware of him — his skin, his hands, his bare feet, the downy hair on his lip and jaw. I caught myself holding my breath for too long and released it slowly so it didn't whoosh out of me like a bellows. "Do you have a girl, Robert?" I asked, hoping to rid my mind of these thoughts by learning what would render them useless.

"Used to," he said. "But she already married some older boy working for the railroad, pulling in good money as a porter. Didn't want to wait around on me going to college." He shrugged. "I can't blame her."

"Do you want to marry? Have children one day?" My earlier tack hadn't succeeded entirely, though contemplating Robert in the light of having a life beyond my family and the way his served our needs continued to fascinate me.

"I suppose I might one day. Right girl

comes along. Patient girl, probably." He grinned at me, and I laughed nervously, for I knew he was laughing at me, too, inside. Not that I thought it would occur to him to compare me to any girl he'd consider. How wrong that would be.

How dangerous.

A cloud billowed across the sky above us, sudden and heavy, and a breeze disturbed the air. I shivered as it raised gooseflesh on my forearms. When a rumble of thunder trembled the earth below us, Robert jumped up from his spot next to me.

"Oh, Lordy, that's a good storm coming." He plunged into the creek, pulled the bottle up, and raced back to the bank. He dropped it in the pail, along with the other minnows, and grabbed the pail up, depositing it with his boots under a nearby tree. "Think we can beat it out of here?" He peered at the sky, and just then it opened wide, a gaping mouth. Spoon-size raindrops hurtled to the ground. "Better take cover, Miss . . . Isabelle. Come get under here!"

I glanced up, too, weighing the practicality of standing under a tree in a lightning storm. But then, pellets of hail began to fall. By the time I'd scrambled to Robert's side, some had increased to the size of the bread ball Robert had used to lure the minnows.

He pressed his back close to the tree trunk, trying to make room for me. When I couldn't get a good spot, he began to move away, but I grabbed his sleeve and pulled him back. "Don't be ridiculous," I said. "You can't be out in that." Not that the tree did much to shelter us from the rain, which was now blowing almost sideways, but at least we weren't being totally pelted by the hail.

I never let go of his sleeve, though I'm not sure I noticed at first. He stood with his back pressed close to me, and my nose barely reached his shoulder. I gazed at the sheets of rain, every other sound silenced by their intensity. I'd never felt as close to another human being. Or as alone. I eased my fingers around Robert's arm and held it at the crook of his elbow.

He didn't react at first, not visibly. He remained still and straight, like the tree trunk behind us, so ancient and wide, it scarcely swayed in the storm.

But when another peal of thunder cracked the sky, I startled, tightening my grip on Robert's elbow. Without a word, he turned to pull me close against his chest. I breathed in his scent, sweaty, natural, but not unpleasant, mingled with the aroma of rain pouring over the leaves and bark of the tree.

The scent transported me, and I was seven or eight years old, huddled under a different low-hanging tree near the creek with Robert and Nell while a summer storm raged, warm rain trickling down our arms and necks in spite of Robert's attempts to shield us with the blanket Nell and I had been using for a picnic. Nell sat between us, but my bare arm snaked around her waist, and my fingers brushed against Robert's crossed feet. He shrieked like a girl when I tickled his anklebone, but he held the blanket steady, doing his best to keep us dry. Was it a real memory? I couldn't be sure, but it seemed so.

Robert and I stayed like that until the storm gentled, until the hail and rain stopped, fast as it had begun. He dropped his hands to his sides and backed away.

I felt naked. Alone, once again.

"I wasn't thinking. I'm sorry." He shoved his hands into his pockets, his face stricken, glancing around as though we might have been observed.

"I'm not," I said. "I'm not sorry at all."

I turned and rushed back to where I'd left my sandals, but of course they no longer rested on the creek bank. They'd likely floated long away by then. I ran home, ignoring my pounding heart, stopping only to release the sides of my skirt before I reached the back gate. I crashed into the kitchen, where Cora and Nell sat at the table, one peeling apples, the other potatoes. Cora pushed her chair back with a scraping and scratching that felt physically painful to me.

"Oh, Miss Isabelle, look at you," she hissed. "Your momma will have a fit if she sees you like this! Hurry on and get out of those wet clothes. Surely she's awake by now, but maybe you can sneak by." I only nodded. I crept upstairs, wondering how I'd explain away my bare feet if I couldn't avoid Mother, wondering how I'd explain the disappearance of my sandals the next time she suggested I wear them. I'd had them a month, and though we were better off than most families in our area, new shoes were expensive. But I also knew I wouldn't trade my afternoon at the creek to get them back. I wouldn't trade it for anything — a thought that shook me all the way to my bare soles.

6
DORRIE, PRESENT DAY

The highway rose and fell in little hilly places now, and I gazed straight ahead, trying to wrap my brain around Miss Isabelle's story. She sat quietly, as though she was still remembering. Who knew she'd had such a prickly relationship with her mother? Before, I'd have pegged her as a typical sheltered white girl, spoon-fed the idea she could do what ever she wanted from birth, then choosing marriage and family. A sweet, obedient daughter with a doting mother. The more I thought about that last part, the more I recognized the assumption it was. Miss Isabelle, meek and tame? Yeah, right. Full of pickles and vinegar, more likely.

I liked this mental version of young Miss Isabelle better. It helped me dismiss my worries about unveiling my own missteps and miseries, made me more confident she wouldn't judge me.

And to think she'd crushed on a black boy when she was a girl. I wasn't sure what to make of that, but if anyone had found out, I bet it was one fine mess. In my head, Robert was beginning to resemble Teague as I pictured him in his younger days. If that was the case, I certainly didn't blame her for falling for him.

"My momma," I said, interrupting my own thoughts, "she didn't care what kind of snags I got into as long as I wasn't making things too hard on her. That is, as long as she didn't have to solve any problems for me or spend any money to get me out of trouble. Oh, and as long as I didn't interfere with her boyfriends."

I guess Momma thought one of those men would be her ticket to a better life. Too bad her choice of men hadn't really worked out.

Four fingers pointing back at me, of course.

But at least I paid my own way, no matter what. No matter how long or how much I allowed a man to mooch off me, I kept things under control. At least the things that mattered. My kids had decent clothes and full bellies, always. They could sign up for most of the extracurricular activities they wanted to. Our house wasn't fancy, but nice enough — clean and neat, so they could bring their friends inside whenever they wanted. I encouraged that, in fact. I wanted to know what kind of kids they hung out with and how they behaved around their peers.

"What made her happy, then, your mother?" asked Miss Isabelle.

"Momma? She was happy when she had a man — and twice as happy when I found somewhere else to be when they came around. She loved me; I know she did. But back then, she preferred not having to deal with me more than necessary. I think she regrets it now. She complains I work too much. Gripes about how the kids don't spend any time with her."

A smile crossed my face. Momma was getting her wagon fixed this week. Finally, I was getting a little return on my financial investment. She'd been headed for the government high-rise, where the county basically stored poor old folks until they died, and as much as Momma frustrated me, I wouldn't wish that place on anyone. I helped her out as much as I could so she could stay in a decent little apartment in a safe neighborhood.

Now, Miss Isabelle's mother, she sounded more hands-on than was strictly good sense. Of course, things were different then, but I don't believe Miss Isabelle had even been given room to breathe.

We'd left the rain in East Texas. Up ahead was a sign for a rest area, and the iced tea I'd downed every time Susan Willis stopped by to refill my glass at the Pitt had come back to haunt me. If there was one thing Arkansas did well, it was public rest stops; obviously, the state spent all their money on those instead of the roads.

As Miss Isabelle and I approached the building, waves of nostalgia surprised me. Yes, it was a public rest room. But it was constructed of the same rustic, Pine-Sol-smelling materials as the buildings at the government-funded summer camp I'd attended as a kid. I'd been glad to get away from home for those two weeks each summer. In a bunk house crowded with squealing girls — even when there were mean ones, and there were always mean ones — I could drop off to sleep mostly without worry. Being pranked in my sleep didn't bother me much. It usually made me laugh.

At home, my mother was wise to try to keep me away from her boyfriends. When she was flush with a new man — fairly often, as they never lasted long — I jammed an old metal folding chair I'd rescued from a trash pile up under my doorknob. It didn't always stick, but at least the falling chair gave me a warning. And usually the clatter woke my mother. "Jimmmmy?" she'd call down the hallway. Or Joe or Jake or whoever he happened to be. "Is that you, honey? You coming back to bed?" The footsteps would recede — if we were both lucky, and Momma was good and awake. But more than one man learned not to mess with me the harder way. I was thankful Momma seemed to avoid the worst ones — ones who wouldn't have been intimidated by a scrappy girl with a good set of lungs and a pair of sharp scissors in hand.

I'd been careful with my kids. My daughter knew she was safe at home. My son knew no matter how many of his so-called friends tried to talk him into stupid, all he had to do was come home to be talked back around to smart. Even so, he had me worried.

Miss Isabelle and I took a moment to stretch after we toured the facilities, then sat at a bench out front so I could clear my head from the three hundred or so miles we'd already come.

"You seem like a good mom, Dorrie. But do you think it's working? Doing things differently from how your mother did them?"

Miss Isabelle's forthright question startled

me. But after I considered a second, I knew she wasn't trying to put me on the defensive, and I could have asked her the same question. She'd outlived her son. She rarely mentioned him, but kept his photo on her dresser, next to that tiny thimble, as well as a family portrait of her and her husband and the boy when he was a teenager. He'd died before I met her. Maybe it was just too painful to talk about.

I took my time thinking through my answer, though.

"My little girl, she makes me so proud," I finally said. "Middle school is the pits, but she's keeping up her grades and doesn't let the other girls influence how she acts. Yet." I smiled, thinking of Bebe, with her awkward eyeglasses and her refusal to wear trampy clothes like so many other girls her age did. Sometimes, she still let me do her hair in ponytails and little natural poofs, and I'd do it as long as she didn't complain. She was like me, except smarter. I prayed she'd be able to stand stronger, too. It was damn hard these days. "Stevie Junior, though, he's too much like his daddy. A ladies' man. He's a good boy, but Steve hasn't set much of an example."

My boy was so close to graduation, I could taste it. In half a semester plus a few days, he was supposed to walk the stage in his cap and gown with lots of pomp and circumstance — a second-generation high school graduate. But lately, I'd been getting automated calls from the school, saying he'd skipped this class or that. I also got reminders about tutoring sessions for kids who weren't expected to do well on their exit exams. Those calls were made by a computer, too, but they were tailored to those who needed them. I checked.

And his latest little girlfriend, Bailey, who was always hanging out at the house with him, she seemed sweet, polite — always Mrs. Curtis this and Mrs. Curtis that, even after I told her she should call me Dorrie. But lately, she'd been dragging in behind Stevie Junior with a long face. I recognized the look. They'd been planning to go to the prom together, but it had been weeks since I'd heard her gush about a dress she'd seen or pester Stevie to go for a tux fitting.

"I think my son's girlfriend might be pregnant," I blurted out to Miss Isabelle, and a big, ugly sigh rattled me to the core. There. I'd said it out loud for the first time. And now I saw it clearly: my biggest reason for wanting to run away.

"Oh, Dorrie. I'm sorry." She gazed across the parking lot, where a family emerged from an economy car like a clown troupe. The little ones ran so fast, I couldn't count them, and they screeched so loud, it appeared they'd been trapped in that thing for days. The momma and daddy looked like they might fall over with exhaustion, yet they soldiered on, rationing drinks and chip bags and rounding up the ones who needed to pee before they could settle down to eat their roadside picnic. "Sometimes babies come at the wrong times, but they can still be blessings if they are welcomed and loved."

"Don't I know, Miss Isabelle," I said. I'd be furious if my son confirmed my hunch, but who was I to talk? I couldn't imagine my life without him — a child who'd showed up two or three years before I ever dreamed I'd be a mother. "I don't know if I'd survive losing him. You must miss your boy so much."

She answered after a time. "You'd think the pain of losing someone would go away after a while, but it doesn't."

We pushed ourselves up from the bench and headed back to the car, settled in, and pulled our seat belts tight around us. Then she said, "You love that boy of yours, Dorrie. And you'll love any child he brings into this world, no matter how or when it happens, you hear?"

The thought of being a grandmother at age thirty-six was almost more than I could take. But Miss Isabelle said it as if I had any choice about whether I'd love my own grandchild.

7
ISABELLE, 1939

The day after the storm, I was helping Mother sort house hold linens, pulling worn ones for the charity box at church. I suggested we ask Cora if she could use them. Robert's comment about the meat still bothered me.

"Oh, no, dear. Cora has plenty for her family. We pay her good wages. You should see how some of the other people in our area live. It's a shame, really." Mother's voice faded as she resumed counting napkins. It was true. Decrepit shacks at the edges of Newport looked like the ones that appeared on magazine covers from time to time, worn-out mothers sitting on sagging porches with sickly, skinny babies. But I honestly couldn't comprehend how a set of snowy white napkins or a hand-embroidered tablecloth could help folks who mightn't even have bread to put on the table, much less meat. I figured Cora would be pleased to have pretty things to set hers — especially ones she or her daughter had laundered and pressed with care for years.

But perhaps she'd be too proud to take them. Everything had become confusing since I'd spent time alone with Robert. Things I'd been sure of before, I questioned now.

Mother sent me to the kitchen for glasses of milk over ice. The day was sultry again, and there was no escaping the house this time. I didn't mean to do it, but when a girl neared a door and heard mumbled conversation, she naturally slowed and tuned her ears to it. Especially a girl who'd had the kinds of feelings I'd had in recent days. Especially when the conversation might have something to do with the object of her interest.

"You see that pile of soaking wet clothes your brother left out last night?" Cora said.

"Ugh. No. What excuse did he give?" Nell asked.

"Says he got caught in the rain. Down by the creek."

The silence swelled like bread dough rising. My feet felt mired in it. "I told that boy he better stay away from foolish. I said he better watch himself, or could make things bad for us all again. I'm happy he finished school, thrilled he's going off to college, but I'll swan, some days I fear he's grown out of his britches. Forgot his place. People round here won't cotton with that, no more than they ever did."

"Oh, Momma, he ain't gonna do something stupid. He knows better." Nell's faint voice wavered, as though she was unconvinced of the certainty of her own statement, as if she needed persuading, too.

"Let's hope, Nell. Let's hope. Finding other jobs like this, these times. It'd be near impossible. We've been lucky so far."

What could Robert do that was so dangerous it could threaten Cora's standing with my family? The brief meetings between the two of us had been pure coincidence — unless my theory that something bigger had brought us together was true. And innocent. Sure, I'd been bold, behaved in ways that surprised even me, but it seemed harmless enough. . . .

Flirtation.

That's what it was. I was flirting with Robert, and his mother and sister could lose their jobs over it. It could cost all three more than I was able to comprehend in my own little insulated cocoon.

I sagged against the wall, torn by my ambivalence, and the floorboards squawked with my shifting weight, setting off a flurry of activity in the kitchen. Nell hurried through the doorway but stopped short at the sight of me in the hall.

"Nell. I . . ."

The words died on my lips. I didn't know what to say. I wanted to assure her I wouldn't do anything to cause trouble for her family. But to do so would be to admit there was even the possibility. For once, loudmouth that I was, words failed me.

Nell simply cast me a look of contempt, then lowered her eyes and went on, leaving me adrift in the wake of our growing distance. I wanted to sneak into the sitting room, wind the clock in reverse, back it up to that last night she'd helped me with my hair. I would hold my tongue with her. I would stay at the party. I would not be foolish. I would not be selfish.

And Robert would be nothing more than a boy I'd once tickled in the rain.

The heart is a demanding tenant; it frequently makes a strong argument against common sense. The very next week, with my nerves soothed by time and having tucked my misgivings away as only a sixteen-year-old can, my selfishness resurfaced. I spied Robert leaving our house. I raced upstairs, grabbed my recently finished library books, and slammed out of the house, shouting as I went, "Off to the library!"

The library was one place I could still go without Mother asking endless questions about my every potential move, even if she thought I read too much. I'd intended to go that day, so my leaving wasn't unexpected. My method might have raised eyebrows, however, had anyone been watching — and noticed who else left the house.

I scurried downhill. At the end of our street, I covered my eyes to peer through the sun's glare; my pupils hadn't adjusted fully after rushing away from my home, which was kept as dim and cool as possible with drawn curtains and lowered shades each day now until dusk lumbered in like a relief worker who was already spent.

Robert's receding figure was still visible, and I breathed more easily, turning to follow him toward Main Street. I hurried to keep him in sight, but at the library, I rushed inside and dropped my books at the returns counter. I turned to dash out again.

"No new ones today, Isabelle?"

"Afraid not. Be back later. Or tomorrow. Sorry, Miss Pearce, I have to go." I was afraid by the time I made it back outside,

I'd have lost Robert's trail, but there was no way I could lug seven heavy books up and down the hills in this heat.

Miss Pearce wrinkled her nose and harrumphed. "Always a first time for everything."

"Yes, ma'am," I called, slamming back out the door, imagining her pressing a finger to her pursed lips at the noise, though I was already gone and it was too late to mind her warning.

I gazed in the direction I'd last seen Robert, spotting only a few businessmen smoking in doorways. I picked up my pace, nearly breaking into a run. Eventually, I slowed. I'd lost him.

Only then, he emerged from the hardware store. He pushed a small paper bag into his pocket once he cleared the storefront and continued toward the edge of town. I fell into step again, twenty yards or so behind, though I needed to take three steps to match his every two.

His destination wasn't foremost in my mind. All I knew for certain was I wanted to speak to him again, to be lulled again by his flannel voice, to be amused by his wry humor.

Beyond that, I had no plan.

Robert crossed the city limit, me sneaking

behind like a poor imitation of a private investigator. After a half mile or so, he turned into a dirt lane leading to the steps of an old building. Faded lettering on the whitewashed sign posted out front identified it as Mount Zion Baptist Church. Below the name, the sign read ALL WELCOME HERE.

Yet I hung back, sheltered behind a huge yellow buckeye tree, watching until Robert climbed the sagging steps and entered the church.

I pressed my forehead against the knotted tree trunk, then plucked a piece of fruit from a low branch. I rolled the husk, flexible and green and unlikely to split open in the middle of summer, between my palms. I yearned to discover what business Robert had in a lonely church on a sweltering July afternoon. But in spite of the sign's promise, I knew following Robert inside would be a blunt invasion of privacy. I stepped back and tossed the buckeye fruit against the tree trunk, the earlier nerve I'd felt so keenly now lost, and started back toward the road. But then I heard a creaking and glanced back over my shoulder. Robert emerged from a side door, carrying ungainly wooden and metal tools. His back was already to me; he'd obviously not seen me on the path, and he headed around the building. I plucked up all the courage I'd believed gone and followed. Behind the faded clapboard structure stood a brush arbor, its original frame hidden within the twisted and gnarled fingers of overgrown vines. Robert ducked under them to enter the arbor. Presently, I heard vigorous clicks and snaps, and the vines quivered.

I gathered a breath and went the last few yards toward the arbor, ducking under at the same spot he'd entered. He startled when he saw me, his arms frozen high in the process of hacking away a particularly thick branch that had wormed its way through the arbor roof and hung so low in the space, it scraped the dirt floor.

"My God, Miss . . . Isabelle!" He released the stubborn branch from the clippers and dropped the tool at his feet, then clutched his chest and backed away from me. "You about gave me a heart attack. I thought maybe I saw a ghost."

I covered my mouth, trying not to giggle at the shock on Robert's face. "I'm sorry. I should have . . . made noise?"

"Or something." He mopped sweat away from his forehead and reached for a jar of water resting on the rustic wooden pulpit. A jar that could have held preserves put up by his mother at my house. He turned his chin to the side and studied me. "You follow me from town? Oh, Lordy, why am I asking dumb questions? Course you followed me. How else would you end up in the middle of nowhere, trying to kill me off early?"

I raised a palm in the air. "Guilty. As charged."

"And why? What on earth were you thinking? Oh, yeah, I remember now. You don't think ahead much, do you, Isabelle?" It was the first time he'd managed my name without the infernal "Miss" in front of it, or even the slightest hesitation, but I wasn't flattered.

"Guilty on count two also." I dropped onto one of the weatherworn benches that lined the arbor.

"Watch for splinters, now."

I smoothed my skirt under my legs. "I'm not scared of splinters. And I followed you because I wanted to talk to you. I like talking to you. I like watching you do things."

Robert shook his head and took another swig from his water jar, then retrieved the clippers and resumed hacking at the branch. "Don't know what you want with me. Your folks would be hysterical if they knew you followed me out here. Well, your momma. Your daddy, he'd be concerned, wondering what you're thinking, talking to a colored boy, even if that colored boy is me. Not the wisest proposition."

"Daddy talks to you all the time. Why can't I?" We hadn't been tutored together in years — my mother had put an abrupt end to those joint sessions long before Robert entered high school — but I still saw my father and Robert together frequently. Daddy quizzed him while they worked side by side, to be sure Robert knew all the basic math and science he'd need to declare a major in biology at college. While they painted house trim together, laid a walkway to our backyard gazebo, dug limestone from the earth to create a retaining wall in the soft, steep slope to our front porch, Daddy groomed Robert, too. He had hopes Robert would follow in his footsteps. Northern Kentucky needed Negro doctors. The few in practice — added to the small number of white doctors who would consent to treat colored folks — were never enough.

Robert twisted his head to gaze at me as if I were too dense to walk the earth. "You know that's different."

"I mean it. Why can't we talk? Be friends?"

"You know why. Don't play dumb on me, now."

"I'm tired of people saying what I can or

can't do, Robert." I puffed air out of my mouth and dropped my chin against my hand, drawing circles in the sand under the arbor with the toe of my shoe. Then I plucked the shoe off my foot and threw it against the vines over my head, hard. Its impact released a shower of dead plant matter onto my head, which would have been fine had it not been laced with a few living creatures. When a spider plopped into my lap I screamed and jumped up from the bench. I brushed wildly at my skirt and backed away from the spot.

Robert threw his head back and belly-laughed, deep waves rolling from inside him. I hadn't seen him so expressive in years. It was as if in my town and on our property, Cora and Robert and Nell filtered their emotions through a fine sieve. If I hadn't been so startled by the spider, I would have marveled simply at Robert's laughter. As it was, I narrowed my eyes at him while stamping my feet and shaking my shirt, still worrying that the spider roamed in its folds.

"Oh, you got him, Isabelle. That spider ran as fast as all his legs could carry him away. But, my, that was funny," he said, mirth still wrinkling the corners of his eyes. He leaned on his knees until his laughter subsided. Then he reached for my shoe where it had fallen. He carried it to me and held it out. I took it from him, and his fingers brushed mine, barely, but enough to make a shiver run from my finger all the way up my arm to the back of my neck.

He felt it, too. I knew he did. He dropped his hand, then froze in place. I'd heard the other girls whisper about boys they liked, heard them describe how they felt when they first really and truly knew the boy liked them back, but I had never experienced it for myself. Now? I knew what I knew.

It flowed between us — even if we couldn't say so aloud. It was no longer one-sided, no longer just a daydream, however treacherous, in my own mind.

I broke the awkward silence. "Here's a question — what are *you* doing here?" I motioned to the arbor and his tools. "Well, mostly, why?"

"This is my church. And this is my church job."

"Your church job? How many jobs do you have?"

"Well, not my paid job. Every member pitches in to get things done. It's coming up on time for revival, and my job is getting the arbor trimmed and looking good and not so full of *live* things before the meetings

135

start." He grinned, and my cheeks heated up as I recalled my hysterics.

"Everyone?" I asked Robert. At my church, everyone was pulled into service on scheduled work days, of course, and the women and girls cooked and served and cleaned up for special dinners or events, but the rest of the time, it seemed the place ran itself — with old Mr. Miller's help. Mr. Miller slept on a cot in an alcove in the basement. He cleaned and maintained the building in exchange for his keep, and the ladies of the congregation rotated carrying him meals, cooking extra when they cooked for their own families, or, as in our case, having their house keepers prepare simple meals to deliver. Every couple of weeks, Cora sent Nell or Robert over to the church with a pail filled with sandwiches and fruit for Mr. Miller's dinner, along with fresh milk and coffee. He'd been there as long as I could remember, though I'd heard whispers about a wife and family and a paying job lost in the early years of the Depression. He kept to himself, mainly, and we kids avoided him, frightened of his long, dour face. But the older I grew, the more I wondered if his expression was not meanness, but grief. After all, I never saw him truly angry, not even when he huffed and grumbled at the boys for leaving shoe-polish streaks on his freshly waxed floors from running and sliding along them in their Sunday shoes.

"From the time they're old enough to walk," Robert said, "even the littlest ones have some chore or another. Straightening the singing books or the pencils, pulling weeds, whatever the mothers and Brother James divvy up between them. I've been making this arbor ready for meetings since I was thirteen." He gestured to the branches over him, then pulled at a button on his shirt, his face an awkward version of proud.

"Well, now, it's a fine-looking arbor, if I do say." I strutted around the edges, studying his handiwork. "But it looks as though you've missed a spot. Here."

Robert rolled his eyes and went back to work. "Oh, now you're the expert on arbor tending, I see."

"The expert of many things, master of none." I sighed. It was true. Sure, I was smart, a good student, but I had no special talent, no burning passion to even present to my mother as an option to her plan. I envied my classmates who were already learning trades and the few who would attend college, pursue careers they'd dreamed of for years — mostly the boys, but a few of the girls, too, whose mothers were more modern than mine. And though I did want a family one day and dared to dream of romance and true love, I feared it wouldn't be enough. I longed for something more, but I had no idea what more looked like.

"Why the sigh?"

"I'm envious of you. Of your opportunity to go to college and *be* something."

His regard balanced between amazement and amusement. "You? Jealous of me? Oh, you don't want to be me." He shook his head and grabbed a rake and started scraping together the branches he'd lopped from the underside of the arbor, dragging them toward one edge. "Trust me there on that. You have no idea."

My cheeks felt flushed as I pondered this truth. I couldn't imagine being a boy, much less a Negro — a second-class citizen in every way, or so my upbringing had taught me, though I questioned this more every day. "Well, no, maybe not. But I want the chance to do something important. Something truly important."

Robert chuckled. I followed as he pushed the trimmings toward an indention in the dirt across the yard. From the bundle he'd carried away from the hardware store, he pulled and lit a matchstick, then tossed it onto the brush pile. Eventually, leaves and branches smoldered in the afternoon sun. "You'll do something important," he said. "Too stubborn to do otherwise. May not be what you're dreaming of, may not be important in the way you think, but still."

"See? You don't laugh at me when I say things. Well, yes, you do laugh at me — you're in big trouble for that. But you take me seriously nonetheless. That *never* happens."

He seemed to withdraw a fraction, though he never moved from the stance he'd adopted, his hands on his hips, watching the fire and watching me. "What if I didn't take you seriously, Isabelle? Am I allowed that? Not taking you seriously?"

My heart seemed to shrink inside my chest like a punctured balloon. Of course he wouldn't disagree with me or poke fun at my dreams. Given who each of us was, it wouldn't be acceptable. Yet I wanted him to be honest with me, more than anything. And it seemed he was honest, no matter what he claimed. "You decide," I said, my voice hardly above a whisper. "It's not mine to allow."

My words crossed an invisible line, one that could change things between us. One that invited trust.

8
DORRIE, PRESENT DAY

We pulled into Memphis earlier than expected that evening, having made good time in spite of our stops. Still, I was surprised when Miss Isabelle asked me to drive past all the tourist spots before we found our hotel, just to look. Elvis's house was smaller than I'd pictured — considering all the fuss. His songs weren't generally my style, but some of them could move even me. (Seven down, five letters: "unaffected by joy, grief, pleasure, or pain." *Stoic*. That was me.)

I yearned to slip away later to one of the blues clubs we eyed along Beale Street. I listened now and then to the stuff my kids liked. The verdict? I liked the beat, but most of the lyrics offended my delicate sensibilities. The blues, now, that was some genuine grit. But I didn't think it would be wise to leave Miss Isabelle alone, and the vision of us together in a place like that only made me laugh. We needed to get some shut-eye anyway.

I'd helped Miss Isabelle set up a computer and an Internet connection around the time I started doing her hair at home, and she'd more than mastered it. Her online skills left me coughing in her dusty wake. She'd been all over the Web, planning our journey. I'd volunteered to find us places to stay, but she'd already taken care of it, reserved our hotel rooms and everything.

Miss Isabelle waited in the idling car in the pull-through of our first hotel. I gave the guy at the sign-in desk the reservation name and Miss Isabelle's credit card. He eyed it and asked me for ID. I handed over Miss Isabelle's. He checked it out, then gawked at me. Like he thought I was trying to *pass* for her or something. And let me tell you, passing wasn't something I'd ever be able to do. My color was plainly there for the world to see.

He pointed to the picture. "This isn't you."

"Really?" I shook my head and chuckled, but not too loud. I imagined those night-time hotel clerks got all out of whack when someone questioned their limited authority, like they were on some kind of power trip or something. "Kindly look to your left," I said. "That is Mrs. Isabelle Thomas." I pointed out Miss Isabelle sitting in her car just outside the entrance. I waved at her, and she waved back and shrugged her hands in the air, like "What's the holdup?"

"This is her credit card and her ID," I said. "She made the reservation."

"Well, ma'am, I can't take ID for someone else. We require the person who made the reservation to show the ID."

"You're kidding, right?" I said. "She's sitting right there. You can see she's the same person as the one in this picture."

"I'm following our company policy, and you need to calm down, ma'am. I will have to call security if you continue to argue with me."

"Calm down?" Really? He said that? And security? For telling the truth? Hot damn. I *was* calm until right about then, just commenting and halfway laughing. But after he said that, I knew the only thing I could do that wouldn't conclude with my hands around his neck and me getting cuffed and carried off to jail was to bring Miss Isabelle inside.

I huffed out a big breath and grabbed her ID and credit card back before I headed out to the car. I wasn't going to leave them sitting there when he might walk off and someone else could snatch them. I hardly trusted the idiot alone.

Miss Isabelle lowered the window when she saw me coming. I'm pretty sure my ears were steaming like an old-fashioned pressure cooker going good. "What is it, Dorrie?"

"Mr. Night Manager isn't confident you are the person in the ID. He would like to see you up close and personal. Mr. Night Manager probably assumes I've kidnapped you, considering we don't exactly look like we're related." I growled. I actually growled. "And whatever you do, do not tell me to calm down."

"You look calm to me, Dorrie — well, mostly — and Mr. Night Manager is going to wish he'd dealt with you, because he's not going to like dealing with me. Not at all."

I pulled open the door, and Miss Isabelle unbent herself from the passenger seat. Every time she emerged from the car, it seemed her joints were stiffer and giving her more trouble. Driving cross-country had to be hell on her skeleton and muscles after nearly ninety years of use.

But eventually, she drew herself up to her full height — all something like five feet two inches of it. That woman was tiny, but when

I squinted just right, I imagined a hat and gloves, like she was Queen Elizabeth about to walk in there and give that kid what-for.

"Young man, is there a problem with my credit card?" she said, and the night manager blushed and scraped at his Adam's apple with his grimy fingernails.

"Oh, no, ma'am. No problem at all. As I was explaining to your — your friend here, we can't take the credit card and ID from anyone but the holder."

"Well, here I am, then, ten feet closer, and I'm sure you can see clearly now I'm the person in the picture. So do your magic. And be quick about it." She turned toward a stripy upholstered chair a few yards from the desk. "You can bring me the signature slip."

"Oh, yes, ma'am. I can do that. I'm sorry for —"

"Now. Pay close attention. Tomorrow morning, we expect your complimentary breakfast buffet to be hot and the coffee fresh and strong. No leftovers from today or shriveled-up stuff that's been sitting there for two hours. We'll be down at eight sharp. Or maybe eight-fifteen. We'll need extra towels and pillows brought to our room within the next ten minutes and help with our luggage. Any questions?"

144

He tried to run his fingers through his hair, but they got stuck in what was obviously too much Dippity-do. I almost felt sorry for the guy by then.

Not really. But I did laugh a little inside at the expression on his face. He was probably some poor college student who worked the night shift so he could go to class, and I doubted he was paid enough to give us the five-star treatment. But he'd asked for it with his earlier pomposity. I bet the next time a customer was plainly sitting in the passenger seat, giving obvious permission to her companion to use the credit card, whether he followed company policy or not, he wouldn't tell anyone to calm down.

In the elevator on our way up to our room — Mr. Night Manager followed with the luggage cart on the next trip — Miss Isabelle said, "I hope you don't mind sharing a room."

You know, up until then, I hadn't thought about it. What sense would it make for Miss Isabelle to pay for separate rooms when one room with two perfectly good beds would do fine?

But I wondered how she really felt. I wondered if she'd ever spent a night with someone like me — a person of another race. I wondered how many people in general had spent the night with a person of another race.

"Well, I'm okay with it, Miss Isabelle. Of course I'm okay with it. How about you?"

She gazed at the floor numbers. Making eye contact in an elevator is hazardous to one's health. "It'll be nice to have someone else there, Dorrie. I miss having company in my house sometimes. It can be awfully lonely and quiet." She shifted her point of view to the doors as they slid open at our floor. "But God help me if you snore."

I snorted. Miss Isabelle's sense of humor was sharp as a needle fresh out of the package. I could only hope I'd be as shrewd when I had nine de cades of experience. "Me, snore? I'm more worried about you."

"Oh, you don't have to worry about me snoring. Tossing and turning, maybe, though I can't even accomplish that efficiently these days. I don't sleep much anymore. More like little catnaps all night long. All day long, too."

I'd heard people talk about that happening when a person grew older. I wondered what Miss Isabelle thought about between naps. When I lay awake at night, unable to sleep, my mind mostly raced with worries about my children staying out of trouble — lately, Stevie's unacknowledged predicament — or whether I could trust Teague, week after week, year after year, to be who he appeared to be now.

Mr. Night Manager placed our overnight bags in appropriate spots around the room, and I wondered if he expected a tip. Miss Isabelle thanked him with another Queen Elizabeth look down the end of her nose — even though he was a foot taller than she was — and gave it a twitch, as if the room didn't smell so great. I deduced he didn't get many tips; he didn't look at all surprised.

It was still early. We'd stopped for dinner outside Memphis and our stomachs hadn't completely settled. I waited while Miss Isabelle carried her nightgown and house coat into the bathroom to dress for bed. Once she was settled in the easy chair with one of her crossword puzzle books and the TV remote in hand, I said, "I'm going to step outside and make a few phone calls, Miss Isabelle. Anything else you need right now?"

"Oh, no, dear. I'll be fine. You don't have to baby-sit me. Go do what you need to do. And Dorrie?" She paused, and I saw the exhaustion in her face, extra lines I didn't remember having been there the last time I did her hair. "Thank you. I couldn't have done this without you. You're — you must be a good daughter." Her voice trembled on the last word, and my heart welled up with affection and sympathy. Something told me what ever lay in wait for her — for *us* — at the other end of this journey was going to be harder than I'd imagined so far. I was glad she wasn't alone, even if it meant I had to study my own problems from afar. I was beginning to feel I was a critical part of this thing for Miss Isabelle — even if I had no idea why yet.

I dug through my purse for my cigarettes and lighter and dropped them into my pocket when I was sure Miss Isabelle wasn't watching. I hadn't had a smoke since that morning, before I arrived at her house. I wasn't as antsy as I thought I'd be. I'd been trying to quit for the thirtieth time and was down to about three most days. Our conversation in the car had distracted me from the cravings, and I hadn't wanted to draw attention to my bad habit when we stopped for meals or rest-room breaks. I'd told myself I could live without my lunchtime smoke for one day, and I guess my ornery old self had listened. I carried my cell phone conspicuously so Miss Isabelle would think I'd been digging for it.

"I know you smoke, Dorrie," she called from the easy chair.

Busted.

"You don't have to hide it from me. I can smell it on your fingers when you fix my hair. Don't worry, it's not unpleasant. Reminds me of the old days. Everyone smoked everywhere."

"I'm trying to quit," I said on my way out the door, my automatic response to anyone who said anything about my smoking, ever. The habit embarrassed me. It was something I'd sworn I'd never do in all the years growing up around my mother and her boyfriends. I'd rarely seen any of them without a cigarette hanging off the ends of their hands like extra finger joints. My mother was half-dependent on the oxygen canisters Medicaid delivered once or twice a month now, but she continued to smoke, like the oxygen was a treat and not a necessity.

I subjected myself to mental self-abuse every time I lit up, yet I'd never managed to make it all the way to done. I'd started in high school, one or two a day, snuck in the alley behind the vocational ed room with the other cosmetology students. We weren't supposed to smoke, but the instructors turned a blind eye. They were career addicts and knew it was in our forecast as future beauticians. Smoking went with the territory. They likely hoped our cravings would end at smoking — not something worse. Too often, hairstylists turned to stripping on the side, desperate to supplement measly beginner's wages with so-called easy money. Then it was a few casual steps from stripping to hooking up for cash to finally doing the hard stuff just to forget about it — cocaine, heroin, eventually crack. A lot of my old friends from class were strung out now, barely existing from fix to fix in the worst parts of my hometown.

I was one of the blessed. I was only a smoker, and I still had my livelihood.

But even though Miss Isabelle hadn't said a negative word, my smoking suddenly seemed such a waste of income and energy. I could hardly believe — as soft and silky as her skin still felt, and as healthy as her hair still seemed for her age — she'd raised even one of those deadly bones to her lips like she'd described doing at that nightclub.

Now I wondered if Teague, too, realized I smoked. I hadn't let him too close yet, but we'd watched a few movies together. He'd pulled my hand into his, warm and lanky like the rest of him, and held it loosely. When we parted company, did he press his palm to his nose, breathing in the scent of me as I'd done with his? If so, my secret sin might not be so secret. I held the cigarettes far from my body, always outside, letting the smoke drift away from me, not realizing it lingered on my palms and fingertips like the scent of lotion might on someone else. Leave it to Miss Isabelle to make the first mention of it in all my years of hairdressing.

I'd told myself I'd quit for good before Teague had a reason to find out — if our relationship lasted that long. Now I was determined. But it wasn't just about Teague. I never wanted my kids to watch me struggle for breath like my mother did. If I quit now, I'd have leverage when I advised them it was dumb to ever begin the habit. Not that I had any reason to believe my oh-so-innocent son hadn't ever smoked a cigarette. I was sure his troubles already went deeper than sneaking cigarettes behind my back.

I brought the almost-empty pack close to my nose and took a draw of the bittersweet tobacco aroma. I counted to five, then dropped it into the swingy-door trash bin outside the elevator. I almost dropped the lighter in, too, but then convinced myself a lighter might come in handy for all kinds of emergencies. It could come in especially handy for lighting the cigarettes in the two extra packs at the bottom of my suitcase. But I wasn't going to think about those —

not if I could help it.

I couldn't imagine throwing away two unopened packs. I'd spent good money on them, and I was too married to my money. Quite possibly, to my bad habit, too. Throwing away my current pack was one thing. Going complete cold turkey was another. I still had over a thousand miles to drive in the next several days. I wasn't crazy.

9
ISABELLE, 1939

Mother began pushing me to interact with the boys at church. Why now, I wondered, when in the past she'd been satisfied to send me off to Sunday school socials or see me seated with a row of girls at church, the boys behind us, their hair slicked back and shoes shined, as if that would keep them from poking at the backs of our necks with sharpened pencils to see if we'd disturb the quiet while Reverend Creech droned on and on. Now, when Mother dawdled after services, pretending to gossip with the other women, my neck prickled. I'd catch her observing me, watching to see whether I singled out any particular boy for attention. After I reminded one boy in my grade that we had a book to read before school started again, she swooped in like a vulture and invited him to our house for homemade ice cream that evening. She gushed at Daddy later, insisting he prepare the ice-cream freezer and chip the ice while she made a rare venture into our kitchen to mix up cream, sugar, eggs, and vanilla.

The boy showed up early, and Daddy cranked the handle of the freezer, grinning, while I attempted small talk with Gerald, who flushed from the top of his skinny collarbone to the roots of his Brylcreemed hair whenever I so much as looked at him.

My brothers guffawed from across the patio, where they reclined on chaise lounges, one of them flinging an entire deck of cards at the other when he lost a game. I'd be sorting cards again soon, I could see.

"Hey, Gerald," Patrick called, "you better treat Bitty-Belle right, boy. We'll be keeping an eye on you. No monkey business, ya hear? We'll come after you. . . ." Daddy's arm stopped turning the crank on the ice-cream freezer. Both my brothers doubled over in laughter, and Daddy started cranking again.

Gerald's face turned an even brighter shade of orange. Mortified at my brothers' rudeness, I attempted a spontaneous but ill-chosen rescue. "Gerald," I said, "what do you think about the unrest in Europe?" I'd pored over the Sunday paper all afternoon, trying to understand events across the ocean.

He had no thoughts on this, but my question uncorked him. He proceeded to speak for more than ten minutes — never once looking me in the eye — about the newly opened Baseball Hall of Fame in New York, which he hoped to visit before summer's end. Daddy winked as I sank lower in my lawn chair. I wondered if Gerald might die before he took a breath, or whether I'd die of boredom first. The only thing that saved me was comparing him in my mind with Robert, who, though only a year older, looked like a man compared to Gerald, and certainly acted more like one.

Mother emerged from the house, and Gerald transferred his attention to her. He successfully deflected each of her attempts to steer him back into conversation with me while he raved about her ice-cream recipe, claiming it was the best he'd ever had, when we all knew she used the same basic ingredients as everyone else. He finally departed, his sleeve smudged with ice cream where he'd dragged it across his mouth.

"Mother," I begged. "Please, never invite him to our house again, for any reason! That was painful."

She sighed. "I guess it wasn't a particularly successful date."

Date? I growled. "It was *not* a date. I'll arrange my own dates, thank you very much."

She smiled and patted my shoulder. "Mother knows best, dear." Daddy shook his head when our eyes met, and I shrugged off her hand and escaped inside, where I could pretend to read my book while I continued my inner life, uninterrupted.

I dropped my books — sometimes now only half-read — at the library each Wednesday afternoon, then returned in time to pluck more from the shelves before Miss Pearce locked up. My new routine baffled the librarian. I'd always spent hours in summer with my elbows on the uncomfortable ancient tables, a leg curled under me in one of the straight-backed chairs, too impatient to wait between picking new books and carrying them home to dive in. Books had been my solace, my dearest circle of friends.

I told Miss Pearce I had weekly errands now and that it was too hot to tote my books along. I did not explain I had a new friend who wasn't hidden in the library stacks. That, in fact, he wasn't even welcome in the building.

I'm certain it was no accident Robert appeared at Mount Zion Baptist Church at the same time, more or less, each Wednesday, ostensibly to clip and hack away at the tangled vines over the arbor in preparation for his church's August revival. It became quite an artistic effort.

According to our tacit agreement, each of us was there, ready to resume our conversation where we'd left off the week before. Robert studied branches, eyeing the arbor for straying members of its knotted congregation, or collected freed limbs into piles for burning. I followed him or sat on a bench, watching him while we talked. I volunteered my help eventually, and I guess he trusted I'd guard the secret of our meetings — or he'd have laughed away my offer. I trailed him with rake or broom, saving him a few steps by gathering debris. My mother had always turned up her nose at physical exertion, though I suspected her restraint was due more to lethargy than gentility. I found the work, though not especially strenuous, exhilarating. The company likely helped.

Under the arbor, I discovered that my father gave Cora extra wages so Robert might remain in school, when so many of his peers dropped out to help support their families. I wondered what my mother thought. I wondered if she even knew. I suspected not. I might have been jealous, but Robert's humility about my father's generosity made jealousy impossible. And my father's generosity wasn't simply for the sake of soothing some guilty itch to help those less fortunate. He'd spotted something special in Robert long before I took notice. The more time I spent with Robert, the more his intelligence astonished me. I'd never met a boy at church or school who'd read as widely as I had, who dared speak to me of current events — indeed, who cared to speak to me much at all, as Gerald had recently proved.

And now, Robert allowed himself to do what I'd asked in our first conversation under the arbor. He trusted me.

When I asked him the same question I'd asked Gerald, he had opinions. We'd each huddled over our family radios for weeks, listening to the building tension — new alliances between Britain and Russia, a broken treaty between the United States and Japan, news trickling in of atrocities happening to Jews in Germany and beyond.

"War is worthless," I declared. "Men are simply looking for an outlet for their natural tendency to barbarianism! We need to stay out of this mess."

Robert shook his head. "Isa," he said. He'd been calling me the shortened version of my name for weeks now. I'd never had a nickname beyond the patronizing ones my brothers had called me. I loved how "Isa" rolled off his tongue, ending in a soft, grown-up-sounding syllable instead of the childish "-belle," which made me feel like a princess held captive by convention. "America will regret leaving her head in the sand too long. Mark my words."

The thought of war frightened me — the ones who would fight were my peers, no matter how they frustrated me. Still, I tried to view it from his perspective. "Would you go to war? If you could fight?"

"If I believed it was a worthwhile cause? In a heartbeat," he replied, and I fought the urge to pummel him myself, not believing he'd go to his potential death so easily. Of course, I wouldn't have to worry much — Negroes weren't allowed in combat, as though they were incapable of the same decisions white soldiers made to kill or let live.

I steered the conversation to a less uncomfortable topic, but inevitably it veered back toward a stickier one. I was delighted to find someone besides my father who would spar with me, who would engage in conversation as though I had valid things to say — even if we disagreed.

Finally, the arbor looked more than serviceable again. I wished I could attend the

159

revival services, if only to share in Robert's sense of accomplishment when his church family gathered under the neatly trimmed umbrella of our handiwork. I'd developed a sense of ownership after our weeks of labor, though my part, of course, was negligible. One day, after clearing the last section, we rested.

"Why do you trust me?" I asked.

Robert pulled a faded bandanna from his trouser pocket and dragged it along his gleaming forehead. "I trust who trusts me," he said.

I'd come to the arbor week after week, spent several hours alone with him, a Negro boy older than I was by almost a year and stronger by a long shot. I could only imagine my mother's horror or that of her friends and my peers if they discovered us. There was a prevailing mistrust of colored men, especially young colored men — even those we allowed into Shalerville to run errands or do our heavy lifting. By day, we treated them as weaker, as lower than ourselves, but when the sun set, we banished them. Then, simply the sight of a young Negro male wandering too close to the edges of town raised a collective shiver in our spines and a call for vigilante gatekeepers to run him far enough away that he couldn't be a threat.

Considering it now, I couldn't exactly finger that threat. I knew every crowd had good and bad, but I'd been as guilty as anyone, lumping entire groups under one designation. Now I questioned how a young Negro man, traveling the short distance across town in the dark of night, could pose any greater danger than one of our own. And now that I'd grown to trust Robert and considered him a friend, I wondered how the notion had originated. I supposed it was a calculated ploy to keep the Negroes in their place after they were grudgingly awarded their freedom, to prevent them from taking jobs or encroaching on living space whites had claimed.

I understood this suddenly and clearly; it was misguided fear.

I asked Robert about the signs, too, whether he knew how long they'd been there. He was even less forthcoming than my father, shrugged when I asked if he'd heard any history from his mother or anyone else. I suspected he knew more than I did but wouldn't say so.

I asked one last question. "Do you wish I were different?"

"What do you mean?" Robert said, his

voice more guarded than it had been in weeks.

My cheeks flamed, though I'd been thinking about *this* for weeks. "Do you ever wish I were more" — I paused — "*like* you?"

"Depends."

"On what?"

"Do you ever wish I were more like you?" He cocked his head, waiting.

With my inquiry turned back on me, first I sighed. Then I shrugged. Finally, I clambered up from the bench and paced. The answer eluded me. It was tricky, laid with traps. If Robert were a privileged young white person, what would I see in him? Would he still be Robert? Or . . . did I want to be with him, to cultivate our relationship, simply because he was different?

"Never mind," I said, but Robert caught my elbow as I brushed by him, intending to reclaim the broom I'd discarded when we'd stopped to rest, though there was nothing left to sweep — we'd already cleared all he'd cut that day away from the arbor, where he would burn it later. In spite of the agonizing late-July heat, I shivered at the sensation of his fingertips, calloused and unexpectedly cool, pressing against my skin.

"Only reason I'd ever wish you were different, *Miss* Isabelle," he said, intentionally emphasizing the word he never used any-more when we were alone — not even by accident — "is so we could do this in public, out in front of everyone, no worry the wrong somebody might see us. Otherwise, I think you're perfect. Every last thing about you." He released my arm and nudged me toward the broomstick, though when I grasped it, it was all I could do to stand upright with my heart going *whoosh whoosh,* a wild bird, captured and locked away in a cage smaller than its wingspan.

"Now, you get to answer my question, too." Robert leaned back, his chin tilted at me, impudent, but his eyes serious.

"I — I think you're perfect, too, Robert, but I do wish . . ."

"You wish what?"

I plunged ahead, reckless. "I wish Mother would invite *you* to the house instead of the boys she asks, trying to marry me off when I'm not even out of school. In fact, I wish we'd gone to the same school. I wish we attended the same church. I wish you walked me home from the library after we studied from the same books. Or drank sodas together at the drugstore. I wish —" I flung my hands high. "I wish for all of that, and" — I closed my eyes — "much, much more." With no backward glance, I gathered my book bag and the crumpled waxed paper that had covered a slice of pie I'd shared with him — a pie his mother had baked — and sped away down the lane, accelerating until I was running by the time I reached the road. I traveled the route home as fast as I could, not once looking to see if Robert followed.

I crashed up my steps, then stopped short, not only because my book bag dangled limp from my fingertips, reminding me of my omission, but because my mother, motionless on the porch swing, furled hand resting on her hip, observed me. "I sent Nell to fetch you home," she said. "She returned alone. Said Hattie Pearce only saw you a moment this afternoon — much earlier. That, in fact, she expected you'd be by after you finished your other errands. As you do every week."

The screen door revealed Nell peeking around the frame, eyes frightened and apologetic. I didn't blame her for telling my mother the truth — assuming she'd even want to cover for me. I wasn't sure anymore. But we both knew if Mother had caught her in a lie — and there's no doubt she would have — it would have spelled disaster.

"Isabelle? Where have you been spending your Wednesday afternoons?"

I fished for an excuse, for some plausible fib to diffuse her anger. A lie from Nell would only have made things worse.

The truth, coming from me, was impossible.

10
Dorrie, Present Day

The kids were fine. Well, Bebe was fine. By which I mean, she was her usual sweet self, showered, ready for bed, and reading one of her favorite books for the millionth time before she went to sleep, even though another one of my longtime clients brought a new stack every time she came to see me. She knew Bebe loved to read.

Bebe handed the phone over to her brother. "How's it going, Stevie Wonder?" I asked. That usually got at least a snort from my boy.

"Fine."

Now, everyone knows when your kid says that and then sits there silent, nine times out of ten it means he's anything but fine. Otherwise, he'd be rushing to get off the phone and back to what ever he was wrapped up in, or he'd be talking my ear off about the dope car he'd spied down the street, just the one he wanted, with a FOR

SALE sign and a price of only four figures, well, slightly under five, but what a good deal, Mom, and how after he bought that car, or any car, he and his buddies could take off on a six-week road trip to celebrate graduation, and it was only going to cost about a thousand bucks each, the way they figured it.

Cost *me* a thousand bucks, that is, if you looked at the fine print.

But no. He said, "Fine."

Not that I was surprised.

I tried to pick something out of him. I asked about Bailey, how she was doing and why she'd had such a long face lately, but all he said was, "She's fine, too, Mom. Damn, you're nosy." The "damn" part hurt. But I licked my wounds and let him go.

I waited a few more minutes before I dialed Teague. I didn't want to interrupt his bedtime routine with his kids. Yes, those kids, those three . . . adorable . . . *little* kids. This was another catch — a major part of my hesitation. My kids were nearly raised, Stevie Junior about to graduate (maybe) and Bebe coasting along as fine as a middle schooler can. The thought of chaperoning three more all the way from elementary school through the teen years made me slightly lime around the lungs.

And it wasn't like Teague had his kids every other weekend. His ex-wife had flat left them, no warning. Turned out she wasn't ready to be married or tied down with children after all. She'd rearranged her priorities. First, third, and fifth weekends, she and the kids played house, and the rest of the time, Teague was daddy *and* momma.

I'd wondered, at first, if maybe he wanted someone to pick up the slack the woman had left in his household. But I was slowly becoming a believer. He hired a baby-sitter when we went out, paid the going rate — and finding out the going rate made me choke. Went to work every day. Fed his children chicken nuggets and Tater Tots, like all the single moms. Went to soccer games and dance recitals, not to mention practices. He'd negotiated a deal with his company that kept him local most of the time, with all his accounts right in the metro area. On the rare occasions he traveled, he made child-care arrangements — generally, not with his ex-wife.

I took a deep breath and dialed, praying, after my little spat with Stevie Junior, for a conversation filled with sweet and light instead of hateful and spite. And oh, my goodness . . .

Teague's kids were already asleep, and

cool jazz played in the background. I pictured him stretched out barefoot and bare-chested on his leather sofa, balancing a glass of red wine against his sculpted six-pack. He'd take a sip, then set it down to run long fingers over his taper fade and down the back of his neck. His hairstylist was *good,* if I did say so myself.

Ohhh, his voice. A balm to my road-weary soul. From *hello,* I floated far out past the breaking surf in a warm, salty sea, hardly having to support myself as gentle waves washed around me. Kind of like the Gulf of Mexico down at Panama City Beach, Florida. The only beach I've been to.

If I'd called Steve while he was keeping my kids when they were little, here's what I would have heard: Stevie Junior and Bebe bickering, beer commercials blaring from the TV between penalties and goals, and Steve moaning and groaning about when I'd be home, because they were about to drive him crazy. I would have disconnected at my earliest opportunity.

But a man who had his children under control, happy, and in bed at a decent hour? Mercy. How sexy was *that*?

I tried to remind myself there was no way he was perfect. That his kids puked sometimes and misbehaved sometimes and that he had bad days, too. But it wasn't easy. I asked myself at least ten times in the course of a single conversation why a guy like Teague would be interested in me.

The obvious answer was, he was too good to be true.

He asked politely about our trip so far, how many miles we'd made, if we'd had any trouble with the car or the route or the stops along the way. I relayed the story of Mr. Night Manager — a lot funnier on the back end — and Miss Isabelle's little obsession with crossword puzzles. But in the middle of sharing a laugh over how many snacks an eighty-nine-year-old woman barely bigger than a Chihuahua could put away, my stomach flip-flopped, my scalp tingled, and I stopped mid-chuckle.

"Dorrie? . . . Hello?"

"Yeah, I'm here." I tried to cover the panic in my voice. It didn't work.

"What's wrong?"

I took a deep breath and pressed my elbows against my churning insides, weighing the wisdom of making this confession. Then I plunged ahead, not even trying to keep my voice steady now. "Oh, Teague. I just remembered I never deposited my cash take from Saturday. Not good. So not good." And then I wanted to take the words back. This wasn't something he needed to know.

Or was it?

"Uh-oh," he said. "You going to be in trouble with the bank if you don't get it in for another few days?"

"No, no, I didn't pay any bills ahead, so I'm good there. Nobody'll be hunting me down, but oh, man, I'm an idiot. I left the envelope at the shop."

"Is it locked up somewhere? Would anyone know it was there or be able to get to it easily?"

"The money's locked up, but you know my shop's not in the best neighborhood. If anyone notices I'm closed for a few days, they might decide to investigate. It wouldn't be the first time, but I usually don't leave any money there. And *crap,* if they find my cash, I *will* be in trouble next week."

I sighed and fumed, even more furious with myself — and embarrassed — than I'd ever admit out loud. I'd forgotten the money Saturday, and was lucky. Then, in the midst of all the other preparations for the trip with Miss Isabelle, I'd left it again Monday when I went by the closed shop to rearrange my schedule. I'd done a few cut and colors that Saturday in addition to some unexpected walk-ins and pulled in

171

several hundred dollars in cash. Not a huge amount in the scheme of things, but enough to pay my power and water bills, and I was counting on it. Kids had vandalized the shop before, but they rarely did more than rough things up, looking for money. Professional criminals knew the payoff for breaking into a one-chair salon — not a big venture, not worth the risk.

"Can I help? I mean, I could . . ." Teague's words trickled off, and I could hear him wanting to do something but worrying anything he offered might be taken the wrong way.

My response surprised me. "Listen, what does your morning look like tomorrow?"

"After I drop the kids at school? I don't have any appointments, and I can get to the office whenever. It's right down the hall, remember? Nobody will miss me if I'm a little late."

He worked out of his house as a sales rep for a pharmaceutical company. He made his own schedule most days — one more thing we had in common.

"Well, could you do this? I left the shop key with my mom. She's staying at the house — she'll be there in the morning. Would you run by and grab it, then check on things? I can tell you where the money is, and you could hold it for me until I get back. Or you could leave it at my house, but honestly, I trust you more than I trust my mother." I laughed nervously, wondering how he'd take that. Who didn't trust her own mother?

He rolled on like it was nothing. I told him how to find the key to the file cabinet where I kept the cash, said that I'd let Mom know he'd be by first thing in the morning. I crossed my fingers and held my breath and hoped to God I hadn't done something even more stupid.

"I'll take care of it, Dorrie. It'll be fine. If your landlord stops me, thinks I'm a hoodlum, I'll have him call you to confirm I'm on the guest list" — he thought of *everything* — "and I could even deposit the money if you'd like. I bet your bank will take cash without the account number if I tell them your name and address and the situation." He was bending over backward, reading my mind, trying to help me understand he wasn't going to pull a fast one.

After we disconnected, I stood still, gazing through the glass windows into the hotel lobby, thinking how big this was for me. I watched a cute little couple check in, the young woman waiting by the elevator with all their bags while the guy paid. They both looked so happy to be there, they had to be newlyweds, or practically so. How long had it been since I'd trusted a man that much? How long had it been since I'd trusted a man at all?

Back in the room, Miss Isabelle had drifted to sleep in her chair while I made my calls. When I opened the door, she startled. Her reading glasses tumbled off the end of her nose and onto the floor next to the bed. When I rushed over to retrieve them for her, I saw her purse, stashed way under her side of the bed. Honestly? I wouldn't have thought anything about it, except in my side vision as I bent over, I saw her almost translucent cheeks turn the tiniest bit pink.

"I'm always worried," she said quickly. "I thought, What if someone breaks in here during the night and tries to take my bag, then what will we do?"

"You sure, Miss Isabelle? I mean, you're trusting me with your whole life, more or less, letting me drive your car and sleep in the same room and all. But, okay, so I am mighty jealous of that big thing you carry around. I might sneak it into my suitcase and take it home with me."

I winked and handed over her glasses. I knew she wasn't worried about me. But still, it made me sad that she felt she had to explain herself, that she worried things might be misconstrued. We were close, that's for sure — and getting closer every minute of this journey — but, realistically, that little gap would always be between us, simply because we were different.

We'd been conditioned that way.

11
Isabelle, 1939

If my mother was overprotective before she discovered I hadn't been spending Wednesday afternoons at the library, now she scrutinized my every move. The day she confronted me on the porch, I mumbled something about wandering along the river on Wednesdays without permission because I knew she wouldn't allow it and losing track of time. My disheveled clothing and my face, flushed and sweating after running home, supported my story. She didn't question me, but whether or not she suspected the true nature of my activities, she obviously believed my reputation was at risk.

In the following days, I hovered around corners when Nell and Cora worked together in various rooms, straining my ears for a mention of Robert. I'd seen no sign of him since my confession, and my pride shrank each time I remembered the foot I'd crammed inside my mouth, apparently embarrassing both of us. Even if every word I'd spoken was true.

I heard cheerful snippets about which neighbor had finally landed a job, hushed gossip about a cousin who'd kicked her drunken husband out for the last time, quieter whispers about an unfortunate girl who'd come up pregnant, shaming her family in the worst way. But not a word about Robert, as if they'd agreed not to mention his name in my house. I knew he wouldn't have told them about our afternoons at the arbor or the feelings I'd admitted. Rather, it seemed, some hunch permeated their collective subconscious, motivating them to draw an invisible line of defense between the two of us.

I attempted to regain Nell's trust when we happened to cross paths. I hoped she'd give me a glimmer of news about Robert, but I also missed her desperately.

She kept me at arm's length, answering my inquiries with no more words than necessary, keeping her eyes focused just below mine — high enough she didn't come across as disrespectful, low enough I knew I was still on notice.

Then, one day, I was curled up in a corner of the porch swing, pretending to read. In truth, I was moping and daydreaming of

Robert. The screen door creaked open, and Nell emerged with mop and bucket. I thought she saw me. She didn't acknowledge me, but that was nothing new these days. I returned my gaze to the pages of my book, my eyes crossed slightly and the letters blurred in the laziness of my wandering attention. The heavy scent of honeysuckle drifted up from the beds bordering the porch. I inhaled the aroma and expelled the frustration my situation had created in my chest, hoping for a productive exchange.

Nell plunged her mop into the bucket, wrung it out, and moved it back and forth, back and forth along the porch's dusky gray surface in a soothing rhythm. Eventually, she hummed in time with her work, and finally, she broke into a song.

Her back was to me. I listened, entranced. We'd sung childish rhyming songs as girls, but I'd never realized how beautiful her voice was. When she drew out the lower notes, my heart contracted, and when she soared on the high ones, my heart soared, too. She was marvelous. When she stopped, I dropped my book and jumped up, applauding.

Nell jerked as though she'd been shot between her shoulder blades. She whirled, and her eyes met mine for the first time in weeks. They flashed both humor and irritation. "My goodness, Miss Isabelle, you about scared the grits and gravy out of me. How long've you been watching me act like a fool?" This was the Nell I'd missed. The one not scared to tell me most of her thoughts and many of her opinions, until I'd ruined it by brushing her away as carelessly as if she were an outgrown dress.

"Oh, Nell. I had no idea you sang so well. What's that song?"

She lowered her gaze again as I gushed compliments. "Just something I'm practicing for our revival meetings. A new song by Mr. Thomas Dorsey."

"I've heard of Tommy Dorsey. He wrote that?"

"No, not the big-band guy. Mr. Dorsey writes gospel songs. Me and my pastor, we just love everything he writes." She glanced up quickly to check my reaction.

"It's beautiful. And you're going to sing it as a solo? Oh, that's wonderful, Nell. I wish I could hear you sing it there." My voice trailed at the ridiculous suggestion. I sighed.

Nell dunked her mop back into the suds.

A tendril of an idea stretched up in my mind. I spoke in a controlled voice, as though my inquiry was born of good manners. "When is that? Your revival. It's coming up soon?"

"All next week. We'll have a picnic supper, then begin the meetings about sundown every evening, starting Sunday. I'm singing the altar call at the end." She couldn't conceal her pride, and a smile transformed her face like the sun touching water.

"Oh, Cora must be so proud, Nell. Your whole family — they must be practically bursting with excitement to hear you."

At my nonspecific mention of Robert, Nell's smile fell away. First, it deserted her eyes, and then her lips curved down. "I don't let it go to my head, Miss Isabelle. It's for the glory of the Lord." She turned with a dismissive shrug and mopped the rest of the porch in silence. Eventually, I gathered my things and went inside, her renewed coolness unbearable even in the blazing afternoon heat.

But my idea wouldn't leave me alone.

Sunday afternoon, I contracted a sudden sick headache, so bad I took to my bed and stayed there while the rest of the family played cards and drank lemonade in the shade of the back patio.

Mother checked on me as the sun finally began to sink in the sky. It blazed through my bedroom window, floating on the horizon like a giant melon ball. "Are you feeling better?" she asked. Her hovering felt more like concern than suspicion, almost as if she worried that her constant surveillance lately had actually caused my headache. I felt guilty — briefly. "Can I get you anything else before I go to bed, sweetheart?"

I already had a basin of cool water to freshen the rag on my forehead, and my father had given me aspirin — which affected my feigned illness not at all.

"Better, Mother." I sighed and shifted the rag to a new position. I'd observed her sick headaches long enough to know what to say. "What I need is dark and quiet. Sleep. I'm sure I'll be good as new tomorrow. Don't worry about me."

"Fine, then, dear. I'll leave you alone." She kissed my cheek and left, though she paused in the doorway and watched me in silence, her face void of its perpetual fussiness — a suggestion of what she could have looked like. Her softened gaze made me want to call her back, pretend I needed her after all. But I allowed my eyelids to droop, and before long, she tiptoed away.

The hushed noises of my family scattering to their various rooms finally dwindled into silence, and I slipped out of bed. I plumped up the bedding and pillows to make it appear as if I were curled on my side, my face hidden beneath the covers. I prayed Mother wouldn't venture beyond the door if she happened to check on me again.

I shrugged off my summer nightgown and pulled on trousers my brother had outgrown years before. I tucked a tailored plaid shirt I thought could pass for a boy's garment — at least from a distance — into the waistband and cinched up the trousers with a belt. My school oxfords were obviously girls', but the trousers almost covered the toes. Last, I gathered my bobbed hair as tight as I could and stuffed it under my brother's frayed fishing cap, then studied myself in the mirror. Anyone close enough would realize immediately I wasn't a boy, but I didn't plan to get that close. Already sweating in the stifling, stagnant air of my room, I wondered how men could stand wearing long pants every day in summer, as if the seasons hadn't even changed.

I rolled up the trouser legs and pulled my bathrobe over my ensemble. Carrying my shoes and the cap, I tiptoed to my door. I knew where and how to hold it — from years of experience and from practicing that afternoon while my family was in the yard — applying pressure in the right spots to keep it from groaning as I opened it only enough to slip out. When I returned, I'd shinny up the latticework on the side of the house and crawl through my window, but I could leave the conventional way if I was very quiet. We rarely locked doors, but no telling who might be up and about later, in the hallway bathroom or down in the kitchen for a cool drink. My brothers might have left, and if so, who knew when they'd return.

I managed the stairs without telltale creaks, and the back door closed neatly, without its ever-shifting threshold sticking. I leaped off the back steps and raced down the drive and away. I paused only to stuff my bathrobe under a shrub. It was reminiscent of another journey I'd made recently, only this time, I hoped, I would be running toward Robert instead of away from him.

Near Main Street, I slowed and unrolled my trouser legs and stuffed my feet into my shoes. Downtown, I hugged the buildings, slipping from one dark entryway to the next. The street was deserted except for huddles of young men smoking and shooting the breeze. Younger boys hung at the edges of some groups, hands deep in their pockets as they dreamed of being invited into those circles. Whenever I passed too close, I sped up, pointing my chin at my chest and pulling my brother's cap low in case someone should recognize me. I breathed easy when the buildings thinned and turned residential again. At the city limit, I slapped that ugly sign hard and let out a whoop. It seemed dressing as a boy had given me permission to act like one, too. It never occurred to me to be nervous about what might lurk at the dark edges along the road. Lightning bugs flickered, but always off in the distance ahead, as if they were leading the way — though my feet knew the direction even in the purple darkness.

The preacher's voice and the rhythmic, almost singsong responses from his congregation reached my ears long before I arrived. I slowed at the unfamiliar chorus, my intentions cloudy now. It wasn't as if I could simply duck under the arbor and become part of the congregation, no matter what the church's sign claimed. What a commotion I'd cause, a skinny white girl dressed in her brother's trousers.

So I crept around the side of the church, careful to hide in the shadows. I scanned the small crowd gathered under the arbor, searching for familiar silhouettes. I could see only the backs of most of the congregation, sitting or standing as they were, facing the preacher, except for those seated in a few rows of benches behind him. I spied Nell's profile there in the makeshift choir loft. She was gazing at the preacher and, along with the rest, responding with nods, amens, hallelujahs, and longer phrases I couldn't distinguish from where I watched. The preacher was younger than I'd expected — no more than a few years older than Nell — and I understood her enchantment. Not only did he speak apparent truth but he was quite a handsome fellow, too.

My eyes adjusted to the darkness, and I leaned against the church's weather-beaten clapboards. Then I started at the discovery of a young woman seated on a tree stump less than three yards away. She held a bundle close, and in a rare pause in the sound from the arbor I heard the unmistakable noise of an infant releasing from a mother's breast and then soft baby sighs while the mother lay her over her shoulder to burp. I knew immediately I'd interrupted a private moment, but I also, by then, saw the gleam of her eyes, wide and gaping at me. A young white man hidden in the shadows of a Negro church was probably not only far from ordinary but also threatening as a general rule.

I gulped once, twice. How could I ease her mind without giving away my hiding place to the others? "Don't — don't worry," I whispered, at a near loss for words and stumbling over the few I could find.

She pulled the infant closer, and her eyes opened wider, if possible. She shrank back as I stepped near. "Don't hurt my baby. Please, just leave my baby alone."

Her terror that I might do some unimaginable thing to her infant knocked the tie out of my tongue, and I rushed to reassure her. "I'm not going to hurt your baby. I'm not going to hurt anyone. I'm here for the service, like you." I yanked off my cap and closed the gap between us, leaning to study the baby. The woman hurried to cover her bosom. Some of the young mothers in my town fed their babies by breast, but always in seclusion, never acknowledged aloud, as though it were a dark secret to be concealed. I harbored a hope that one day I'd be a mother, too, and that I might feed my child that way, yet the sight of an exposed breast still flustered me. I'd never even seen my own mother's naked chest.

"It's a beautiful baby," I said, hoping to diffuse her tension and my embarrassment.

"Oh, you're just a girl," the woman said, clucking now that she could see and hear me clearly. "She's a girl, too. My baby girl." She held the baby away from her, beaming at the tiny face. The little one had already fallen asleep in the peaceful shadows, and her mother dabbed a line of milk pooling at the corner of her rosebud mouth. In spite of her relaxed pride, though, I knew I still puzzled the woman. I knew what question would come next before she spoke it. "What you doing here? I mean, you said you come for the service, but —" She shook her head.

"Well . . ." I paused, giving myself time to come up with a better reason than the ones I'd thought of so far. I settled on two truths. "That sign out front? It says 'All Welcome Here.' "

Her eyebrows rose, but she shrugged. "Can't argue that one, I suppose. Just never been tested before, far as I know. Course, here you are, hiding in the shadows."

"Well, yes. But" — I took a breath and plunged ahead — "that girl in front, in the choir? The one on the left in the pink dress." I waited to see if she followed me.

"Nell Prewitt?"

"Yes! Nell. She works for my family. She told me she was singing tonight, and I wanted to hear her. She practiced her song at my house one day, and, oh, it was like an angel on my front porch. I wanted to hear her sing at church, where I'm guessing it will be even more heavenly."

The woman pondered my answer, then nodded, and her shoulders relaxed fully. It seemed my explanation contained too many inarguable details to be a lie. I didn't tell her the third reason — that I also hoped to glimpse Robert, and, if it wasn't too much to ask, to speak to him. I'd missed him so much.

"Well, you're not too late, and it won't be long now. Preacher's almost done."

"Do you know Cora? Nell's mother? And her brother?"

"Course I do. All the Prewitts been coming to this church long as I remember. We're all raised up here. Baptized and married and buried. Their family, mine, plenty others."

"Have you seen them to night? Cora?" I hesitated. "And Robert?"

She pointed. "Cora's there on the front row, her and her man, Albert — Robert's and Nell's daddy. Probably sat down an hour early to get the best seats so they can hear their girl singing like an angel." She smiled as she echoed my compliment of Nell. "Robert, I don't know. Either sitting with the boys in the back, cutting up and being obnoxious like they do, or off somewhere doing something Preacher asked him before service. Probably that. He's a good boy. They're kind of tight, and they'll be in-laws soon, if I guess right. Brother James and Nell got their eyes on each other more than strictly necessary lately."

My powers of observation weren't half-bad. I smiled for Nell. She loved her church, and I couldn't imagine a better life for her than to be a preacher's wife instead of doing domestic work forever like her mother. We'd both been hiding things from each other — though the fault was all mine.

"Baby girl's happy now. It's time I go sit with my family. Should I tell Nell or Cora you're hiding over here?"

"Oh no!" I took a physical step back, and my heart hammered my ribs. "Cora would be worried if she knew. She'd probably feel like she had to tell my mother or my father tomorrow, and I'd be in bigger trouble than you can imagine." I shook my head furiously, picturing any of the four of them if they found out. I almost regretted fibbing about being there after all. But I felt sure the young mother wouldn't give me away.

"Okay, then. Don't you worry. But you gonna be safe getting back home? Where do you live?"

"Shalerville."

Now she shrank back. "That's a good hike in the dark by yourself. What can you do, though." It was not a question. We both knew what she meant. I wondered how she'd react if she knew Robert had walked me all the way through my town in the dark before.

"There is one thing you could do," I said. "If you see Robert, tell him I'm here? I'll wait around the corner there, near the building. After the service, perhaps he and Nell can walk me partway. But let him tell Nell. Don't worry her by saying you saw me."

Studying me, she pulled the baby tight again and pushed herself up from the tree stump with her free hand. I could envision the wheels turning in her mind as she contemplated my request, but eventually she nodded. "You be careful, young lady. I'll tell Robert you're here. Enjoy Nell's singing."

"Thank you," I called softly as she moved away. "Your baby is lovely."

The worry on her face vanished, and she beamed back at me.

She approached the arbor, slowing to study the young men grouped near the back. She whispered to a seated teenager. He pointed off to the side, and I spotted Robert then, leaning against one of the thick wooden posts that supported the arbor; he stood on the outside, not under its shelter.

190

Hands deep in his pockets, he gave the appearance of listening to the preacher, except I could see his face, which wore a faraway expression. Was he thinking of me? Of our time in the arbor? I shook myself. He had more worthwhile thoughts than mooning over me — even if I mooned over him more than I cared to admit.

The woman eased toward him and tapped his shoulder. He reached back as if to swat a june bug, then realized she was there. She whispered, pointed toward the church and the corner where I'd promised to wait. His face flashed from distant to wary. The young mother squeezed his arm, then skirted the arbor to the other side, where she slipped past a man to sit beside a toddler, who covered her with kisses, as though she'd been gone for days. She might have argued, but she was the second person I could have compared to an angel in one evening.

I hoped Robert considered her a messenger of good tidings. More likely, he was fuming about my increasing boldness. He crossed his arms and hunkered against the wooden support, almost as if he wished to mold himself to it and blend in until he disappeared. I almost ran. Even if the dark seemed formidable now, his expression brought me face-to-face with how ridiculous

I must seem — a careless, stupid child, sneaking here, placing not only myself in danger but also him, once more. I shrank into the deeper shadows, though, and backed toward the corner. If I left, he'd feel responsible to go looking for me along the dark road back to Shalerville. I leaned my forehead against the rough boards of the building to wait.

Eventually, though, hands still buried in his pockets, Robert strolled to the back of the arbor and cut diagonally across the property. Away from me. My breath caught. Would he simply leave, sidestepping my foolishness? Or had he misunderstood the young mother's instructions?

I sank against the building and sighed loudly. If the preacher had paused then or moved into silent prayer, the whole crowd would have discovered me.

Then I heard a frantic whisper. "Isabelle!"

I jerked my head around, nearly losing my balance in the process. Robert shushed me with one hand and steadied me with the other. Then he stepped back and studied me a full five seconds before he shook his head. "You crazy girl."

I clasped my hands behind my back and forced a smile. I hoped I could charm him, or at least disarm him. "You're right. I am crazy. But you're always tempting me into these silly situations. I must be losing my mind."

"Well, if you're here to listen to Nell, like the lady said you were, we'd best shut our mouths. There she goes." I swiveled, and sure enough, Nell stood at the front now, mere yards from the preacher. He'd stepped closer to his congregation and was issuing an altar call, his arms reaching toward them. He nodded to Nell, and she opened her mouth. Then out floated the notes and words she'd practiced on my porch the week before, so pure and sweet they hovered in the air all around us, even here, so far from where she sang.

She didn't look at Brother James and he didn't look at her, but a nearly palpable connection flowed between the two of them as they issued an invitation for the members of the congregation to respond to the message.

Clearly, they were meant to do this. Together.

My heart ached. My throat swelled. Tears pricked my eyes. Would I ever have such a partnership with a man I loved? So far, the interest my mother had tried to stir in me with the local boys had fallen flat. I'd met only one fellow with whom I could imagine sharing my life and living my dreams, and it was an impossible notion.

Yet here I was.

My shoulders shuddered, my sigh now broken by tears.

"Powerful good together, Nell and James," Robert whispered.

I could only nod. Nell began a new verse, and several people moved forward to line up before Brother James, where they spoke and prayed with him one at a time, some openly weeping. Others knelt where they were, heads bowed toward the rustic benches, issuing unspoken requests directly to God, without a human intercessor. It was beautiful and more inspiring than anything I'd seen in my own place of worship, where we sang the same hymns over and over, and our minister, who'd been there more years than I'd been alive, delivered the same fire-and-brimstone messages Sunday after Sunday, so monotone, nobody shook with fear unless called out publicly by Reverend Creech for dozing during his sermon.

When the last one reached Brother James, and no others stood to follow, Nell began humming the song's chorus quietly, and the choir joined her in a soothing, almost lullaby. James raised his hands high again, beckoning his congregation once more, and when no one else responded, he lowered them and clasped them behind his back. He offered a spoken prayer to end the service.

After his benediction, the choir sang again to send out the members, this time in a fast and rhythmic chorus. Some sang and clapped along; others gathered up sleepy children or embraced one another. I'd never seen such a joyful group. The state of their clothing, threadbare and outdated in most cases, indicated they struggled with poverty, barely hanging on even as America finally emerged from terrible times, yet they seemed thankful regardless.

"So, Miss Isabelle."

Robert's voice startled me. He seemed amused even in his annoyance, and I knew he'd reverted to "Miss" only to tease me. I'd temporarily forgotten him behind me, and he tilted his head now and eyed me with curiosity. I struggled to speak, my voice momentarily lost after watching his family and friends worship. Finally, I said, "I know you think I'm stupid for coming here. Isabelle and another one of her dangerous ideas." I sighed. "But that was the most beautiful thing I've ever seen. I do envy you sometimes, Robert, even if you can't believe it. Your family and your church and all the people who surround you, they amaze me. That young mother who found you? Once she got over the fact that I wasn't a white boy come to cause trouble, she was so gracious, just like that sign out front says. I didn't even know what I longed for, but now I know. This." I spread my hands, indicating the last few lingering under the arbor and more. My voice became ragged and I nearly wept. "If only I could have it."

Robert laced his fingers together and rested his chin on them awkwardly, as though uncertain what to do with his hands. "Be careful now, Isabelle. You might make me feel something I shouldn't. Make me want to do something I can't do." He took a short step back.

"What, Robert? What do you feel? Was I *not* wrong that day in the arbor? It's not just me? Tell me. Show me."

The crowd behind the church had dissipated quickly at this late hour, and the lanterns hanging near the arbor swayed in a light breeze that had begun to stir, the only other movement visible now. The current raised gooseflesh on the back of my neck where my hair, freed from my brother's cap, clung to my skin, damp with perspiration.

"You know I can't," he said. "You know it would be wrong, cause all kinds of trouble."

He was right. I knew he was right. So why didn't his protests cool my feelings? Why couldn't I step away from this folly and ask him to walk me to the outskirts of Shalerville, once and for all, back where I belonged — even if it no longer felt like home.

"Robert," I said, and shook my head the tiniest bit and gazed up, bolder than ever, into his eyes. Then he was there. He erased the space between us. Slid his hands around my waist to pull me close, then lifted one to press my head against his shoulder, just as he had during the storm. I stayed there, almost not breathing, listening to the *tum tump, tum tump* of his heart beating against my ear. I felt safe there, harbored in his embrace, and I didn't want to be anywhere else, ever again. I didn't want to move.

But then he lifted my chin with his finger and met my eyes with his, asking a question I'd never been asked, all with those simple gestures.

I leaned my head back, still cradled by his hand, and raised up on tiptoe. Yes.

He pressed his mouth to my mouth, gentle and hungry, and his lips, soft and warm, against mine. I gasped when his tongue gently prized them apart to explore the very edges of their interior. He drew back again, then dropped barely perceptible kisses on my forehead, my cheeks, my jaw line, and even on the underside of my chin, where

I'd never dreamed the nerves could be so sensitive to a touch lighter than the tickle of a blade of grass.

I was unable to contain my giggle. He stopped. Held me away from him and studied my face. I wondered if I looked different now.

"Where did you learn to do that?" I asked. I was serious. I couldn't picture him reading the racy stories my classmates hid from their mothers. Perhaps he'd seen movies — a love story in a Cinchy cinema that permitted Negroes in the balcony.

He tilted his head. "Maybe I'm a natural. Or maybe I can't reveal my sources." I felt a twinge of something. Was it jealousy? Jealousy of the other girls he might have kissed this way before? But what right did I have to think I should be the first? The only?

What right did I have at all?

He must have detected my sudden doubt, because he slid his fingers down to my elbows, then pushed me slightly away and rested his hands on his hips. "You make a right pretty boy, Isa, but I suspect it's time you were getting home."

We walked in silence at first. I'd forgotten my worries again and was so caught up in the euphoria of the evening, I didn't notice when his steps began to drag. His face grew more serious and anxious the closer we came to that sign at the edge of Shalerville. "Isabelle?" he asked finally, and dread wormed its way through my stomach.

"Don't say it. Don't," I muttered, and pulled his hand to mine, not caring we were mere feet from a place opposed to his very existence except for the services he could perform by daylight.

But he did say it. "That can't happen. It didn't happen."

"I don't care about them, you know." I jutted my chin toward town, then leaned my head back and gazed blatantly into his eyes. "I don't care what anyone thinks. I meant everything I said. Every word."

"Isabelle. What happened tonight? It can't ever be more than that — a nice memory. For the both of us. You know it. Anyone ever finds out I kissed you, you know what they will do to me? What your momma will do to you? It's impossible."

"But —" I drew a breath. "Robert Prewitt, I think . . . I think I might love you." My heart raced and my face burned and my fingers, wrapped around his, trembled.

"You just — you're just a girl, Isa. A child. You don't know what you're saying."

I flinched at his dismissal. But I was convinced it was his way of denying what I believed he felt, too. He was right; I was only a girl, not even seventeen, but I couldn't deny the feelings I'd finally acknowledged, feelings that had grown each time we'd met. In my yard. At the creek. Every week under the arbor. Tonight. More than ever, tonight.

"But I do know what I'm saying. I do, Robert. Can you tell me you don't feel it? That you don't feel the same? I have to ask. I know you're afraid. I'd be afraid, too. I *am* afraid." He tried to turn away, to fix his gaze elsewhere, but I let go of his hand and reached to turn his face toward mine. "Do you love me, too?"

He shrugged. "What if I said I did? What if I said, yes, I — I think I might love you. What good would that do either of us?"

I couldn't and didn't answer his question. All I wanted, more than ever, was to know my feelings weren't unfounded. His statement, in its roundabout manner, gave me enough of a hint to understand he felt them, too.

12
DORRIE, PRESENT DAY

I twitched around on the bed all night, worrying about my money. Then worrying about trusting Teague with my money. Then worrying about anything else I could think of to worry about. By morning, I felt as wiped out as if I'd spent all night walking a newborn baby who never stopped fussing. Not something I planned to do for real anytime soon, see, so I worried about my son and the probability he'd knocked up his girlfriend, too.

I hoped my restlessness hadn't kept Miss Isabelle awake, especially since she said she didn't sleep well anyway. What a pair we'd make on the road, trying to stay awake.

But she surprised me again, pert and ready to hitch an elevator ride to the complimentary breakfast buffet she figured she'd actually paid for as part of the room charge. She liked to get her money's worth. When I did her hair, she always pointed out any spots I missed — not often, please note.

"Rise and shine, Dorrie Mae. Sun's up."

I groaned at her voice and said, "Damn you, Susan Willis." When Miss Isabelle shoved open the blackout drapes I dragged a pillow over my eyes, because, sure enough, the sun was right there glaring at me. I reluctantly pulled the pillow away and swung my legs over the side of the bed, burying my face in my hands as I ordered the rest of my body to wake up. It didn't work so well.

"I heard you over there worrying all night. I'm sorry we have to get going so early, but we need to get on the road or we'll be running behind schedule." I'd always figured her for a morning person, and now there was no doubt. But I also figured she had on her game face, and this was no vacation.

"No problem, Miss Isabelle. Just doing a limb check here to be sure I'm alive. I'll be fine once I get a caffeine drip going." I forced myself up and dressed quickly. I'd taken a quick shower before bed, and since I couldn't do much about my hair on the road, I patted it flat as I could and promised I'd do better when we arrived at our destination.

People were often surprised that, as a hairdresser, I wore such a simple hairstyle.

Early on, I'd discovered I had no inclination to devote much time to my own hair. I kept it trimmed evenly all over, short and natural, sometimes with a deep auburn rinse. In my humble opinion, I had a nicely shaped head, and my style always got plenty of compliments — if mostly from white folks. Momma ceaselessly complained that I was letting a head of good hair go to waste, believing I should advertise my services by making the most of it. I disagreed. My customers came to me for one thing — to leave feeling shiny and pretty, like a new penny. They didn't give a rat's anything how my hair looked as long as it was neat and unobtrusive. (Seventeen across, eleven letters: "inconspicuous, unassuming." *Unobtrusive.* Big, fancy word.) I was the vehicle to get them from zero to beautiful in sixty minutes or less. Along the way, if we became more than casual acquaintances, then hallelujah and pass the potato salad, because then my hair ought to be the least of their worries. I counted on that from my friend Miss Isabelle as I gave it one last pat.

Downstairs, we settled ourselves before plates of steaming eggs and toast, cold milk over cereal, and lukewarm coffee. Miss Isabelle turned her nose up at the cinnamon rolls, saying she figured they weren't worth the fat it took to frost them. No wonder she kept so trim. I'd seen photos around Miss Isabelle's house of her at various ages, and in every one, she looked like she'd just come off six months of Jenny Craig, her waist tiny and cinched in by belts the likes of which I hadn't worn since before Steve Junior came along. Or never. I sighed and passed up the rolls, too, figuring it wouldn't hurt to follow her lead. I could smell them, though, and it nearly killed me not to have one between my lips. Or a cigarette.

"How do you know a good man when you see one?" I asked. Abrupt, yeah, but I needed to know. I hadn't had enough sleep to ease into the question.

"A good man," she said, and raised her fork to nibble scrambled egg. So much for a quick answer.

"See, I know how to find the scummy ones, no problem," I added. "Well. I don't even have to look — as soon as one leaves off, the next comes running. I'm a loser magnet."

"A good man," Miss Isabelle began again. "For starters, he treats you well. But just as important is how he treats everyone else."

"Like, how do you mean? His kids? His momma?"

"Sure. But there's more. Whenever he

takes you to the movies, does he thank the ticket takers? When you're riding in his car, does he hog the road? Even after two weeks, or two months, is he respectful to his fellow man, no matter that person's position in relationship to him? In other words, does he still tip the waiter?"

"That's good, Miss Isabelle. That's really good." She was right. I'd never thought about it before, but nearly every man I'd dated had treated me like a queen the first few times we went out, but griped at servers about food being cold or bland when it was just fine, or cut off drivers who were desperate to enter the highway, even if there was plenty of time to get wherever we were going. Eventually? He treated me the same.

"I've known a few good men in my life. They're out there." Her eyes went a little hooded and soft, as if she'd drifted into a memory, and her lips curved in a small, private smile. I wished I could climb inside her memories beside her. I wanted to see the things that still gave her happy thoughts after so many years. "My husband was a good man. But he wasn't the only one," she said. Then she focused sharply. "You think you've found a good one, Dorrie?"

"I don't know. I'd like to think this man I've seen a few times — Teague? — is a good guy, but I don't trust myself anymore. I almost prefer the known evil — the guys I can tell will spoon-feed me whatever I want to hear, then break my heart one more time in the process. But this one? Miss Isabelle, you know that saying, If it looks too good to be true —"

"— it probably is," she said, finishing for me. "But maybe not every time."

I told her about asking Teague to check on my shop, about how I wanted so much to believe he was trustworthy and would do what he said, no more, no less. About how my batting average in picking trustworthy men was about as low as you could go.

"How long have you known him?"

"We've been going out a little while, but —"

"When's the last time you asked anyone to do something this big for you?" she asked. "Any man," she added.

I sipped my coffee and inventoried my past relationships. "A while." I shook my head. "Okay, a long . . . long . . . time."

"You know more than you think you do, then. Give yourself credit."

"Maybe. But damn — *darn* it, if he lets me down, I am through with men. I'm done. Who needs them?"

She sighed and shrugged, her gaze fuzzy

and unfocused. We finished eating in silence.

I'd refilled the tank and climbed back into the driver's seat at a gas station near the Memphis hotel when my phone rang. Miss Isabelle sat patiently while I dug the thing out of my pocket.

"Hey, Teague, what's the news?"

"Hi."

I could tell by his voice, by the ginger way he greeted me, by what he didn't say and the silence drawn out long and heavy over the line. "Just tell me."

"I'm at the shop."

"Yeah?"

"Someone definitely broke in since you left. I'm sorry, Dorrie. Wish I had better news."

I closed my eyes and sighed through my nose. "The money?"

"Gone."

I slammed my palm on Miss Isabelle's steering wheel, and she jumped an inch in her seat. "Sorry," I muttered, my hand over the receiver.

"It's okay, honey," she whispered, motioning for me to continue my conversation.

"What else?"

"Well, they jimmied the lock to get in. The file cabinet is messed up pretty good, too.

207

Pried open with a crowbar or something. Knocked over a few things here and there. That's it."

It was more than enough. I never left the file cabinet locked overnight — probably a dead giveaway where I kept the money. I cursed myself for not putting in an alarm system. Every month I swore I'd do it. Until I paid bills. Then I decided to wait another month. The doors in the old-fashioned strip mall were too easy to burglarize. It hadn't mattered much, though I'd spent some money fixing the lock the other times. In the long run, it had cost me less to replace locks than it would have to install and monitor an alarm system. But I'd never forgotten money before. The scales had tipped.

"Still there?"

"Yeah." I sighed. "Look, would it be too much trouble for you to make a police report?"

"Of course not. I'm also going to run by Home Depot for something to board up the door until you get back. Work for you?"

"Oh, Teague." I shook my head. "You're a lifesaver. I'm sorry to get you involved."

"Don't apologize. It's no trouble at all, and I'd like to think you'd do the same thing for me if the tables were turned."

I wondered. Honestly, I'd probably run

the other way, faster than a bullet. I'd had enough of needy men to last me a couple of lifetimes and then some. Then again, none of them had been Teague. He blew me away. He wasn't just kind; his concern had legs that walked.

As soon as I disconnected, though, I started second-guessing. Miss Isabelle watched me. She could probably see the little nerves running up and down my stomach muscles, clenching their fists and pumping them in the air, chanting, "Run away! Run away! Run away!" Telling me Teague could have done the damage himself, then pocketed the money and lied right across the phone line. I pulled onto the interstate and stared at the flat road out of Memphis.

"I'm sorry, Dorrie. I feel responsible. But for me asking you to bring me on this trip, it never would have happened. Between this and your worries about Stevie Junior, I feel like we should go home. At the very least, I'd like to reimburse you for the money you lost." I shrugged. I wanted to scream and throw a hissy fit about the money. Even worse, I knew I might have to put down my pride and take her up on the reimbursement — as a loan, of course. But going home wasn't going to change anything right now.

She didn't speak again for a while. About ten miles down the road, she pulled her crossword puzzle book out and flipped to a clean page. She peered at the clues and scribbled a few answers. My hand was clenching the armrest, and she reached over to pat the back of it. "Try not to worry, Dorrie. About the money or the man. I have a feeling both will work out fine. Now, help me. The first one is two across — which hardly *ever* happens — and it's six letters. . . ."

I listened with half an ear while I rattled around my head for another kind of answer.

13
ISABELLE, 1939

Two weeks.

Two weeks since I'd seen him. Two weeks since he'd kissed me. Two weeks since I'd told him I loved him.

I began to imagine he'd seen my confession as the ridiculous and dangerous ravings of a schoolgirl. He wouldn't humor them. He'd never set foot near my house again, and he'd avoid any possibility our paths would cross if he could help it.

But then one day, he showed up to help my father repair the retaining wall. The sand packed around the grooved chunks of limestone was eroding, and my father feared their hard work from the previous summer would go to waste, the stones would eventually loosen, and then the front yard would slide slowly south until it simply fell away from the house, leaving us teetering on top of the hill.

Monday, the hardware store delivered

three bags of cement at the bottom of the steps. Late in the afternoon, Robert met my father there. He instructed Robert how to mix the concrete. I watched from an upstairs window, hidden behind lace curtains. The sun sank lower, and Robert shook hands with my father. He went away down the street, away from me again.

But the next morning, he returned before I woke to mix concrete in the wheelbarrow, then scoop and force it carefully between the stones, using a damp rag to wipe away traces from their outside surfaces so their textures remained visible from the street. My father, busy with patients, left the work to Robert's capable hands.

My tension swelled while I waited for an opportunity to speak to him, for a workable excuse. When my mother retired for her rest after our midday meal, I rushed to the kitchen. Cora was peeling eggs to devil for our supper. Nell was occupied somewhere in the house, maybe even absent. I hadn't seen or heard her for several hours.

"It's miserable outside again," I said to Cora, and dropped into a chair across from her.

"Lordy, yes, Miss Isabelle. This summer's about to kill me. I feel for my son out there in that blistering heat, but I expect he'll survive. You young people tolerate weather better than us old folks."

It had been a long, long time since she'd mentioned Robert in my presence. "Do we have lemonade, Cora? I sure could use a cold glass."

"We do. Give me a minute, and I'll pour you some."

"I'll get it." I hurried to the cabinet and pulled out two glasses. Cora raised her eyebrows when she saw them, but she said nothing. I chipped ice off the block and filled both glasses, then poured Cora's fresh-squeezed lemon goodness over it. "Thank you, Cora. I'll carry Robert a glass, too. He must be thirsty in the heat."

"Oh, no, Miss Isabelle." She'd peeled the last egg and hurried to wipe her hands down her apron after rinsing them at the sink. "No need. I'll take it. And you can't use that glass for —"

"I've got it," I said. My look gave her no chance to argue, though I hated pulling rank to get what I wanted. I cringed at the loud sigh emanating from the kitchen behind me as I hurried down the hallway. I used my arm and hip to push open the screen door, then left my glass on one of the flat slabs jutting away from the porch on either side of the steps. It would give the impression I hadn't intended to do anything more than deliver Robert's drink. I carried his glass down the walkway and descended the steps to the street.

He blinked when he saw me, then buried the blade of his trowel in the wheelbarrow. He'd just mixed a fresh batch of concrete. He waited wordlessly; I felt suddenly shy.

Finally, I offered the glass of lemonade. Confusion clouded his eyes as he looked from the glass to his hands and back. As Cora had pointed out, I'd unthinkingly used one of our nicer glasses. Obviously, he worried he'd ruin it with the half-dried mess on his hands. But I had a handkerchief tucked in my side pocket. I pulled it out and wrapped it around the glass.

"How's that fancy thing any better? I'll mess it up, too."

"It's an old one." Or maybe it was one of my newest handkerchiefs, cut and edged by me in a fit of boredom earlier that month — and likely laundered, pressed, and starched by his mother or sister a day or two before.

He glanced around dubiously, but I thrust the glass closer, and he took it. The contrast of the back of his hand against the snowy square was startling in the harsh sunshine. I reached to shade my eyes.

He gulped the lemonade and returned the glass before I could even lean against the stones he hadn't begun to repair yet. But lean I did. He turned back to the wheelbarrow and pulled his trowel from the quickly setting glop. "Have to hurry. This hardens fast."

"Don't let me keep you from working. Pretend I'm not even here." It was a directive, not a pleasantry. He craned his neck to look up at the front windows of the house, but his mother was the only one aware I was there. She couldn't see me even if she happened to be looking. And the street curved slightly before reaching my house at the end of a narrow lane, so even our nosy neighbors couldn't see me wedged against the wall. The lane ran into a meadow too damp for building on and eventually met the creek where Robert taught me to catch minnows, where we'd been caught in that fateful thunderstorm.

"So, what've you been up to these last few weeks, Robert? Since I saw you."

He pressed the lumpy mixture between stones rhythmically, smoothing it around each, then wiping them clean. "Nothing out of the ordinary."

"I've missed you," I said, wasting no more time with small talk. Any second, someone could interrupt us, looking for me, wondering why the ice melted in my lemonade on the porch while I'd wandered off.

His hand, holding the handle of the trowel, paused against a stone with fossils clearly embedded in its surface. "You can't. It's a bad idea. I told you. That whole night — you know it was a mistake."

"Don't tell me what I feel. I did miss you. Horribly, the last fifteen days. I counted. I thought I would fade to nothing before I saw you again."

He turned and I detected a gleam in his eyes at my drama, but when he saw my sober face — I meant every word — the amusement fell away. "Okay, then," he said. "I admit it, I missed you, too. I hear you. I understand it. But, Isa, I asked you then, what can we do about it? Nothing. You know it. I know it. We're like that concrete there. Mix you and me together, and we make something too hard to work with in the wrong place. This here" — he gestured around him, indicating more than the street in front of my house, his hand encompassing the town, maybe even the whole world — "is the wrong place. It's flat illegal. We'd be crazy to even consider it."

"It's too late. We've already considered it. It's a good thing, Robert. You know it is."

"You might think I'm being mean and ugly here, but, Isabelle, you've got to leave me alone." He'd returned to his work, but he stopped again now and looked me full in the face. "You want to get me killed?"

I trembled. He spoke the truth.

His rejection had already rubbed me raw, torn me open — even if it was a rejection of what could be and not what we both felt. The truth blistered my heart.

My eyes filled, and he turned away fast, but not before I felt the full force of his own emotion and reaction to my sadness slam back into me. I gripped the empty glass, though my handkerchief slipped loose and fluttered to the ground as I turned away. When I paused to retrieve my glass from the stoop, I saw him bend to pick up the delicate fabric, and he raised it toward me. I shook my head and he dropped his hand, then lifted the hankie again and pressed it into the pocket sewn against his heart.

Inside, I nearly plowed through Nell, who stood frozen by the door, her face stricken. I knew she'd witnessed what she could see from there. The last, important part. She bowed her head as I pushed past. I crashed the glasses down on the kitchen counter, neither bothering to empty mine nor wipe up the sticky mess I created as lemonade splashed over its rim. Cora was nowhere around now. I ran past Nell again and up the stairs to my room, where I threw myself on my bed, my face pressed hard into my pillow. But anyone in the hallway might still have heard my angry cries.

I'd so longed to see Robert again, where I could force the matter into the light of day. I'd known there was a greater chance he'd turn me away than welcome our forbidden relationship. But the reality hurt more than I'd imagined.

I'd allowed myself to dream of the two of us sneaking behind our families' backs if that's what it took, stealing time where we could. I'd not thought past that to the inevitable end — for we'd have had to end it eventually.

Robert was right. Marriage between Negroes and whites was not only taboo but also illegal. What good was our love if consecration in the eyes of God and the law was forbidden?

But in my selfishness, I was devastated that Robert wasn't willing to borrow what we could. I was furious, not only with him but with myself, for allowing my heart to dream. I was embarrassed and ashamed.

For days, I went downstairs only for meals when my mother or father insisted, or to go out for church on Sundays.

My mother fretted, afraid her tendency to sick headaches was hereditary. My father seemed resigned, although disappointed, as I'd always possessed an adventurous spirit, nothing like the pretty flower he'd married, only to discover she wilted daily at noon.

Daddy insisted I accompany him on a house call that required a long drive into the country, as I often had in the past. Back then, more often than not, I'd simply wandered his patients' acreage, thrilled to explore new spaces, or read in the car with the top down under the shady canopies of wise old trees. If there were children, I'd played with them, their parents grateful for the diversion while my father examined or treated, the kids delighted to have company in their isolated surroundings. On occasion, Daddy even let me watch while he performed minor procedures, allowing me to hand him supplies as long as I'd washed up beforehand and the patient didn't object. Daddy affectionately called me "Nurse" when we were out, claiming he'd rather have me assist any day.

But this time, I refused to leave the car, even when the upholstery threatened to scorch my arms and legs. I turned away when he asked me to tell him what was wrong, afraid he might read something other than physical pain in my eyes — afraid he might discover my secret.

I longed to share it with him. My silence violated our connection, the one he didn't have with my brothers, who spent their days and nights carousing, wasting his money, and getting into senseless trouble. I knew, even though he'd never declared it aloud — instead, gently, subtly prodding me toward it — he hoped for greater things from me, his studious, curious daughter. If nothing else, I think he believed I'd make an excellent physician's wife, more suited as a help-meet for a small-town doctor than his own wife had turned out to be. If he'd known about Robert and me, he'd have been surprised how accurate his prediction could have been — if only that relationship wasn't impossible.

But I realized now that he'd never stood up to my mother when it came to the big things. Even if he understood the emotions that tore at me like milkweed against flesh, I couldn't trust that he'd offer any more help than a shoulder to cry on, and I was out of tears.

Wind seared my face as we drove home. I kept my eyes on the blurred landscape at the side of the road. I felt Daddy's gaze upon me when he'd glance away from the highway, and it occurred to me to wish, maybe for the first time in my life, he were different. I wondered if my mother wished he'd be stronger, too. Maybe that was all she'd ever wanted.

One dull day ran into the next. The heat still burned like smoldering ash, though the bitter scent of summer's finale now permeated the air. A timid knock startled me from a restless nap. I'd dozed off reading *Little Women.* My favorite stories distracted me from self-pity — temporarily. As quiet as the tap was, I sprang from the bed, crashing my book to the floor.

She peeked around the edge of the door. "Miss Isabelle? Can I come in?"

I waved her in and settled back on my bed. "I think my heart just stopped," I said. Of course, it was already broken, but how could she know that?

"I'm sorry, Miss Isabelle. Didn't mean to scare you." She retrieved my book from the floor, her finger marking the place where it had landed facedown. I reached for it and closed it, then returned it to the shelf over my bed.

She carried nothing — no laundry to put away, no cleaning supplies. She stood before me, threading her apron between her fingers.

"What is it, Nell? Did you need something?"

"Yes, ma'am," she said. Yet stayed there, no explanation.

"Oh, Nell, for pity's sake, you needn't call me 'ma'am.' It makes me sad we're all grown up now and you feel you must address me as if I were my mother. Be assured I am *not* my mother." I shuddered.

"I know it, Miss Isabelle. But Momma says I must pay you the same respect now you're a young lady."

"Hogwash. You respect me. And I respect you. Now, tell me why you're here. I can hardly stand it."

"Well. You know that day? The one you talked to Robert while he patched up the retainer wall?"

I nodded and waited.

"My brother, he's moped around the house ever since. Like you've moped around here. Something ain't right with either of you. It's got me so worried."

I weighed her words. After all our years growing up together, I knew I could trust her with anything, yet the situation seemed hopelessly silly when I considered telling her. I fiddled with a pencil from my night-stand.

Nell nudged the side of my bed with her knee. "So. You think of anything I should know about Robert? Anything that might help him not be so moody? So down?"

"Oh, Nell. I won't involve you. I can't."

She straightened her shoulders, her face stern. "I'm *asking* you to involve me. I can't stand to watch you two this way."

She stood still while I considered. Finally, I checked to be sure the door was closed tight. I spoke in hushed tones, carefully guarding every syllable of my confession. It surprised me to find the telling wasn't awkward at all, speaking of my deepening affection for Robert — even if he was her brother. I didn't tell every detail, but I sensed she comprehended the depth of my feelings. And every second, she was stoic. It was obvious none of it surprised her.

I finished. She shook her head. "It's what I've been afraid of. I asked Robert what it is, why he's so blue, and he brushes me away. But I know what a young man looks like when he's in love." Her voice trembled, and the glow in her cheeks heightened.

"I know, too, Nell. I saw it that night at the arbor. It's obvious you and Brother James love each other, and he's a good man.

I'm thrilled for you. It's just — it's a shame things aren't so simple for me and Robert." I pulled at my bangs and twisted a lock around my finger — I was probably nearly bald from this habit I'd long held but only recently perfected.

"It's not smart," Nell said. I nodded miserably, twisting even tighter.

"But I'll be thinking on this while I do my work today, Miss Isabelle," Nell said. My head snapped up. "My two favorite people in the world, so down in the dumps . . . this makes me blue, too." She stepped closer to the bed and touched my shoulder. As young girls, we'd held hands, dancing and playing together in the garden, or huddled so close our foreheads touched while we whispered secrets. But in recent years, we'd begun to observe our mothers' conventions, and I'd become careful not to do anything to cause my mother to scold me — or worse, to scold Nell. Since the night I'd brushed her off, we hadn't touched except by accident.

My throat swelled at her fingers pressing on my shoulder. The pressure hurt, making me painfully aware how thin I'd become. Too thin to begin with, I'd probably courted danger with my refusal to eat more than I had to lately, and I cringed to imagine what Robert would think to see me now — a wraith. But in this moment, I was more conscious of the regret I felt for the breakdown between his sister and me. I was thankful. Nell had returned to me.

14
DORRIE, PRESENT DAY

We made good time leaving Memphis, and I drove three hours before we needed to stretch our legs. We weren't ready for lunch yet — still full of complimentary breakfast buffet — but Miss Isabelle asked me to pull off the road in Nashville. We parked in a visitor's space at the front of a college I'd never heard of.

I checked my phone, eager to see if Teague had called back. *Damn.* I'd missed four calls and a whole slew of text messages. But not from Teague. My heart raced when I saw Stevie Junior's name on every single one. If he was calling me, it couldn't be good news. The messages were ambiguous, though. "Call me," or "Mom, call me ASAP," again and again. My fingers shook as I hit the call-back button. Was it my mother? A heart attack or a fall while I was on the road? Or, heaven forbid, had something happened to Bebe? My sweet little girl was an innocent.

If anyone had done anything to her, so help me God.

It wasn't any of those. But it was worthy of my panic.

"What is it, Stevie? Momma okay? Bebe?"

"They're fine, Mom. But you better brace yourself. I got two things to tell you, and neither one's gonna make you happy with me. In fact, I'm probably lucky you're not here, or I'm pretty sure you'd go ahead and kill me now."

It'd been weeks since Stevie Junior had made a speech that long in my presence. It had been all I could do to pull guttural *whats* and *yeahs* out of him when I asked him to do something or, heaven forbid, inquired about his life. This was not a good sign.

"Okay. Well. Hit me."

He breathed a little heavier. "Mom, uh, are you sitting down by any chance?"

I wasn't. I was pacing back and forth next to the historical marker Miss Isabelle was studying in front of the college. I suspected it was about to turn into a hysterical marker. "Nope, got nowhere to sit. Come on, now, Stevie. Spill."

"I have to tell you this in order, Mom. First part first, so the second part makes sense. Not that it's going to make sense either way or make you any less mad."

He was trying my patience. "Stevie. Spit. It. Out. Now."

"Mom . . . Bailey's . . . she's . . ."

"Pregnant?"

Dead silence on the other end for a full thirty seconds. There was my answer.

"You knew?" he asked finally, wonder in his voice. And relief.

"You think I've spent the last thirty-some-odd years wandering around with my hands over my eyes and ears, son? Think I've learned nothing about boys and girls and the ways they get themselves into trouble and how they act when they do? Shoot, Stevie. I've just been waiting for the news. But I wish you'd told me earlier. Like in the privacy of our own home. Not when I'm on the road, trying to help my friend here at a very serious time. For the love of God, Stevie, we're on our way to a *funeral*."

"Momma, I'm sorry."

"Yeah." Ouch. I wasn't shocked or surprised, but I wasn't lying, either. I was disappointed in my boy. I'd done my best to provide everything he needed to come up better than I did, to make sure he knew how to take care of himself and the girls he hung out with. But each generation of teenagers, it seems, is no smarter than the one before.

Still.

"Oh, Stevie. I'm sorry, too. I know it was an accident. I love you, and we'll figure this out." There. I'd said the proper words of support and encouragement, the right thing to do, even if I wanted to jump through the telephone and strangle the dickens out of my kid.

"Well, that's where the other thing comes in. We, uh, Bailey and me, we decided she's too young to have a baby. It's really bad timing for both of us. She — *we* made an appointment. To get, you know, an abortion."

My heart stopped. I know it did. I heard leaves rustling around me. What the *hell*? An abortion? No. Freaking. Way. And *bad timing*? Hell, yeah, it was bad timing. Too bad they weren't thinking about timing when they couldn't keep their hands off each other.

"I know what you're thinking, Mom."

"Yes."

"But Bailey, she's already made up her mind. She can't imagine being big and pregnant or having a baby, what with starting college next year and all. Plus, her parents would seriously freak. They'd probably kick her out if they knew."

"Her parents don't know?"

"No. As of now, you make the third person, counting us. Well, maybe she told Gabby — her best friend. I don't know for sure."

A girl named Gabby keeping a secret? I would have laughed if I hadn't needed to cry more. "Oh, baby. We have to think about this. Can't it wait until I get back? I'll be home in just a few days. The three of us can sit down. You know how I feel about this."

"Mom, people do it all the time."

"I don't care what other people do. That's their business. I care what we do. *Our* family. I think about *you,* Stevie."

I heard him breathing hard, and I knew he was reflecting on what I'd said, what I'd always said. That I'd considered it myself for maybe ten seconds. That I was so thankful I had him. That I couldn't imagine my life without him.

But I also knew — and this was hard — that this time it was not my decision. "I'm not saying you have to do what I want, but I think we need to talk. A couple more days won't make a difference."

"The appointment's tomorrow."

My heart sank down low, somewhere around my navel. Suddenly, I felt powerless, like I was circling the planet with next-to-zero gravity, barely hanging on, watching everything on my part of the marble spin right out of control.

"So, Mom? Here's the second part."

"The second part? That wasn't the second part? Stevie . . ."

"No. There's more. See, the appointment costs about three hundred. Neither of us had any money. You know I don't."

Fingers of dread curled up and pinched the back of my neck. Then I did find a place to sit. A concrete bench, in fact, conveniently tripped me in my stumbling around, and I sank down, not even caring its surface was covered with bird droppings. At least they were dry.

"Oh no, you didn't. Oh no."

"I haven't even told you yet."

"Oh, Stevie. Please tell me you didn't." The silence deepened between us. I knew, and he knew that I knew, even if he wasn't ready to admit it.

The money at the shop. Oh God. He'd been the one to break in and take it. My baby son, who'd up until a year or so before never been able to look me in the eye and lie. The one all the teachers said they counted on to do the right thing even when they weren't looking.

Unplanned pregnancy? It happened to the

best of us. Like I could talk.

Burglary? Lord. Have mercy.

Finally, he began talking again, in a raggedy voice, and I knew it cost him to tell me the truth, but I cut him no slack on this one.

"I was there when Teague came for the key this morning, Mom. Gran gave it to him, and I just sat there and watched, feeling like I was going to puke. I thought you'd come home and figure out someone broke in and fix the door like you always do. But I wasn't thinking at all, was I? I couldn't believe you left any money" — his voice went north — "and I was kind of hoping you hadn't. Because then I could have told Bailey we were out of luck. We'd have to figure something else out or wait. But there it was. Three hundred dollars. Mom, I couldn't figure out what else to do."

So now it was my fault. But then, Stevie Junior's voice caught, and my son broke into the caliber of sobs I hadn't heard in years, not since he'd figured out his daddy was gone for good, that he wouldn't come dragging his tail home one more time, begging me to take him back. "I'm so sorry, Mom. I'm stupid. I hate myself. I didn't know what to do." He sobbed for a few minutes while I let him suffer. While I let *me* suffer.

Anyone who thinks a seventeen-year-old is mature enough to always know the difference between a smart choice and a dumbass decision hasn't been a mother to a seventeen-year-old. The reminder sucked. And I did blame myself, too. Why, oh why, had I left the money? I pounded a fist against the rough concrete bench, the pain of the impact hardly tempering the pounding in my head.

But then I sprang up again. *Crap.* While I sat there wasting time, Teague was probably leading the cops through my shop, showing them the mess I'd assumed some unknown juvenile delinquent had made.

Good Lord, I'd sent my own son to the gallows. Even minor trouble with the law could be the start of a long, hard journey for a young black man — first offense or not — and I had to keep him away from that sentence. We'd work this out on our own.

But I wasn't letting him off the hook. I was furious. What I said, I said fast. I told Stevie in no uncertain terms to take my money and put it in a safe place. I told him if Bailey wanted to argue about that part of this mess, she could take it up with me. Then I cut our conversation short. I needed

to get him off the line and have Teague call
off the dogs.

15
ISABELLE, 1939

Later that afternoon, Nell suggested carrying a note from me to Robert. Her voice trembled when she said it, but she hushed me when I tried to argue.

I spent the whole evening composing a letter in my head, and the whole next morning recording it on paper. What could I say that would make a difference? He'd asked me to stay away, and I'd complied until his sister broke our miserable silent truce. I decided to blame Nell, citing her pity for our gloomy attitudes, but then decided that was the coward's way. I tore up my letter and began again. And again. Each time I read what I'd written, I tore the previous effort into tiny shreds.

Finally, I managed an epistle that I hoped struck a balance between pitiful and courageous. Epistle, because the length was probably over the top. But I'd scrutinized it from every angle and couldn't find anything I could bear to leave out.

Nell and I had agreed on signals. When I was ready for her to fetch the note from me, I found her in the hallway. My mother looked on, clueless as to what a tap of my index finger against my chin meant, as though I were deep in thought about something I needed to do. Nell acknowledged me with a tug on her ear, as if she were answering an itch. I returned to my room later for a "rest," and she came for the blank sealed envelope.

"Oh, Nell, you've no idea what this means to me. I only hope Robert isn't angry. He told me to stay away."

"This was my idea," she said. "I don't care if he's angry with me. I'll just say I threatened to quit if you didn't do it." She stared me down. She'd never quit. "Besides, it's just a letter."

Maybe it was just a letter, but we both knew it held more importance than that. Her cavalier attitude freed me and tied me in knots at the same time.

I waited for Nell's ear tug to tell me she'd brought me a response from Robert. I sunk back into my gloom when, day after day, she shook her head as we passed in the house. Eventually, her face held regret, as though she wished she hadn't suggested the note. I couldn't blame her. It had been worth a try, but Robert's silence stung.

Then, early one morning, while I forced down a breakfast of dry toast and coffee at my father's insistence, Nell entered the dining room.

"More cream, please, Nell," my mother said, her nose buried in the social section — all she cared about in the daily newspaper. My father pored over better news of the domestic economy, the only bright light amid rumors of war, while the rest of the world tumbled into chaos over the failing Treaty of Versailles and Germany's increasingly aggressive chancellor. I worked the crossword puzzle until he passed me the front section. He finished the puzzle while I read the news.

Nell returned with the cream pitcher and lingered, fussing over the bread basket. "That's all," my mother said, her voice impatient. It caught my attention. Nell eyes met mine, and she tugged her ear. I thought I might fly through the ceiling. I tapped my chin and inhaled the rest of my breakfast.

"May I be excused?" I asked.

My father regarded my plate, empty but for crumbs. "Now that's what I like to see, ladybug. You're feeling better. Go on."

"Thank you, Daddy." I counted silently and matched my steps to the rhythm, forcing myself to walk as straight and steady as I had when balancing a book on my head in the cotillion classes I'd attended at age thirteen. But after the swinging doors fell into place behind me, I clattered through the kitchen, cocking my head at Nell as I went, indicating I'd wait in the backyard.

While she finished her breakfast tasks, I paced by our old play spot, between the kitchen garden and the clothesline, where Cora — and a granddaddy oak tree — used to keep an eye on us while we played and she worked. I rose on tiptoes when I saw Nell, clasping my hands tightly at my waist to keep them polite.

Nell withdrew a tightly folded sheet of paper from her dress pocket, hidden well beneath her apron. Only one sheet, I could tell, and my cheeks burned as I remembered the stack I'd sent. But boys were different. In writing as well as in conversation, they honed their thoughts into succinct paragraphs, void of the emotional excess girls tended to.

"Hope I've done the right thing, Miss Isabelle." Nell pressed Robert's note into my hand. "I don't know what all he has to say here."

"But did he seem happy when you told him? And when he sent you with his answer?"

She wrinkled her nose and seemed to think back over time. "Can't say. He's better, but it's almost time for college to start, so no telling. I know he's happy about that."

I appreciated her honesty, though I'd hoped she'd have more confidence in Robert's pleasure at hearing from me. He'd told me to stay away, though, and I couldn't imagine he'd changed his mind simply because I'd written him and told him I'd be happy to hear about his studies now and then, or what ever new adventures kept him busy at school.

But I intended to wear him down until he couldn't stand not seeing me any more than I could stand not seeing him. Perhaps it was desperate and selfish. I suppose I *was* desperate and selfish.

Robert's first letter honored my request — a dry replay of his activities since he'd finished work on the wall. No more, no less. Eyes not meant to see it couldn't have faulted what he reported, even if they'd discovered the note lying about. He didn't even address it personally — no "Dear Isabelle" or salutation of any kind. He dated the corner and signed it, simply, "Robert

Prewitt." Anyone might have mistaken it for a journal entry carried by accident into our house. Of course, if they'd discovered it between the pages of what ever I happened to be reading, it would have raised eyebrows.

So it went, into fall. I began my last year at school, and Robert started at the Negro college fifty miles away in Frankfort. He traveled home most weekends. I knew to expect letters only on Sundays or Mondays — or two weeks in between when he remained at school to study for exams or write papers. Our letters began to overlap, which could be confusing when their delivery criss-crossed.

Robert's remained impersonal, but over time, another tone crept in, and the way he shared about his classes and classmates and the things he learned expressed not only the facts but also his feelings about them. Then one day, I sat down with a thump on the floor of my room, where I'd been pacing while reading his latest, so shocked was I to notice he'd used the personal pronoun *you.* If someone found this letter, they'd no longer be fooled into thinking it was a journal entry. To my joy, he'd slipped up and addressed me as a human being. I hugged the letter to my chest, my hands wrapped around the backs of my arms. I felt as though I'd been embraced.

Now I dared pour even more of my feelings into my letters, mentioning often how I missed seeing him and how I wished things were different. Another day, another shift occurred. He admitted he missed me, too, more than ever, and believed his head would burst with thoughts of being with me, of walking together openly, of holding hands. A burning made its way from deep in my belly to my heart when I read his words.

We saw each other a few times after that. Nell alerted me to Robert's long weekends home, and we met at the arbor, though it was chilly and often damp and muddy from rain — and the threat of snow as winter approached. I'd claim a study date with a friend after school on the Thursdays Robert arrived, then would hurry after the final bell to meet him there. Our rendezvous were innocent, mainly spent gazing at each other with great silly grins, stumbling over our words in a hurry to share everything we didn't dare mention in letters. At visit's end, we shared chaste yet passionate kisses before parting — no more than our first kisses after the revival.

But, of course, after each visit and kiss, I found it more difficult to return to life as usual. I existed on two planes, two separate lives — one, the same I'd led forever, yet where I felt like an alien now, walking as I did in a daze, as though I no longer fit in the spaces I'd once occupied well enough, even if always slightly off-kilter. The other felt like real life, and I lived for the moments when I could transfer myself into that reality by repeatedly reading letters from Robert or spending what stolen moments we could arrange.

After a late fall visit, I needed a glimmer of hope it wouldn't end.

"I pray every night we'll find a way to be together," I told him, leaning into him for another embrace after we'd already said it was the last that day. "There has to be a way, one that won't cause trouble for your family or put anyone in danger. There has to be." My voice broke.

Even as he drew me into his arms, he scoffed, gently, yet with impassable resignation. I knew in my heart it was fantasy, but his scoff hurt more than I could graciously bear.

I jumped up from the bench he'd covered with his jacket so moisture wouldn't ruin my skirt and walked furiously away, at first toward home, but then in a direction I'd never gone, down a path worn through dense woods. I wanted to be alone, away from anything familiar. But Robert came after me, struggling to shove his arms into his damp jacket while he tried to keep up.

Finally, he caught me, grasped my arm from behind, and halted me in the middle of the woods. His jacket flapping, he tugged me to him and pressed my cheek hard to his chest, so tight his heart pounded against my pulsing temple. I breathed deeply until their rhythms almost matched — or at least until they weren't in opposition, and the chaos in my head calmed, too.

"I don't know how to do this, Isabelle. I can't promise anything but the next letter, or the next visit. You knew when you sent me that first note after I told you to stay away that all I could offer was the present. The moment we're given. That's all we've ever been sure of."

His speech was more refined each time I saw him. College had polished him, revealing a gleaming gem. I wouldn't have cared if he still spoke like his mother or sister at times, dropping consonants or using the wrong verb tenses — that was the young man I'd fallen in love with — but I considered him now, marveling that anyone could find anything lacking in him. He was the perfect match — except for the color of his skin, beautiful and precious as the black sapphire in my mother's wedding ring. Color was all that stood between us. The injustice made me want to scream. I wanted to climb the highest hill I could find and shout until our world saw its error. But I came to a crossroads that afternoon. I rendered a promise in my heart, and I said it out loud. It was my time to turn him away.

"I'm finished with this, Robert. The sneaking around. The hiding. The way my heart breaks, little by little, when I believe this is all we'll ever have. It's not enough anymore. And I won't see you again. Not until we find a way to be together."

I understood now what I hadn't before the letters, before I fell deeper in love with him. Our relationship as it stood, the creeping around behind our families' backs to steal conversation and kisses, could only continue so long before we'd both hover at the brink of insanity.

Now it was Robert who watched in disbelief as I turned and left him, this time without even a handkerchief to tuck close to his heart, clinging only to my pitiful pledge.

I didn't regret the deal I'd made. It only made me angrier at the situation and more determined to conjure a plan to bring us back together. I schemed and plotted for weeks, considering such ridiculous ideas as staining my skin with permanent dye and taking on a new identity. Laughable? Yes. I was that desperate.

One day, though, a guest speaker came to my school. The teachers were concerned that the boys in my community lacked ambition, that they'd be drawn too easily into the organized-crime gangs that had begun to infiltrate even our quiet town, creeping up the hill from Newport like a contagious disease. They found easy work running errands for the bosses — making deliveries, acting as valets at the mob-run Beverly Hills Country Club just off the highway. Our principal invited career men to speak to our class. We girls were expected to listen quietly or study while our guests answered our male classmates' questions. This plan was fine, in theory, but a visiting attorney from Cincy — some uncle or cousin of our teacher — met a wall of silence when it was time for the boys to quiz him about his work.

I poked my hand up, disregarding my teacher's displeasure, until the man noticed me. "Yes, young lady? Have a question about how to meet and marry one of our bright young associates, do you?"

I ignored my friends' titters and my

teacher's glare. "Mr. Bird? I know you need to go to college, but what must you know to be an attorney?"

He seemed taken aback by my question, which was not simple, and which came, of all things, from a girl. Finally, he recovered. "Well, Miss . . ."

"McAllister. Isabelle McAllister."

"Miss McAllister, when your young men here enroll in various fine law schools after completing their baccalaureate degrees, they will read and study more than they ever imagined while sitting here in class, so spoiled have you all been."

I doubted my teacher appreciated his remark or the scare tactic — it likely negated any effect she and her colleagues hoped for in motivating the lazy boys. But I voiced another question before she could distract him. "Reading and studying what, sir?"

"The law." He said it simply and ominously, as though referring to the Bible. As though every conclusion could be drawn from his short answer.

"The law?" I said, hoping he would elaborate.

"You, child, have no idea how many volumes reside in the libraries of the best law schools in the United States. Trained reporters painstakingly record the details of each case — the facts, the issues, the precedents, and the decisions."

"And in order to know what the law is, you'd have to read every one of these books?"

I wasn't sure I understood. But I'd piqued the visiting attorney's curiosity by then. I didn't suppose a girl had ever questioned him this way, and he seemed determined now to give me a satisfactory answer. "We start with the U.S. Constitution. It has jurisdiction over every American state and city. But what is not defined in the Constitution is defined by individual states and municipalities. I suppose you could go to any local government office and request a copy of its laws. You might even find constitutional and local law in a public library — if it's a fairly large one. But, my dear, the trick lies in interpreting the law. That's what attorneys and judges do. We learn the laws, then try to apply them fairly. In the process, new laws are created."

He had no idea that, curious as I was, I'd tuned him out by the time he reached the end of his answer. I needed only a simple answer to a simple question: if and where Robert and I could legally marry. His lengthy explanation contained the one detail I'd hoped for. We'd learned the Constitution in school, and it said nothing about marriage.

Before that day, I suppose I knew on an intellectual level that each state made its own rules about many things. But it had never occurred to me that while marriage between a Negro and a white was illegal in Kentucky, it might not be elsewhere.

My teacher eyed me as I gathered my books and schoolwork at the end of the day, then shook her head and went back to cleaning the blackboard.

Later that week, I forged a note to the school office, saying I'd miss classes the following day to accompany Mother on out-of-town family business. The secretary hardly glanced at it before sending it on to my teacher.

The next morning, I started for school as always, but when I reached downtown, I turned the other direction, boarded a streetcar that would connect me to another that would carry me into Cincinnati proper, where I'd visit the office that issued marriage licenses. I had a question.

16
DORRIE, PRESENT DAY

I was too embarrassed to call Teague after all. I texted him, crossing my fingers he'd confirm he received my message right away. If he didn't, I'd have no choice but to talk to him.

"Teague. Big mistake. Please tell police never mind. Don't want to press charges."

The message was like an old-fashioned telegram. I didn't have time or energy for more.

He tried to call me back immediately, but I ignored Marvin Gaye's sultry voice. I couldn't face Teague, even over the phone. I knew once I explained what happened, he'd take off as fast as his never-ending legs could carry him. Volunteering to help me with the sorry actions of a stranger was one thing. Dragging him into my mess of a son's new career in crime was altogether different.

Pretty soon, the text messages started.

"Um . . . okay?" said the first.

Then: "Dorrie, what happened? I did what you asked, but I don't get it."

"You still want me to fix the door, right?"

"Dorrie. Call me. Please? I'm worried about you."

"Dorrie?"

They piled up, one after another. Miss Isabelle pulled a couple of tissues out of her purse and spread them out along the bench before she joined me there. Her face said she'd heard enough to understand what had happened, and that I needn't elaborate unless or until I was ready.

I sat there and snuffled away. I swatted the stupid tears rolling down my face, not sure if I was angrier with my son for what he'd done or because he'd made me cry for the first time in who knew how many years. Miss Isabelle's only nod to my tears was passing me another tissue she dragged out of that bottomless handbag without a word when I couldn't catch any more salt water with my hands and my nose was dripping, too. She understood.

Eventually, she rose and walked farther down the sidewalk, tiny, careful steps. I sighed and followed her, thinking I might as well get my mind off myself for a minute. We'd stopped for a reason, so I turned my attention to her as we made our way a half block or so.

I reached the marker about when she did — I walked faster even when I wasn't trying. But I hung back while she studied the inscription. Then we both moved closer. A large stone sign marked the entrance to one of the campus buildings. The sign was etched with the weatherworn image of a kneeling soldier who supported the head of a fallen soldier and held a stethoscope to his heart. Below the etching, fifty or so names were carved into the stone's surface and labeled *Murray Medical College Wartime Class of 1946.* Miss Isabelle traced her finger down a column of names until she paused on one and smiled up at me, tears shimmering in her eyes now.

Robert S. Prewitt.

I looked from her to the name and back again. Tilted my head and asked a question with my eyes, then whispered, "Oh, Miss Isabelle, that's him? Your Robert?"

She straightened. "Attending med school at Murray was his biggest dream."

Whatever trouble Robert and Miss Isabelle had experienced together — and I still didn't know the whole story — he'd achieved his dream after all.

Back in the car, we nested among the

drink cups and crossword puzzle books and all our other traveling detritus (or twenty-seven across). I turned the ignition, though I was almost too drained to back out of the visitor's space. Miss Isabelle watched me shore up my energy. "Oh, Dorrie. This is too much. You have to go home." She waited for me to respond. "I mean it. Let's turn around now."

Bless Miss Isabelle. Here we were on the way to a funeral, and she'd forget it all so I could go clean up the mess waiting for me at home. And I knew it made some sense to take her up on the offer. Things were falling apart without me while I was on some kind of mystery trip, driving toward a funeral for someone I'd never even met — someone whose identity was still unclear, though my suspicions were growing stronger.

"Miss Isabelle . . . this funeral . . . it's pretty important to you, right? It's someone special?"

She didn't answer immediately, as though she was really thinking through my question. "It's important, of course it is. But Dorrie, nothing — *nothing* — is more important than a mother's responsibility. I'm telling you, if we need to —"

"No," I said, interrupting her. Her statement made everything crystal clear. "It's better for me to be anywhere but home right now. *That's* taking care of Stevie Junior. My son's right. If I saw him right now, I'd surely do things — *say* things — I'd regret. Teague told the police not to bother with the burglary. Burglary . . ." I laughed bitterly. Was it still burglary when your own child robbed you? Seemed like there ought to be a more serious classification for this kind of crime. And it sounded like Bailey was going to do what she was going to do no matter what — but not with *my* money. "Let's go, Miss Isabelle. I'll deal with Stevie Junior when I get home."

I'd never answered Teague's text about fixing the door, but knowing him, he'd handle it anyway. I hoped I could count on Stevie Junior to go by and check on things after I spoke to him next. It was the least he could do to start making up for his official worst choice ever.

17
ISABELLE, 1939

I jumped down from the streetcar onto air, so light I felt I could run forever and never deplete the energy that pulsed through my veins, my muscles, my bones — from head to toe and back again. The leaves were changing, and I dragged my fingers through them as I ran; their pungence delighted me and their varying shades seemed translucent, brighter, and more hopeful than any I'd seen before, even as they prepared to return to the earth.

Robert and I could be together. Forever. It was simpler than I'd imagined. It was across a river. A wide river, but one with plenty of bridges.

Ohio had no statute against intermarriage. It had been legal for whites and Negroes to marry there since 1887. In fact, it had only been illegal for a few years at the beginning of the Civil War. Kentucky's law against intermarriage, on the other hand, had been in effect since the state was constituted. Who could have imagined that less than one mile across water could make such a difference? I was both astonished and amazed.

And I was assuming that Robert would want to marry me. I was only seventeen, having celebrated my birthday that fall, and he was eighteen by then, but it wasn't uncommon to marry young. Folks our age were considered grown for all practical purposes. Several of my friends had left school early, were already a year or two married, and more than a few of the girls we knew — especially those from less fortunate circumstances — had one or more little ones clinging to their skirts.

I hadn't planned on being a child bride; my original goals, however unclear, had placed marriage farther down my time line, a few ticks after doing something important with my life.

But understand this: When you fall in love, every kind of reason flies out the newly opened window of your brain.

I was confident I could convince Robert it made sense.

After all, if we were legally married, who could keep us apart? Perhaps we wouldn't get to court as long as we wanted, to take time to learn each other's qualities — and foibles — thoroughly before taking such a final step. Perhaps I wouldn't know Robert as thoroughly as I might have had our circumstances been different and we'd been allowed that privilege.

But I knew one thing: I loved him, and I couldn't imagine that anything or anyone could change my mind. I wanted to spend the rest of my life with Robert. If that took marrying immediately instead of meandering toward wedded bliss, I'd do it.

I prayed he'd feel the same.

I savored the knowledge, unblemished, as long as I could stand it before putting pen to paper to write my first letter to Robert in nearly a month. I waited through dinner, where I choked on creamed peas when Father inquired how my research had gone that afternoon. In the midst of my euphoria, I'd forgotten my excuse for being late — staying after school to find sources for a term paper. For a moment, I feared I'd been discovered — maybe spied by a colleague of my father's while I pored over the fine print in the instructions to apply for an Ohio marriage license. Finding nothing that spelled a dead end in them, I'd asked the clerk to be sure. Her expression was unreadable, but her silence was telling. Finally, she'd replied, "Well, I don't suppose there is any law against it, no." She sniffed. "Not that I've seen."

"So, if these two people I've described wanted to fill out this application and receive a license to marry, it would be permitted here?" She'd shrugged and returned to her work, as though she couldn't bear to acknowledge it aloud. I hoped for another clerk when Robert and I returned — though I supposed another could be horrified rather than stymied or might even refuse the application for other reasons.

"My studies are swell, Daddy," I answered once I regained control over the unfortunate wedding of oxygen and peas in my windpipe.

When the day's small talk died down, I asked to be excused. In my room, I sat against the wall next to my bed and chewed my pen while I contemplated how to inform Robert of our impending nuptials.

"My love," I began. No. It seemed too precious, in spite of my overflowing heart.

I settled on a straightforward approach: "Dear Robert." Anything else would paint me as a child, immature and floating in the clouds, instead of a grown woman who was down-to-earth and dead serious.

At my signal the next morning, Nell stopped short in the middle of polishing the hat tree in the hallway. She tugged her ear, but with such a questioning expression, I tapped my chin again to be sure she understood. I'm sure she'd wondered why weeks had passed with no exchange of letters, but she'd never questioned it. Later, in my room, she greeted me with an apprehensive expression. I wondered if Robert had repeated my ultimatum in the woods.

"You must take extra care with this, Nell," I whispered. "Nobody can see it but Robert. If anyone did, there would be trouble." I hated to worry her more, but my letter had to go straight from my hands to his, with hers the only others touching it.

She sighed and tucked it into her pocket. "You scare me with talk like this. I feel like I started something maybe I shouldn't have. I only meant for you two to —"

I cut her off. "This means the world to me, and to Robert." For me to speak for Robert must have seemed odd to Nell. She was the one who'd grown up with him, so close in age they were often mistaken for twins. I patted the side of her apron that hid the letter, but I also felt dismayed at the mantle of wariness that shrouded her face again.

"Best get back to my work," she said, and turned away.

"Isa, have you lost your mind?" he wrote back.

"Yes, my mind is lost in love for you," I replied.

"It can't work. You're too young. You have too much to lose," he responded.

I crumpled the paper into a ball and threw it into a corner. I retrieved it and smoothed it and stared at his reasoning, then pulled out a clean sheet of stationery.

"Don't think of me. There's nothing here for me. You're the one who will have to postpone your studies. You're the one they'll come after. You're right — it's hopeless. Forget my insane rambling."

He didn't forget it. Instead, he sent a detailed list of every conceivable argument to prove the plan wouldn't work. His analysis told me it wasn't a lost cause.

"I know these things. Could it be you really don't want to be with me? Am I the reason?" I wrote.

I knew it was manipulative, and I regretted it as soon as I sent Nell away with the note. I sent another the next day. "I'm sorry. It was wrong of me to say that. Please forgive me for doubting you."

A weekend passed without any word, and I resigned myself. Finally, I'd proved exactly how selfish I was. But then, a week later, came Robert's response.

"I can't think of anything I'd rather do than join my life with yours — even if the thought terrifies me. But marriage won't solve most of the problems we'd face as a couple — not even in Cincinnati. Just because the laws are different doesn't mean the people are. And it wouldn't be only me they'd judge."

"I'm not an idiot," I wrote, "even if I frequently act like one."

But I chose, like an idiot, to dream only of the hat and dress I'd wear the day we were married, of scenes of domestic bliss. I chose to ignore thoughts of what vicious folk might do to a pair such as us. I didn't allow myself to envision our life without my family's support — especially the support of my father.

Robert didn't rush his decision.

"Isa, you must be patient while I investigate the process for marrying in Cincinnati myself, for my own peace of mind. I would have to find work, a place for us to live. It would take time. I already miss you more than I can bear," he wrote.

Though I missed him desperately, too, I

distracted myself with school. If he agreed, I might not complete my final year at my own school; but wherever Robert and I lived, I could enroll and finish, even if late.

Through the remaining days of fall, I waited for confirmation. Instead, Robert's letters were still about his schooling — unspoken and unintentional reminders that marriage would suspend his own coveted education, for my father would surely cut off his financial support. Without it, Robert would have little hope of paying for school, not to mention that he'd be busy supporting the two of us. But I believed that, like me, if he was meant to return to school, we'd find a way.

Finally, the day came. During the Christmas holidays, Robert wrote that he'd found employment in a dockyard on the Cincy side of the river. The pay wasn't much, but enough to secure lodging in a boarding house. He hoped I wouldn't be ashamed to live in the West End neighborhood popu-lated mostly by Negroes — with a few Orientals and Cherokee-looking folks sprinkled here and there. He had no choice; women who took boarders in other parts of town had closed their doors in his face when he inquired about living space for him and his wife.

His wife. The phrase both terrified and mesmerized me.

"Isa . . . will you marry me?" he wrote.

"Yes, yes, yes! I will marry you, Robert."

I sealed the letter and pressed it to my heart before I sent it with Nell.

Robert believed we needed an ally to help with our scheme. Nell eyed me with even more caution, passing letters — more quickly now that Robert was home from college — with hardly a word or a glance. The distance between us grew again, until I couldn't stand it.

I pulled her into my room as she passed one day.

"Nell, please. Don't look unhappy. This is what we want, your brother and I. Imagine if you and James couldn't be together. Imagine if you couldn't see each other in public places."

Her shoulders drooped so low, it seemed they'd collapse in upon her ribs. I pressed her down on my bed and sank beside her. It had been years since we'd sat on an equal level like that, but I feared she might fall over if I didn't brace her up. "Oh, honey," she said. "I'm so scared for Robert, and for you, too. It's got me all knotted up right here." She poked her fingers against her stomach and grimaced as though her innards were in literal turmoil. I understood, though the dose of joy mixed with the turmoil in mine made it possible to bear. "There's mean folks out there . . . going to be ready to make things ugly and dangerous for you two. Just because they say it's legal in Ohio doesn't make it safe." She dabbed at tears with the corners of her apron, then looked away, as though she were ashamed.

I wanted to reassure her we'd be fine, that once we had our license and a minister of the gospel had signed it, we'd be like any other married couple she knew. But I knew it would be a lie. Instead I appealed on a different level. "Nell, you're like a sister to me. I can't wait until you are my sister — when Robert and I marry, you will be." Her eyes widened, a fleck of plea sure lighting her irises, even as she denied our plan could work, or that if we succeeded in marrying, anyone would see my logic.

"And we'll take care of you and your mother. I promise we will. No matter what my mother does, we'll take care of you." Our marriage would surely mean Cora and Nell would be fired, and they couldn't survive on Albert's income alone. Robert and I had agreed he'd work two jobs to replace what they'd lose. I'd work, too. His

mother would find other employment eventually, and Robert even felt it would inspire
Brother James to propose to Nell sooner —
which seemed imminent anyway. We'd
planned for every contingency we could
imagine.

Her shoulders lifted a fraction. "It's
mostly Momma I'm worried about. James
and I, we'll be okay."

I nodded. "I'll need things if I'm going to
be married," I said. "Will you help me?"

This asked more of her than anything. It
wasn't just asking for help. It was asking her
to align herself with what would cause a rift
between our families — even as it joined
them at one tenuous point. Nell grasped
my hand and squeezed.

18
Dorrie, Present Day

Hearing about Miss Isabelle so young and so sure it would work took my mind off things. It gave me something to root for in my head, even though I had a feeling the story wouldn't end well. There she was, the same age as my Stevie Junior, and she and Robert were trying to think of a way to change the world for the better, while Stevie was thinking of ways to ruin his life as fast as he could. I suppose at the time everyone thought Miss Isabelle and Robert were trying to ruin their lives, too. I was thankful times had changed. More or less.

When we pulled away from Nashville, finally heading north instead of east, I thought about my childhood in that small East Texas town. The schools had integrated at the last possible minute, and we all knew the middle school used to be the black high school, closed down and renovated only a few years before I was born. There was still a definite color line in the town, signs or no signs. You knew where the blacks lived and where the whites lived, and though a house or two might deviate along the fringe, nobody truly crossed the line.

One summer, I took my kids home for a visit before my mother moved to the city to be closer to us. We were playing in the park one day. A cute little white girl befriended Stevie Junior on the playground and invited him to the annual Vacation Bible School at the big Baptist church the next morning. My jaw about popped off when her mother said sure, that she was the teacher for their age group and that she'd be glad to pick up Stevie and take him as their guest. Bebe was still in diapers and too young to go. The next morning, Liz honked her horn outside my mom's door, and I packed Stevie into her car, and they all toodled off to the church. Stevie had such a great time. He came home sticky from snacks and stained with finger paint and glitter and so tuckered out, he took a long afternoon nap for the first time in years. We walked back over to the park later, and little Ashley and her mom were there again. Only this time, Liz met us with a long face.

"I hate this town," she said. "Ever since my husband got this job and we had to move here, I've been feeling this undercurrent, but I never could put a finger on it until today."

I felt worse for Liz than for myself. I knew what was coming. I'd grown up there. I'd figured this deal was too good to be true. "Someone tell you Stevie wasn't welcome at VBS tomorrow?"

Her mouth fell open and she closed it again with an angry snap of her teeth. The pastor had come by to tell her an anonymous caller had threatened to do something horrendous if they allowed black kids at VBS again. Only they didn't put it that nicely. The pastor said he felt bad, but his hands were tied. "Geez. Us. This is ridiculous," Liz said. "I'm not even believing it. What is this? The Dark Ages? Makes me wish we'd rented instead of buying. I can't get away from this place soon enough."

"Well, Stevie had a great time today. I'm glad you invited him. Sorry it won't work out for the rest of the week, but don't feel bad."

"Oh, Dorrie. I don't care what they say. I want you to send Stevie anyway."

"Nah," I said. "It'll cause too much trouble for you down the line. You'll have a reputation as 'that woman.' And trust me?

267

You don't want to be that woman around here."

Next thing I knew, she was sniffling, and her eyes welled up with tears. I knew she was battling between wanting desperately to do the right thing and understanding I was right, too.

"It's okay," I said. "I promise. Isn't anything I haven't seen around here before or won't see again. I appreciate you trying."

She threw her hands up in frustration.

Later, when I explained to Stevie Junior that he couldn't go to VBS the next day, first, he cried, and then, he pestered me about it until I finally broke down and stopped making excuses. I figured at almost seven, he was old enough to know the truth if he was old enough to be the victim of it. "Son, some people still don't think black folks are as good as white folks. They say and do ugly things that make it hard for us to get along."

"But Miss Liz, in our class she said Jesus loves *all* the little children of the world. We sang a song about it. Black and red and yellow white . . ." He sang all the different colors in crazy order, and I smiled through my heartbreak, remembering how I'd sung the same song as a kid. It wasn't politically correct anymore — calling people red or

268

yellow, or even black some days — but I figured Liz brought the song out of storage and dusted it off for Stevie's visit. It sure as heck probably wasn't in any new curriculum.

"You're right, honey, he does. But some ignorant people don't believe it. Miss Liz does, and she's very sorry you can't go back tomorrow. She still wants you and Ashley to play together at the park, though."

Even now, in the sprawling metropolitan area of Texas where Miss Isabelle and I lived, we ran into racism. A young white girl who had rented a station from me in the shop for a while had a child who was biracial. Her little girl had come home from school crying more than once because she didn't fit in with either the black kids or the white kids. And one time, she'd been invited on an after-school playdate, but when the other mother came to pick up the kids, she made some excuse about having an emergency and not being able to take the little girl home with her. The school secretary called Angie to have her pick her daughter up at the office, because the woman had just *left* her there.

My own mother fussed at me for doing white hair. She couldn't understand why more than half my clientele was white. I explained that in school I'd learned to work with all kinds of hair, and I'd discovered over time I was *good* at doing white hair. I certainly wasn't going to turn down a customer because of the color of his or her skin. I'd always worked in shops with a mainly white clientele, and when I opened my own place, most of my clients moved along with me.

Worse yet, when we were driving along, me thinking my own thoughts and Miss Isabelle wrapped up in her crossword puzzle book again, my own prejudices jumped right in my face.

The one time I'd been inside Teague's house, I'd seen photos of his kids plastered everywhere. There was one old picture of them with Teague and his ex before they split. She was white. The kids were golden. That's the only way I could describe them. Their skin and hair practically glowed in that photo, and his little girls had eyes the color of a warm ocean.

As progressive as I claimed to be, with my white clients, and the fact that I wasn't freaking out over my son's white girlfriend — not because she was white, anyway — who might be the future mother of my half-white grandbaby, I wondered how well I could mother children whose biological mother was white — if it came down to that. Even more, I wondered what she would think. Sure, she'd run off and left Teague to care for them most of the time, but how would she react if some black woman — a *very* black woman — started playing the role of mother in their lives?

Stevie's mess gave me yet another excuse to cater to these fears now. I kept ignoring Teague's text messages, and when the phone rang again and I saw it was his number, I silenced it and turned it facedown in the console.

19
Isabelle, 1940

On a chilly Saturday in late January, the sun barely peeking through the clouds at midday, I left home with my book bag, giving studying at the library as an excuse. Mother had been less vigilant the last few months, too busy with the holidays to note my comings and goings. The library had become my kingdom again, when I wanted it. I retrieved a small suitcase I'd hidden under a hedge that morning before anyone else woke, then placed the tote full of library books in the empty space. I apologized silently to Miss Pearce; the books might be moldy by the time they were discovered.

Nell had laundered and pressed my good dresses, along with other things I'd need. I'd folded my best dress carefully around a matching hat in my already-stuffed case, though I feared the hat would be squashed beyond repair. I hoped I'd have time to duck into a public restroom to change.

Chances were, I'd have to make do with the outfit I wore — a nice-enough dress — when Robert and I exchanged our vows. Mother would have been immediately suspicious if she'd seen me leaving for the library in my holiday dress.

The Monday before, Robert and I had met at the Hamilton County Courthouse, where we'd persuaded the clerk — despite her obvious misgivings — to accept our application for a marriage license. Robert and I each marked our ages as eighteen on the application, though I'd barely passed my seventeenth birthday. As the clerk studied the information we'd completed, I prayed she wouldn't ask me to prove my age. We both claimed we were residents of Hamilton County. Robert listed his employer's address as his residence and I gave the address of the rooming house where we planned to live. This wasn't the clerk I'd spoken to before. This one was less horrified than worried. She studied us with curiosity, and even, I think, a touch of sympathy. I was afraid she saw right through our misinformation, but she issued the document. We told so many lies that day, I felt sick by the time I returned home. By Saturday, those lies seemed small compared with the deception it took to get me out of

Shalerville and on my way to Cincy.

After riding one streetcar into Newport, then another across the bridge and into the city, I met Robert at the entrance to a church. A workmate had told him the preacher performed last-minute weddings, but there'd been no opportunity to talk to the man in advance. We held a collective breath as Robert knocked at the side entrance, near the pastor's study. He'd been told the pastor often worked Saturday afternoons, polishing the next day's sermon — or maybe to supplement his paltry minister's income with fees collected from couples who showed up unannounced.

The man answered Robert's second, louder series of knocks. He peered around the edge of the door, looking past Robert to me, then beyond. I knew he was looking for a third party — someone besides a young Negro man escorting a white girl.

When he didn't see anyone else, he barked, "Who is it? What do you want?"

"I'm sorry to interrupt, Reverend. We were told you perform marriage ceremonies. Do you have a moment?"

The man gawked, first at Robert, then at me, his eyes boring into mine, questioning whether I'd come of my own will. I nodded, and he turned his scowl back on Robert.

"Who told you that? I require an appointment, but I wouldn't give you one anyway."

Robert swallowed hard and plunged ahead. "I work at the docks. A man there told me."

"Well, he told you wrong. I never married a white and a niggro. Never will."

He moved to close the door in Robert's face, but Robert slipped a gloved hand into the gap, forcing the man to either crush his fingers or leave the door open a crack. Thank God the man chose the latter.

"Sir, begging your pardon, sir, but can you tell me where we could be married, then?" I marveled at Robert's temerity.

"Why didn't you try your own kind first?" The man sneered and rolled his eyes. His tone left no uncertainty as to what he thought of our relationship, as though it were somehow perverted. I felt my cheeks flame as he shot me a look filled with disgust. Then he seemed to reconsider. I didn't quite trust the change. "St. Paul's, maybe."

"St. Paul's, sir?"

"African Methodist Episcopal is what you people call it. Now, go on. I don't have time to waste on the likes of you." He spat on the pavement, then crashed the door closed.

Fortunately, Robert removed his hand in time.

We trudged back toward the trolley stop. Likely, St. Paul's was in the West End, Robert figured, not far from the rooming house where we'd live. He asked a colored news vendor where to find it. The streets were crowded, even for a late Saturday afternoon, and he hung a half step behind me, as if he were an escort of last choice rather than my future spouse. I knew he didn't want to draw attention, but I hoped one day we'd be able to walk side-by-side, freely — and not just when we were deep in the woods.

On a quiet street lined with the dreary houses that dominated the area — stark two-story dwellings with narrow porches, covered in false-brick tar paper or dingy clapboard — St. Paul's rose from the middle of the block, a beautifully ancient red brick Italianate structure trimmed in white stone. I gazed up, pleased — if the angry preacher's advice held — I'd be married in a lovely setting. The other church, drab, mud-colored, had blended into the dreary January surroundings.

A few Negro children played jacks or bounced balls on the wide sidewalk in front of St. Paul's, and they gaped as we studied the building, unsure where to enter. One tiny girl popped her thumb into her mouth and hid behind an older girl, but she peeked out to one side, her left eye still studying me.

"Hello, young gentleman," Robert said to the tallest boy in the group, who ducked his head at Robert's greeting and studied the toes of his shoes. "Can you tell me where we'd find the reverend? Is he around on Saturdays?"

The boy looked to the older girl. She swept her jacks together and dropped them in her pocket, then stepped forward, the toddler still clinging to her skirts. "Don't know if he's at the church today, but he lives right there." She pointed out a narrow house, covered with the same red brick as the church and so close to it, they practically shared a wall.

"Thank you, young lady." Robert bowed, which made the girl smile shyly. He indicated I should lead the way toward the front door of the humble residence.

"What do you want him for?" another boy called, not so shy as the other one. "Getting hitched?"

The older girl covered his mouth and shook her head furiously. "Shhh. Course they ain't getting married. Can't you see? That's a white girl he's with." She said it low, but I heard. My stomach twisted, but I smiled nonetheless.

"Have too seen white girls here, getting married to Negroes. And the other way around." The boy whispered this so loudly, anyone within a half block might have heard. The girl grabbed his hand and the toddler's and yanked them into a march down the street and away, but I caught her looking back at me, an apology on her face. I wiggled my fingers, and she snapped her head around and continued her little parade toward a narrow stoop at the end of the street. The oldest boy lagged behind, bouncing his baseball as he went.

Robert tapped the door knocker. Soon, a woman answered. She smoothed her skirt when she saw us. Obviously, she'd been expecting kids; her glance started waist-high, then rose to our faces. She took a step back. "Oh! Pardon me. I thought it was those young'uns again. Always knocking on the door, all Saturday long, asking if they can help with anything at the church. Really, wanting to see if I've baked them a treat." She beamed, though her eyes flicked in my direction more than once — sizing me up, I could tell. But she was the first adult all afternoon who hadn't looked horrified at us together. I liked her immediately.

"What can I do for you, then?" she asked.

"Is the reverend home?" Robert tugged off his cap and held it nervously between his hands, as though even mentioning the man who might join us in marriage unsettled him.

"He is. May I say who wants to see him? Maybe a word about why?"

"Oh, yes, ma'am. We —" He indicated me with a flutter of his cap. "We wanted to see him about a wedding."

"I see," she said. "I figured as much. Come on inside, honey." She waved me into a tiny entryway, then gestured for Robert to follow. "I'll get my husband."

I breathed easier, glancing through a doorway to a small parlor, not fancy, but neat and filled with furniture that was probably the best in the house.

The woman returned. "He'll be right with you. Won't you please take a seat? I need to check on my supper, if you'll excuse me." She pointed us into the parlor, and Robert and I settled gingerly at the edge of an angled settee covered in dark green mohair, careful to leave a full foot of space between us.

We dared sneak a look at each other — the first time we'd really looked all afternoon, it seemed. Robert wrinkled his brow and leaned toward me. "Are you okay?" he asked. "You sure about this?"

"Never more sure," I said, though inside I'd never felt more nervous or terrified. As anxious as I was to become Robert's wife, as desperately as I wanted to be with the handsome and gentle young man I loved more each day, reality was coming into sharp focus. Everywhere we went, if we didn't get outright verbal abuse, we were the object of funny looks and comments, even from children. The children were the tipping point against my illusion that everything would be fine.

"How about you?" I said. "Do you want to go through with it? If they —" I didn't finish. A tall man whose belly proved his wife's claim about the children looking for a treat entered the room, and Robert and I both sprang up from the settee.

"Good afternoon, madam. Sir." He shook Robert's hand. "Reverend Jasper Day."

"I'm Robert Prewitt. This is Miss Isabelle McAllister."

"Pleasure to meet you, ma'am." He made a tiny bow in my direction but didn't reach to shake my hand. He gestured for us to return to our places on the settee, then dragged a matching chair closer. "Now. Sarah says you're here about a wedding.

That right?"

"Yes, sir," Robert said. Reverend Day looked at me, and I nodded. I'd yet to say a word.

"Well. You've come to the right place, then. I suppose you heard I've married a few couples like you." His use of the phrase "couples like you" seemed worlds apart from the other pastor's. Less an insult — more like he didn't know how else to frame it without being blunt. "Understand, however, that even though I will marry you if that's your genuine wish, I'm going to try to talk you out of it first." He smiled, but it seemed filled with something far from the joy that ought to accompany a wedding day.

Warning.

My heart didn't know whether to sink low or rise into my throat.

He took us through the arguments Robert had already made with me, though the examples of what could happen may have been more frightening even than what we'd already imagined. He described how we'd be treated every time we emerged in public as a couple — and sometimes even in the privacy of our own home by people we thought were friends, colored or white. He described how a young black man had been lynched recently by a white girl's family for attempting to marry her. The girl had been thrown out on the street, left to become what girls became when nobody else would have them. I shuddered, and Robert clenched his hands, his face unnaturally gray as the pastor described the boy's fate.

I finally spoke. "My family will not be happy. They'll be shocked and disappointed, of course. Angry, no doubt. But I can't believe they'd ever do anything like that to Robert. They love Robert — his mother practically raised me, and his sister's like a sister to me."

Reverend Day nodded, but he explained that even those who claimed to be "like family" often retreated behind enemy lines when someone violated the family code. "I'm sorry, Miss McAllister. I don't relish scaring you, but I must tell the truth. It's not that I think you're doing anything wrong by marrying Mr. Prewitt, but I'd do you a disservice if I didn't ensure your awareness of what you're getting into."

He studied our marriage license, asked if we'd encountered trouble at the courthouse — his countenance said we were lucky we'd made it as far as his church and parsonage without more harassment than the other pastor gave us, and he seemed surprised — and wary — that the man had given us the name of his church.

He left us alone to make our final decision. I repeated my question to Robert. "Do you still want to do this?" His opinion was more important than mine. After all, he was the one who could suffer most at the hands of those angry about our actions and our union.

Robert paced near the window, gazing into the street. The children had returned, and beyond him, through the shining panes of glass, I watched them bounce a larger ball between them now, chanting a song I couldn't hear. Now and then, one would gaze toward the front of the house, craning their necks, as if they might see through the walls.

I joined Robert at the window and fixed my eyes on the tiny girl who'd hidden behind the older one. Her skin was like Sarah Day's — palest brown — and her eyes seemed illuminated as if from within. If Robert and I had children, they might favor this little angel. Perhaps she had a parent or grandparent who looked more like me. I suspected such things happened, even if nobody spoke of them or condoned them.

The beauty of her little face convinced me. I wanted to be with Robert. I wanted to bear his children. I was prepared to live with the consequences.

But I was terrified for him. I couldn't ask him to make this choice.

"Robert, you can't do it," I said, pulling him to face me. "I'd never forgive myself if what happened to that young man happened to you. I'd die, too. This is a mistake."

Robert focused on the corner of the room, where a unique display shelf backed into it at an angle, built to fit. The shelf held photographs — the young pastor and his wife in their wedding finery, others I assumed were parents, siblings, relatives. Robert drew closer, his attention caught by one of a family gathering — a faded photograph from an earlier generation — in which a lone white woman held a baby on her knee in the midst of the others. He beckoned me and pointed. Her eyes were filled with both joy and sorrow. "Here's why he marries folks like us."

"Maybe so. It doesn't change things, Robert."

"Maybe we can't change the world, Isabelle. But we can't change what we feel for each other, either. I can't anyway." He looked into my eyes. "Can you?"

I knew then I could never, ever lie to him, no matter what happened. I shook my head. "You know I love you, Robert. With all my heart, my soul, and every last ounce of my strength."

It was as if we'd exchanged our vows then, solemnized our marriage in that moment, though Reverend Day returned and accepted our request. His sweet wife knew what I needed, too. She asked if I wished to prepare for my wedding. She led me upstairs to a small bedroom, where I pulled my best dress from my case, smoothed my hair and rested my hat over it, gazed at myself in the mirror atop the dressing table, knowing the next time I studied my reflection, I would no longer see a girl. I'd see a married woman.

"It's a shame you can't get a picture of your wedding day," Sarah Day whispered as she showed me back to the parlor, where Robert waited with her husband. She patted my arm. "But you'll have a picture in your mind. That's enough."

"Wait, though," she said, and hurried to another part of her house, returning a moment later with something tiny, which she handed to her husband. She whispered to him while he slipped it into his pocket. During the ceremony, when the reverend asked if we had a ring to use as a symbol of our love, Robert shook his head and his chin fell a fraction. But I didn't care. He'd worked hard to pay the first month's rent on our room and the fees for the marriage license and the wedding, there was nothing left over.

"It doesn't matter," I said.

But then Reverend Day reached into his pocket and retrieved a tiny silver thimble, engraved with an intricate design of interlocking flowers. Three words encircled its band.

Faith. Hope. Love.

It was beautiful, polished to a high shine, though loving use showed in its surface — some of the indentions on the top had worn all the way through. I wondered if it was a family heirloom; it had been so obviously cared for and treasured. "We can't take it," I protested.

Sarah brushed away my objection. "I won't take it back. It's small."

So Reverend Day took my hand and turned it up, then pulled Robert's close beneath it and laid the thimble carefully on my palm. He said, "Whatever happens, wherever this life you've chosen takes you, these three remain."

He folded our fingers tightly around the thimble and stepped away.

We were married.

20
DORRIE, PRESENT DAY

The story of Miss Isabelle's simple wedding gave me goose bumps on my heart. As I drove through southern Kentucky, I remembered standing up before old Brother Willis, my mother, and a few friends when I pledged my love to Steve on a muggy day nearly two decades earlier, my belly already pooching out some — Stevie Junior attended the wedding, too, though we wouldn't see his face for several months. I loved Steve, but I already worried about his ability to take care of a family. He spent more time running around with his friends than hanging out with me. He even disappeared for hours on our own wedding night, returning so drunk, I pushed him away when he tried to kiss me. I was already pregnant; what did it matter?

But Miss Isabelle's wedding, plain as it was, young and alone as they were, without family or friends other than kind Reverend

Day and his wife, Sarah, seemed like the real deal. They'd married for all the right reasons — in spite of what anyone else thought.

I saw women in my shop who married for all kinds of reasons — and plenty discovered their mistakes before the ink on the license had dried. They told me things they didn't tell anyone else. Some of those stories would make you shiver, and not in a good way, about husbands and the things they did sometimes.

I was often the first to see bruises hidden behind hair purposely brushed forward, or scabbed-over places where it had been pulled out by the roots. The state licensing office mailed letters explaining how I might be the first line of defense — I could refer clients to agencies that helped victims of domestic violence. They said it was my responsibility. So I kept little stacks of brochures in the waiting area and on my front desk, where clients could casually slip them into purses or pockets. The trifold pamphlets rarely left my shop, but the top few were creased and soft from handling and maybe — I hoped — committed to memory by those who needed the information. I thanked my stars Steve was never violent to me or the kids, even if he wasn't much good at being a husband or father.

Domestic abuse wasn't the only secret I knew about. In fact, being a hairstylist was kind of like being an unlicensed therapist.

I recognized the sorrow in a woman's eyes when she came in, hoping a pretty new style or hair color would pull her wandering husband back to her. I never said it probably wouldn't work. I held my tongue when women fantasized about turning their men around — if they could only lose a little weight or get a boob job or tummy tuck or some other fix that had no bearing on a man's ability to be faithful. They believed it was their fault their men couldn't stick to the commitments they'd made. I'd believed it myself for years. Then I wised up. The only thing that made a man keep his word was the man himself.

I mainly listened. Now and then, though, a customer would ask for my opinion or advice. Then I was blunt and honest. It made me happy to see the same woman a visit or two down the road, glowing and sure of herself after a good decision that filled her with self-confidence and purpose — whether doling out tough love to her partner or starting a brand-new life, where she might have a chance at real love.

But the customers who really broke my

heart were the ones who shared in tiny, terrified whispers how they'd discovered lumps in their breasts. And sometimes I had to tell them I'd noticed a dark, scaly patch on a scalp or a new scary-looking mole on a neck or shoulder. Sometimes I was the only one who saw those stretches of skin on a regular basis. And sometimes I was the only one who knew about secret appointments for second mammograms or biopsies — they were too scared to tell their spouses or children; telling might turn possibility into reality. I was their safe place.

We rejoiced or mourned together when they returned with news, good or bad. I helped with new cuts or styles to compensate for hair falling out in handfuls, and more than once, I shaved a head bald and gloriously smooth when a woman decided she'd rather boldly embrace her new identity than watch it emerge, strand by strand, clump by clump.

There I was, an uncertified therapist, social worker, and diagnostician, and I couldn't keep my own family from falling apart or find it in my heart to trust another man.

I admitted it now: I was terrified.

Seventeen-year-old Isabelle had been so brave, determined to follow her heart and spend the rest of her life with a man I was sure had been the real thing — one who would care for her and love her and their children to the best of his ability, no matter what life flung their way. How on earth had that girl — *child,* really — done it?

I wanted to listen carefully now, to figure out how she'd handled the mess she surely got herself into with that wedding. I wanted to find a graceful way to navigate Stevie Junior's disaster. I wanted to see if there was a way to salvage the muddle I kept making of my love life along the way.

If anyone knew how, it was probably Miss Isabelle, and if she could do it, maybe I could, too.

21
ISABELLE, 1940

Sarah Day fed us an early supper from the plentiful meal of roasted pork and potatoes she'd prepared. "You need a celebration. Most folks come in here with friends or relatives, and maybe they have a little party somewhere after. But it's just the two of you. You stay. We'll celebrate with you!"

I was thankful. Her invitation allowed us a buffer between the ceremonious signing of our wedding certificate and the hour when Robert and I would be alone. Suddenly, I felt shy. I had little idea what to expect when we reached our rooming house. Whispers among the girls I knew were the sum of my preparation for my wedding night.

We finished our meal, and Reverend Day wouldn't hear of us leaving alone. For our first venture out as a married couple, he insisted I must be escorted by another woman. As darkness fell, the neighborhood where Robert had rented our room would become rowdy with both Negroes and whites visiting less than respectable businesses nearby. He and Sarah would walk us to our new residence.

Robert and I spoke at once, protesting, but Reverend Day insisted. "We'd like an evening stroll, wouldn't we, Sarah?"

Sarah's smile exposed her nerves, but she didn't disagree. Her face revealed the truth: Their evening strolls didn't usually reach my new neighborhood. But still, she said, "Just for tonight, we'd like to be sure you reach your destination safely."

They donned their coats, and we retrieved ours, along with our luggage. As we left their warm, cozy home, Sarah insisted she and I walk ahead of our husbands. *Husband.* The word took me by surprise; it was the first time anyone had used it in reference to me. I'd dreamed it, but spoken aloud, it sounded different.

We were weary by the time we reached the rooming house, though our journey was uneventful, aside from a few curious looks from folks we passed by. I was sorry the Days had to turn around and walk the same distance home.

On impulse, I hugged Sarah, though I'd known her less than twelve hours. She pulled me close and whispered, "If you need anything — anything at all — you know where you can find me. You've got a tough road ahead, but I'll be saying a prayer for you every single day, you hear?"

Robert waited with Reverend Day near the steps that led to our new home. He shook the preacher's hand, then leaned to grasp our cases.

A Negro woman answered the door. She inspected me with surprise but led us upstairs to a plain but clean room. The faint aroma of food left simmering on the stovetop too long lingered throughout the house.

"No fires, no candles, even when the power goes out — which is more often than you'd think. This is old wood, and I can't have nobody burning down my place. I take laundry on Wednesdays, but it'll cost you extra. I don't do meals on Sundays, so you're on your own tomorrow, and it's too late for the rest of this week, too — I already shopped. Be sure and turn off the hot plate after you use it. Anything I forgot?" She waited a half second, then hurried out the door and down the stairs. It seemed our new landlady was a no-nonsense kind of woman — fine by me — but she was also a bit hard around the edges. I already missed Nell and Cora. But Nell and Cora were family now, for real. I longed to see them soon and hoped they wouldn't be too furious with Robert or me.

My new husband pointed out empty drawers and wardrobe space where I could store my belongings, which appeared even more scant now. It took me all of a minute to hang my dresses and tuck my other garments into the creaky, mothball-scented dresser. I left the drawer open a crack, hoping the aroma would dissipate and my clothing wouldn't smell too much like chemicals by morning. I didn't want to complain or make Robert think he hadn't found us a fine place.

He watched from a chair near a tiny table in front of a built-in pantry while I explored. On a small wooden chest nearby, I found a one-burner electric hot plate, an enamelware cooking pot, and basic utensils. The chest contained two each of chipped crockery plates, bowls, cups and saucers, and dull metal flatware. I knew even before I scanned the room that I wouldn't find any place for cold storage. We'd have to consume dairy products or other perishable items we purchased almost immediately. My family had been one of the first in Shalerville to get a refrigerator. I was spoiled.

But I could manage.

I'd learned basic homemaking and house-keeping skills while watching Cora and Nell work around the house. The things I'd learned from my mother, on the other hand — embroidery, fancy needlework, flower arranging — would be useless here.

"Will it do?" Robert asked, interrupting my inspection of the compact space. It was short steps from the bed to the eating area, and one easy chair crowded the room's remaining corner, though its springs looked none too springy.

"It's our home — I love it." I tried to reassure him with a nervous smile.

Robert cleared his throat. "The, um, bathroom is down the hall. We share it with two other lodgers." He shrugged his hands apologetically, though I would have been surprised had it been any other way. In my family home, one bathroom was shared by all the upstairs bedrooms, too. This wasn't so bad. We were lucky it wasn't in an outbuilding.

"Of course we do," I said. "What do you think I expected? A suite at the Palace?" I didn't even know anyone who'd stayed at the fancy downtown hotel.

Robert pulled me down to sit close to him at the edge of the bed. "That's my girl," he said. "Now."

His voice trailed off, and it became obvious the piece of furniture on which we sat caused his sudden loss for words. I waited. I didn't know how to put him at ease any more than he knew how to voice what he wanted to say.

"Isa. You know I love you."

I nodded, my eyes growing wide and the muscles of my cheeks and chin cold and stiff as though from lack of use, though I knew it was simply fear of the unknown that immobilized them. But I'd never loved him as much as I did at that moment. He smoothed a hand across the coverlet. "Been a long day for both of us. You are probably exhausted. We can ease our way into this part of things. If you like."

I appreciated his concern. I was grateful for his patience. He was more of a gentleman than any male I'd known in my life — though I still believed my father was a gentleman, too, and would prove it once he discovered my elopement. I answered Robert with a kiss on his lips, long and lingering and — I hoped — leaving him with no doubt I was prepared to participate fully in every aspect of our marriage.

Preferably, the sooner the better.

I carried a small bundle — nightclothes, hair and tooth brushes, toothpaste, and a rough towel from the drawer — to the shared bath down the hall, where I prepared myself for bed and Robert. When I returned, he waited in the dim room. He'd shut off the overhead light, but a reading lamp glowed on the nightstand.

I regretted not having a proper negligee to wear for my wedding night, but Nell had laundered and ironed my best summer nightgown, sewn of white pin-tucked lawn with narrow ribbon straps that barely covered my shoulders. She'd rinsed it in rose water, and I felt as much like a bride as I could under the circumstances. What had she thought as she prepared the garment for me? Had her face glowed when she considered its purpose — especially given that it was for her brother's bride? I pulled my old, worn bathrobe tight. It had taken more room in my valise than I'd wanted to sacrifice, but now I was glad I had. Our room was chilly, and I was grateful for the extra coverage.

Robert had pulled down the coverlet, and I slipped between the sheets, still encased in the robe, but too embarrassed to remove it. Robert went down the hall, and when he returned, he stripped off his trousers and shirt and climbed in beside me, wearing only his white shorts and undershirt. He smelled of soap and water.

We lay in the dim lamplight together, and I wondered whether Robert was any more educated in the art of lovemaking than I was. I imagined he'd had opportunity at some point to gain more experience, but something told me he hadn't taken it. He'd been driven by his dreams of college and medical school; perhaps he'd been so busy, he hadn't availed himself of those opportunities. I also struggled to picture him in the company of the kinds of girls who would provide them. As quick as he'd been to defend my honor in the dark alley in Newport, I guessed he'd kept company only with girls more like me — even if they'd had different-colored skin.

"Robert," I finally said, almost whispering. "Have you — have you ever —" I couldn't finish the question.

"No." His simple answer both comforted and terrified me. I'd halfway hoped one of us would have an idea how to go about things. But I also breathed a sigh of relief that I'd never need to contemplate his being with anyone before me.

"But," he said, "I, uh . . . I talked to some people. Well, not girls. I talked to some of my good buddies. I think I have the mechanical aspects under control."

I chuckled at his description, and it served to relax us both.

Suddenly, Robert sat up and then dropped to his knees beside the bed. His long arms still reached me, and he gently scooped his hands beneath me and pulled me closer to the middle of the mattress. He stayed there, still, for a moment, stroking my hair and shoulders through my bathrobe. He slipped a finger beneath the threadbare cloth to touch the skin of my shoulder where the ribbon did no more than divide its span. I shivered.

He looked up and into my eyes. "I have a promise to make, Isabelle Mc— Prewitt!"

I smiled at his correction. I waited.

"I love you more than anything, anyone, anywhere. I never dreamed I could love a girl as much as I love you. I suspect it started up a little bit that night in Newport, when we walked along, and you weren't ashamed of me, when you wanted me next to you, not following. I'd never seen a white girl act like that." Now he chuckled.

Ashamed of him? I'd been so grateful for his appearance, I couldn't imagine being ashamed. I almost interrupted, but I held my tongue so he could continue.

"Believe it or not I am thankful for every crazy thing you've done, even if at times I wanted to strangle you. Now, I want you to be proud of me. I want to make you happy and take good care of you. I want to protect you and keep you safe. I don't want to hurt you. Not now, not tonight. Not ever."

How could I deserve this man? My breath caught, and I tried to keep the tears that had threatened during his beautiful speech from slipping down my cheeks. I didn't want him to imagine I was scared, or worse, regretted my choice. One lone tear broke loose, though, and it drifted lazily down my face until Robert caught it with the edge of his finger and swept it to the side.

I pulled his face close to mine then, forcing him to lift himself back onto the bed. His weight against my ribs and hipbones reminded me of the thimble I'd carried all evening, first in my dress pocket and now in a pocket hidden in the seam of my robe. I reached for it and handed it to Robert. He placed it on the nightstand, where it glimmered in the lamp's faint glow, a whole range of hues reflected in its surface.

He switched off the lamp and reached across me to raise the blackout shade over the window. My eyes adjusted to the light from the moon, and in it, eventually, I studied the contrast between our clasped hands. The nuanced differences of our skin tones, the browns and pinks and creams, were indiscernible now — everything was black or white, with few shades in between. Just as the world would see us. But I reveled in our differences in spite of the slightest tremble of nervousness I experienced as Robert began to make love to me.

I sighed at the brush of his skin against mine, smooth and silky, the downy hair on his legs stroking my smooth ones, exposed when he untied the sash of my robe and gently pushed each side away.

I marveled at the sheer number of nerve endings that stood on end when he ran his fingers and palms over every inch of my skin, bared when he gently released my arms from my robe and lifted my gown over my head.

Small sounds of pleasure and pain and pleasure again slipped unguarded from my throat when he entered the secret place of my body, using the instrument I'd scarcely dared imagine even in the darkened privacy of my old bedroom to create an eternal union between us.

There was no doubt about it now. I was his. And he was mine.

22
DORRIE, PRESENT DAY

"Oh, Miss Isabelle, it was so romantic." I felt a lump in my throat as we continued up the southern Kentucky highway. Her sweet story of her wedding night made me regret many of my stupid teenage decisions. Times had changed, that was for sure, but maybe all those folks with their talk of abstinence had a point. Still, you had to tell kids how to protect themselves.

It was too late for me, and, obviously, too late for Stevie Junior. He'd crossed so many lines in the last few days — most of them far worse in my mind than premarital sex.

I still hadn't decided how to approach Teague with the news that Stevie was the one who'd robbed me. I couldn't believe he hadn't given up on me yet, though his texts and calls were coming with less frequency now. He would quit calling eventually — I was counting on it — but I had to admit a small part of me hoped he'd hang in there while I figured it all out.

"I'm glad we had our romantic wedding night, yes." Miss Isabelle's voice interrupted my thoughts. I glanced over, and her eyes seemed to fade in an instant, their silver blue going a little more gray. "It changed my life and his, without a doubt."

"What happened next? What about your families? I bet your mother totally flipped a wig."

"You could say that." Miss Isabelle pulled her crossword book close to her reading glasses. She appeared to puzzle over a spot that still lacked a few letters, as if she were struggling to combine the clue with the letters already there to find the right answer. Then she sighed and turned her head to gaze out the window for a while. Eventually, I turned the radio up a couple notches, hinting that I didn't need to hear the story if she didn't want to tell it. She was worrying me. We were on our way to a funeral, what had to be a sad and painful occasion for her already, and here she was, baring her soul, telling me a story I suspected she'd never shared in full before. I felt honored she trusted me with it. But I was scared it wasn't good for her.

It was clear things had changed dramatically at some point for Miss Isabelle and

Robert. Every face in the photos on her tables and walls was white — her husband, her son, extended family members. There wasn't a single shot of a black person. Something bad had happened. I was amazed Miss Isabelle was so giving and had such a positive attitude anyway. If I'd lost my soul mate — I had no doubt Robert and Miss Isabelle had been soul mates and that they had lost each other — I wasn't sure I could have gone on like she had. I was dying to know what happened between that night and when she met and married the only husband I'd known about.

But I could be patient for Miss Isabelle's sake. If I never found out, well, I'd live with it.

After a while, I asked whether she was ready to stop for lunch, but she wanted to press on. She studied her travel atlas, then determined we could make it to Elizabethtown. Seemed like every other town in Kentucky was either somebodytown or somebodyville. By her estimation, we'd have a little more than a hundred miles to go after that — maybe an hour and a half — and we could snack before bed in Cincinnati. I didn't care. My appetite had taken a hit from all the thinking about Stevie Junior. As far as I was concerned, the sooner we arrived in Cincinnati, the sooner I could take stock of things and figure out what on earth I was going to do.

I studied the scenery while the radio played in the background. To my surprise, Arkansas, Tennessee, and Kentucky had all looked much like East Texas so far. I'd never traveled this far from home by car, and somehow I'd expected things to look different. There were plenty of trees, of course, but those started just west of my old hometown. I'm not sure what else I'd expected. I guess I thought bluegrass might actually be blue. Miss Isabelle had explained it only looked blue if you let it grow two or three feet tall — like anyone would do that. The land rolled gently around us, off to the east and west of the interstate, but I was hoping for something a little more exotic. Older, maybe. More antique. More something. I spied a few of those little split-rail fences — causing me to fight an unnatural longing to stop the car and shoot a few pictures. I smiled. I was never one for taking pictures of anything, much less scenery. I didn't even own a camera.

"Some of the next part is hearsay," Miss Isabelle said out of the blue, interrupting my thoughts about grass that color and picture taking.

"Hearsay?" I pretended to peer at the book in her lap. "Is that one in your puzzle?"

"No. Hearsay . . . what you hear through other people — what I heard from Sarah Day and others, eventually."

Sarah Day? A creepy-crawly feeling in my stomach scritch-scratched its way up to my heart. I'd hoped for at least a little bit of happily ever after for Miss Isabelle and Robert following that beautiful wedding night, as impossible as it seemed. But I had another feeling that what had actually happened would make my troubles with Stevie Junior and Teague look like a Sunday drive.

I gripped the steering wheel tighter.

23
ISABELLE, 1940

When I didn't return home the night I was married, Father wanted to contact the police immediately. Mother suspected the truth.

Cora and Nell had come in early Sunday to prepare dinner, and my mother cornered Nell in the dining room while she was laying the table. She questioned her repeatedly, but Nell pretended ignorance.

Mother ransacked my room. Nell watched, terrified anything my mother discovered would incriminate her, too. She slipped away and told Cora what we'd done. Cora led her back upstairs, where she stuttered through her confession. I'm sure Cora hoped Mother would spare their jobs. I'd left a note on my father's desk in his office, and Robert had left one with Nell for his parents. We didn't say where we'd be living, only that we'd found someone who would marry us in Cincinnati and that we would be in contact eventually. Nell handed over the note to Mother — a note in which Robert had named the church where we planned to marry. He'd wanted Cora to know we'd be married in the eyes of God, and not just the law.

Mother dispatched my father and brothers there immediately, and, of course, the hostile preacher sent them right along to St. Paul's.

Reverend Day had just finished Sunday service. He was enjoying a quiet dinner with his wife when they arrived. Sarah hurried to the kitchen to clear away the mess left by her meal preparations, leaving her husband to answer the door. Members of their congregation often showed up unannounced on Sunday afternoons, bearing desserts or problems that couldn't wait for Monday. She rushed to wash pots and pans and wipe down the counters to prepare for guests, but she froze at the sound of angry voices in the entryway.

One of my brothers ordered Reverend Day to tell them whether he'd married Robert and me on Saturday. The reverend tried to divert their questions, but their voices grew loud and furious.

Sarah peeked around the kitchen door to see my brothers crowding her husband, their fists in his face, threatening to injure him if he didn't tell the truth.

My father tried to intervene. "Boys, this isn't the way to do it. Now, Reverend, you can see we're very upset my daughter is missing. She's only seventeen and didn't have permission to marry. We just want to find her and see what this is all about. We want to bring her home."

"Pop, we'll handle this. We know how to make this niggra talk." Jack — I know because Sarah later described him as the shorter, stockier one — dismissed Father and continued to harass Reverend Day. I was relieved to learn that my father had attempted reason with Reverend Day instead of intimidation. I was heartbroken he hadn't been more forceful with my brothers. But I guess I should have known he wouldn't stand up to them — not even then, not even for me. As a child, I'd watched him shake his head and turn away when he found the dismembered carcasses of bugs my brothers left in their wake, or the remains of baby rabbits they'd skinned for fun, then thrown carelessly in the grass. I'd cried and begged him to punish my brothers, to make them suffer as much as the lesser creatures they'd tormented, but my mother had simply said, "Boys will be boys, John. Let them play." As

310

always, he bowed to her directive.

From the corner of his eye, Reverend Day spied Sarah, and his frantic look signaled she should go to warn Robert and me.

He delayed them as long as he could. My brothers roughed him up. They slapped his face and punched him in the gut, while my father stood by, helpless, his protests ignored. But when they threatened to hurt Sarah, the reverend surrendered. He gave them the address for the rooming house — and prayed Sarah would reach us in time.

Robert and I had spent a lazy morning lounging in bed — or perfecting what we'd discovered we did very well together. But by early afternoon our stomachs rumbled. Robert reluctantly pulled on trousers and a shirt. He went down the hall to clean up, then returned to drop a last kiss on my lips. I still lay in bed, savoring the dream it seemed I was living. "Don't you move," he said. "I'll be back before you can count to sixty-three, and then we'll have a picnic, right here on this mattress." I sighed and smiled. He left, then threw open the door again to peek in and throw another kiss. Finally, his steps receded down the hall, then the stairs, and I drifted, half-sleeping, half-awake. I knew I should rise soon to straighten my hair and brush my teeth, but

I was too contented to move. I drifted back to sleep.

Later, I learned Robert had difficulty finding an open shop; in our bliss, we'd forgotten it was Sunday. He regretted turning down Sarah Day's offer to send leftovers with us the evening before. Finally, he found a café serving lunch and spent too much money on a meal that was expensive to carry away. He wouldn't return empty-handed on our first full day of married life.

A nervous tap startled me fully awake. I knew it wasn't Robert. I threw on my robe, tying it clumsily as I moved toward the door.

"Who is it?" I said in hardly more than a whisper.

"It's Sarah Day. Hurry now, open the door."

My insides went cold and steely at her voice. I feared right away something had happened to Robert. Somehow, Sarah knew and had come to inform me. My second thought — that my family had found Reverend Day and made him talk — was the correct one, of course.

I pulled Sarah inside. The apron under her overcoat increased my dread. She hadn't bothered to remove it before leaving her house — and I knew in my gut that Sarah Day wouldn't wear an apron in public. I clutched at her arms. "What is it? Is Robert all right? What happened?"

"Oh, honey, you've got to act quick. Your brothers, your father, they were at my house, and they're probably headed here now. They know about the wedding. I came to warn you — I'm sure there isn't much time."

I heard her words, but in my shock and terror, I simply sank onto the mattress. "What do I do? Robert's gone to get us something to eat. What can I do, Sarah? I don't know what to do."

"Robert gone is probably the best thing. I don't know about those brothers of yours. They were angry when I left, threatening my husband. I think maybe I should go watch for Robert, head him off. They could hurt him real bad — if they even leave him here." I know we both saw pictures in our minds of the boy the reverend had described the day before. "Your daddy, he just stood there, not wanting to cause trouble, but I don't believe he's a match for those boys."

She was right. My mother's insistence on leniency had ruined them, had made them confident to a fault. I knew they weren't scared to fight or hurt anyone who got in their way — not even our own father.

"You're right. Please go, Sarah. Go watch

for Robert. Tell him not to return until — I don't know when. I'll deal with my brothers."

She hesitated at the door. "Honey, your father said you're only seventeen. Is that right?"

I nodded, ashamed of my lie.

She shook her head. "Oh, honey, that wasn't the smartest thing to do. You lied, not only to your parents but to us. It's going to be hard for this marriage to stand up to that, much less everything else you're facing."

I doubled over in a sob, and she let herself out. I'd lied before God, too. All my plans were useless now. What I'd done so far was all I could do. I prayed Robert was far enough away he wouldn't run into my brothers, and that Sarah would find him and warn him in time. Robert knew my brothers wouldn't hurt me, even if they were furious. I was almost certain he'd do the smart thing and stay away as long as he needed to.

Finally, though, I pulled on the dress I'd worn before our wedding and tidied up the place so it wouldn't look as though I'd spent half the day in bed with a man. Even though I had. Even though he was my husband and I'd had every right to.

I could have left. In the spare moments after I straightened our room, my heart could have pointed it out as the obvious course. Gather up what I could, find Robert, and race toward the place where we could begin again, where we could live peacefully as husband and wife.

Was there such a place?

But in the back of my mind, I knew running wouldn't work. I knew if my brothers didn't find me, they'd find both of us eventually and it would be even worse. I knew that if they didn't find us, they'd hurt Reverend Day, or, God forbid, Sarah, as they'd threatened, and I couldn't be responsible for bringing such pain to folks as kind and generous as the Days. In the light of day, I saw it plainly: It wasn't just the two of us. It was Cora. It was Nell. It was a whole circle of people we respected and loved.

I sat in the easy chair and waited for the second knock — this one, no timid tap.

The knock became a crash. My brothers kicked in the door, desperate, I suppose, to rescue their sister from the monster they believed Robert to be. Why else would a Negro think he had the right to marry a white girl?

I sat in my chair, scared but resolute.

Thankful when I saw all three — and only the three. My brothers hulked in the door frame. My father stood behind them, not exactly apologetic. Perhaps he was entitled to be displeased with me for leaving home without permission, for making a choice that could alter irrevocably what he'd worked so hard to create.

If all three were there, it must mean Robert was safe, distracted from returning to our room. I hoped Sarah would have the sense not to tell him right away, perhaps to act like she'd encountered him by accident, then keep him busy talking for a while before she told him the truth. A part of me still feared he might take it upon himself to come inside the house and up to our room, to try to protect me, when he'd be the one in danger.

"Are you crazy, girl?" my oldest brother yelled. "Where's that boy? Where is that nigger boy? Soon as I see him, I'm going to wrap my hands around his neck and squeeze until he can't feel it no more."

My father finally stepped forward. "Now, Jack. That's not necessary. We found Isabelle. We can take her home now." He placed a hand on Jack's arm, but Jack pushed him away.

"That boy ruined our sister, Daddy. Your

316

little girl's been ruined by a nigger. We won't let him get away with it, will we, Pat?" He looked at my younger brother. Patrick shook his head and threw me a look of contempt. "If he argues, I got something better than my hands."

I gasped when Jack withdrew a handgun from his coat pocket. They wanted blood. I could almost smell it. But now I desperately wanted to know if my mother had sent them with her blessing, knowing what Jack carried in his pocket.

"Remember now, you're in Cincinnata, boys," my father said. "Things are different here. You might not get away with what you can at home. You want to end up in jail over this? Both of you, let's just gather up Isabelle and go on home. Come on now, Isabelle." Daddy's eyes pleaded with me to do as he asked.

"I'm not leaving. Daddy, I love him."

Jack and Patrick stepped forward. The looks in their eyes said they thought I was an animal for admitting this much. But I knew better; they were the animals.

"Isabelle, sweetheart, you don't have any choice. You're a minor. Your marriage is invalid. And you're coming home with us." He stood up to me, when he'd refused to stand up to anyone else. And I was the one he'd loved most. How could he?

So what choice did I have then, my brothers willing, maybe eager, to let blood over this, my father unwilling to intervene? At that point, I believed the best thing I could do for Robert was to leave quietly, without drama. We would have to find another way to be together. We were married now, at least in the eyes of God. We had the right.

But I was wrong. I should have refused to go. I should have run as fast as I could, far away from the ones who'd always claimed to love me.

24
DORRIE, PRESENT DAY

I couldn't imagine how Miss Isabelle must have felt, leaving the place she and Robert thought would be home. Robert must have been out of his mind with worry and heart-break when he returned later to that empty room, and when he imagined what lay in store for Isabelle at home. But if he hadn't gone for that meal, who knows what might have happened when those louts showed up with their fists and a gun. (*Louts,* sixty-two down. The definition might as well have said "Jack and Patrick McAllister.") And I'd so wanted to like her father. He'd seemed like a fair man — one who loved his daughter more than anything. I supposed his hands were more or less tied because of the times, and if he'd tried to help the two of them, he'd have been powerfully outnumbered. But I hated him, too, for letting those nasty brothers of hers get away with what they did.

We'd blown right past Elizabethtown while Miss Isabelle talked. I hadn't the heart to interrupt her. Up ahead, an exit pointed toward another little town — named after someone else, of course. "You ready to eat?" I asked, though the timing felt insensitive.

Miss Isabelle heaved a tiny sigh, as if revisiting that day had worn her out. I hoped again it wasn't a mistake to let her share her story with me. But what could I do? She wasn't a child, and I couldn't stop her if she wanted to tell me.

"I *am* hungry." She seemed surprised.

Faced with the usual three or four small-town restaurants right off the interstate, we went with a familiar breakfast-food chain, even though we'd had our fill of breakfast food that morning. The hostess seated us quickly.

But more than seventy years since Miss Isabelle's wedding, some folks still weren't ready for us — and who some of those folks were would surprise you. This old boy and his wife were eating at the table next to ours. Before we even got settled, he proceeded to stare, nudging his wife's foot with his toe when he thought I wasn't looking and quirking his head at us, trying to get her attention. She just looked, gave a *tsk* with her tongue, and shook her head, then went back to buttering her pancakes, but her fool husband kept ogling me and Miss Isabelle like we'd each sprouted an extra nostril.

Maybe the best response would have been for us to ignore him and carry on with our meal. Miss Isabelle and I were both more than a little tense after she told me the part about her brothers forcing her to leave Robert. Maybe what occurred next in that restaurant would not have happened if not for our emotional state.

Maybe Miss Isabelle projected a bit.

And what could I do to stop a nearly ninety-year-old angry woman from expressing her entirely valid opinion?

"Young man," she said, and I almost cracked up. The guy was sixty if he was a day, but he was a baby compared to Miss Isabelle. "Haven't you got better things to do than stare at people?"

He did a double take, then looked over at his wife, who was obviously trying her best to ignore the whole situation. She scooped another dollar-size pancake into her mouth, licking her lips to catch the dripping syrup. Mr. Eyeballs contemplated his own food while the waiter delivered our ice water and menus. But before long, there he was again, sneaking glances, shifting his weight so he could hear our conversation — not much, given we were both weary and drained.

By the time the waiter came back for our order and went off to clip it up over the grill, the man was outright gawking again. And Miss Isabelle might have ignored him at that point had he not leaned back against the pleather seat, toothpick hanging out of the side of his mouth, legs spread so far apart in his tight jeans I could have seen the outline of his boys if I'd looked close enough — which I didn't, thank you very much — and said to his wife in a stage whisper, "I never saw a black girl and an old white woman together in a restaurant around here. You think she's her maid?" He scoffed. "Lady's taking her out for a birthday or something? Otherwise, I can't imagine why —"

Miss Isabelle stood in the narrow space between our tables. It took a while for her to draw herself up to full height, naturally. Long enough for me to think, Oh no, he didn't. Fool really should *not* have said that. But what're you gonna do? I waited for the fireworks.

"No, she is not my maid. She's my granddaughter." I'm sure my jaw dropped as far as the man's did at that. "Furthermore, I'm almost a hundred years old, and I can't believe they still permit idiots like you to walk the earth. In case you missed it, it's now perfectly acceptable for whites and blacks to have relationships. To be friends or relatives. Or lovers."

Our waiter hovered nearby, and Miss Isabelle waved him over. "Sir, we'd like our food to go. I can't stay in this building another minute."

Our waiter stood there, hands flapping, unsure how to handle this obviously sticky situation. Miss Isabelle dug her credit card out of her pocketbook, then waved me to follow her. We sat in the waiting area until the waiter brought us steaming to-go boxes and cups with lids.

"I apologize, ma'am. I'm not sure what happened there, but I am really sorry. Are you sure we can't seat you somewhere else to enjoy your meal?"

"Oh, honey, it's not your fault," Miss Isabelle said. She looked past him to the manager, who hovered behind him. I'm sure the woman entertained visions of her corporate race-relations officer grilling her about the events. "But may I suggest you post a notice on your door that says 'No bigots served. Of any color'?"

The waiter packed our food containers into a handled bag. He returned Miss

Isabelle's card. "There's no charge. We're so sorry."

"Oh, well, I don't mind paying for the food," she said, but he waved her away.

We found a little picnic area on the town square. Monuments and markers dotted the area. The whole scene, bordered by old buildings, was downright quaint (eleven across), and, finally, completely different from anything I'd seen at home. Eating from those flimsy Styrofoam boxes was awkward and messy. Miss Isabelle fumed. But eventually she sighed and relaxed her shoulders.

"I'm sorry, Dorrie. I shouldn't have caused a scene back there, but you know, there's no call for that kind of —"

"Oh, hush. As of right now, you're officially my hero." It was true. I couldn't have said what she had better. "I can't believe sometimes how people act — even black folks. Some of them have this idea it's being disloyal to hang out with white people. If you hadn't said it, I would have." That's right. Those folks looked a lot like me. If you'd squinted just right, I could have been their daughter. Which reminded me . . .

"Miss Isabelle. *Granddaughter?*" Surely she was just messing with the guy, but I had to ask. Was there some bigger reason she'd invited me on this trip — one I'd never even considered?

"I couldn't think of a better way to wipe the judgmental look off that jackpot's face, pardon my French. So what if I want to call you my granddaughter? You *are* the closest thing to family I have these days."

Miss Isabelle's compliment touched me, but it saddened me, too. I drained my Diet Coke, hoping the emotion would pass.

"Oh, stop looking at me like that, Dorrie. I know what you're thinking, and all that's in the past. You've got more to worry about than an old woman and her ancient history. What I want to know is what you're going to do about Stevie Junior. Have you decided? What about your boyfriend? Are you just going to leave him hanging until he gives up? Is that smart?"

I sighed and scraped myself together. "I'm still thinking things over. I'm taking my time on this, instead of flying off the handle and trying to fix things the first way that comes to mind. Unless — God forbid — Stevie's decided to go ahead and spend that money and make things even worse, he can sit there and stew for another couple of hours about all the sh— the *trouble* he's gotten himself into. Teague, well, he's probably already given up."

"I don't know," Miss Isabelle said. "Sometimes the good ones surprise you. Sometimes they stick around longer than you'd think — after they should have given up."

We were finished eating, though Miss Isabelle had only consumed about half of her double-decker club sandwich and fresh melon balls. I crammed our litter down in the bag and tossed it in the trash can by the table. We wandered back to the car, each lost in our own thoughts.

25
ISABELLE, 1940

If home had felt like a prison before, now it was maximum security. In fact, it was solitary confinement. When my brothers delivered me to Mother like bounty hunters, she took my suitcase and led me upstairs. She gestured to the bathroom door, waited while I relieved myself, then followed me to my room, where she dropped my case at the end of the bed and left without a word. The door had a double-sided keyhole. I heard metal twist in the lock, then her footsteps receding deliberately down the stairs.

Patrick was already at work outside, tearing latticework from the side of the house, lopping the frail arms from the tall cedar tree closest to my window. Attempting to descend those flimsy branches would have been madness. Perhaps they thought that was the case; by then, they mightn't have been far off. Soon, I wasn't surprised to hear the ladder scrape my windowsill. I peered out. My brother hammered long, thick nails into the window frame to prevent me from raising the sash.

Mother and Daddy argued in the distance, her voice steady and harsh, his hushed and pleading. I'd always thought Daddy was in quiet control of our household, that he'd *chosen* to leave the running of things to my mother. Now I knew the truth.

At first, Mother brought meal trays, three times daily, and waited at the bathroom door while I bathed or relieved myself. I learned not to drink much water or tea at once as I was required to take care of life's most basic and private needs on her schedule. I sipped until shortly before I knew she'd appear for another meal and bathroom break, for I refused to call out.

Eventually, she allowed me some meals downstairs, but only those where my brothers were present, instructed by her, I'm sure, to pursue me if I bolted. Not that they needed reminding. Mother looked at me with no expression; they still looked at me — when they acknowledged me at all — with disgust. I much preferred the meals I took upstairs.

I had no plan yet. When Mother finally spoke, it was to assure me if I had any intention of trying to contact Robert, she'd make certain he and his family were punished more severely than I could begin to imagine. Nell was conspicuously absent, and I saw Cora only for seconds at a time when she scurried in and out of the dining room to pour coffee or refill dishes. She never looked at me. I scarcely tried to make eye contact, so ashamed was I of all the trouble I'd caused her family.

All that kept me within sanity's margins during those weeks was writing letter after letter to Robert, though I had no idea whether he'd ever read them. I realized that, in my haste to gather my things at the rooming house, I'd left the thimble on the nightstand. When I remembered, I sank to my bedroom floor and wept for hours. I couldn't identify a single physical reminder of Robert. Everything was gone. I prayed Robert had found the thimble and saved it. I worried, too. Perhaps my failure to take it had telegraphed an unintentional message — one of rejection. I regretted now not having had the presence of mind to leave him a note. I wondered if Cora had told him how I was being kept prisoner.

I finally spoke to my father when Mother stepped into the kitchen briefly while Jack and Patrick, who had already finished eating, smoked on the front porch. Since my capture, she no longer complained about their smoking or sent them out back. I guess she considered them men now, due to their act of heroism.

I begged my father to explain why he'd let them come after me, why he hadn't left us alone when he discovered I loved Robert. "It's not fair. It's *so* unfair. I thought you wanted more for me, Daddy. You wanted me to be happy. And you wanted more for Robert, too. We love each other. He can still be a doctor. I could help him. You always said I'd make a good nurse. How could you let her do this?" I babbled in my desperation, rushing through everything I'd waited to say until we were alone.

"Isabelle, my girl . . ." He sighed, shrugging as though I should understand. I understood, certainly, that he'd allowed the others to decide the fate of my marriage — no matter that he respected Robert, no matter that he'd trusted him for years, encouraging his education and providing for it.

"I'm not your girl anymore, Father," I said, and looked away. We didn't speak for a long while after that. I never called him "Daddy" again.

Another day, I managed a conversation with

Cora. Father had left hastily after she poked her head into the dining room to report someone's emergency. I wasn't sure where Mother had gone. She'd complained of a headache; I assumed she'd gone to bed. She would never have left me entirely on my own. My brothers were absent. I gathered a few dishes and carried them to the kitchen under the guise of helping to clear the table — something I'd done often in the past.

I pushed through the swinging doors, startling Cora. She looked up from soapy dishwater and saw me with my load of dinner plates. She looked away again and didn't acknowledge me other than jutting her chin to indicate where I should place the dishes, but I kept the china in hand. If anyone entered the room, it would appear I'd just arrived.

"Is Robert all right?" I asked, my voice low and hurried. I didn't give Cora a chance to answer, though, gathering speed as I poured out my apology, fearing it might be my only chance. "I'm sorry for everything, all the trouble I've caused you and your family. But I love him, you know. It's the only reason I did it. I love him, Cora."

She dried a hand on her apron and raised it to rub at what could have been an itch near her eye but may well have been a tear.

"Can't talk about it, honey. You go on now, take care of yourself. Don't worry none about us."

"But Robert —"

Cora swung her head around. "We're all fine now, but if your brothers get wind of you trying to talk to me, they're gonna follow through on their threats. Day after they bring you home, they come to the house looking for Robert, and they mean business. He's likely not to survive what they'll do next if he touches you again or any of us try to talk to you. Not just Robert. They mention our house, the church, talk about accidental damage, burning things. Miss Isabelle, you've got to leave us alone."

She turned away. I couldn't see her face, but her breath caught, as if she were trying to control her emotion. My hands trembled. I set the dinner plates on the counter, the leftover splotches of gravy already congealing, their scent turning my stomach as the words Cora said squeezed my heart into my throat.

Mother inquired whether I needed sanitary supplies for my monthlies. Her concern surprised me. Then the subtle knock and scrape of the metal wastebasket against bathroom tile enlightened me. She was waiting for a sign — a sign my body hadn't been altered to a point that would visibly shame my family.

One day, I told her I needed napkins, and she sighed audibly, relief plainly relaxing her body from head to toe. She thrust a box past my door within minutes. I felt my face flush. We'd never discussed their use beyond what was necessary. I'm sure she assumed I was embarrassed.

But it wasn't embarrassment that drew the color. It was fury.

26
DORRIE, PRESENT DAY

Irony was the answer to forty-two down, and it hit me as we started the final stretch to Cincinnati. My Stevie Junior in a panic and doing stupid things because his girlfriend was pregnant. Miss Isabelle's mother in a panic over whether she was pregnant and doing stupid things.

The thought of Stevie conjured a call from him. I wasn't exactly ready to talk, but there was no time like the present. We were on a straight stretch of road, so I dug my phone out and hit the answer button. He was yapping before we connected.

"Okay, Mom, this here's the deal. Bailey is seriously freaking. She told me she better have the money by tomorrow morning, or she's gonna tell her mom, and then her mom is gonna tell her dad, and then her dad's gonna come over and bust my ass. Or worse —"

"Hold up! Hold up a minute now." I

reminded myself how to breathe — inhale, exhale, inhale — trying to keep my eyes on the road and my hands on the wheel, when all I really wanted to do was find two little adolescent necks and wring them. It was becoming a fairly regular desire, and not an especially healthy one.

" 'Hold up,' Mom? You have *no* idea what I'm dealing with here."

"Really? Is that so? You mean I have no idea what it's like to deal with teen pregnancy? Yeah. You're right."

His brief silence acknowledged my subtle reference to his own birth, but he went right on. "Okay, Mom, but you have to let me use that money. Her dad might kill me or something. I'll pay you back. I promise. First job I find, I'm there. Mom. *Please.*"

" 'Have to'?" Fuming was a mild way to describe me by then. I considered pulling over before I caused an accident, but I wanted badly to get to Cincinnati so we could settle in for the night. We were road-weary, and there was no telling what we'd need to deal with before the funeral activities started the next day. So I kept driving, only semiconscious of the speedometer inching up. "Son. That was my money. I earned it. And you stole it from me. You think I'm going to pat you on the back and let you keep it?"

He went off on me, screeching what a horrible mother I was for endangering his life and how it was probably my fault in the first place he was in trouble because all I ever did was work, work, work and ignore him and spoil Bebe, while he just tried to find someone to love him and . . .

A cop car merged onto the road, pulling behind me. The flashing lights served only to enhance the red I was already seeing.

I stretched my hand toward Miss Isabelle, my phone flat on my palm. She took it, then studied it, wrinkling her forehead at the angry sounds still spewing forth. I should have disconnected before I handed it over — I'd already seen her in action once that day — but it was too late.

"Young man?" she said. The noise from the phone stopped abruptly. I eased over to the side of the road, trying my hardest not to sling a string of my own expletives.

"Your mother is an angel," she said. "An angel of *mercy.* All your yelling and carrying on is unproductive. Now, your mother's done you a favor by not letting the police drag you off to jail for taking her money. You think about that and speak to her after you've cooled down. She has something else to deal with right now."

I'd pulled onto the shoulder by then. I kept one eye on the patrolman approaching my window while watching Miss Isabelle search for the way to end the call. "The red one," I said, then lowered my window and dropped my head against the headrest.

"In a hurry, ma'am?" the officer said.

"Oh, you have no idea." I shook my head. A model of restraint.

"May I see your driver's license and proof of insurance?"

I pulled my license from my wallet while Miss Isabelle located the little scrap of paper from State Farm. We waited in silence while he returned to his car to check my rap sheet. Finally, he reappeared at my window.

"I'm citing you for excessive speed. You were doing almost *ninety* in a seventy-mile-per-hour zone." He eyeballed me, like speeding was an uncommon *offense.* "Also, I'm issuing a warning because your driver's license expired two weeks ago. You need to handle that right away. Maybe over in Texas, you get a grace period, but here in Kentucky, I could haul you in." He glanced past me to Miss Isabelle, as if she were the only reason he'd decided not to.

My face went hot and the backs of my hands tingled as if they'd been spanked. I glared at the little plastic card I mainly used for a good laugh at the picture. My birthday had passed with a minimum of fuss, and thanks to debit cards, I couldn't remember the last time anyone had asked to see my ID. The state of Texas sent reminders for everything else — why the hell not an expiring license? Officer Shocked and Appalled passed me the electronic clipboard so I could acknowledge my exponential stupidity. (One can guess where I found *exponential,* though I have no memory of whether it was down or across.) He wished us a good evening — ugh! — and I groaned after he walked away.

"I'm sorry, Miss Isabelle. I can't believe I've been driving you with an expired license. And damn Stevie Junior. He's going to pay for this ticket, too, as soon as he finds that job he probably won't bother to look for." I glanced over at her. "What do we do here? You gonna drive?"

Miss Isabelle sighed. "Oh, honey, my license expired three years before yours, so I expect we're better off with you at the wheel. Take it easy, and we'll be fine." She patted my hand. "By the way? In case you wondered? I'm not sorry for what I said to Stevie Junior."

I shook my head and growled low in my throat. "Somebody needed to say it."

I signaled to get back on the road, feeling paranoia tighten my chest like it always did right after a cop pulled you over, like there was a hidden camera on the car, watching your every move to be sure you were doing it right — even worse when you didn't fit the system's ideal picture of a good citizen. And why did I open my mouth just then? No telling. "Only reason that cop didn't take me to jail was because I had a white woman sitting next to me, Miss Isabelle. I guarantee."

Miss Isabelle looked at me. All she did was look at me. But her look spoke those words uttered too many times before, by too many people, in too many places: *You people. Always thinking we're out to get you.*

I thought I might lose it again. I knew if I didn't leave the car, I might do something I'd really regret later. I pulled over, and Miss Isabelle gaped as I grabbed my purse from the console and bolted out, slamming the car door behind me as hard as I could slam the heavy hunk of metal. I walked off along the breakdown lane, dragging my cigarette pack and lighter from my purse as I went. I couldn't fire up that thing fast enough, and I took a big drag as soon as the flame caught. I threw my purse over my shoulder and kept walking until the Buick's license plate was a tiny dot behind me. Then I walked some more, replaying those unspoken words over and over in my mind.

When I was a kid, this one security guard worked late afternoons or evenings at the public housing project where my mother and I lived — an off-duty Texarkana police officer who'd grown up in my little town and still lived there. He befriended the kids in the complex — the ones who didn't already mistrust the cops, who hadn't already had run-ins with the law for stupid stuff like graffiti on trash bins or keying cars. Or much worse. I liked him. I trusted him. He'd stop me when I trudged back in from school, my backpack dragging at my shoulder. I was always wondering what shape my mother would be in when I walked through the door. Happy and in love? Depressed and asleep? Or cooking dinner for the first time in a week?

"How was school, young lady?" he'd ask. "Got a lot of studying to do today? Your teachers working you hard enough?" He asked questions a parent would, though more often than not these would have been the last thing on my mother's mind. She was usually concerned with whether I had a plan to meet up with a friend to do homework — not whether I actually *had* homework, but whether I'd be preoccupied so she could go out. Hoping the friend's mother would offer me supper.

"I've always got homework," I'd say.

He'd nod. "What's your favorite? I hated science, but I was a whiz at math."

I groaned. Math was never my specialty. "You're crazy. I guess I like social studies. I like to learn about how other people live in other places?" I made it a question, then checked his reaction. Most of the men I knew — except the few at school, who were mostly gym teachers or administrators — were my mother's boyfriends or the other losers who hung around the single women in our complex. They weren't much interested in me before that year, when suddenly I'd sprouted breasts and curvy hips like my mother's, and now I mostly wanted to get away from them as fast as I could find an excuse.

But Officer Kevin wasn't like that. He seemed genuinely interested in what I thought. And I never caught him looking me up and down, judging my chest and hips like I was a berry ripe for picking. "Social studies was fun. Now, when you get to high school and start really learning history, it gets trickier. You have to study hard then. You planning to study hard in high school,

Miss Dorrie?"

"Yes, sir," I replied, not in the way I said "Yes, sir" to get the stalker managers at the dollar store off my back — the ones who followed me around, asked if I was doing okay, looked at me as if I already had merchandise stuffed down the back of my jeans. I said it to Officer Kevin like I meant it. Yes, sir, I planned to study hard. Yes, sir, I planned to get the heck out of my hometown at the earliest opportunity. And yes, sir, if studying hard would get me there, I was on it. Like all the other girls in my complex when we were ten, eleven, twelve. Until the boys started playing with our hearts. I'd held out longer than some so far.

Officer Kevin told me once how he was saving the extra money he made doing security to make a down payment on a nicer house for him and his wife and kids. I liked picturing that. They lived over on the white side of town, of course, but the house was just a crummy little starter thing. He had four kids of his own, and I imagined they were spilling out the windows with all their toys and activity. He wanted to build them a nice big place in the country — where they'd have room to play, maybe even a real swimming pool instead of the little molded plastic or blow-up things they bought every summer at Wal-Mart. I kind of wished I'd had one of those, but I didn't say so out loud. Officer Kevin was nice and I liked that he talked to me — like I was a real person, not a delinquent in training. I suspected he didn't like whiners.

But then one afternoon, I came home from school, and he was standing next to a local police cruiser. My mom sat in the backseat. I ran to the car, dropping my backpack on the sidewalk.

"See what your so-called friend went and did?" my mother screamed through the window of the police car as I approached. "See what happens when you trust white people?"

Officer Kevin leaned up against the car while the local cop took his statement, his back to me, hands deep in his pockets, like he was embarrassed for me. And maybe for him, too.

Momma kept ranting, and I hushed her. "Momma, please don't yell." All the neighbors gawked over their railings. This kind of thing was nothing new around our complex, but she had never been the source of entertainment before. She kept her nose fairly clean when it came to the law, even if she wasn't the most attentive parent. "What happened?" I asked.

"Officer Kevin, here," she said, nodding toward the man I thought had been my friend all this time but who now acted like he didn't even know me, "he called the cops on me — said I was in possession of an illegal substance. I told him it wasn't mine. It wasn't mine, Dorrie. I promise."

"Marijuana smoke comes drifting from your windows, it's as good as yours, ma'am," the local officer said, and my mother snorted through her nose.

"It was my boyfriend's. What was I going to do? I can't control what he does."

"Oh, Momma, I told you not to let him do that in the house." I wasn't sure which of them to be angrier with — my mother, for letting another idiot come in our house and do something stupid, or Officer Kevin. Sure, it was his job, but what was I supposed to do if they carted my mom off to jail? How was I going to study hard if I had no idea what was going to happen next? I had visions of foster homes. My mom was probably telling the truth — the pot probably *was* her boyfriend's. She couldn't afford it. But I wouldn't have been surprised if she'd taken a hit off it, too.

And where was that boyfriend now? "Where's Tyrone?"

"Gone. Lit out not five minutes before

344

Deputy Dog here called the police and they came for me. Wouldn't be surprised if your Officer Kevin timed it that way. He's just been looking for a reason to get me in trouble, get me kicked out of this place. He's been using you to watch me. Trust me."

I couldn't believe it. Why had Officer Kevin blown the whistle on my mom, of all people, not even giving her a chance to explain? There was illegal drug activity in our complex every single day, and it wasn't like my mom was wandering outside in a heroin daze. So maybe she took a little hit of reefer. A rule is a rule, sure, but why *my* mother and not one of the real criminals? Maybe he needed brownie points that day and she was an easy target.

My mother pleaded down to a minor offense. She spent three nights in jail because she couldn't pay the fine. But we were also booted out of public housing for a year. You couldn't live on government hospitality with a documented drug problem. Momma had to attend a supervised rehab program, and we had to live with her drunk old pop — my grandfather, though I never really thought of him that way, because there wasn't much affection wasted between us — in a falling-down shack on the edge of town until we got our eligibility back.

The day she got out of jail, Momma told me Officer Kevin had waited until Tyrone left, then knocked on the door and said he'd trade a little something for not turning her in. She refused and he called the police.

My face burned like fire. My Officer Kevin? The one I'd trusted? The one who'd left me alone when the other creepy men leered at me? The one I'd pictured at home with his nice wife and four cute kids?

I wasn't sure whether to believe her. But she was my mother. There had to be at least a grain of truth in what she said. I learned this: not to trust someone just because they treated me nice. They were probably waiting like a snake in the grass to strike me down. That was the year I started studying only enough to get by.

So okay, maybe I lied when I said I never judged someone based on the color of their skin. I tried not to — most days, I convinced myself I couldn't judge a whole race by one person's actions. But sometimes, something triggered that old memory. It came bubbling up, and suddenly, all I saw was Officer Kevin when I looked at another white face. My heart told me to watch it. My heart told me that white face would go only so far for me. My heart told me I couldn't trust men or people with white faces.

And now I took all the hurt I'd balled up and hidden in the very back of my heart for so many years and spewed it into a million pieces behind me, at Miss Isabelle, as I walked.

Finally, when my cigarette had burned down to a nub, I headed back. Angry as I still felt, I also felt cruel when I arrived at the car. Miss Isabelle sat there, her face pale, her heart beating so hard, it fluttered her blouse like a little bird hidden beneath the fabric.

"I'm sorry," I said as I pulled away from the shoulder. "I wasn't going to leave you alone here. I just needed to get out so I wouldn't do something stupid. *Say* something stupid."

"I didn't think you'd leave me alone. I knew you needed a minute. But why were you so angry with me?"

"You thought I was just saying that, Miss Isabelle. About being guilty just by existing — DWB, you know, driving while black. You have no idea what it's like sometimes, always living under this cloud of suspicion, someone always ready to string you up for the least little thing, like you just proved what they thought to begin with."

"I didn't think that, Dorrie. But you're

right. I don't know what it's like. And it makes me sad that in this world we still do this to each other."

My face burned again, all these years later. I thought back and pictured her look. I'd jumped the gun. Assumed. I was probably right about the cop, but maybe I'd misjudged Miss Isabelle. Maybe I really had.

My shoulders finally began to relax again. We were thirty miles outside the town where we'd eaten, had skirted Louisville on a loop and passed a sign that said it was about a hundred miles to Cincinnati. A little more than an hour and we'd be there.

Except . . .

A clang and a squeal erupted from the front of the car; then a thumping started up and the steering column started to tremble like an earthquake in my hands.

"Good Lord, what's that noise? You'd better pull over," Miss Isabelle said.

I ignored my impulse to throw a sarcastic "Oh, really?" her way. I gingerly steered the car to the shoulder, shut the engine off, sniffed, listened, and watched for smoke or flames to erupt from beneath the hood.

Nothing. At least we weren't about to explode.

I turned to her. "Now what?"

27
ISABELLE, 1940

I was furious with my mother — for the obvious reasons, but even more for watching so carefully to see if I was bleeding. I lied about needing the napkins. I carefully counted off days, timing my requests for supplies at the proper intervals. Each time I made a trip to the bathroom I held my breath — certain I'd see what I didn't want to see — then released it, both joyful and terrified. I wrapped the napkins carefully in toilet tissue, as though they really were soiled with the blood my mother believed would save her.

The road would be perilous when she discovered the truth. But I was ecstatic to have one souvenir of my time with Robert. One tiny piece of him I could cradle in my soul, and eventually — when my abdomen refused to give easily — in my hands. One living, growing reminder that I had once freely loved the man I would carry in my heart always, whether we were ever together again.

Mother informed me my marriage had been annulled. It was easy enough to prove I was underage, didn't have permission to marry, and came from a place that wouldn't recognize our marriage anyway.

At first, I felt dead inside at her news. But she couldn't steal my marriage, even if the paperwork had been destroyed. We'd made our vows. It was enough.

And now I had something else she couldn't undo. When the baby came, she would send me away. She would have no desire to keep me in her house, no wish to see the daily reminder of her failure. She would turn me out. Then I would find Robert, and we would begin again, this time with the precious product of our union to bind us together.

Eventually, of course, she confronted me. Then the nausea I fought was less from my pregnancy and more from the thought of her examining the contents of the waste-paper basket. I said nothing, waiting, expressionless, for her wrath.

Instead, she left.

Later, they argued in the hallway, their voices hushed, but flowing under my door like oil and water, my mother's rising, my father's low.

"You know people who can help us, John. People who will keep things quiet."

"I won't do it, Marg. It's no use beating me over the head."

"What will we do, then? What about when it's time for her to deliver? This can't continue."

My father paused at the bathroom door and shushed her. The door frame creaked in the same old spot it always creaked, and I pictured him leaning against it, waiting for my mother to leave him to his nighttime ritual. She sighed, and her shoes scraped the floor as she continued to their room, as though she had no inclination to lift her feet in complete steps.

What did she wish my father to do? Who were the people she spoke of, who would help and stay quiet? A chill in my spine needled the back of my neck.

This I knew: Even if my father wouldn't help her, Mother was determined I would not have Robert's baby.

I knew little about my mother's upbringing — only that she'd been desperately poor, reared in another small Kentucky town, sired by the town drunk. He'd impregnated my grandmother, then promptly absolved himself of paternal responsibility by falling from a bridge while sleeping off a bender. Documents I'd snooped out listed my grandmother's occupation as washerwoman, but Mother's refusal to speak of it, and, more clearly, her birth order — eldest of four — hinted that taking in laundry wasn't the full scope of her mother's business.

Mother obtained her basic school certificate, then moved to Louisville, where she made herself over, clerking in a millinery shop until she met and married my father. He'd just finished medical school and planned to take over the retiring physician's practice in Shalerville. I pictured my mother remaking herself again, this time as a physician's wife. She'd already come a remarkably long way; my father likely believed he'd swept her off her feet.

I recognized now how her half sister — my beloved Aunt Bertie — had nearly wrecked Mother's careful positioning of our family in Shalerville society. Aunt Bertie had escaped their dreary life, too, coming to live with us after she finished school. She worked hard but was carefree and tempted by worldly things. When Mother could no longer conceal Aunt Bertie's impropriety, she asked her to leave. Her eventual fate, plunging from the cliff in a careless driver's car, seemed more punishment than she'd deserved.

It seemed Mother always balanced on the precarious edge of respectability, but if she'd thought Aunt Bertie's rebellion would be what tipped the scales, she'd thought wrong.

I was the one who might bring down the entire house of cards. The image she'd cultivated and projected for so many years was in jeopardy, and after overhearing her conversation with my father, I couldn't fathom how far she might descend to keep the McAllisters on Shalerville's pedestal.

One afternoon in late spring, Mother observed me leaning to retrieve a book I'd dropped. The fabric of my dress pulled tight against my waist and belly, and it was obvious our little secret would soon be impossible to hide. My father had always said I was built like a sparrow. It hadn't taken long for my growing abdomen to jut from the narrow space between my hips. The next morning, a dour, thin white woman served breakfast in Cora's place, wearing a handmade gingham apron over her own worn dress instead of one of the neat uniforms my mother had provided for Cora and Nell. The woman couldn't have been more their opposite.

"Where's Cora?" I asked. She sniffed and went about her business, pouring coffee, stirring the scrambled eggs to bring steam to their surface so they'd appear freshly plated.

"Where's Cora?" I asked my mother, who had entered the room behind me. My father shuffled in last, bedroom slippers paired with his dark trousers. He usually struck out early for the few Saturday visits he made. Apparently, he hadn't been needed this morning — or Mother wanted him there to give the impression they were a united front.

"This is Mrs. Gray. She keeps house for us now," Mother said.

Mrs. Gray? It was an appropriate name. But I was less concerned about her presence than about Cora's absence. "But — what happened to Cora?" I asked, looking carefully from Mother to Father. He settled into his usual spot and sorted through the morning papers, reading glasses low on his nose, immediately preoccupied with the stock market report. Studied ignorance.

"Cora has a new position." Mother's gaze darted between my father and me. I was certain she was lying; Cora's absence was additional fallout from my actions. She'd been let go as soon as my mother found a suitable replacement. I wondered if she really had been able to line up other work in time — whether she'd been given any warning at all.

Then my mother's eyes flicked toward my waist, and I saw the truth. Cora's departure had coincided with my shifting silhouette. She would not witness the bloom of my pregnancy. Had she any idea when she left that Robert was going to be a father? I'd hardly seen her since our last conversation. I'd left her alone — as she'd requested.

My mother intended to hide my condition.

I had longed, desperately, for a way to contact Robert or Nell, to learn how they'd fared. Did Robert still work at the docks, replacing the income he and Nell — and now Cora — had lost? Had he walked away from our rented room, leaving the memory of that bittersweet night and day behind? Or had he stayed on, choosing to live as an adult instead of returning to his childhood home? And what was the fate of the tiny precious thimble I'd forgotten? Cora's warnings, however, had echoed louder than my longing to know.

I realized now that my mother would not turn me out as I'd assumed when I kept my early pregnancy a secret. I was four months along; she would have done so already. I still worried she'd find a way to rid us of the baby, but with each passing day, I grew more confident I'd be allowed to give birth.

My original intention — to escape when I found an opportunity — changed to maternal instinct. As long as I remained at home, my unborn child would receive the nourishment and shelter he or she needed, even if the situation was cold and unbending. And my father was a source of medical care. If I left without a workable plan and was unable to be with Robert, my baby would have none of these things.

For now, staying put seemed the only solution. My mother sensed my resignation and relaxed her guard, allowing me to roam the house freely. I had no desire to venture out. My brothers skirted me, shooting accusing looks at my belly. I'm sure my pregnancy was a perversion in their minds.

Originally, I counted by days and weeks, then by dragging months as my figure grew unwieldy and my center of balance shifted.

Mrs. Gray rarely spoke — only when propriety dictated. I often came across her standing still, dusting the same curios over and over. Clearly, my mother had hired her less for her house keeping skills and more for her discretion.

Even as time stood still, summer arrived, bringing intense, unpredictable weather. One moment, it was so hot and humid that I moved, heavy and languid, as though through a dream. The next, the crash and flash of thunder and lightning jarred me into too much awareness.

One afternoon, the heat exploded into a storm, as though the sky was throwing a sudden, inexplicable fit of temper. I paced, beginning in my bedroom. I'd reread every book I owned — and the few Mother had fetched from the library — until I was certain I'd lose my sanity between boredom and the growing discomfort of the baby crowding my lungs and ribs and hips. I walked the hallway and back again and again, pausing only to study the storm through a window and to wonder whether it would exit as quickly as it had emerged or linger all evening in moody surges.

In the front room downstairs, my mother addressed correspondence from the church's benevolence committee. At their weekly meetings, the women penned cheery little notes to shut-ins — frail widows and the terminally ill. My mother brought the notes home to address and mail. I amused myself by imagining how her committee would react if I slipped an extra note into the basket for their next meeting, one which offered our family sympathy for my unenviable condition. I was certain she'd conjured up some story about my absence — that was what happened when young girls went away in the bloom of health and returned, with pale faces and sad eyes. It was said they were on extended visits to help distant family with, say, an aging relative. I wondered whether anyone questioned my mother, surprised I'd been sent to help in my last school term. I assumed she'd worked out all kinds of excuses.

How many of those girls had, like me, been prisoners in their own homes? How many had been sent, instead, to places where their babies were taken from them and parceled out to new families like eggs or milk?

I doubted many shared our dilemma, where the racial identity of my baby's father would be apparent the instant I gave birth. Perhaps those places made stipulations when the girls arrived — that the child produced must be acceptable to any young couple eager to adopt a newborn. What did they do with babies with unexpected characteristics? Perhaps a physical defect — a cleft lip? — or exotically turned-up eyes that hinted at lifetime supervision. Or a baby with dark skin, born to a young white girl. What happened to those babies?

I was tentatively relieved I hadn't been turned out or sent away. Not yet.

After a dozen or so of my endless circuits, Mother climbed the stairs, her steps as heavy and worn-out-sounding as mine as she approached the top.

"Please stop pacing," she said as I returned from my latest pause at the window to peer across the street into the woods. Water pooled in the street, the gravel-covered surface no match for the torrent the sky had released, and I wondered if the retaining wall Robert had reinforced the summer before would hold.

"I'm restless, Mother. I can't help it."

"I wish you'd thought of that when you —" She stopped abruptly.

"When I what, Mother? When I fell in love? When I married him before I got myself into this condition? When I destroyed your careful plans?"

She shook her head. My insolence appalled even me, especially when I knew it wouldn't make a difference. It seemed impossible to shame her into empathy, into caring for more than her reputation.

My speech wasted energy, and I had little

these days. Still, I pressed on. "Have you finished your notes?" I asked. "All those old women and sick people believe you're a model citizen. Your concern for the suffering is astounding. What if they knew you kept me here, hidden as though I were a leper?"

She didn't think long. "You know what they'd think. You know where we live and how people would feel if they knew the truth. How can you not see that this is all for you?"

"If not for your interference, I'd be with Robert. We wouldn't care what people thought."

"Oh, Isabelle. You'd be nothing more than fodder. By now, you'd have been chewed into tiny pieces and spit into that dirty river. Your brothers wouldn't have tolerated it. Robert would likely be dead."

"Only because you allowed this town to brainwash them. You're brainwashed by your own fear."

She'd started for her room after her last words, but this called her back. I grasped the banister where it curved around at the top of the stairs to catch my breath.

"My fear?" She edged closer. Her face betrayed what she tried to deny as she strained to remain expressionless, but it pulled at her forehead and the skin around her mouth.

"What would happen if your benevolence committee knew the truth? What if they knew your daughter had married a Negro man and would bear his child? What other secrets might they drag to the surface, Mother?"

She stepped near enough that I could smell her breath, sour, drawn quickly and released again. "Enough. You have no idea what you're saying, Isabelle. You've brought this family more shame than you can begin to imagine."

"Your father? A drunk who impregnated your mother, then fell off a bridge? A mother who did whatever it took to feed you and others who came after you, no fathers listed on their birth certificates? You keep everyone around you under your thumb to prevent anyone from knowing. But I know *all* your secrets, Mother. And I'm the one you can't blame on anyone but yourself."

She gasped. "Isabelle, stop! Why are you doing this? You have no —"

As I confronted her with my frank assessment, she seemed to shrink before my eyes. "It's true, isn't it, Mother?" I felt small, too, as I aimed straight at her vulnerability, but also in control where I'd had none before. "You're afraid of what will happen if they find out. To you, not to me."

I'd pushed too far. She grabbed my bodice — loose around my ribs, as I'd been forced to start wearing cast-off dresses of hers that would still fit my swelling belly — and she shook me. My foot slid around the post and lost traction. My body followed the foot, pitching into air, then crashing along each step until I thudded to a stop where the landing topped the turn into the last few stairs.

Later, I clearly remembered gazing up at my mother where she stood still clutching the blue-flowered print of her old dress, the piece that had ripped away with an almost human shriek as I fell. I remembered struggling to decide whether she'd reached to stop my fall or had simply let me go, allowing bare wood and sharp angles to batter not just me but my unborn child in our descent. Was the terror on her face for me? Or for herself because of what she'd done?

As the pains began in my abdomen, as liquid rushed between my legs, fast and warm like the summer rain flooding the street, I heard a wail. It began somewhere in my chest and emerged from my throat like that of a keening child.

28
DORRIE, PRESENT DAY

Miss Isabelle's voice shook, and I sat in stunned silence. She didn't cry, but her pain cloaked the air between us.

We'd been at the side of the road, waiting for a mechanic, for nearly an hour, but thank heavens for Triple A. Miss Isabelle had rummaged in her pocketbook for her member card, and I'd called the toll-free number to report our breakdown. They'd promised someone would come out to survey the damage. Most likely, they'd tow us back to the suburb we'd passed outside Louisville. Yes, backward. We'd be going the wrong direction, but at least we wouldn't be sitting on that highway all night picking our cuticles and trying to figure out what to do. Sometimes, I was learning, it was a blessing to be prepared. I'd always lived by the seat of my pants. It was the cheapest way to go. Unless you had a problem — then it was expensive.

"Call them back and see if they're going to be here soon, would you?" Miss Isabelle said, her voice cranky and tired and a little querulous now. (*Querulous:* "whining or complaining in tone.") Not her usual old-lady style. It took my mind off her mother.

I started to hit redial on my phone, but it was the same button to answer an incoming call. I had just enough time to register the scrap of Marvin Gaye and the name on the caller ID as my finger pressed the button. Teague. Now?

But what could I do? Hang up? I closed my eyes and gathered a big breath and said hello.

"Dorrie! *Finally.* Girl, I've been worried about you all day, thinking you might be stranded somewhere or hurt or I don't know what. Do you know what you put me through?"

Our silences blended awkwardly.

"I'm sorry," he said, finally. "I overstepped there. I was worried because, well, I care about you, Dorrie." He sighed. I cringed. I hated that I'd stressed him out, when I was just trying to salvage my own pride in the name of keeping him from having to deal with my mess. And I'd never had anyone apologize for overstepping boundaries before. In fact, I'm not even sure I realized

I was entitled to boundaries until that very moment, when someone acknowledged pushing them.

I forced myself to smile, hoping it would come through in my voice. "It's okay. As a matter of fact, we are stranded, but we've got the Triple A coming any minute now. Probably a belt, nothing serious. I'm sure we'll be on our way in no time."

"Dorrie?"

My smile fell away. I knew what was coming. Boundaries or no, he had that note in his voice. He was going to ask about the break-in again.

"Why didn't you want the police involved in your burglary?"

And I still didn't have a good answer. If I told him the truth, he'd back out of my life faster than he'd become a part of it. That might hurt more than ignoring him, letting him think it was all about me until he dropped it and went away. Either way, he was going to bolt. I guarded my voice. "So you called them back? Told them to forget about it? They said okay?"

"Yes, but —"

"And the door?"

"It's boarded up tight until you get home, and I'm planning to run by every day to check on things, but Dorrie —"

"I appreciate it. I really do, and — oh, hey, I see a tow truck in the distance and I'm willing to bet it's for us, so I've got to go. I'll talk to you . . . later, okay? Thanks again, Teague."

I disconnected and dared to look over at Miss Isabelle. She shook her head enough for me to detect it. "What?" I said, and gestured behind us, where a tow truck was rapidly approaching. It pulled around us and parked on the shoulder.

"Nothing, Dorrie," Miss Isabelle said. "Nothing."

She didn't need to say anything.

Eventually, the mechanic called from under the hood, "Yep. Gonna have to tow her in. And I know for a fact I don't have that belt in stock. I'll have to chase it down in the morning, but it'll be a quick fix. Sorry, ladies." He dropped the hood and brushed off his hands.

He drove us to a hotel near his shop and promised to call first thing in the morning. Miss Isabelle fretted while I paid for the room — this time aided by Mr. *Nice* Manager — and rolled our bags down the hall. She was worried we'd be late for the viewing and visitation the next evening. But I assured her if the guy fixed up the car as fast as he'd promised, we'd arrive in plenty of time. It was only a hop and a jump across a river to Cincy once we got back on the road — even I'd begun calling it Cincy in my head after hearing Miss Isabelle say it enough times.

I bought our dinner at a convenience store down the street. After a few hours of television, I went out for the cigarette I'd been telling myself I wasn't going to smoke, checked in with my mother, and had a quick word with Bebe. I didn't bother asking for Stevie Junior. We went to bed early. There was nothing else to do. I settled into the scratchy pillows and was drifting when Miss Isabelle sighed.

"Don't worry. We'll get there," I murmured across the few feet between us.

"I know, I just —" Another sigh made me nervous. Even when the doctor had made Miss Isabelle quit driving, she'd seemed completely in charge. She'd adjusted. But now her inability to let go of her worry concerned me. My temper tantrum earlier probably hadn't helped.

"Miss Isabelle. Trust me?"

"I do. I'm tired, that's all." That was better. A minute later, she even chuckled. "Hmmph. Imagine your Teague if he heard you talking about trust. Hello, pot, I'm the kettle, and just so's you know? We're both

367

black." Then her bed shook as she silently laughed at her own joke backfiring. Full recovery — or maybe slight hysteria.

I flipped to face the other wall, pulling the extra pillow over my eyes to block the street-light glaring through the crack between the dusty blackout curtains. Where was a hair clip when you needed one?

The only person I needed to trust was myself. The other road had too many curves, and I wanted to see straight ahead.

29
ISABELLE, 1940

Mother called for Mrs. Gray, and together they managed to walk me to the claustrophobic room behind the kitchen where we kept an old bedstead. Cora had slept there overnight when it had been too late for her to walk home safely and my father wasn't available to drive her — though I'm sure nobody ever admitted it.

Mrs. Gray spread a sheet over the lumpy mattress, and I fell onto my side, drawing my knees high, groaning at the pains, which were coming faster now. I heard Mother dial the telephone in the kitchen and speak. A short while later, another woman entered the room. My pain had begun to peak. If it hadn't already stolen my breath, the sight of her face would have.

A Negro.

A midwife, come to deliver me of my baby. Apparently, colored was good enough now the baby was coming. I might have laughed had my insides not been boiling like molten lava trying to erupt from the volcano of my body.

I closed my eyes, thankful for someone with a notion of how to get me through this. Later, I realized I never saw my father the whole time I was confined to that tiny room. As a physician, he should have checked how things were progressing — especially given how early the baby was. Perhaps he stayed in the kitchen, advising the midwife, too ashamed to examine his own daughter.

She prodded me, gently explaining each step. I was too focused on the pain to be self-conscious. She assured me the baby would emerge as it should — even if I felt I was going to split in two — and that it wouldn't take long.

Her worried eyes, however, revealed that her expectations were low. Perhaps she sensed if she voiced her worries about the timing of the birth, I might stop working to get the baby out. As it was, I struggled to follow directions, distracted by my fear for the baby and anger with my mother, which recurred every time she entered the room. Mother stood to the side while the midwife briefed her, then left again. Finally, the midwife said she should remain. I would need to push soon, and the pushing would be more productive if she functioned as an anchor.

My mother took her place at my knee, her face a muddle of anger and concern. I looked away, focusing on the midwife's features as she alternated instructions to push or wait or push again. My lower body seemed to have a mind of its own by then, disconnected from my mind, and though I tried to do as she commanded at one point — to wait and gather my strength for the next wave — I had a sudden, uncontrollable need to push the baby out.

The rest passed in a blur, the midwife reporting I'd delivered the head, then the shoulders and body, and this series of events I couldn't see or comprehend resulted in a tiny bundle wrapped in white toweling and rushed from the room. I strained to hear a cry, a wail — something to tell me my baby was alive. Silence pierced silence.

The midwife left me alone with my mother, and I shook, suddenly cold, even enveloped as I was by the sweltering heat. My body was foreign and new again. The shock chilled me.

"The baby?" I asked, and Mother remained silent.

I asked the question several times, and each time she turned away, until I became frantic, pleading for a simple answer. Finally, she studied me with what seemed the smallest measure of pity. "It was so early," she said, shrugging. "It was for the best."

Another cramp clenched my abdomen, and this time it seemed it came from the pain of learning my baby was gone, as though my body were mourning the loss before I even knew of it. A wail budded low in my chest and emerged from my mouth whole. Though I wanted more than anything to prevent my mother from witnessing my anguish, I couldn't conquer it.

"No," I cried. And again. "No. I want my baby. My baby." I turned my face from hers and moaned into the pillow, tears mingling with the sweat of my labor. She left the room.

The midwife returned and reseated herself at the end of the bed. She pressed on my abdomen, as though she were trying to expel my grief from my body, and with each wave, my sobs diminished, until they finally ran out. She explained that the afterbirth had been delivered. She took it away, and when she returned, I clutched her arm, my eyes asking the question I couldn't voice again.

She barely shook her head and looked away, and my eyes flooded again, though this time my cry was silent.

"Was it a boy or girl?" I asked. I watched her battle with the question, her eyes flicking toward the door, though it was firmly closed.

"A girl," the midwife whispered.

"I want to see her." I struggled to sit up, but the woman pushed me down again, though gently, her hands and arms strong and versed in the care of new mothers. But without my baby, what was I?

"Honey, you lie still now. I need to check things and get you cleaned up. And . . ." She hesitated and looked toward the door again and shook her head. "I'll do what I can."

"Mother!" I screamed, and the woman started at the force and volume of my cry.

Mother opened the door only enough to let herself in.

"I want to see my baby," I said, my voice dead calm now.

"It would be a bad idea, Isabelle."

"Maybe just for a minute, ma'am?" the midwife said. "Just to say her good-byes? Sometimes that helps."

"It would only make things more difficult. And it isn't your concern." Mother's voice was flat, too, her face harder than I'd ever seen it. It was impossible to believe I'd once been *her* baby girl.

When she stepped out of the room again, I grasped at the midwife. "What will they do with her? I need to know where she'll be." I knew my mother would never tell me. Someone might see me mourning, and our secret would be no more.

"She'll be in a good place, don't you worry." She paused to listen to the rain, which still drummed against the roof. "Safe and dry . . . and in God's hands. You'll see her again one day. I know it."

Her platitudes didn't help. I screamed again, over and over, long after Mother had left the room, through the whole process of the midwife bathing me and soothing me with warm cloths as though I were an injured child, through the examining and stitching of the jagged tear that would take weeks to heal properly, that throbbed constantly like a separate heartbeat, reminding me of what I had lost.

30
DORRIE, PRESENT DAY

The mechanic reclaimed us at the hotel the next morning and sent us on our way. Miss Isabelle had been tight-lipped about the day she went into labor, but once we were settled into our route again, aimed the right direction and an hour and a half or so from Cincinnati, I'd quietly asked her what happened after she fell down the stairs.

My questions felt cruel, but more and more, it seemed she needed to tell this tale, to purge some of her pain before we arrived. (Forty down, five letters: "to flush out or eliminate." *Purge.* Even thinking the word was painful.) As though in the retelling, she would work her way through a kind of healing.

When she told me about her mother's refusal to let her see her baby, her monotone exposed her grief. This time, tears did drip from the sides of my eyes as she fell silent. I blinked as long as I could, then casually reached a finger to rub them away, hoping she'd think my eyes watered because of the late-morning sunlight gleaming through the windshield.

"What made her that way?" I asked, a lump in my throat choking my voice. "I'm so afraid I'll let my kids down, Miss Isabelle."

I thought of Stevie Junior, home alone with his dumb mistakes, faced with ultimatums from both sides, right or wrong, but equally critical. How was the kid supposed to deal?

I'd talked to him briefly that morning. He'd been subdued and embarrassed that Miss Isabelle had witnessed his temper tantrum. He apologized for screaming at me, which made me feel hopeful. I told him I felt like I ought to be there — *wanted* to be there now that we'd both calmed down some — but he said it was okay and promised to sit tight another day or two. Bailey had agreed to wait to tell her parents and to not do anything hasty — at least until I returned home, as it would only be a few more days. He'd given Bebe the money for safekeeping, and though she'd pestered him to tell her where it had come from, all he told her was that he needed her to keep it in a safe place he didn't know about. I chuckled a little over that. My mom was there, but twelve-year-old Bebe was the one you could trust with the money. We all knew it.

"All you can do is act the way you'd like them to act," Miss Isabelle said now. "They'll watch you, and then they'll make their own decisions. You cross your fingers over your heart and hope to God they make good ones. But you're not going to let them down, Dorrie. No more than any imperfect mother who loves her children more than she loves herself."

"But how did she cross the line? Why did your mother let you down so hard?"

"It was a different time, Dorrie. And I had crossed an unforgiveable line, too . . . for that time. Though it's hard to accept, any other mother we knew might have reacted the same way. And you're hearing this story through my eyes — my seventeen-year-old eyes. It's an irony that young people mostly see things as black and white, Dorrie. All or nothing. Sometimes, in spite of their enthusiasm for embracing change, it takes years of experience before they truly see the whole picture. Still, I don't believe my mother ever really learned how to love me properly. Her basic needs were scarcely met as a child, and all she could do as an adult was clutch at the status she believed would save her. I really do think it all boiled down to fear. She was so worried about what the people around us would think, she forgot about . . . *me.*"

I hurt for her. As much as my own too-young, too-ignorant single mother had bungled things — and made me nuts with her dependence on me now — I'd never, ever, questioned her love. I always knew that, in her weird, unreliable, impulsive, ridiculous way, she loved me. I'd seen the pride in her eyes when she watched me with my own children, or watched me work my magic on a customer's hair — even if she didn't understand my methods or relate to my self-determination. Sure, Momma had let me down, plenty of times, but never in the way Miss Isabelle's mother failed her.

Up ahead and over to the east, in the now-visible distance, a series of bridges spanned the Ohio River and skyscrapers rose in a clump on the other side, creating the illusion we were about to cross over onto an island — though, from studying the map along the way, I knew it wasn't so.

Miss Isabelle's eyes filled with something I struggled to identify. Like a ball of rubber bands, all mixed up in their colors and textures, the emotions in her eyes were a jumble.

Finally, there it was: Cincinnati.

The City of Seven Hills, Miss Isabelle had said they called it. There were more hills than that, if you were counting.

31
ISABELLE, 1940

My skin was young and elastic. I hadn't put on much weight during my pregnancy; first the depression and then the humidity and heat had stolen my appetite. Between that and the baby's coming early, I'd hardly shown, and my hip bones had scarcely shifted. Unclothed and up close, my faint stretch marks could have been detected by an experienced eye, but nobody was looking. Perhaps my breasts were fuller, but the midwife had instructed me to bind them tightly with rags when my milk began to come in, and with no baby to suckle, they were no beacon of motherhood. My old dresses soon fit again.

When I emerged from the cocoon of my bedroom, Mother said I could come and go freely — under one condition: I must never admit I'd been in Shalerville during the time she'd claimed I was gone. Otherwise, she showed no interest in my whereabouts or anything I did. I suppose she was relieved to be finished with the distasteful business of ridding us of my baby.

Granting her wish was easy. I had no desire to explain the last seven or eight months to anyone. Nor did I initially desire to leave. It wasn't that I was content to stay home, reading, sleeping, or — more often — gazing out the windows. If anything, I was numb. I was unmotivated, uninspired.

Undone.

Finally, though, after a month or so of doing mostly nothing, and when the heat let up, I became unsettled.

I don't know what flipped the switch. I simply woke to life again — even if it meant feeling the pain intensely while my mind explored ideas and plans. Suddenly, another minute in the house where I'd been tried, convicted, and held prisoner for the crime of following my heart was too long. And after my eighteenth birthday that fall, my mother could do little to keep me under her thumb, even if she'd wanted to.

The Reds were nearing their first World Series victory in twenty-one years, and everyone was obsessed with baseball. No one paid attention to me as I began making daylong journeys to the city. I purchased coffee or tea in exchange for café seats,

where I combed through secondhand newspapers, flipping past the ragged sports pages
to the nearly as ragged classifieds. Debates
over the fine points of the most recent loss
or victory were my background noise as I
scanned for jobs available to a bright young
female with no real training or specific skills
— but none that would transform me into
one of the eerie young/old women I witnessed streaming from factories or plants
when end-of-day whistles sounded. My soul
felt ancient, but I would need a strong,
healthy body if I must support myself
indefinitely. If I couldn't have Robert, I
wanted no other man, and I would no
longer depend on my family. I would take
care of myself.

But I kept one eye on the newsprint and
the other on the teeming sidewalks, praying
one day I'd glimpse him.

After a time, I felt bold enough to stroll
past the rooming house where we'd spent
our wedding night. I did so several times,
on different days, desperate to spy him
climbing the steps to the porch at the end
of a workday. But I didn't see him. Finally,
I dared climb the steps myself. The landlady
stepped back, seemingly startled, perhaps
even frightened to discover me on her
doorstep. She peered past me — to see if I

was alone, I suppose, or whether the angry men who'd barged into her home and business accompanied me.

"What do you want?" she said. I asked whether Robert still lived there. She shook her head, avoiding my eyes. "He never came back since that day," she said. "Took everything and never came back at all. Told him I couldn't refund the rent he'd paid ahead, but he didn't mind." She cocked her head. "Not here for that, are you? Can't do anything for you if so."

I assured her I wasn't looking for money, though I asked about the thimble. She denied having seen it on the nightstand or under the bed when she cleaned. I hoped that meant Robert had gathered it up with whatever he took when he left. The woman closed the door on me as soon as I gave her the opportunity.

Sarah Day invited me into her kitchen, clucked her tongue, and gathered me close. I didn't mention the baby, but something told me she knew, the way she released me carefully from her embrace and studied my hips and bosom when she thought I wouldn't notice. But her story was no different. Neither she nor Reverend Day had seen or spoken to Robert since the day after our wedding, when she headed him off while my father and brothers took me home.

I tried to summon the nerve to go by the house in the small community where Robert and Nell had lived with their parents, the courage to walk to the church, to the arbor where I used to meet him and where we'd shared our first kisses, but fear paralyzed me. I didn't know how Cora or Nell would react to seeing me. I was afraid I wouldn't be able to withstand their fury at me for costing them their jobs. I wasn't even sure Robert would want to see me. I wondered if he'd been angry that I hadn't tried to contact him. I wondered if he knew my mother had kept me prisoner. I wondered if he had any idea I'd carried his child . . . and lost her.

Though I contemplated the best course of action, though I hoped for a twist of events — coincidental or celestial — to bring us together again, I resigned myself to creating a life alone. I'd caused enough trouble already.

One day, an ad ran for a job, not giving many details other than it was a new business that needed one additional steady employee, no experience necessary. Everywhere else, I'd been summarily dismissed upon walking through the door to ask about a position. My slight stature must have put potential employers off — not to mention my lack of experience when the unemployment rolls still hadn't recovered completely from the Great Depression. There was no telling how many people competed for a single position. I assumed this business owner would react the same way.

But not this time. He looked me over, asked to see my hands, studied how I held a few small tools, then told me about his new endeavor.

A popular camera company had introduced a new film that produced beautiful color slides, and the price of the film included processing and returning the slides to the customer already mounted and ready to project. People enjoyed showing off photos of vacations or family events, but mounting their own old-fashioned slides was tedious. This was the latest, greatest thing, a major time-saver, albeit a luxury. And the price reflected this luxury. This Cincy entrepreneur saw his opportunity. He'd perfected his own system of mounting the old-style glass slides. He produced large quantities of pressboard frames similar to the other company's. People could bring batches of glass slides, and he would mount them at a fair price. And if they dropped them off one day, he guaranteed they could pick them up the next, instead of waiting on the postal system as the other film's users had to do. To his great delight, business was booming. He couldn't keep up. That was where I'd come in.

Mr. Bartel declared my small, nimble fingers a good fit for mounting slides. He warned me I'd better show up for work every day and on time, but I could start the next Monday, with Saturday afternoons and Sundays off.

It was Friday. I sped back to the coffee shop where I'd found the ad, hoping the newspaper was still, by some lucky chance, where I'd left it. If I were to start a job in Cincy on Monday, I would need a place to live and a way to pay the rent until I received my first wages.

The newspaper was scattered in sections around the shop, but I found the ads for rooming houses and scanned them for a few promising ones that claimed suitability for single young women, quality only. It was anyone's guess whether the description fit now, as used and dried-up as I felt so soon after giving birth, emotionally bereft after losing my dream of love and family, but I could surely give the illusion of wholesomeness.

I walked right past the first house after

noting its disheveled appearance — oily-looking men in undershirts hanging around the porch, smoking cigarettes, and a young woman leaning from a window in nothing more than a slip, calling to another man on the street. Quality?

The next house, though, was in a quiet neighborhood. It looked recently painted, and the stoop had been swept clean. The woman who answered the door was friendly and youngish, with two toddlers clinging to her skirts. She scanned me up and down and studied my shoes and clothing, apparently coming to the conclusion I would do. She agreed to hold the room until three o'clock the next day. If I returned with two weeks' rent, the room would be mine. Her small attic-level room was pleasant, sunny, and clean. I could eat with the family for an extra fee or take my meals elsewhere, provided I notified her a day in advance.

My heart thumped as I calculated the amount — seven dollars for two weeks, nine if I included suppers. A small fortune. I realized now how hard Robert had worked to secure the rent for our room — only for it to go to waste almost right away. I'd never saved more than a few coins at a time from birthday or Christmas envelopes, and I'd spent what little I had accumulated on coffee, tea, and streetcar fares while looking for work.

The only solution I came up with was to approach my father. His inaction in the face of Mother's determination, his refusal to speak a word against her, had finished me with him, but I figured he owed me at least this. I could talk him out of a measly ten dollars.

I hurried back to Shalerville, hoping to catch him before he left his office. He spent Friday afternoons there, catching up on paperwork and reading his medical journals, unless an emergency called him away. Patients with mild complaints were instructed by his nurse to call again Monday.

In my haste to exit the streetcar, I marveled at my body's recuperation. Only weeks earlier, my insides would have protested, jarred by the thud of feet against curb.

I didn't speak, gave the nurse no chance to stop me as I passed her, only rapping my knuckles hard against the solid door of my father's consulting room before opening it. I caught my breath while he studied me, emotion seeping from his eyes. An odd mix — sadness, trepidation. "Isabelle?"

Is it really you, his eyes asked, *or the phantom of your former self?* I wasn't sure myself.

"Hello, Father." The formal address still irritated my throat, dragged over my tongue like sandpaper, like the accusation it was. "I need ten dollars. Please don't ask why."

His gaze stayed on my face as he fumbled in his pocket for his wallet. He withdrew a slender stack of bills, only glancing down to identify a five and five ones. Before he bent them together and slid them across the desk, he added another five.

"Oh, Isabelle." He sighed. "I won't ask, but I will wonder. I suppose you've earned the right to your secrets now."

His mouth's droop got me. I admitted I'd found employment and a place to live in the city. I reminded him I was an adult now, eighteen, and that I hoped this time — if he knew where I'd gone and that I wasn't doing anything to offend my mother, my brothers, or their strange moral code — they would leave me alone.

"I'll tell your mother what you've decided. You'll leave in peace," he said. "And, honey . . . I'm sorry . . . for everything."

Oh, Daddy. I nearly cried the words aloud. Almost ran to his side to throw my arms around his neck and cling to him like a child. But I wasn't, and I couldn't.

Money. Apologies. Running interference with my mother — at last. Even his own self-loathing.

It would never be enough. I started toward the door.

"Isabelle?"

I turned back reluctantly.

"Do you remember asking about the signs?"

I nodded, cautious. It seemed he wanted to make amends by engaging me in this conversation. Again, it was too late. But I waited.

"We're not the only town with them, you know."

I knew. I'd seen them here and there when we'd made road trips — as often in Ohio as in Kentucky. Intermarriage might have been legal there, but it didn't mean there weren't towns just like Shalerville.

Daddy continued: "Here in Shalerville, it was considered a more civilized action than some others you might hear about. Long before you were born, the good citizens of our city ran every Negro out of town." His lip curled around the word *good*.

I gaped. Negroes had lived in Shalerville? I'd assumed they'd simply never been there. Why would anyone have run them out?

"It was an era of fear. In many places, people didn't know what to do about the freed Negro slaves. They felt they were encroaching on the land, threatening their livelihoods, so they used whatever excuses they could trump up to run them out of places — false accusations, making entire communities a scapegoat for one person's crime. But not in Shalerville. Here, it wasn't about that, they said. When Shalerville incorporated, the leaders thought the appearance of exclusivity would draw high-class residents. So they gave the Negroes one week to pack and leave. Not many, you see. But they'd been here as long as any white family." He shook his head. It seemed unbearably wrong. But my father's eyes told me his story wasn't finished.

"You know, Cora's family served the physicians of Shalerville for generations."

I remembered that Cora had talked about her mother working for the family that came before us, in the very same house. I nodded, and I suddenly felt sick.

"So far back, they were the property of the doctor that came before the ones that came before us. Her grandparents were slaves, honey. Given their freedom, they chose to stay on. They were good, loyal workers, and the doctor was a fair employer, paid them decent wages. And the doctors who came after. Cora and her brothers were born and raised in a little house that used to be on the back lot — her family had been given title to it. And Doc Partin was better than most around here. When Cora's family was forced out, he paid them for their home, helped them find a new one in a safe area. He disagreed with the policies — and especially the signs — but he was outnumbered. They said it was about making the town better. But truly, those men were just itching for a reason to hurt someone — like everyone else. No telling what would have happened to Cora's family if they hadn't complied with what those folks demanded. And you know, honey, things haven't really changed."

My father's story sent a warning, subtle and clear at once. I must abandon my illusions. I could never be with Robert — not if he and his family were to remain safe. And it was more than a warning. My throat ached. A family home had been lost as a result of blind prejudice and ignorance. To add insult to injury, a family tradition of service and mutual respect, generations old, had ended with our actions — my mother's, and mine.

Saturday, I packed, afforded far more room this time than when I'd left before. I used my small suitcase, but my mother spared a few carpetbags, too, sent upstairs via Mrs. Gray. I had more time to tarry, but less inclination to be sentimental. I took only a few mementos that required little space. The rest, I packed into a battered, unlabeled box, then hid it in a corner of the attic, assuming it would be overlooked there unless I decided to return for it.

Father kept his word, and I exited without fear or fanfare. My brothers were as scarce as ever. I endured a short embrace from my father, careful to look over his shoulder and not into his eyes. My mother's farewell was a cautious nod. She turned away, back at her busywork before the screen door slapped the heels of my shoes.

On Monday and Tuesday, on my way to the Clincke house at the end of each day, I struggled against the flow of traffic, fighting the crowds walking in one solid mass of celebration toward Crosley Field for the final two games of the World Series. It seemed an appropriate metaphor for the previous year.

But soon, I found the routine of my new life reassuring, if not exactly comforting. Work and home. Work and home. My landlords were pleasant but not invasive. I satisfied Rosemary Clincke's desire for a respectable boarder with my early departure and early return, before the sun even thought about setting throughout that long fall. My willingness to pitch in pleased her. I stirred the supper pot or set the table while she tended to one of her many chores involving the children, who seemed to multiply like rabbits in the days after I arrived. I was thankful she didn't have a tiny one — I knew it would make my loss that much harder to bear. But the bulge at her waist, which I'd assumed was weight left over from her last pregnancy, began to increase, reminding me soon enough.

She seemed happy with her growing brood, and her husband acted proud, coming home from his job as the superintendent for a bricklaying company to pat the older children as they finished their schoolwork, or toss the littlest ones in the air while they spewed pure glee. But one evening, as we watched, Rosemary said quietly, "When you find a fellow, wait a while before you start thinking about a wedding and making a family. You need time together, before the kids come along. It's my only regret, God bless 'em." She waved fondly at the children, but the weariness in the gleam of her eyes said it was sometimes too much. I nodded and smiled, never feeling a deep-enough bond to share my secret and not desiring to burden her with it.

Work was easy enough. Mr. Bartel showed me the procedure the first day, how to carefully fit the pressboard frames he'd constructed around the two-layered glass squares, glue them, label them, and pack them into small boxes. By the next afternoon, I'd mostly perfected it. The shop was quiet, other than the occasional tinkle of the bell over the door when customers dropped off or reclaimed their orders. I also performed various housekeeping or organizational duties Mr. Bartel didn't have time to do himself. Eventually, he allowed me to help customers if he was busy. Mainly, I perched on a high stool at a table bare of anything but the tools and supplies essential to my routine, numbly organizing others' memories. The aroma of the pressboard and cement was strangely soothing.

I quickly checked the mounted slides for flaws that needed correcting by Mr. Bartel before I boxed them, but if I happened to get ahead of him or I had but a small stack of slides to build and no other chores waiting, I slowed. Sometimes I held a few close to the lamp to study them more intently. Most often, the subjects were landscapes or small groups of people, sitting or standing

shoulder-to-shoulder, posed to commemo-
rate some occasion. I considered the expressions on their faces, the level of tension in
their shoulders, the space intentionally left
between their respective ribs and hips. I
tried to discern whether they were truly
happy, or if they, too, breathed cautiously,
guarding secrets like mine in their hearts,
close and prickly and numb and distant, all
in the same inhalation and expulsion of air.
A glimpse of something too familiar spurred
me quickly on to the next slide, and I buried
my emotions in the routine.

One late-fall morning, a particularly stubborn slide, cut crooked, refused to fit the
frame as it should. I was supposed to wear
the soft cotton gloves Mr. Bartel had provided to protect both the slides and my
fingers, but when I struggled, I sometimes
removed one or both to gain more control.
That morning, I tugged off my right one. In
my attempt to align the slide with the pressboard, I knocked apart the two glass layers,
then dragged a fingernail across the emulsi-
fied surface.

I cursed under my breath and glanced to
see whether Mr. Bartel had noticed my
consternation. He was occupied, so I hastily
pulled on my glove, then lifted the slide
toward the light to see how badly I'd dam-

aged it. I cringed at a long diagonal scratch. A good picture, now ruined. I studied several of the slides that preceded it in sequence, as well as a few that followed. As often happened, the scratched slide was sandwiched between nearly identical shots. Photographers were inclined to shoot a scene several times to capture the best composition. In this informal family portrait, the same tiny figures appeared in each of five slides, in more or less the same poses. Before I'd scratched it, I'd noticed the faces were black. Slides of colored folks were not common, but neither were they unexpected.

I glanced at Mr. Bartel again, then tucked the ruined slide in my dress pocket. He'd never know. Surely the customer who retrieved the finished slides would never notice one shot missing among several similar, or that the count returned was off by one.

I could have admitted my error. But I was still new at my job. I was afraid if Mr. Bartel knew I'd disregarded his instructions to always wear the gloves and that I'd ruined a perfectly good slide, he'd be angry at the least, perhaps even dock my pay. At the worst, he might let me go. I'd just begun to breathe easily, knowing I could afford my room and board at the Clincke house, with a bit left for practical needs and occasional inexpensive entertainments. I was also strangely drawn to this family portrait, almost as though I'd been meant to ruin it so I'd have to take it home. Maybe I wanted to study it more, imagine it was my family. It could have been.

I hurried to finish that order, then the others, scarcely glancing at the slides I framed. I held them up for quick quality checks, then packed the trays, keeping one eye on Mr. Bartel to be sure he wasn't waiting to scold me until I'd finished my work for the day. I sighed with relief when I left that evening and he gave his usual half wave, murmuring, without so much as a glance at my face, that he'd see me in the morning.

After I dressed for bed that night, I withdrew the damaged slide from my pocket. I studied the group under my desk lamp, wondering what occasion had called for this tangible, visual memory. I imagined myself among them.

Eventually, I folded the tiny square of pressboard and glass into a handkerchief and tucked it far back in my dresser drawer.

The next morning, I dragged my feet all the way to work, worried again that Mr. Bartel would somehow discover my misdeed, likely when the customer came to retrieve the slides. After I arrived, I glanced in the drawer by the register, my eyes searching out the name I remembered from the order.

Mr. Bartel performed his morning activities behind me. "Looking for anything in particular?" he asked.

I glanced to see how closely he was watching me. "I thought I'd forgotten to place the order slip back with a tray yesterday."

"They all looked fine to me."

"Oh, well, good, then."

"Several pickups this morning before I even turned the sign around."

My heart lightened. Mr. Bartel often arrived early to get a head start on the day's work, and he'd help early customers, too. I'd missed whoever had picked up the slides. All was well.

But at night, alone in my room, I often pulled the damaged slide from my dresser drawer, carefully swaddled in my handkerchief, and fell asleep clutching it to my chest.

On my days off, I wandered the nearby Cincy neighborhoods, strolling through the markets where butchers and produce men hawked their wares and housewives sorted to find the best quality before handing over their coins — more plentiful amid the recovering economy and rumors of war in Europe.

One afternoon, when winter's chill was taking a firm hold on the city, I found myself straddling the invisible line between white and colored territory — a marketplace where the boundary wasn't as clearly acknowledged as elsewhere. I wasn't the only young white woman in the place, nor was a young woman who skirted me indifferently the only Negro one. But when we collided, startling each of us from whatever we studied separately, we both gasped.

It was Nell.

Her face hardened, but when I didn't look away, when I forced her to maintain eye contact with my helpless and hope-filled gaze, her eyes went soft, gleamed at their edges, exposing a vulnerability she likely resented, but couldn't help. Her voice was cool and steady, though, when she answered my cautious hello. She nodded curtly. "Miss Isabelle."

"Oh, Nell, there's no need to call me that. It's just you and me now. I'm a working girl, living in a rented room. I never cared for it anyway."

"Fine, then," she said. "Isabelle."

"I don't blame you if you despise me. I

ruined your life, your mother's. Robert's."
Even saying his name was painful. I missed
him so. Our story's end had defeated me.

Her eyes shuttered. "We're doing fine, taking care of our own." Doubting she'd say
more and recognizing that it might be my
only chance to get news of what had happened to them all, I plunged ahead. I
grasped her left hand and pulled it close,
studying the silver band encircling her ring
finger.

"You're married?" She nodded.

"Brother James?" She nodded again.

"Oh, Nell, I'm thrilled for you. It was your
dream. You must be so happy."

She pulled her hand away, but a tiny
twitch at the corner of her mouth betrayed
her. She and James were destined to be
together — even if my actions had acceler-
ated their plans.

"Starting a family soon?"

Nell pressed a palm to her abdomen, just
below her ribs. Her belly swelled no more
than mine now, and she seemed stunned, as
though I'd guessed she was expecting,
though it was only lucky fishing for information on my part. I didn't press for details.
"Congratulations. I'm thrilled for you, Nell.
And . . . your mother?" I no longer felt
entitled to use Cora's first name casually.

"Momma's okay. Got a position over in the new places, up the hill here in Cincy. They treat her fine, but it's a long trip two times every day." Though Nell's voice was tinged with accusation, I was happy Cora hadn't been entirely blacklisted from the only kind of work she'd known.

I knew Nell wouldn't bring up that final name, the one she surely knew was the hardest for me to say — the one I was most curious about, however deep my affection and concern for his family. And after a painful silence, neither could I in good conscience. I remembered the conversation with his mother before I began to show. I remembered the unspoken warning from my father. I remembered my debt to Nell's family.

"Well," I said. "It's wonderful to see you, Nell. I'm pleased you and your mother are doing well. And I'm sorry. For everything." I turned away before she could see the tears that wet my eyes and threatened to overwhelm me.

But she surprised me. She caught my elbow as I began to step away, and I turned slowly back to face her. "Robert, he's joining the army soon as he finishes up school in Frankfort. Maybe in just a year. They've got special programs to speed things up for enlistees."

Every sinew stilled, in my hands, my spine, my face. I was thrilled he'd returned to school and could finish so soon, but this other? It was the last thing I'd expected. The news of war in Europe and rumors that we'd be in it soon had led to a peacetime draft, and now young men were joining up in record numbers, on standby and waiting to plunge into the fray. But I'd never pictured a life in the army for a young Negro man. What would it be like? What would he do? How would he be treated? If there was a war, would he live?

"He's hoping to serve as a medic, but he'll take what he can get — picky's not allowed."

I finally spit out words, all lies. "That's . . . wonderful. I suspect he'll be happy if he can start his medical training while he serves." Nell's chin tilted, showing her uncertainty. "And I suppose the girls will be lined up to see him off. Maybe even a special sweetheart to wait for him to come back home." My words stung my throat. I couldn't ask outright, but I had to know. Did he think of me still?

"I expect you're right," she said, and I'm sure she sensed my gasp, though I fought to keep it inaudible. She lowered her eyes, and now she turned to leave. The moment had grown too awkward for both of us. I watched her, though. Eventually, she paused at a greengrocer's stall, pretending, I could tell, to inspect a bunch of broccoli before exchanging a coin for it. Her evasive response and her body language was clear. Robert had moved on — in more ways than one.

32
DORRIE, PRESENT DAY

I refused to believe Robert had forgotten her so soon. If he'd soldiered on as if he no longer cared, if he'd taken up with another girl, it was only to dull the pain of losing Miss Isabelle.

It wasn't even lunchtime when we crossed into Cincinnati. We could have checked into our bed-and-breakfast early — after all, Miss Isabelle had paid for the night before. But she asked if I'd like her to show me some of the places she'd talked about along our journey. I hesitated, wondering, once more, whether this would make her feel better or worse. But she said she wanted to see how they'd changed in all the years she'd been gone. She pointed me this way and that with little hesitation. The streets of old Cincy were narrow and congested, the houses tall, skinny, and crowded together, many with only a few inches between if they didn't share a wall.

We slowed in front of one. Miss Isabelle pondered it for a time. The last time she'd seen it, she said, years after she'd lived there with the Clinckes, the paint was peeling off the trim in strips and there'd been a stack of cinder blocks for a front stoop, the orginal bricks having disintegrated from neglect. Long before, when the neighborhood had started to turn, Rosemary Clincke had moved her family to a small house in the suburbs. The new house looked as though it had been shaped with a cookie cutter, then baked, Miss Isabelle said, with only the surface decoration setting it apart from the ones on either side. But it was safe and had a yard for the children.

Many of the houses in the Clinckes' old neighborhood had been subdivided into apartments or cheap rooming houses, but they were gradually returning to loving hands, being restored as single-family homes. Now their old house had bright paint, neat trim, and flowers tucked into boxes hanging below the windows, like it had when Miss Isabelle lived there. She showed me a window on the top level. A modern fire escape ladder dangled nearby. "Mine for almost a year."

We drove up and down hilly streets to a neighborhood between the newer suburbs and the older parts of Cincinnati and stopped before a red brick house with a peaked roof and a porch running halfway across the front. On the other half, metal awnings shaded two windows like green-and-white-striped eyelashes. A skinny drive led to a one-car garage in the back. The houses on this street, tended well over the years, must have looked much like they had more than fifty years earlier — though massive trees rose before and behind them. Miss Isabelle said they were Cape Cods.

"I thought Cape Cod was on the East Coast," I said, letting the car idle because NO PARKING signs lined the street.

"It's Cape Cod *style*."

"And you lived in this one?"

"This isn't just a tour of the architecture." Her reaction here was mixed. She looked sentimental, tender, as she studied it. But a note of frustration and bitterness tugged at her face, too, doing funny things to her cheeks and lips — and then mine, too. I'd been having too many of these unexpected urges to cry the last few days. I coughed. "So that was . . . after the Clinckes? Did you live here with another family?"

"Yes. Another family," she said. "For five or six years before we moved out to Texas."

"We?"

She didn't elaborate then. Instead, she asked me to drive on so we could find some lunch. She pointed me toward a little restaurant — the Skyline Chili Parlor. At the counter, she suggested I order a Cincinnati four-way — a big plate of chili over spaghetti noodles, covered with cheddar and onions. Apparently, chili was more than just a Texas thing. It was a Greek thing, too. The chili was different — I kept tasting hints of cinnamon . . . or chocolate. And the funniest part? After I ordered that mess, Miss Isabelle chose a Coney — a plain dog on a bun, half the size of a regular one. She preferred Dixie Chili, she said, but that was on the Kentucky side of the river. Plus, she'd never sleep that night if she ate something spicy. I shoveled my four-way like an obedient child, then groaned in the car while she found her directions to our bed-and-breakfast.

Miss Isabelle was drooping by the time we entered the fancy secluded neighborhood back in Cincy proper. The owner apologized for charging us for the previous night, but policy was policy. Miss Isabelle graciously shrugged it off. (She would have been gracious to Mr. Night Manager, too, if he'd been gracious first.) The innkeeper offered us a complimentary night at the other end of our stay if nobody else had booked it, but, of course, we wouldn't need it.

While I moved our luggage, I insisted Miss Isabelle relax in an odd little corner jutting off the edge of our room, where two easy chairs sat catty-corner.

The room held two double beds covered with puffy white comforters and pillows printed with blue drawings of old-timey ladies wearing long skirts and carrying umbrellas. After the generic hotel beds we'd slept in, they looked like heaven. I couldn't wait to sink into one, but bedtime was hours away. We had things to take care of, places to be. First on my list, though, was convincing Miss Isabelle to rest awhile, even if I wouldn't. The longer we'd been in town, the tenser she'd grown.

"Come sit over here." I pointed to a low-backed chair in front of the antique vanity. "It's been nearly a week since I touched that hair. We need to give her a face-lift before we go back out in public."

I couldn't give Miss Isabelle a shampoo and set, but I could certainly freshen up her curls with my curling iron and brush. Getting my fingers on her head and massaging her scalp and temples and the back of her neck might loosen muscles stretched so tight I could see them.

She moved, dazed, not bothering to speak. She sank into the chair. "I'm tired, Dorrie."

"I know," I said, brushing gently through tangles that had managed to make flimsy nests in her silver hair in spite of the old-fashioned silk case I'd stuffed her hotel pillow into each night on the road. "What'd you do with that slide, Miss Isabelle? Did you hang on to it?"

"I'm not sure why, but I did. I kept it in my old handkerchief, always tucked in the back of my dresser, no matter where I lived. It comforted me, as if I had a portrait I could study when I felt lonely for Robert and the baby." She closed her eyes and settled into the cushioned chair while I worked. She nodded off. I watched in the mirror. Her lids twitched as her eyes moved back and forth beneath them. I only wondered *what* she was dreaming. It was easy enough now to guess whose faces she'd see.

33
ISABELLE, 1940–1941

Nell's news meant my spirits sank even lower, but soon after I saw her, a girl I'd met in a lunch diner invited me to attend a public weekend dance with her. Dancing didn't interest me. All that interested me was getting through each day, paying my room and board, and counting the minutes until I could forget my heartache during the few hours I slept deeply.

My new friend persisted. "Think of all the handsome guys that are sure to be there," Charlotte said — not knowing it made me even less inclined to go. But she added quickly, "It's mostly soldiers on their way to Fort Dix." America's first-ever peacetime draft meant men were leaving in hordes, with little advance warning. "The point is keeping their spirits up before they leave home," Charlotte said, "or maybe so they can find some gals to write to. It's just for fun — you wouldn't want to get too attached." She'd noted my disinterest in dating, though I'd never expressed the reasons for it. But the part about soldiers caught my ear. I knew I'd never see Robert at these dances. From what Nell had said, he was still safe at college in Frankfort — not to mention he was colored and wouldn't be granted entrance to them. But I desperately hoped to learn something, *anything,* about how life would be for a Negro in the army.

With the naïve reasoning that going with Charlotte to the dances might be the way to hear such things, I threw myself into the frantic parade of young women who primped and preened and attempted to catch the attention of the freshly barbered conscriptees.

It was also a strange relief — when I listened to the bands, when I danced. The men didn't care who I was or where I'd come from. They cared only that I was someone they could hold close and imagine thinking of them if they went overseas. Some offered scraps of paper listing their names and general delivery military addresses. I promised to write — along with the others they asked.

Some dreamy-eyed girls met their soul mates — after one evening. They were ready to march to the altar with young men they'd only seen cleaned up, dressed up, and on their best behavior. I thought they were fools.

Every now and then, a fellow became too attentive, asking me to dance too often, pressuring me for my address or a photo, hinting he'd enjoy care packages — or a little more than dancing that very evening. I'd laugh, promise to write while crossing my fingers behind my back, and insist I wasn't interested in a long-distance relationship.

One night, a skinny guy in a plain flannel suit asked me to dance, once, twice, and later again after watching me from the refreshments table while I danced with others.

I figured it was time for the brush-off. But he surprised me. He admitted he wasn't a soldier. He'd failed the physical because of a mild heart murmur. "Don't tell anybody, but I'm not going anywhere."

"Then why are you here?" I asked. "Most fellas are trying to line up as many girls as they can before they go off to Dix."

He shrugged. "Oh, you'd be surprised how many aren't soldiers. It's as good a place as any to meet gals. The draft is twenty-one and over. You think all these guys are that old?"

He was a fake. Like me. I answered his shrug with my own. He wasn't strictly playing by rules. Neither was I. "You're right. It's a free country. Who's to say who's allowed or not? You just took me by surprise."

Max — that was his name — often surprised me over the next couple of weeks, showing up consistently, asking me for a decent but not overwhelming number of turns around the dance floor. We grew comfortable together. I looked forward to seeing him, not in the fluttery, rumble-in-my-stomach kind of way I'd looked forward to seeing Robert in the old days, but in the sense of recognizing a friend. Someone reliable. Someone to shoot the breeze with if Charlotte had a whirlwind of dance partners while my card was mostly empty.

He asked to escort me home each time, and finally, I agreed. But on the short walk to Mrs. Clincke's, I felt a keen sense of betrayal toward Robert — though I hadn't encouraged anything other than friendship with Max. Or so I'd told myself.

He reached for my hand, and I gazed at our clasped fingers. This was well beyond the scope of a standard brush-off now. I'd allowed him to court me without realizing it because I'd enjoyed our casual no-strings-attached friendship. "I'm sorry, Max. I'm in no shape to be with a fellow right now. You wouldn't want me like this, I promise." I looked at him, helpless, hoping my eyes conveyed genuine apology.

He dropped my hand gently and shook his head. "It's okay. I'm not in any hurry. Remember? I'm not going anywhere."

So there he was, a friend walking me home, but with something new implied: He was patient and would wait for me to be ready.

He began asking me out to weekend movie matinees; for walks, munching Busken's pastries along the fountain esplanade; for rides up and down the Mount Adams Incline on the cable car because it was too cold to visit the zoo. I felt lucky. But worry still nudged my conscience when I caught him studying my profile. I knew he was falling for me. And I was empty. Max's attention filled me in a small, if temporary, way.

"Someone must have hurt you real bad," he'd say as we walked home in the progressively colder evenings. "You gonna keep that heart of yours closed up tight forever?" He asked gently, never pushing, and he seemed content with my shrugged response.

What should have been my first wedding anniversary passed in the midst of a record-breaking January snowstorm, with me bundled in bed to stay warm — and where my misery could go unnoticed. The next day Mr. Bartel and I struggled through icy drifts to wait on customers, but not a single one came. I went straight to bed again that night after telling Mrs. Clincke I wasn't feeling well, then cried myself to sleep. I rose the next morning to face the cold, numb again.

Saturday afternoon, Max wouldn't identify our excursion ahead of time. The snow wasn't expected to melt for days, but people were beginning to emerge again. Life had to go on.

The January sun, though bright, did nothing to warm us as we hurried along the street after Max arrived. He tugged me up into one of the new trolley coaches that were slowly replacing the old double cable cars, then down again at a city park. He presented a sledding hill, crawling with adults and children alike, rosy-cheeked and enthusiastically climbing the slope and sliding to the bottom.

Max wrapped torn rags around my boots to keep my feet warmer and drier, then pulled me up the hill. We soared down on a rented sled. We likely appeared in love, like other young couples on the hill. How could the crowd know my heart was as cold and still as the frozen snow we traveled? I was only physically present, attempting to match my facial expressions to Max's while my mind drifted to another January day.

Eventually, Max pulled me over to a concession stand an entrepreneurial citizen had rigged and settled me on a bench with a cup of warm cocoa between my gloved fingers.

Silently, we watched the merrymakers. Toddlers fell in the snow and pulled themselves back up without complaint, drawing smiles from even my cold lips. Max studied my smiles, as if gauging my mood according to the degree of their arcs.

Finally, he took my gloved hands between his, rubbing vigorously, ostensibly to warm them — a rare physical contact he could initiate without my awkward rebuke.

He stopped, though, his hands still wrapped over my fingers, and I studied them together. Robert's hands could completely encase mine. Max's fingers, even in their bulkier men's gloves, were hardly larger than mine. Robert's hands could awe me with their power, make me shiver at their touch. Max's instilled a simple sense of meeting halfway, stirring nothing in my heart beyond gratitude for our friendship. But for Max, I suspected, the time had come. Friendship no longer sufficed. When I saw how far he'd fallen — in his eyes, in his smile, even in the set of his shoulders — I knew it was unfair to string him along.

"I've been patient, Isabelle," he began. I nodded miserably. "I'm a good man. I'd take the best care of you."

I could only reply with silence. I knew what would come next. Our quasi-courtship was ages old in the context of our time — some couples we knew of had married overnight. The threat of war sped everything up, even for civilians. But I feared the tentative steps I'd taken back into life were about to be reversed and that I'd sink back into the misery from which I'd risen at least a few feet. I breathed the frigid air, the fragrance of muddy sled blades. The cold breath caught in my chest.

"You're the girl I've waited for. I know it. I want to marry you."

He released one of my hands and reached his gloved finger to press it to my lips when I began to protest. "Not today," he said. "When you're ready. I'm not stupid — I know you don't feel the same way. But you do care for me. We make a good team. I earn enough to buy us a nice little house — maybe with an extra room to start a family one day."

He couldn't know those words were the worst he could say. A tear formed in the corner of my eye. It froze in place and stung my skin.

"Think about it? Please, Isabelle?"

I wanted to explain that marriage between us could never be anything but a mistake. But he was right. His thoughtful proposal deserved my careful consideration.

We walked home in silence, as though it might be the last time we'd walk together.

Max was steady, dependable. A good man. Handsome in a quiet way.

I had great affection for him. But I didn't love him. No matter his good points, I didn't love him.

I had loved Robert with my whole being, and that marriage had ended.

Ultimately, I realized my heart was closed to love or marriage because I'd been tending a glimmer of hope that Robert would return for me. Some way, someday. Seeing Nell should have doused that glimmer. To think he might have fallen for another girl battered me. Like a hard-boiled egg slammed against a countertop on all sides, my heart was cracked and ragged.

I left Mr. Bartel's lab in early February, wind cracking around my uncovered ears.

I'd forgotten to stuff my hat in my handbag that morning. After a few blocks, I ducked into a café. I knew I'd never make it home without filling up on hot coffee. The scent alone warmed me, rushing to greet me when I dragged the heavy door open against the wind.

I waited at the counter, observing those seated at the café's small tables. One couple shared a newspaper. The young man read over his girl's shoulder. Occasionally, she'd nudge him away, as though he'd encroached on her space. Good-naturedly, he'd nudge her back but give her room. Eventually, he slid around to face her. A ring sparkled on her finger, but the flames between them seemed more like embers. They seemed content and happy to be embarking on life together. They seemed the best of friends. I saw Max and myself in them.

At another table, a young woman crossed her arms and hugged herself, petulant lips poised to issue a sharp word. Her uniformed fellow leaned past her to chat with a man at an adjoining table. She was jealous. She didn't want to share her beloved. Yet, when he turned briefly and slid his hand up her arm, she relaxed, dropping her hands into a calm lover's knot in her lap. Now she watched him with admiration and obvious, fiery passion. I saw Robert and myself in them.

Neither couple seemed right or wrong. They just were.

It had been long months since I'd lost what mattered most — first Robert, and then our baby. I'd made it clear to Nell I was independent now, able to make my own decisions. If Robert had been going to seek me out, he would have done so by now.

The metaphor played out by the couples in the café seemed clear. I could stay frozen in place, grieving my losses forever, or I could take steps to try move on, too. The answer seemed dictated by the signs around me.

34
DORRIE, PRESENT DAY

Miss Isabelle had awakened from her nap in the chair in an unusual mood — *pensive,* said the puzzle book. We were going to a funeral, so who wouldn't be pensive? But this was something extra. I'd wanted her to let things rest for a bit, but she seemed driven now to finish her story, so I'd finished touching up her hair while she talked.

I struggled to imagine Miss Isabelle giving up on her forever love. Hadn't there been any other way she could have found Robert? How could she have given up on him? Given up on *them*? Had Max really been the best answer?

But I knew how this turned out. I'd seen the photos at her house. It was kind of like a sad movie: You'd heard what happened — maybe you'd already watched it five times, so you *knew* what happened — but you kept hoping the end would be different.

After I finished with Miss Isabelle's hair, I

changed clothes. I'd brought two nice outfits — one for the funeral service, and a pair of dress pants and a silky top Miss Isabelle had said would do for the visitation. I dressed, then fussed with the little fuzzies springing up all over my hair. It was time to see my own stylist, but obviously there wasn't much I could do about this in Cincinnati.

"Dorrie?" Miss Isabelle called across the room. "I haven't been forthcoming about the details for this funeral."

No, she hadn't. We'd established that. I kept going about my business, doing my best to make my fingers work the microscopic clasp on my necklace. I never wore much jewelry, but this was a special occasion — even if it wasn't mine. I didn't want her friends or family assuming I was some low-class companion she'd hired to drive her out to this funeral.

"I'm nervous. And I don't want you to think badly of me, but I have to tell you —"

"What? You nervous? No way, young lady." I squinted at her, trying to beam a little light into the conversation. She was making me nervous, too.

"I'm serious now, Dorrie. You're going to think I'm a horrible old lady."

"I'd never think you were a horrible old

lady," I said. "Well, maybe there was that one time, back when we met." I chuckled. "But we got that straightened out."

"I may be the only white person at this funeral."

So. She'd finally spit it out. I can't say I was shocked. I'd figured that all this remembering had to be going somewhere. In fact, I had a pretty good idea whose funeral we were attending, and I completely understood it was going to be difficult all around — for me, too, now that I knew the story. I hated how things had turned out for her and Robert.

But nervous because she might be the only white person? I couldn't help it. I snorted a little. Which I regretted when her face crumpled in on itself like I'd poked her with a sharp needle and let all the air out. She was serious.

"I'm sorry. I didn't mean to laugh." I hurried over and squatted down next to the chair. I grabbed her hand and squeezed it. "Thank you for being honest with me, Miss Isabelle. I always appreciate that about you. But what are you afraid of? I mean, all anybody will think is how nice it is you've come for this funeral."

"I know, Dorrie. I just had to say it. I don't want anyone to believe I'm some uppity white woman riding in on her white horse. I know it sounds ridiculous."

"But you were invited. Your friend knows you're coming, right?" This worried me. I could see her point. If she showed up at this funeral unannounced, some people might be curious about her presence. And was she right? Might they even be offended?

"Yes," she said. I released my breath.

"Well, that's settled, then. Don't worry." I patted her hand and stretched up, groaning when my back muscles clenched into a little knot halfway up. All the standing I did every day wasn't just hard on my feet; it killed my back, too. One of those massages the brochure on the nightstand mentioned sounded very tempting. But who was I kidding? Massages were on my to-do list for when I was rich and famous. Or maybe married again.

Teague. I hadn't thought of him for at least an hour. In fact, I'd only thought of him in snatches between worrying about my kid's foolishness and Miss Isabelle's sad history. But hearing that she'd likely given up on her one true love sent me into action. "Miss Isabelle. It'll be fine. You'll see. Do I have time for a phone call before we leave?"

A tiny bloom of hope transformed her face. Maybe she saw something in mine that made her optimistic about my own seemingly hopeless situation. Who knew? Maybe she had a reason for telling me her story, besides explaining this funeral.

I glanced around outside our room. A door led to a long, deep porch with lots of comfy chairs. I felt funny checking the door to see if it was unlocked, as if I were in someone else's house, doing things I wasn't supposed to, but the innkeeper had told us to make ourselves at home. On the porch, I paced before hitting the speed dial code I'd set up for Teague a few weeks before.

Voice mail.

That was fine. More than fine, actually.

"Hey, Teague. It's me, Dorrie." I paused, already feeling silly. "I just want to say I've been doing it all wrong. I don't know if we can work this thing out, whatever it is, but I want you to know how much I appreciate you. I assumed you'd think the worst when you found out my kid went and did something dumb. In fact, maybe you're freaking out right this minute, putting two and two together — and, yes, you're getting the correct answer. But I didn't even give you a chance. For that, I am truly sorry. I don't have time for the whole story right now. I'm kind of getting on my knees here — even though I'm actually standing on a porch at a bed-and-breakfast — and begging for your patience. The next few days are about Miss Isabelle, about finishing this journey. Then, when I get home, it has to be about me dealing with my kid and figuring out whether we can salvage his life, clean up this mess, and move forward. But there's something else . . . I really dig you. I really, really do. So. Will you be patient with me? Will you let me play this by ear for a while? I realized all this a few minutes ago — though I think it's been in the back of my mind all along. Teague, I don't want to lose you, whatever it is we —"

Teague's message system cut me off with another beep and I slapped the porch railing. I'd used up my allotted time. And that never happened unless you had something important to say.

But I'd said what I needed to. For that moment. He'd get the gist, and hopefully . . . well, hopefully, he'd give me another chance.

I said a silent thank-you to Miss Isabelle. Her story couldn't have the ending I'd hoped it would, but if nothing else, it had shown me something important.

When the right guy comes along? Don't blow it.

35
ISABELLE, 1941–1943

I gave Max an out. I told him he would not be my first, that I was not a virgin. He was not put off. He said I wouldn't be his first, either, and it seemed fair and reasonable that we begin on level ground.

Both my weddings were simple, quiet ceremonies. At the second, like the first, only four people were present. This time, it was me, Max, the justice of the peace, and my friend Charlotte, who took full credit — she'd invited me to the dances where we met. In the photos, she and Max beamed, as if they were the happy couple, whereas my face appeared pasted into a half smile.

In the second, as with the first, I didn't notify my parents. I'd proved I could live without their approval. Max's parents lived hundreds of miles away. He telegrammed the news, saying he'd understand if they couldn't attend.

My attire was simple again, but the good

dress I'd worn for my first wedding remained in my closet, the bittersweet dust of memory settling on the fabric, for I never brought myself to wear it again — nor to discard it.

One wedding was in bitter January. The second was in late, bright spring.

My mood had been spring the previous January, and was January that spring.

Max brought me a plain gold band — though I thought of nothing but the symbolic thimble Sarah Day had provided. I still wondered what had become of it. Had Robert retrieved it, or in my haste to leave, had it been knocked under the bed and rolled into a crevice, where it still remained? Or perhaps the landlady used it now for sewing and mending, unaware of its significance.

No warnings were spoken before Max and I exchanged vows. The justice glanced at our paperwork and pronounced us married. He'd wed countless couples by then who had met only weeks or even days before, but he was one of few who didn't question why Max wasn't shipping out, and he didn't seem to care.

As we left city hall, the crowd flowed around us without a glance. Nothing set us apart.

Max had mortgaged a small house in a newer section of Cincy. One trip had transferred my still-meager possessions there before our wedding night.

And that, our wedding night, was altogether different.

I didn't enter the house with anything like the fear I'd experienced the night Robert and I climbed the stairs toward our wedding chamber. I wasn't afraid anyone might chase us down or deem the union unfit or illegal. I wasn't afraid as Max took me gently in the modest bed he'd installed in our tiny master bedroom. I can't say I was an enthusiastic bride. I was resigned to the act, and over time, I even enjoyed its mindless, numbing pleasure.

I took care to avoid pregnancy, and Max agreed to a delay in starting a family. With the uncertainty of war and the newly recovering economy, I insisted we should hang on to our stable jobs and not even consider it until we'd established our home and accumulated a cushion of savings.

It would have been fair to say outright I didn't want children at all. I'd never shared my history with him, had never breathed a word about Robert. I hoped I'd never have to. The thought of another pregnancy terrified me — even without the possibility of someone tearing my child from my arms before I'd even had a chance to kiss her too tiny, too quiet lips goodbye. I also worried the fall had permanently damaged my womb. Perhaps I'd never carry a child to full term. I didn't want to know. I couldn't imagine seeing another newborn emerge from my loins without conjuring my daughter's face — one I knew only in my imagination.

The United States entered the war in December. It changed everyone. The bombing at Pearl Harbor, though far away in Hawaii, challenged the belief that our country was invincible. The news sent me to bed in tears. Max thought I wept because of the inevitability of war; he couldn't have known I was weeping for Robert. I wondered whether Robert would survive now that we were really and truly at war, just in time for his departure if Nell's information held true. Max attempted to soothe me when he came to bed, caressing my shoulder, trying to draw me close, but I turned away. I felt as unfaithful to Robert as ever.

I worked fewer hours each month as Mr. Bartel's business dropped in response to the inevitable tightening war brought. Max's job as an accountant in an industrial supply firm was regular as clockwork. The war only increased demand for the goods his company produced. I cooked his breakfast each morning and packed his lunch box. He pecked me on the cheek, as though we'd already reached our silver anniversary, and waved as he walked toward the stop where a trolley bus would pick him up. We were saving for an automobile, but with fuel rationing, we wouldn't hurry.

On weekends, we still attended movies or went to concerts by local civic orchestras — though so many men had left for the war, the music was thin.

I could see far into the future: Even at the war's end, our life would continue as it already was, slow and steady, year after year, decade by decade.

Max thrived on predictability. I withered inside. I cursed our dull utopia. Max wasn't interested in conversation that kept my mind alive — there was no discussion of current events, popular fiction or the classics, music or film. I tried to draw him in, to lift him — as I began to view it, self-righteously — to my level. He seemed puzzled, but not overly frustrated by my attempts. He chuckled, insisting he really didn't desire to look beyond the surface.

He was a good husband, but for his inability to stir any wonder in me — wonder at who or what lay beneath his surface. After less than two years of marriage, I felt I knew him completely, and the knowledge could be poured into a single coffee cup. Conversely, he knew me little beyond realizing he'd married a woman who seemed to enjoy sparring for the sake of it. He took that in stride, like everything else, with an amused sense of pride.

On a day like that, in 1943, Max strolled away to the bus stop. I spent my frustration on the innocent potatoes and carrots I peeled for our supper, on sweeping the porch, on trying not to explode in my desire to engage someone — anyone! — in conversation more stimulating than a discussion about the weather or the price of a dozen eggs. I turned to an unruly rosebush we'd planted the spring before. The country was deep in the war by then, and most of our gardening efforts went into growing lettuce, beans, and anything else we could cultivate to preserve commercial produce for the troops and cut transportation costs to move it. But we'd splurged on one rosebush for a barren corner of the front yard. We never expected it to be such a needy plant, however, forever demanding attention. If I wasn't fighting mildew, it was time to fertilize. If I wasn't fertilizing, I was pruning.

It seemed an awful lot of work for a medium-size plant that hadn't given much in return. A few buds had opened after we'd planted it, but mostly, it had remained dormant all summer, fall, and through the winter. I'd read that pruning it in the spring would encourage the prolific blooms I longed to see — perhaps they'd give me hope for more than just the rosebush.

His voice came from behind me. "You were never great at trimming bushes."

I dropped the shears clutched between my bulky gloves and pulled my hands to my belly. I sank to my knees, my legs collapsing beneath me. I'd never expected to hear his voice again. But even after nearly four years, I'd have known it anywhere.

I didn't dare turn around. I wondered whether the sound had issued from my imagination, an illusion born of the images that still haunted me. Of course I would hear Robert's voice as I pruned a bush, dreaming of the hours we'd spent grooming the arbor. Of course I would.

I let my eyelids droop closed and sat still, commanding my mind to do it again.

I heard throat-clearing, and I turned my head only enough to glance over my shoulder.

Robert waited, resplendent, in military

uniform. He held his sharply angled cap between his hands and moved it out a bit, jiggled an awkward greeting.

Emotions flooded me, some directed at Robert, some simply at the situation: relief, shock, joy, fury, skepticism, hope, bitterness.

Love.

Still love.

"Hello, Isabelle." Quiet, confident. Whereas he'd been a bit of a boy before, he was a man now. The passage of time I saw in his eyes must have been reflected in mine.

But his greeting also conveyed caution. Not the worried fear of discovery or harassment. He seemed unconcerned what my neighbors might think, yet wary of my reaction.

I forced myself to rise, pushing up from the ground against the odd sensation that gravity might win. I stepped toward him, studying him as though he might yet fade, a mirage conjured by my internal longings — or from leaning into the roses too long with the sun pulsing at the back of my head.

"You are real," I said when close enough to touch him, though I didn't.

"Of course I'm real," he replied.

I wanted to throw myself at him, beg him to say why he'd never tried to contact me, plead with him to save me from my mistake of a marriage. I didn't. I simply stood and drank in this sight of him in uniform.

The events he'd witnessed and the demons he'd wrestled across four years etched his forehead and jawbone like stories written in fine lines and tense muscle.

Though his voice was unmistakably Robert, the rough edges had been sanded away, leaving something verging on refinement. I wondered where he'd traveled since enlisting. He had already sounded different after he'd attended college — before we married — but this surpassed that. Wisdom resonated in his deep baritone, even in the few words he'd uttered.

"Why are you here? What are you doing? How . . ." How would I begin?

"I'm not sure I know the answers myself," he said. "Though I believe it was providence that led me to you. Again."

" 'Providence'?" I was confused at first, then thought of my words to him all those years ago, when I'd gushed childishly about kismet and fate. I'd been so naïve.

"I saw your father downtown. He told me about your — your marriage. Your husband's name was easy enough to find in the telephone directory."

He knew I was married again. And my father knew, too. I'd ignored his attempts to

436

contact me through the Clinckes, but he'd apparently been keeping tabs on me. The mention of him stirred the ice in my heart. "Where have you been?"

"Where have I been lately?"

"I'd like to know where you've been since the last time I saw you. For now, lately will do." I hated how a chilly tone crept into my voice. After all, it wasn't as if he could have done anything differently; my brothers and mother had been determined to erase him from my life. Anything else would have been madness. But I was bitter. I couldn't help it. Had he even tried?

"Working in army mess halls, along with other fellows who look like me — if they're not moving supplies." He crumpled the edge of his hat into his fist. "So far, on the home front. When I joined up, they said I'd never be allowed on a medical unit, but now they're talking about training a group of Negro medics for the European theater. I'm throwing my name in."

This announcement crushed the air from my lungs. Even though I was married again, I had harbored some kind of fairy-tale fantasy he'd come to rescue me. I couldn't speak at first. When the silence between us became unbearable, I scraped up a brief question. "You're going . . ." I stopped. The phrase "over there," sung patriotically in songs, angered me. He'd found me, but only to say he was sacrificing himself to the enemy, when he could stay safely on home soil, even if his skill and training was wasted. I wanted to ram my hands against his ribs and shove him to the ground.

"Not much call for medics here. I want to do my part. There's a unit of Negro soldiers training for Europe. They'll need medics. Right now, nobody'll hardly touch our injured boys. They don't get much more than a look when they're wounded. Most are left to die."

I felt shame at his use of *our boys*. It was my people doing this. I shuddered, thinking of men like Robert abandoned in the field simply because of skin color. But this was the same country that had erected signs like the one outside my hometown, warning Negroes they'd better be gone before dark. The same country where violent men took "justice" into their own hands while others turned a blind eye.

On an intellectual level, I understood Robert's need to go, to care for his brothers when they were hurt. Of course I did. Any other reaction would have shamed both of us.

On an emotional level, though, where I

wanted to cry out for Robert to right my dismal error in marrying Max, to gather me to himself and love me for the rest of our days, I couldn't stand believing he intended to leave me again.

"I wish you'd never come here, then." I spit out the words. "I wish you'd left me ignorant of the fact that you're even alive. Finally, I can stand living without you, and now my heart is going to break all over again."

I dragged my gloves off and threw them at the base of the rosebush, kicked my pruning shears out of my way. I ran along the walk, then clambered up the steps toward my front door, leaving Robert speechless in my wake.

"Isa!" he finally cried. "I'm here because I had to see you. I still love you. Every day, every minute, I love you."

I faced my screen door, slowing at his words, at the sound of his name for me.

I shook my head. He wasn't here for me. He was going away, as soon as he'd appeared.

Even if he loved me still.

I buried my fists against my eyes, trying to contain the scalding tears that threatened to betray me.

"Nell, she told me . . . she led me to

believe you'd found someone else." I said the words so quietly, I wasn't sure he'd hear them. But his voice came over my left shoulder.

"You saw Nell?" he asked. "She told you — Oh, Isa, there was never anyone but you. Never, from the day I saw you at the creek, screaming and beating your fists on the ground."

And now when I pictured Nell, I saw her clearly, doing what she thought was best for both of us, leading me to believe Robert had moved on. *Always* trying to do what was best for both of us.

"Is that why . . ." His voice faded, but I knew the question he left hanging.

I turned and faced him. "Yes. That's why I live here in this pleasant picture of hell. I watched for you. Waited for you. But you went away. You gave up and went away. So when I met Max and he didn't demand more of me than I could give, I married him."

"I wanted to come back for you. I would have. I wasn't sure I'd tell you this. But . . . there's something else you should know." Robert looked down at his shoes now, almost as if he were ashamed. "I wanted to come back for you long before now, Isa. I planned to. I thought I was brave enough to break the rules. I stayed at the docks, saving money to go back to school in the summer — I knew your daddy wouldn't be paying my tuition again — and hoping I'd think of another way for us to be together. I tried so hard to think of a way.

"Summer was coming on . . . already so hot and humid, tempers were short everywhere. Felt like if I sneezed wrong, the boss would fire me. I was walking home from the job one afternoon when out of nowhere, two men jumped me. They grabbed me by the arms and dragged me to a car. It was Jack and Patrick. And it was your daddy's shiny car."

Robert stopped, gazing off down the street, looking at nothing, really, as though remembering my brothers' faces — or maybe that afternoon we'd flirted with water while he washed my father's car. I thought of the timing. When my pregnancy started to show, Jack and Patrick never gave any indication they'd noticed. Not the day I gave birth. Not after.

But they'd noticed.

"They shoved me in the backseat. This guy in the front seat — I didn't know him — he drove, and they kept pushing my head down, though I fought it at first. By the time the car stopped, I had no idea where we were. On a dirt road — really just a path with ruts — in the middle of some woods. They yanked me back out of the car, and I tried to run, but all three pounced on me, nearly beat me to a pulp. Then they dragged me by the ankles into a clearing. Three or four more waited there.

"I begged your brothers to tell me why they'd taken me there. I said I'd done everything they asked. Left you alone, Isa. Didn't come around asking about you, didn't try to contact you — even though I wanted to. Still intended to. Momma and Nell were gone from your house by then, Nell, a long time before, of course, and Momma a few weeks.

"They said, 'Shut up, nigger.' Said it was about time they taught me a lesson for defiling a white woman."

I leaned on the screen door, afraid my knees wouldn't support me. Robert's words made them quiver, made them useless. The flimsy door wasn't much better, but it held.

"By then, I was past scared. I figured my best chance was to be quiet, to go along with whatever they had planned. It was six or seven against one — what else could I do? I prayed it wouldn't involve a rope or a tree.

"There was a rope. They tied my hands

and ankles together — one big knot, me laying over on my side. One of them, he wanted to gag me, but Jack said, 'No, I want to hear this coon scream. I want him to scream good.' I knew then what I had coming wasn't going to be no picnic. I could only pray I'd come out alive."

As his words came faster, Robert sounded more like the boy I'd known so long ago.

"One of the other guys was stirring up a fire I hadn't paid any attention to until then. He called over to Jack, said it was good and hot. I started sweating, wondering what were they going to do. Burn me alive? I would have preferred hanging to being a human barbecue. And I'm not too proud to admit I begged for mercy then. I cried like a baby. I thought I was going to die."

Tears covered my cheeks, but I didn't move a muscle or make a noise. Robert was in front of me — 100 percent alive — yet I felt the terror, as if it were happening now, as if it were happening to me, too.

He released a breath through his nose. "They had something else in mind. Jack said, 'Go get the thing out of the car.' Patrick returned with a long metal tool, like a fire poker. I didn't know what they were going to do. Rape me with it? Blind me? What? When I think what could have happened, I guess I was lucky. Jack took it from Patrick and went to the fire. Then I figured it out. It was a branding iron."

I gasped.

"Jack heated it up, a big thick glove on his hand — I knew how hot it was going to be when he couldn't handle it bare-fisted. It glowed orange-white. I shivered, the temperature of my body ice-cold now compared to what I knew was coming. 'Scared, boy?' he asked. When I didn't respond, he walked over and kicked me in the kidneys.

" 'Yes,' I finally spit out when I stopped coughing.

" 'Yes, what?' he said.

" 'Yes, suh.'

" 'That's better. Now, boy, this here will be a reminder — in case you ever think about even looking at a white woman again, hear?'

"I nodded. 'Yes, suh.'

" 'And any white woman who dares to look at an animal like you will be punished, too.' I jerked my face up, and Jack stared me down. I don't think the others knew, except Patrick. They never spoke your name, but Jack meant they'd hurt you, too. It killed me, thinking of them touching you in any way, punishing you because of me.

"Jack said, 'This won't hurt at all —

you're an animal, after all. A big hairy animal who can't keep his hairy thing in his pants around white women.' Pardon my language, but that's what he said, only not so politely.

"The others laughed along with him. But I wasn't laughing. Not then, not when he jabbed the iron hard into my side, into the thin skin of my rib cage. Last thing I remember before passing out was the sizzle and smell of my own flesh cooking."

I pressed my hand to my mouth, afraid I might vomit. I backed into one of the metal chairs on our porch — chairs with shell-shaped backs and seats, which Max had painted cheery yellow. The yellow made me even more nauseous, and I shielded my eyes from the empty one. Robert stepped close, bent on a knee, and continued in a low, quiet voice.

"Next thing I remember, I'm waking up where they tossed me out of the car somewhere in those woods. They'd untied me, but I could barely stand from the pain in my side. I crawled, following the sound of trickling water until I found a slow-moving creek. I tore a strip off my trousers and soaked it in the water and held it to my skin, though I could hardly stand it. I hoped the cool water would take away a little of the pain. It was almost dark by then. I lay by that creek all night, wondering if they'd killed me after all — just a slower death.

"I woke the next morning to a voice asking was I okay. I was never so relieved in all my life to see the face of an old Negro peering into mine. I showed him the letter burned into my side. A, for animal. He carried me in his wagon to Momma. They'd left me less than a mile from the house, barely across the line from Shalerville. I only stayed a few days, until I was strong enough to work. Nell took word to my boss. I was lucky he didn't fire me.

"Why they chose that time or place, after all those months . . . I guess I'll never know. But it changed me. I lost my nerve. But then, after I joined up, after I spent months dealing with all kinds of guys who thought they were better than they were, I got it back. I believed again. I found the courage. And I wanted to find the means to get you away from there — from them. To keep you safe no matter what they threatened. Then I found out you were already gone. And that *you* gave up, too, Isa."

I kept my eyes averted, focusing through my tears on the dimples in the concrete of the porch. He was right. What I'd said about waiting and watching? It was mostly a lie. I had given up. Without so much as a fight after I lost our baby. Doing nothing, when I could have sought him out once I'd left my childhood home. I'd given up, believing Nell's hints that he'd moved on.

I'd believed what the world told me. I'd *surrendered.*

Robert reached to cup my chin, to force me to look up. "But I'm here now. You're here now. And I still have this. It proves you're married to me, not him." Robert gestured toward the door, then pulled a slip of paper from his chest pocket.

I recognized the document, the leaf so thin, you could see the sun through it if you held it up to the sky. I said, "My mother had our marriage annulled."

He shook his head. "Not as far as I'm concerned. I swore to love you until the day I died."

"It's no good." As horrified as I was at the story he'd just told me, as sick as I was at the thought of what my brothers had done to the man I loved, as nauseous as I felt at their threats, my voice still emerged sullen. His declarations were useless — no matter how genuinely he felt them. No matter how I wanted to believe them. It had turned me into a hateful mess.

"We could take this piece of paper, Isabelle. Take it where people will respect it and leave us in peace."

"There's no such place. And you're leaving again."

"I'll find that place. But first, I'll take you where you can wait for me and I'll come back to you. I promise."

I allowed myself to contemplate the idea. If I left, Max would surely hate me. And though Robert held our marriage certificate, my mother's actions had made it good for nothing but the scrap pile.

Yet I had made those same vows. His suggestion that he could find a safe place for us made my heart leap in a song it hadn't sung in years. More than anything, I wanted Robert.

"Isa?" He rose from his knee, again using the nickname only he had ever called me. And it was too much.

I rose, too, and flung myself at him. Without looking to see whether a neighbor watched or if a stranger passed by on an errand, I threw my head against his chest, my tears freed, hot, ugly sobs bubbling from deep in my lungs, where I'd buried them too long.

When I'd spent my fury and frustration at my choices, I laid my cheek against the heavy cloth of Robert's uniform shirt. My tears had left damp spots on its starched surface.

Robert held me for a time. Then he slid a hand up my arm and lifted my chin with his finger until I looked straight at him, at those oak-colored eyes I'd believed I'd never see again. At his strong jawbone, so freshly shaved it appeared as smooth as the skin of his lips.

I reached toward him and our mouths collided, as though we'd both been wandering, searching a midnight desert for the last thing that could save us.

I stepped back, tugging him along with me, pulled the screen door open, and stepped inside our house, my house and Max's.

The thought stopped me less than a heartbeat. Long enough to tell myself a lie: that Max was an unimportant variable in this strange new equation.

We kissed — no, we devoured one another — through the living room, the hallway, all the way to the doorway of the bedroom, where I paused and glanced at the simple bedstead Max had installed before bringing me to this room on our wedding night. I pushed away from the door frame and led Robert instead to the smaller second bedroom, where we'd set up a single bed.

My hesitation at the first door hadn't gone unnoticed. Robert questioned me with his eyes and with one simple word: "Isabelle?"

I covered his mouth with my fingers, then led him to the narrow bed, where I sank down and lay back on the pillow, pulling him to me. I remembered the unlocked front door, wishing I'd thought to slide the bolt home. But Max wouldn't return for hours, and he had a key — not to mention that a bolt couldn't keep him from this, whatever it was. A betrayal of Max? When I'd already betrayed Robert with him?

I no longer cared.

It was no simple, innocent wedding night. No Robert afraid he might hurt me. No me shivering beneath my nightgown, hiding under a heavy quilt with nervous anticipation of the unknown. No half-child, half-grown boy and girl playing house, ignorant of what would destroy us so soon.

Our eyes were open.

My fingers hurried to unbutton the shirt that separated his flesh from mine, to push it away from his shoulders, even broader and stronger now than when the same muscles flexed to clear overgrowth from the brush arbor. I pressed my nose against his skin, inhaling everything I'd so bitterly missed. My hands trembled at the resistance

450

of hipbones and long, lean tendons on the backs of his thighs. I shivered as he swept my blouse away from my ribs and unhooked my brassiere to expose my breasts to his mouth, then removed my plain skirt in a clumsy game of lift and tug until it fell next to the bed.

There was no gentle give-and-take in our lovemaking. It was all greed and haste and pressing toward something we couldn't reach soon enough. Matching each other breath for breath. Climbing. Crying out when we reached it. Agony, exclamation, discordant harmony.

After, we lay half-dressed and tangled in the damp of sweat and remnants of our reunion, gasping to regain equilibrium in our lungs and slow the beating in our chests.

Robert wedged himself into the too-small space next to the wall and flung one arm above his head, the other across my chest, covering my nakedness with a stark stripe of skin against mine. I traced the angry scar on his side, over his ribs, purple and puckered, in the clear shape of the letter A, thinking of what he'd suffered because of me. But he lifted his hand and brushed my fingers away, as though the scar were irrelevant. Then he brushed his own fingertips against my abdomen, and I froze when they lingered in the shallow valleys of skin a shade lighter than the plateaus surrounding them — my own scars, the ones that could give away my secret. But he gazed across the room, and I knew he noted nothing beneath his fingertips and saw nothing in the room itself. Rather, he studied the situation, as we both did, in the motes that floated in the sunlight piercing us from the window.

We'd made another decision with our actions.

How could I continue my farce of a marriage after this? Every time Max and I had joined in subdued pleasure paled next to the passion Robert and I shared. Max would have to accept my mistake, acknowledge I'd compromised by burying my love for Robert under the guise of doing the right thing. I'd warned him I was no good for him.

Robert and I each straightened our own garments now, retrieving the cast-off pieces from the floor, silently buttoning and zipping ourselves back into everyday life.

When he asked if he could return — once he'd found that place for me to wait — the answer was clear. I stood in the shadow of my front porch, following him down the street with my gaze, as I'd done that morning with my husband.

36
DORRIE, PRESENT DAY

Leaving the message for Teague had calmed my nerves, and the vision of Miss Isabelle and her reunion with Robert both buoyed me up and put me on edge. We headed out, with me in my dressy pants and top and Miss Isabelle in a sweet little dress that showed off the exquisite figure she still had at almost ninety years old. I'd developed a crush on that word the day before — nineteen across, ten letters: "delicately lovely." *Exquisite.*

We weren't far from the funeral home — it was just across the river in Covington — and we were early. Miss Isabelle requested we make a detour on our way. She asked me to watch on either side of the river for a florist or an upscale grocery that might have a nice floral section.

"Don't people usually send arrangements to the funeral home?" I asked. "Do people carry in flowers like that?" I wasn't sure it was done.

"Dorrie, please humor me. I need flowers."

We were lucky. Before you could spell Cincinnati ten times, right after we crossed the double-decker bridge into Covington, I spied a flower shop in an old building on Main Street. And lucky again — the store wouldn't close for fifteen minutes.

"Are you going in?" I asked.

"No. Just get me a nice bunch of something simple and classy. Nothing fussy. A dozen."

"Roses?" That seemed easy enough.

"Yes. Red roses, if they have them."

"In a vase?"

"Just wrapped."

Now I was really worried. What would they do with wrapped flowers at the funeral home? Maybe she was counting on the fact they'd have vases, or maybe she intended for someone to carry them home instead of leaving them. She was frugal, but not too cheap to splurge on a vase.

But I followed her directions, and soon I was back in the car, carefully settling the sleeve of flowers on the backseat so it wouldn't get mangled when we started rolling. The clerk had bragged they'd been delivered at the end of the day. I'd gotten the pick, before anyone else had dug through them. They were gorgeous, and their sweet scent filled the car.

We pulled away from the curb and drove through the middle of Covington. The streets were lined with ancient buildings, some nice and fixed up, with open businesses, others vacant and rundown, with boarded-up windows. Then they became more residential. Tired old houses sat close to the street, mixed in with mom-and-pop businesses, bars, minimarts, and vacant lots where things had been torn down. I wondered why anyone would choose to live there, but then I'd spy a huge old historic house or school and I'd think how beautiful it must have been, and still could be, at any point in history. It reminded me of sections of Dallas and Fort Worth. Gradually, the color of the folks walking the streets shifted, though the setting remained the same. Miss Isabelle told me we were in Eastside, the historically African-American section of Covington. At a light, we pulled even with an old house that was now a funeral home.

"There it is," Miss Isabelle said, pointing. "But one more stop before we go there. We're still early."

I didn't question. I kept going. Before long, we drew up to a wrought-iron gate leading into the Linden Grove Cemetery. Miss Isabelle peered at a sheet of paper she'd pulled from her handbag, then handed it to me. It was a map. "Can you find this?" she asked, indicating a numbered plot circled in pencil. I studied the map, then eyed the gate and other landmarks to be sure I had a good idea how to locate the grave. Miss Isabelle kept a tight grip on the handle of her purse. Her mood had been up and down all day, but it had changed again. The air inside her Buick hung solemn now, heavy with unshed tears.

My confusion mounted as I drove down the narrow lane toward the section with the grave site she wanted to find. I wondered if she wanted to see ahead of time where the burial would take place. Maybe the funeral home had already set a canopy over the freshly dug hole.

There was no canopy. I parked as close as I could, then insisted Miss Isabelle hold my arm as we walked toward a large marker with a last name etched into it and surrounded by smaller stones, some newer than others. She clutched her roses in the crook of her free arm — I'd offered to carry them, but she'd refused, as though they supported her from the other side.

Then, I stopped. Suddenly, I felt light-headed. Miss Isabelle let go and proceeded on her own. She stopped, then bent carefully, holding on to the top of the granite memorial, stooping to lay her roses carefully at the base of one small gravestone. She drew herself up again and stepped back to study it beside me. She nodded, bowed her head, stood with her eyes closed for a time, breathing slowly in and out, as though fighting for her composure.

On the stone, in lichen-stained etching with weathered edges, was this: *Robert J. Prewitt, beloved son and brother.*

37
ISABELLE, 1943

I ran my hands down my belly, gauging the slight swell below my navel, then over my breasts, flinching at their tenderness, their reaction to even the lightest touch. They'd felt this way once before. I did the calculations in my head again. A woman was supposed to be filled with joy and wonder at the realization she was pregnant.

I'd experienced that once. This time, I was filled with dismay.

The first time, my joy had turned to sorrow when I couldn't share the news with Robert, then fury with my family for tearing me away from my unborn child's father and, in so many ways, from my child herself.

This time, nobody would rush to rip this child from my arms — not at first anyway. I wasn't sure who the father was. I wanted to believe it was Robert, as I'd made love with him without any thought of preventing pregnancy. I'd held Max off in the intervening weeks, making one excuse or another when he slid close in bed and touched his bare foot to mine, our passive, silent signal. But there'd been one night before Robert — I had been angry, but Max had been cautiously optimistic when the condom slipped off, allowing his seed to spill in me.

I was smart enough to have prevented this dilemma. I wondered if my subconscious had brought me to this place. And as much as I didn't want to be pregnant, I knew losing another baby would kill me. I would do what it took to bring this child into the world healthy and strong.

But it was more than a dilemma. It was a crossroads. Robert had sent word only days earlier — a simple envelope posted and addressed to me, with a false return address, as though I'd received a letter from a girlfriend. He was coming for me. He'd found a place I could live without harassment until he returned from the front. I'd alternated between excitement and fear when reading of his plan.

I'd agonized over how I'd tell Max. How would he react when I said I was leaving? Would he be enraged, demanding explanations and berating me for misleading him, for allowing him to support me while I plotted to desert him? My hours at Mr. Bartel's shop had dwindled to almost nothing, while Max worked extra shifts at his war-essential job to pay the mortgage and utilities and put food on our table.

Or would he fall silent, his hurt showing only in his bewilderment, wordlessly observing me as I left behind what he'd lovingly built, knowing I'd never given him my heart?

I'd almost wished for the first, but knowing Max, it would be the second. I would feel worse for it. He was indeed a good man. He'd never uttered an intentionally harsh word to me. He'd been patient with my slow investment in our life as a couple, but I doubted he'd ever suspected I'd throw him over so easily for another man.

Now, though, there was another cog to consider in the shaky wheel of our marriage: a baby. One Max would welcome and cherish, would be proud to carry on his shoulders so he might see above a crowd. He'd teach his son — I sensed immediately this child would be a boy — to ride a bicycle, to throw a baseball. He'd be 100 percent immersed in fatherhood.

If the child were his.

But if he were not? If I stayed? If the infant emerged, looking at first like any other newborn, pale and covered in milky vernix, squalling and reddening as oxygen filled his lungs, then eventually settled into the warmer shade of another race?

Max would have no choice but to throw me out of his house, onto the street, where I'd have to fend for myself and my child if I couldn't find Robert again, facing untold horror as a single mother of a mixed-race child. I shuddered to realize I could be forced to resort to a life of prostitution, selling my body to keep my child alive, for who would hire me then?

On the other hand, what if I left with Robert and the child belonged to Max? My child would be subject to ridicule and constant physical threats from those who couldn't see past his stepfather's skin. He'd grow up on the margin of both societies — the white one, which would punish him for his mother's sin, and the other one, which might mistrust him even if he lived in it from the day he was born.

I considered each way, and knew, eventually, I had one solution — the one best for my child.

Robert's eyes, when he came for me, were wild with grief. As I explained, he stepped backward, as though he'd be unable to contain his fury if he stood too near. He couldn't know how this decision devastated me; the jagged edges of my own heart weren't visible.

"The skin of this child alone will determine our future?" he said. "I would love him, Isabelle. You know I would. Even if he wasn't my own flesh and blood, I would take care of him. Whatever is part of you is part of me."

But I couldn't do it to Max or the child. I'd made a poor decision marrying Max, in not pursuing every possibility for a reunion with Robert, but I couldn't steal Max's son from him.

"What if he discovered I gave birth to his child?" I said. "Don't you think he'd come after the child? Would he let us raise a child who belonged to him?"

I knew, pushed far enough, Max would react. If he learned his child had been taken, as docile as he was, he would not lie down. He would not surrender his son.

Before Robert left, he made a promise. "I'll be back, Isabelle. One day, you'll look up and I'll be walking that sidewalk one more time, coming to be sure you aren't here raising our son on your own."

He stepped forward again. I knew he intended to bring me against him in an embrace. I wouldn't be able to endure it. If he so much as touched me, I'd falter. I'd crumble and deny every ounce of common sense so carefully gathered the last few weeks. I'd leave with him, and I'd do it without a backward glance. I held up my hand. A warning and a plea. "Don't."

His answering look destroyed me. I'd never imagined how difficult it would be to send him away again. Every other time, we'd been separated by family, by circumstance. I'd clung to a barely burning ember of a dream that one day we'd be together.

This time, I knew that ember would be extinguished when he turned to go.

Turn he did, but before he walked away, he said it again: "I will come back for you, Isa. I promise."

38
DORRIE, PRESENT DAY

"But he didn't come back, did he, Miss Isabelle? He didn't keep his promise."

The second line said it all, below *Robert J. Prewitt, beloved son and brother* — the one that said when he'd lived and died: *1921–1944.*

Miss Isabelle pulled an envelope from her handbag, the paper so worn from handling, I worried I'd tear it while accepting it from her outstretched hand. But she pressed it on me. "Please. I want you to read it. I want you to see who he was, by his own hand. Not through some story I told."

Miss Isabelle settled on a stone bench near the Prewitt family plot. I unfolded the tissue-thin sheets the envelope contained, walking, unable to sit while I studied the faded ink, the careful handwriting.

Isa, my forever love,
    This means I'm breaking my promise.

This means I won't be coming back for you or — if the baby you carry is mine — for our child. If you hold this letter, I pray the baby is Max's. Thinking of my child growing up in a world that sees only his skin next to his mother's, and treats him even worse than a black boy is already treated without his father to protect him, it kills me.

I never wanted anything more than to be with you and our child, to live beside you the rest of our days. But now you know it wasn't meant to be. You must be content with knowing I'm looking down on you every day, asking the good Lord to keep you safe and happy. Isa — there is no one like you.

I asked Nell, who still loves you like a sister, to send you this letter if something happens overseas. Nell also promised she and Momma will open their arms and doors, welcome you and any child, no matter what. They love you as much as I do — if it's possible. Find them if you need to.

Now, my Isa, I must say good-bye one last time.

Never, ever, forget that I loved you. It was always you.

Robert

I thought I might actually choke. It was nearly impossible for me to swallow. Why did I keep having some silly hope that things had worked out after all for Miss Isabelle and her Robert, even now, with the engraved date of his death staring me in the face? It was like I went to read that letter, thinking the headstone was some kind of joke, that any minute he'd come out of nowhere and he and Miss Isabelle would go hobbling toward each other and embrace like some happy-ever-after movie couple.

I sank down by Miss Isabelle, speechless, and she spoke.

"Robert did promise, but we both knew he might not return. That when he finished his training, he'd ship out to Europe if the war didn't end first. Before he left, he gave Nell the letter to mail if she had to. It was dangerous even for medics in the war. They were in the business of healing people, not killing them, but they weren't immune to unexpected or unintended attacks that took place off the battlefield. An attached note from Nell said the Americans had turned captured land into an army hospital. Another medic didn't see the tip of an unexploded mine sticking out of the ground until Robert threw himself between it and his colleague. My Robert died saving a life, but he returned home a hero."

Robert had died in the war. Not as a second-class member of the army who cooked and cleaned kitchens or moved supplies across the country, but doing the thing he'd wanted to do since Miss Isabelle's father had begun to groom him as a boy. He'd wanted to save lives.

But this felt so final. So sad, I could hardly stand it. I thought I had problems, right? Maybe my kid had been so dumb, I was afraid to go home, for fear I'd throttle him. Maybe I was scared to death to love a man because I assumed he'd turn out to be a loser like every other one I'd trusted. Maybe I'd had a few hard bumps in the road of my life. Maybe I was about to become a grandma before I wanted to think about it. Or maybe I wasn't. That would make me cry, too.

But all the folks I loved were right there at home, waiting for me, biding time until I could get back and help them patch things up or move along. Oh, Stevie Junior claimed Bailey's father would hurt him if he knew about the pregnancy, but his understanding of hurt had nothing on what Robert suffered at the hands of Miss Isabelle's brothers. That ugly puckered scar she'd described on Robert's side . . . my God.

I couldn't imagine enduring the loss Miss Isabelle had survived again and again and again.

I folded the letter carefully and she slid it back into the zippered compartment on the side of her bag, a pocket I'd never noticed before today. No wonder she'd worried about someone stealing her purse. And I'd been thinking it might be about me.

"So, the baby, it was Max's after all? You and he . . . I suppose the two of you managed?"

"Dane was Max's baby, clearly. I knew the moment he was born. You've seen my boy's photos."

I nodded.

"After Robert left, Max assumed I was depressed because I wasn't ready for a baby. He was right, but mainly, I was sure I was going to die without Robert. We'd found each other again, only to have it end worse than ever. I couldn't eat or sleep. I hardly moved most of the months of my pregnancy. I stayed inside, listless in bed or with my head hanging over the commode, vomiting up nearly anything I ate, all three trimesters. It's a miracle I gained enough weight to keep Dane alive. But he came out fighting, strong and angry and demanding I love him. He fought for his mother's attention, and I was forced to give it, feeding him and changing his diapers to keep my eardrums from bursting with his bawling.

"The neighbors had no idea I'd been pregnant until they saw me pushing Dane down the sidewalk in a pram to the drugstore or library or wherever I needed to go. I was the crazy neighbor lady after that. I never made close friends there."

"Were you happy Dane was white? That he didn't look anything like Robert?" I couldn't help asking.

"It was easier on everyone. I never had to confess my betrayal to Max. Dane never had to suffer what a child of Robert's would have back then. People have changed some, but even these days, I suspect it would be hard at times, especially with both parents being white."

I nodded.

"But honestly, Dorrie, I was devastated. Once again, I didn't have that little piece of Robert to remember him by. The letter came a week before Dane was born. After I read it, I decided I didn't have the strength to give birth. I wasn't sure I cared whether either of us survived. But Max — he was a *good* man — he pulled me along, never questioning why I was so numb and dead inside. He walked me up and down the halls of that house, bathed my forehead with cool cloths, called the doctor to come when it was time. He took Dane in his arms the minute he was born, loving him immediately, as I knew he would, then placed him at my breast and forced me to love him, too. I alternated between anger and fear those first weeks — anger that I would never see Robert again and had no child to remember him by, and fear that I'd be a bad mother, that I'd be unable or unwilling to care for Dane like I should. When Max saw how it was, he never asked me to do it again. Once was enough, for both of us."

She reached back into her purse for something so tiny, I didn't recognize it until she balanced it on my palm. "Of course, I did have something to remember Robert by. Still do."

It was that tiny thimble I'd seen on her dresser when I did her hair. The make-do symbol the preacher's wife gave them on their wedding day.

"Max found it in our mailbox the day after Robert left. I don't know when Robert put it there. Maybe that same day. I didn't watch him go. I couldn't, or I'd have run after him, begging all the way down the street for him not to leave, to take me with him forever."

I turned the thimble on my thumb. The three words told their whole story.

Faith. Hope. Love.

But who lay waiting in the funeral home? All the way from Texas to Cincinnati, I'd assumed it was Robert, but he'd been here in this old grave the whole time. Someone else waited for Miss Isabelle's good-bye.

Nell? As Miss Isabelle took her slow, short steps back to the car, I imagined her saying good-bye to the woman who'd been a sister to her, willing to do almost anything for her — even if it meant swallowing her own fear.

"What about the marker at that college?" I said to Miss Isabelle once we were settled back in the Buick. "I thought it meant Robert finished medical school."

"Robert completed a semester of basic medical training at Murray right before he shipped out the last time. His training and service would have counted toward his degree, and he would have completed his studies soon after the war. He wasn't the only member of his class who died overseas."

I'd assumed they were graduates. Now I understood the list had included all who would have finished in 1946. I wondered how many others hadn't made it back alive that last year of war, when black men were finally allowed in the field.

Our short return drive to the funeral home was quiet. When I switched off the ignition, Miss Isabelle took about the deepest breath I'd ever heard. I went around to her door and peeked in. She looked like she didn't have the strength to pull herself up and out of the car.

"You going to be okay, now?"

"I made it this far, didn't I?"

"You sure did, Miss Isabelle. You sure did."

Farther than I ever dreamed when we set out.

Inside, she studied easels set up outside each visitation room, labeled with the names of the deceased and their dates of birth and death. When she stopped, I didn't recognize the first name. It was a woman's name, but not any name Miss Isabelle had mentioned in her story. She had never called anyone Pearl.

The last name? I knew it well by now.

Who was Pearl Prewitt?

Miss Isabelle had told me one last detail on the way over. She and Max and Dane had moved to Texas shortly after the war ended. How would she know someone who'd been a small child when they moved away? Why would it matter?

Suddenly, I didn't think I could follow her into the quiet room where a flower-laden casket waited, half-open, so the one who lay there could receive farewells from those who'd loved her. But I did. Now, more than ever, Miss Isabelle would need someone to lean on.

39
Miss Isabelle, Present Day

I drink in her portraits. They lean against easels. Portraits of Pearl as an infant, then as a toddler, then as a young woman and, later, a middle-aged one. Finally, a snapshot of her standing near a window. The still figure in the nearby casket favors that one. Perhaps the undertaker studied it, preparing her for burial.

She was old. I was older, certainly, but each of her seventy-two birthdays haunted me. My skin is smooth for an old woman's, and hers was slightly more so. She died suddenly, unexpectedly, unmarked by years of disease. In the recent photo, her eyes are bright, alert and she stands erect, lacking the hesitation I too often observe in women of a certain age. Yet, in her steady gaze, I also detect decades of sorrow.

A tinge of color clearly identifies her as Robert's daughter. The hint of him also surface in her height — by my estimation from the photos, surpassing mine by a good three or four inches — and in her intensity.

But here is what shreds the breath from me, as certainly as a scalpel reaching between my ribs to scrape my lungs and heart: Pearl looked like me.

40
DORRIE, PRESENT DAY

Miss Isabelle gazed at her daughter. The one torn from her all those years ago. The one she never had a chance to hold.

When I realized who lay in the casket, I feared I might pass out. I grabbed the back of one of those overstuffed chairs arranged around the visitation room for guests. We'd arrived thirty minutes before the official start time. The room was quiet and empty except for me and Miss Isabelle, but now, another elderly woman slipped in behind us, pushing a walker along the carpet. I knew she was Nell — alive — not only by her resemblance to Pearl and how close she and Miss Isabelle looked in age but also by her eyes as she watched Miss Isabelle study her lost daughter.

Miss Isabelle had brought me along because she knew I loved her like I would a mother — and because she knew I'd be strong when she couldn't be.

And that was now.

I'd entered the room behind her, but I took a breath and moved close. She reached for the crook of my arm, and I pulled her hand into it and placed mine over hers.

I tried to imagine what she was thinking and feeling. It was beyond my comprehension. How had her daughter survived, this Pearl Prewitt, who'd come too early out of Miss Isabelle's body, too tiny and blue to make it, or so Miss Isabelle's mother had said? Where had Pearl been all these years while Miss Isabelle kept her grief secreted away? When Miss Isabelle married for practicality instead of passion? While she mothered a son she loved, and grieved for the daughter she'd never even seen?

Who had done this?

I turned to look at Nell. I wanted to march right over, demand explanations for the selfishness of whoever had hidden Pearl — in plain view if my gut told me right. For denying Miss Isabelle all those decades of mothering and watching her baby grow into a beautiful woman. For all I knew, there were grandchildren, greatgrandchildren.

This was the cruelest part of the story so far.

But when Miss Isabelle saw Nell, she hurried as fast as she could on her tired bird legs, and the two embraced. It was a picture of sisters, as different as they were, coming together in something so big, so profound, I couldn't grasp it.

Miss Isabelle's eyes filled and overflowed, and Nell's did, too. Miss Isabelle's whispered words cut me all the way inside. "Oh, Nell. She's so beautiful. I've missed her my whole life."

Nell brought Miss Isabelle a photo album that had been placed near the casket. Miss Isabelle turned the pages slowly, studying each portrait or candid shot of Pearl. At one, she clutched her hand to her chest, then motioned for me to look. Like the slide she'd stolen and hidden, it was a family portrait. She named them, resting a finger against each face: Nell and Cora, Brother James and Alfred, and, of course, the infant Pearl on the laps of the women who had mothered her, their bodies so close, you couldn't tell who really held her. Only Robert was missing. Had he known about Pearl? Did he know she was his?

I had to look away.

Miss Isabelle stayed quiet the rest of the evening, sitting, solitary, in a chair that dwarfed her, listening, watching those who came to pay their respects to her daughter and to the family. I had chosen a settee next to her chair. Some folks asked if the seat beside me was taken, then extended their hands, introducing themselves as friends or relatives of the deceased. I gave my first name, didn't offer any relationship. Eventually, they'd move or turn to talk to someone else.

Mostly, Miss Isabelle gazed at her daughter's face, which was plainly visible from where she sat. She knew none of the visitors but Nell — Cora was long dead, of course. The small crowd sent curious looks toward the elderly white woman in the corner who resembled Pearl enough to puzzle them. But Nell didn't introduce her; she allowed Miss Isabelle to mourn in peace, preventing awkward explanations.

Except, near the end, Nell brought someone to her. She introduced him as Pearl's son. Pearl had married late, though she eventually divorced and took back her maiden name. Her son was in his late thirties, a father, married. A small girl, no more than four or five, hung on to his coattails, peeking around to study Miss Isabelle with rainy-day eyes — so like hers and Pearl's — until Miss Isabelle smiled at her. The child skipped around then and squeezed into the chair beside her. She picked up Miss Isabelle's hand and stroked the skin on the back of it, then up her arm. "Your skin is soft," she said, and I saw Miss Isabelle shiver. "Are you my great-granny? That's what Mommy said. You're pretty. My granny is pretty, too. She died."

Her father shifted awkwardly on his heels, allowing the child to communicate for him, while Pearl's daughter-in-law watched with gleaming, happy-sad eyes. The tiny girl whispered to Miss Isabelle after her father moved away to other parts of the room to visit with family and friends. Eventually, she fell asleep in the chair, still stroking Miss Isabelle's skin, sometimes her cheek, and when her parents were ready to depart, her daddy gently extracted her from the curve of Miss Isabelle's embrace. Miss Isabelle tucked her elbow close against her hip, against the fading warmth left by the slumbering girl.

We left as soon as the visitation hours ended, returning to the inn early, where Miss Isabelle was too tired even to consider a snack from the tray the innkeeper had left. She sipped hot water, then asked for help getting ready for bed. She could barely raise her arms as I unbuttoned and unzipped her from her pretty floral dress. It was the first time I'd ever seen her mostly unclothed. She was so small, so fragile-looking, I was afraid her bones might break if I didn't move slowly, carefully, helping her push her arms into her nightgown and pulling it down to cover her again.

"Thank you, Dorrie," she said. "You'll never know . . . I couldn't have done this alone."

I answered with a gentle squeeze on her shoulders. "I know, Miss Isabelle. I know."

She seemed to sleep immediately, but I suspect she only rested her eyes in that big fluffy bed, imagining the life she'd missed, maybe only drifting before the hour came for us to rise and go to the church for Pearl's funeral.

The service was formal, quiet, though in the reading of Pearl's obituary, the crowd stirred when the preacher named Cora Prewitt as foster mother and Isabelle McAllister Thomas as mother. We moved from church to cemetery, where Pearl's coffin would be lowered into the ground next to Robert's grave. All morning, Miss Isabelle was elegantly composed, right up until the preacher said his final words over Pearl. Then her arm quivered against mine, and I turned to see her face crumple up.

I'd never seen anything but tears shining in her eyes at the visitation and in all the days we'd spent together. Now she quietly sobbed, and watching her body racked with such grief was painful. I folded her against me, as if I were the mother and she my little child.

Later, we drove to Nell's home. She was widowed, Brother James having passed years earlier. She still lived in the same little South Newport community where she'd grown up with Robert, in a long, skinny shotgun house she and Brother James had bought after they married. Miss Isabelle said the area hadn't changed much, but the little church where she'd met Robert in the arbor was long gone, demolished to make way for an industrial building.

Folks brought covered hot dishes into the house, plates filled with cold cuts, cookies, and pies. Some approached Miss Isabelle now, encouraged by Nell, cautiously, then confidently when she smiled, speaking of Pearl's life, how generous she'd been. In spite of her unclear heritage, despite a difficult marriage, while parenting a son mostly on her own, she'd been caretaker of so many more. She'd been a teacher, first in a segregated Covington grade school, than later in an integrated school during the turbulent civil rights era. Other than Pearl's beautiful little granddaughter, the few young people present were mostly children or grandchildren of students she'd mentored in a world that would continue to deny them full status in so many ways, even while the civil rights movement was a memory for most.

I marveled at how graciously Miss Isabelle responded to the words of these strangers. Me? I might have been on the floor by then, kicking and screaming about my lost daughter and every minute I'd missed.

Finally, the crowd thinned. Nell closed the door on the last visitors, who'd hugged her on their way out, rocking her through her own grief. She'd been one of Pearl's surrogate mothers, too, though Pearl called her "Sister" all her life.

Nell came to the kitchen table, where I'd settled Miss Isabelle with a plate of food. Miss Isabelle only nibbled. She had no appetite, and though she ate like a bird anyway, I worried she would grow weak. She seemed to be wasting away before my eyes. I encouraged her to drink some decaf coffee, hoping the milk she added would strengthen her.

Nell poured herself a cup, too, and pulled her chair close. The three of us sat there quietly awhile. The scent of strong coffee and relief that the funeral was finished settled around us, mingling with the sorrow that had weighed us down since we'd walked into the funeral home the day before.

After a few moments, Felicia, Pearl's daughter-in-law, returned, having dropped her husband and little girl at home. She sat at Nell's side while Nell explained everything that had happened. While compiling a list to make phone calls, Felicia had been the one to discover a name and number in Pearl's address book — along with cryptic notes scribbled by Pearl. Felicia had questioned Nell about whether Isabelle Thomas was someone they should notify about her mother-in law's death.

Nell had reluctantly told Felicia the story of Isabelle and Robert, and, ultimately, about Pearl's birth. Like so many from her generation, Nell had thought it best to leave well enough alone, to let the past be the past, where it could do no more harm. But Felicia persisted and Nell agreed Felicia should make the call. She had told Miss Isabelle very little over the phone — nearly two weeks earlier, I learned. They'd postponed Pearl's burial until Miss Isabelle could be there, to give her a chance to absorb the shock, then make the journey. Bless her, but I still could hardly stand thinking about Miss Isabelle receiving that call, about her dealing with her grief alone in those days before she asked me to bring her to this place. How had she done it? And how had she kept herself together while we traveled, kept her chin so high, even to the point of being able to laugh at times?

Lord, have mercy. She was stronger than I'd ever imagined — even if she needed me, too.

"After Sallie Ames, the midwife, delivered you of Pearl," Nell said, "she knew the baby was likely too tiny to survive. Your mother made her promise she'd carry her away, take her to the colored orphans home in Cincinnati. Shalerville was no place for a tiny black baby, of course, even if she survived. Sallie felt so sorry for you, Isabelle. She hated taking the baby from you, not giving you a chance to see her or hold her, even if only for a minute.

"But she found out where that baby belonged. Not at an orphanage, where after coming so early, she would surely die. Sallie came knocking at our door late that night. It was sweltering hot, deep of the summer — probably what kept Pearl alive those first few hours, along with her own little stubborn spirit. Sallie wasn't alone by then." Nell quieted, and Isabelle leaned toward her, desperate to learn who had accompanied Sallie. Nell seemed scared to continue.

Waiting, my own breath hung in my chest.

"It was your father, honey. Your father . . . he followed along behind Sallie, watching her safely out of Shalerville in the dark; then he called to her, and the two of them hurried to our house with the baby. Sallie had helped with early babies before, of course, but Doc McAllister, he knew some things because of his journals, knew what they'd been doing, keeping babies that came too soon in incubators. People could even go to fair exhibits and see the babies behind glass in the incubators. The admittance fees paid for their medical care. He instructed Momma to keep her warm and close to a human body every single minute, how to feed her, a drop at a time, with a special formula he made up. We all took turns with her — Momma, Daddy, and me. He came by often to check on Pearl, to bring more formula and weigh her and watch for signs of trouble. It was touch-and-go those first weeks, but that baby girl, she held on, fighting with everything she had in her little bitty body to survive. And survive she did."

Miss Isabelle's face had gone pale as bone while Nell spoke, and I reached for her arm, afraid she might faint and topple from her chair. She spoke slowly, her words drawn out, gaping holes like questions between them. "My father? I can hardly take it in, Nell. I don't know what to think."

Nell nodded. "He did. He loved you, Isabelle, and he cared what happened to that baby — his own grandchild — even if he couldn't figure a way for you to have her. He was a good man, Doc McAllister. But he had one big flaw: He was scared to stand up to your mother."

I wondered who *hadn't* been scared of Miss Isabelle's mother. I had no sympathy to waste on that woman. But now, I found a sliver of respect for her father — even if he'd refused to do his good where all the world could see. Where his own daughter could see.

"Why didn't he tell me?" Miss Isabelle asked. "Why did he keep it from me that she'd lived? No matter how hard it was for him to stand up to my mother, he should have told me."

Nell had gone very still. "That she'd lived?" she asked. "Who told you she died?"

Miss Isabelle sat for a moment, thinking back through her memories. "I remember clearly. Mother said, 'It was so early. . . . It was for the best.' "

"Oh, honey," Nell said. She stood, moving slowly, coming around the table until she was touching Miss Isabelle's arm. "We believed you didn't want her." Her eyes seemed almost frantic as they sought Miss Isabelle's out.

I'd just lifted my coffee to my lips, and I set the cup back down so hard, it clinked and liquid sloshed over the side. I forced myself to reach for a napkin, to stop the spreading stain from running over the edge of the table, though I could hardly move my arm. Miss Isabelle rocked in her chair, her eyes burning holes in her lap, obviously struggling to keep her composure. Nell stayed close, and I saw now that, before, she'd been holding something back. All her reserve was gone in an instant, and in its place was only sorrow.

Felicia pulled Nell's chair next to Miss Isabelle and pressed Nell's shoulder until she sat. Nell's voice shook as she continued.

"Before Sallie left your house, your mother gave her a sealed note, said to deliver it with the baby. Sallie had tucked the note inside the blanket she'd wrapped around Pearl, and we didn't find it until later. It said, 'I do not want this child. Please do not try to contact me.' "

They had all believed she didn't want Pearl. I thought of the time Miss Isabelle had seen Nell in the market, how cool and indifferent she had been. Miss Isabelle assumed it was only because of the trouble she'd caused. It was so much more than that.

"I wanted her. Oh, how I wanted her." Miss Isabelle's voice trembled "And my father knew better. Why didn't he tell me?"

"He never saw that note, but if he had, I suppose he would have been afraid you'd try to go off after her, and between you and me, Isabelle, if you had, I think your mother would have made life even more miserable for all of us. We'd already lost our jobs, though we were doing okay by then — Daddy had gotten a raise, and I was newly married and starting a family myself. But I think your father wasn't just afraid of your mother. He was truly afraid for Robert. It was bad enough, what your brothers got away with, but I believe he felt they would have killed Robert if they could have found a way around the law. It wasn't hard in those days. Black boys and men died for lesser things. *Looking* at a white girl or woman the wrong way was considered a crime. Fathering a white woman's baby? That would have been too much. They'd have had a group of folks lining up to lynch him. We could hardly believe you didn't want her. That nearly killed Momma and me. But, honey, I guess we accepted that in the long run, it was all for the best."

"Did she know about me, growing up? My name, it was in her address book. . . ."

Pearl. Miss Isabelle wanted to know what her little girl knew of her mother.

"We never spoke of it openly as long as Momma was alive. There didn't seem any point. And, of course, we just didn't in those days — that kind of thing happened more than you'd ever believe. The story went that Sallie Ames delivered an early baby in another community and the mother died in childbirth. That she'd brought her to us because Momma was out of work and could care for her better than anyone else around. Your daddy, he brought money for a long time, making sure Momma had enough to provide what Pearl needed — extra food for our table, clothing, so on — even after Momma went back to work and I started keeping Pearl days. Up until he died, little envelopes showed up under the door, filled with cash, no name or anything, but we knew who'd left it and knew who it was for. Before he died, one big pile of money — enough to send Pearl through college. So Momma was able to raise that little girl as if our home was Pearl's own home, and Momma was her mother."

"I know she did," Miss Isabelle said.

"Cora was a better mother to me than my own. I'm grateful to her. But I wish I'd known about my baby. All those years, I thought she was dead. And Robert? Did he know?"

"It's hard to say, but I think he probably did. Robert never moved home after the two of you ran away together, only stayed for a few days that once when he was . . . injured. He worked in Cincy until he went back to school that fall. After he joined up, when he came home on leave, he told Momma he'd found you, that he wanted to bring you to her to wait out the war. I think she would have admitted the truth about Pearl then — she was two or three years old and the spitting image of the both of you — but Momma knew he needed to go, to serve his country. I suppose she thought she couldn't tell half the truth — that Pearl was his — without telling the rest — that you'd given her up, or so we believed. It would have killed him. And then, of course, you never came. We assumed you wouldn't, in spite of what he said."

But if Miss Isabelle had gone with Robert, she would have gone to where her baby girl lived with everyone who loved her — except for that baby's own mother. I understood Nell's reasoning in how dangerous it would have been at first, but by then, would it have mattered?

Who would ever know? It was such a mess, and so far in the past, nothing could fix it now. But I think Miss Isabelle was about to boil over with emotion inside. I was worried for her heart, both figuratively and literally. She held her hands to her collarbone and breathed in and out carefully. The grief in her eyes seemed to dull them and reveal her pain all at once.

"After Momma died, though," Nell continued, "when Pearl was grown, I did tell her about you and Robert. She said she'd always suspected there was more to the story than what Momma had told her, but she'd been afraid to dig. She suspected, as light as her skin and eyes were, that one of her parents was white. She looked enough like us, she'd long wondered if Robert had been her father. She used to study his pictures, matching up his features with hers.

"I never told her you didn't want her. I thought that was too cruel, though I worried about that all along — whether it would be a mistake. I'm thankful for that now. I left it up to her how to deal with it then, Isabelle. It was her choice. Pearl said she'd tracked you down to Texas. She told me she'd started to call you a few times — went so far as to dial your number and wait for an answer. But when you answered, she didn't have the courage to speak. I guess she was afraid you'd reject her — a white woman who suddenly discovered her black daughter was still alive? She worried about your family, too. Your husband. Any other children you'd had with him. She was happy enough in her life, with her son, with the things she did and how she was able to mentor her students. I think she was mainly curious about you, and in the end, she decided not to trouble the waters."

"I remember," Miss Isabelle said, her eyes focusing on something Nell and I and Felicia couldn't see. "For about a year, the phone would ring, and I'd answer and there would be silence on the other end, but I knew someone was there. I never dreamed it was her, though. I had crazy ideas — that Robert hadn't died after all. That he was calling to say he was coming for me."

"He was, in a way," Nell said, and Miss Isabelle's expression took my breath away.

"I wish she'd spoken. Oh, how I wish she'd spoken. I would have given anything to know my daughter." Nell pulled Miss Isabelle's hands close to her and held them while they wept silently, together.

We sat for a while, Miss Isabelle and Nell

thinking of the past and how they might have changed it. Me, waiting and hoping that Miss Isabelle could survive this one last blow. Felicia stood and began to tidy up the kitchen, wiping the counters and rinsing and stacking our coffee cups when we turned down refills.

As we prepared to leave, Miss Isabelle and Nell hugged for the longest time. I think she knew Nell had always had her best interests at heart — had always wanted to protect her and Robert and Pearl from the danger of the truth. Times were different then. What a burden Nell must have lived with all those years.

At the door, Miss Isabelle grasped Felicia's hand between hers and gazed into her eyes, thanking her for bringing everything to light, making her promise to send photos of the precious little girl who had already stolen her heart, maybe even to come visit her in Texas, though I wondered if that would ever happen. How hard would it be to jump-start those relationships, at this late date, with no history to build upon? Though he was kind and polite to Miss Isabelle, Pearl's son didn't seem to know how to act or what to think. Their brief conversations had been stilted, trailing off in so many unspoken and unanswered questions. But I think Miss Isabelle was happy to know that in that man, and in that beautiful girl child and any others yet to come, the love she and Robert had shared finally had a legacy. In spite of everything, it really was meant to be.

As I started the car, I asked Miss Isabelle the question that had been bothering me ever since we'd arrived at the funeral home. "Why didn't you tell me it was your daughter, Miss Isabelle? Why didn't you tell me before we set out?"

"I just couldn't talk about it at first, Dorrie. All I could do was tell my story as much as I knew so far. Then things started happening at home — your mess with Stevie, your worries about Teague — and I was afraid if you knew about Pearl, you'd refuse to return home even if you really needed to. You'd feel like you had to stay on the road, with me."

"Oh, Miss Isabelle," I said, shaking my head. "Sometimes you just have to ask for what you need. But thank you."

We drove away from Nell's house, and Miss Isabelle gazed into the dusk as night fell around us.

41
DORRIE, PRESENT DAY

We left Cincinnati the next morning a different way from how we'd entered it. Instead of crossing the main bridge back into Kentucky, Miss Isabelle directed me back toward Newport, toward the area where Nell lived, except we drove the other way down the main road until we came to a sign.

WELCOME TO SHALERVILLE.

"That's where it was." She pointed her trembling finger at the side of the road. Now, a huge old oak tree was the only thing keeping the welcome sign company. I pictured it in my mind, the sign that would have kept me from crossing the city limit after dark all those years ago — and not that far in the past. Miss Isabelle thought maybe the signs had come down around the late 1960s. But Nell had told us hardly any black folks lived in the area even to this day, except for a small population in Newport and in one little town nearby that had a university.

Back home in Texas, even when no sign stood at the side of the road, I still wouldn't be safe driving through some towns, especially at night — heaven forbid I had a flat tire or something and had to walk anywhere. There'd been plenty of small communities like that near my East Texas hometown. For all I knew, there were places like that close to the big city where Miss Isabelle and I lived now. These little sundown towns had been established everywhere — north or south of the Mason-Dixon Line, east or west of the Great Divide. Maybe it wasn't as in your face now as it had been back then, maybe it was no longer politically correct to keep someone out of your town just because of skin color, but that didn't stop some folks.

We drove up the main street of her hometown, and then Miss Isabelle directed me into another cemetery — the biggest, hilliest cemetery I'd ever seen. Gravestones dotted every available surface, no matter how steep, and narrow driving surfaces ran in every direction, up and down and around the hills. A fancy old stone building rose from one of the hills, and another one in a lower spot housed mowers and landscaping equipment. Workmen performing various tasks ignored us as the car crawled the tiny streets of this town populated by the dead.

Miss Isabelle knew her way this time. She asked me to stop first in an out-of-the-way corner. We stayed in the car, but she pointed out a tiny headstone so dark with damp and age, the writing wasn't visible from my window.

"That's Aunt Bertie," she said. "One time, when I was still a girl, I followed Mother here. She didn't know I was only steps behind her as she walked this road to tend her sister's grave. I wouldn't have known where she was buried otherwise."

She studied the grave for a moment, and when she spoke, her voice broke in places. "I hid behind a tree and watched. My mother lay over this grave and she cried, Dorrie. It was the only time I ever saw her cry."

A moment later, we pulled close to the edge of a road to park, and she pointed out a family marker. McAllister.

"Will you help me, Dorrie?"

I helped her from the car, which seemed more difficult every time she attempted it. She'd brought a cane on our trip, but she had refused it before, insisting I leave it in the trunk. She asked for it this time. We walked as close as we could get to the marker, though we had to stand back a distance. Her mother's and father's names were etched on flat stones nearby, as well as Jack's and his wife's. The stones were skewed on their crumbling concrete bases, her mother's tipped at an odd angle into the grass. Miss Isabelle clucked her tongue. "All those years ago, Mother thought us better than anybody else in town, and now look — nobody even tends their graves." But her eyes were cloudy, emotion-filled again. After a minute, she whispered words I strained to hear and understand. "Thank you, Daddy. Thank you for helping my little girl live."

Tears clogged my throat.

We drove all day and into the evening, only making pit stops for gas and bathroom breaks and sweet snacks — all Miss Isabelle would agree to eat. Along the way, she paged listlessly through her crossword puzzle books when I asked her to read me a few clues. I pretended I was sleepy and needed her to keep me awake.

Somewhere around Memphis, she talked about what happened after Dane was born. Max's company expanded, and he was offered a promotion and a raise, but they had to move to Texas to take it. Miss Isabelle said she was perfectly fine leaving the place where everything seemed to hold excruciating memories.

In Texas, they made a quiet life. She and Max struggled, but they maintained their marriage. Once, though, shortly after their move to Texas, Max made no secret of seeing a woman two or three times, someone he'd met at an office party. Miss Isabelle didn't react. She felt she had no right — still guilty for deceiving him all those years earlier. The affair fizzled when Max realized nothing would change. He was only trying to get her attention. He broke it off and returned his steady, careful attention to Isabelle and their household. They settled into a life with few bumps after that — other than a brief period while Dane served in Vietnam. He returned safe, if cynical.

"What about those big things you promised Robert you were going to do, Miss Isabelle? Did you do any of the things you dreamed about all those years ago?"

"Oh, Dorrie, not really. Nothing too big. I tried to be a good wife and mother."

We talked about the neighborhood where they'd lived in far east Fort Worth. A prosperous new community when they moved there, Poly Heights later fell victim to blight when the racial makeup began to shift. Isabelle and Max stayed even while white flight was in full swing. I could tell she was a respected part of her community, though she didn't say it. She volunteered in her neighborhood, tutored schoolchildren, helped children and adults alike apply for library cards, and encouraged her neighbors to fill out voter-registration forms. She joined civic groups that pushed the school administration to make more efforts to desegregate. The schools had remained mostly segregated by virtue of districting lines, even when the enrollment rules changed.

So in her own little ways, Miss Isabelle had done some pretty big things — things most women like her wouldn't have dreamed of doing. I knew the neighborhood where she and her husband had lived until they finally moved, after Max retired, to the smaller, easier-to-maintain suburban home where I did her hair now. Poly was the kind of neighborhood white folks ditched at the first signs of diversity in those days. It was one of the few older neighborhoods in Fort Worth mostly untouched by young professionals now that it was cool to live in the city again.

Max died peacefully in his sleep at almost eighty. Dane grew up and moved away to Hawaii. He lived and worked there until he passed only a few weeks after a cancer diagnosis. He left behind a wife and a couple of grandkids, whom Miss Isabelle seldom saw while he was alive, and even less after he died and his wife remarried. They sent her cards at birthdays and holidays, but it had been years since any of the kids had visited and months since she'd heard from them by phone. She felt like maybe it was her fault. "It's hard to keep up relationships long-distance these days, Dorrie," she said, "especially if they aren't so strong to begin with." She wasn't sure she'd ever allowed Dane to depend on her as much as she should have. Had she kept him at arm's length? Was her ability to love damaged by her losses?

"It's hard to keep up relationships where they're in your face," I said, thinking about all my fears about trusting men, and the disaster with my child awaiting me at home. These things seemed almost petty to me now. But they were mine.

"I was lucky, you know, Dorrie," she said, surprising me out of the blue the next day. We'd finally stopped overnight in another generic roadside hotel. We'd been too tired to converse after we'd climbed in the car that morning. "I was loved by two good men."

I thought about it. I had to agree. "I hope to be so lucky one day," I said, "but I hope I don't have to experience as much heartache to get there. One good man is plenty, thank you."

"Remember this, Dorrie: Some men are just plain bad news. Then there are good men. They'll do. Then there are good men you love. If you find one of the last kind, you'd better hang on to him with everything you have."

She was right. I had a feeling Teague was one of the last kind. I wondered if he'd heard my message, and if he'd be patient enough to wait while I got my mess with Stevie Junior all straightened out, then patient enough to deal with me. Because I had another feeling. I had a feeling I could love him if I pushed back the barriers in my own heart.

We pulled into her driveway late that afternoon, bone-tired and weary. Before I reached to open my car door, Miss Isabelle put a hand on my closest one. "When I learned Robert had died, I thought my life was over. I eventually loved Max in my own way, and Dane was a good boy and I was a good mother and I loved him, of course. But it always seemed like something was missing, like losing my little girl and losing

Robert had left two holes in my heart.

"But then I met you, and you stuck with me even when I was cranky and acting like a foolish old woman. God gave me a blessing. He brought me a little piece of the family I'd lost. Through you, Dorrie." She shushed me when I started to protest — not because I wasn't honored, but because I couldn't accept that the things I'd done, so small, could begin to touch the empty places in her heart. "Don't deny me now. Dorrie, you've become like a daughter to me."

The tears bubbled up and poured out of my eyes. I couldn't help blubbering like a fool.

"Oh, stop now. You're embarrassing me. I just love you like you're my own child, Dorrie. It's simple and nothing to get excited about. It's not like I have a pile of money to leave you. I'm probably more trouble than I'm worth." I laughed through my choked throat, and she patted my hand.

I pulled her suitcase from the trunk and moved mine to my car. I walked her into the house, checked all the doors and windows. Everything was secure. I put the crossword books on her kitchen table, but she pushed them back at me, saying I should keep them as a memento of our trip.

She snorted after she said it. But I *would* keep them, and I'd remember every bit of her story when I thumbed through them, even while so many of the squares remained empty.

It felt different, leaving her that night, as though she'd changed while we were on the road, going from a feisty old woman who'd needed a little extra help to a fragile thing I was scared to leave alone. I forced my feet to walk to the entryway.

"One more thing, Dorrie."

I turned back. She supported herself against one of the chairs, which looked like it had been in her formal living room thirty years or more. "I'm firing you."

I gawked. What in the hell? I'd been doing her hair over a decade — no way I'd quit now, no matter what she said.

"If you're like a daughter to me, should I be paying you to come over here and do my hair every Monday afternoon? You ought to be doing it for free." She chuckled then, and I did, too, though my heart did a jiggity jig, uneasy about these things she kept springing on me.

She pulled her key chain out of the massive purse of mystery. "There's an extra house key on here. Take it off and keep it. You go ahead and let yourself in whenever you come by. If you have time to work on my hair while we visit, you can."

I shrugged, but we both knew I intended to show up every single Monday morning and do her hair like I always had. I'd never take another dime from her, either. "Okay, Miss Isabelle," I said. "I'll talk to you tomorrow."

It was awkward then. Was I supposed to hug her? Kiss her? Now that I was her honorary daughter, it seemed appropriate, but neither of us was the touchy-feely type.

Maybe, though, one day in the future, I'd surprise her with a quick hug and peck on the cheek. I mean, I'd seen her in her underwear, right? What secrets were left between us?

42
DORRIE, PRESENT DAY

Stevie Junior waited for me at home, subdued and all hangdog, like I was going to tear into him, rip him to pieces right there. A few days earlier, I probably would have. But I'd realized now what was most important. Part of that was not pushing my son away when he needed me most.

"Hey, sugar. What's the latest?" I called out, letting myself in the house, dragging my suitcase behind me and dropping it on my bed. I'd worry about unpacking later. Stevie was sprawled on our ratty old sofa. I'd wanted to replace it for years with something that would make our house look a little classier. Today, it looked familiar and comfortable. It looked like home.

Stevie dragged himself to a sitting position and hunched over his hands, which he clenched in one overgrown fist under his chin. He looked surprised at my casual greeting, his shoulders stiff and tensed up, as if my mood were too good to be true.

I dropped into the recliner catty-corner to the couch, equally familiar and welcoming. My list of what seemed important a week ago had different entries now. "Bailey talk to her parents?"

"Um, no. I actually don't think she'll be talking to them, Mom."

My heart felt like it had stopped for a few beats, then resumed beating dully in my chest, as if it didn't want to but would plug on. So, it was too late to talk over anything. Too late to assure Stevie I'd support whatever choices he made as long as he tried his best to use the brain the good Lord had given him. I sighed.

"She lost the baby."

I jerked my head back and stared at my son. His eyes gleamed. I knew then how seriously he'd taken this whole mess. It wasn't in his plans, but now he was experiencing a loss he'd never expected to deal with at only seventeen years old.

I pushed myself up and dropped down next to him, wrapping my arm around shoulders that seemed so broad, but were the same ones I'd held all the years he'd been mine.

"Honey, really?" I couldn't help feeling the tiniest bit relieved. It was only human, I guess, for the mother of a kid who'd done something dumb to feel relieved the consequences wouldn't be so harsh. But I hurt more than I expected, too. This had been my grandchild, after all. Even if I wasn't ready to be a grandma, a piece of my heritage had passed into another realm without me having a chance to love the little guy or gal.

"She started bleeding yesterday, like a heavy period or something. We went to the emergency room. They said she'd miscarried. It's early enough she doesn't have to do anything else. It's just over. But Mom?" He looked up, pain naked in his eyes. "It hurts. I didn't know it would hurt like this."

"Oh, son, I know. I'm so, so sorry." I held him closer as his shoulders quaked and he choked on his tears, trying so hard to act like a man. "It's okay, Stevie. It makes you more of a man to cry. Trust me."

A last wave of sobs rumbled through his body like a fading thunderstorm. After he'd finally calmed himself and wiped his face clean with a tissue, I talked.

"I'm not going to lie. I'm disappointed, Stevie. Disappointed you didn't come to me to begin with, tell me what was going on and what you thought you needed. Maybe I could have helped you make some logical decisions instead of going against everything I thought I'd taught you — breaking into the shop and taking the money and, basically, letting Bailey's fear corner you into bad choices."

"I know, Mom. I'm so —"

"Now, wait. Hear me. I also know you're still a child in ways. You're going to do some more dumb things before you're all grown. But I want you to try to remember that if you'll include me in the decisions you aren't sure about, maybe I can help. Yes, they are your decisions, and we may not always agree. In fact, I'm sure we will strongly disagree sometimes. But you don't have to do this all on your own, son."

We spent the next hour or so figuring out other things — not so serious, but as important to his future: how to approach the school counselors about getting back on track, how he intended to repay me for the damage he'd done to the shop door and my filing cabinet.

I hugged Bebe long and hard when she came home from her friend's house, and by the time I was ready to pay someone else a visit, it felt like things were at least a little normal again. Like we were going to make it.

■ ■ ■ ■

I asked Teague if he'd meet me at the shop. He jumped on it, sounded eager — as if he not only wanted to talk things over but maybe even had *missed* me. A man who'd missed me after all the messing up I'd done over the last week was maybe a man to hold on to.

He burst out of his car when I got there — he'd already parked and was waiting for me to arrive. He hurried to me and pulled me close in a hug that felt so, so good. Then he tilted my chin up and dropped a kiss on my lips.

It was a welcome-home kind of kiss. A kiss that said more than any kiss I'd had. It said *I like you. I am a patient man. I am willing to wait for you to work all this out.*

I smiled. I couldn't help myself.

"Let's talk." He pulled me toward the shop door. I braced myself before viewing the mess my son had made of the lock and door frame.

One of the first things I did was admit I was a smoker — trying to quit, but a smoker — just in case I'd managed to pull a fast one on him. He laughed, said he'd wondered when I was going to spill the beans.

511

He wasn't crazy about it, but he'd been a smoker, too, for years. He understood how hard quitting was, but he was willing to help me if I was willing to do the work. I'd hardly had time to miss it on the road with Miss Isabelle, but the first thing I'd done when I got in my own car was light up. Of course I had. Old habits were hard to break.

Later, after I'd reminded him of all the things and people I was responsible for in my life — my kids, my mother, and even Miss Isabelle — he'd recited his own laundry list. He reminded me he had three children who depended on him completely because their mother wasn't present most of the time, who would turn into teenagers soon enough, with their own unique problems and issues. He reminded me he had a job that took a lot of time and energy and caused him loads of worry on occasion. Like I did. Then he shared extra burdens I hadn't even known about.

"Wouldn't we make a fine pair, Dorrie? I'd say we're pretty evenly matched here. In fact, I'd be surprised if you wanted to take me on. I'm kind of a handful."

I laughed and swatted his arm.

"Are you ready to trust me?" he asked after he'd drawn me close again, sitting himself down on my hair chair, pulling me

512

onto his lap. In the past, I might have bristled, thinking he was treating me like a little girl instead of someone who could take care of herself just fine, thanks. But I understood some things about love now. I understood he was offering me a deal I couldn't pass up: a good man. One I was pretty sure I already loved, though we still had a ton of getting to know each other to do and a lot of history to build before we could call it a sure thing.

So, it seemed like a good idea to take Miss Isabelle's advice and see where it led my family and me. The answer to Teague's question came easy. I kissed him first this time.

43
DORRIE, PRESENT DAY

Monday morning, I was doing Miss Isabelle's hair, like always, as I had promised to do, even though I hadn't spoken it out loud when I left her. She knew.

It seemed different now, of course. More intimate than before. The shampoo and rinse I massaged into her hair made it gleam. While I waited for the curls and waves to set, I studied her face and marveled at her skin, so soft and unlined in spite of all her heartache and loss.

I let my mind drift. Perhaps I'd be so lucky. Maybe I'd faced most of my demons in my younger years and my remaining ones wouldn't age me quite so fast. Maybe I'd enjoy the rest of my life with people I loved — even if things didn't always turn out how I planned. Maybe the time Miss Isabelle and I had shared on the road had been my education in how to be a happier person.

"I think everything's going to be okay,

Miss Isabelle. My boy — I have a good feeling about him. I think this thing woke him up, scared a little sense into him. I have to believe he'll stick to the values I taught him now and use them to make something of himself. I really do believe that. Now, if only I can get Bebe through the dramatic years, I'll be all set."

I chuckled, trying to imagine my sweet little Bebe girl causing me any real heartache. It was hard to picture now, but I supposed at some point she'd give me a run for my money. I hoped it would be simple things — too much makeup or shorts too short. But I supposed she'd put a few cracks in my heart, too, before all was said and done.

"And Teague. Oh, Miss Isabelle. Sometimes I think he's too good to be true. I keep waiting for him to mess up, so I can say, 'See, I told you so, there's no such thing as a good man.' "

But he'd been there the day we got home from our journey, and the next day, too — Sunday, when I'd needed a real grown-up to accompany me to take care of one of the hardest things I'd ever done. Something I'd never expected to do so soon, but in the end, it didn't surprise me at all.

Miss Isabelle's lips curved in a gentle

smile. They reassured and encouraged me, telling me one more time that everything was going to be fine.

Her hair was dry now, and I gently combed the curls into the soft waves she preferred, framing her face like a silvery blue halo. She'd never been perfect — I knew that for sure now — but she was the closest thing to a guardian angel I'd ever have. My eyes misted as I thought of everything she'd come to mean to me. I hoped I'd been a blessing to her, too.

I used her favorite styling spray to keep everything neat and smooth, the way she liked it, then stepped back to study my handiwork. Pretty good, if I did say so myself. She looked good. She looked beautiful, as always. "What do you think, Miss Isabelle? Should I charge you extra this time? I did my best work today, you know. Yes, I do believe I've outdone myself here. All because . . ." I choked as I tried to say the last few words.

All because I loved her.

I remembered my thoughts from Saturday, when I'd debated whether to turn around for a hug or a kiss. This time, I didn't hold back. I stepped close to her again. I leaned down to reach her frail shoulders, then gathered her as close as I could to embrace her. She didn't seem surprised at all. Not at that, and not at the kisses I gingerly placed first on her forehead, then on both of her papery cheeks, which were scented lightly by the products I'd used to style her hair, as careful as I'd been to shield her face from them.

I ran a finger over her lips, then covered her hands, which were clasped carefully at her waist around her tiny silver thimble, with my own. I marveled at our differences again, at the contrast between our skin tones, like rich earth and sun-bleached sand.

So different. So much the same.

I heard a rustle at the doorway. I looked up to see Mr. Fisher, who waited there, patient, but with a question in his eyes.

"She's ready. As pretty as ever. Between us, we did good," I said.

The undertaker nodded and patted my arm. I stepped back.

She was with Robert now. And Pearl. And probably Max and Dane and everyone else who'd loved her but had gone on ahead.

I believe Miss Isabelle *was* ready. This time, she wore a celebration dress.

ACKNOWLEDGMENTS

I owe so many people a debt of gratitude, I hardly know where to begin. The order will seem wrong no matter how I do this.

I've been blessed with amazing literary agents. Elisabeth Weed, you were my first choice all along, and I still can't believe I'm lucky enough to have you on my team. Foreign rights agent Jenny Meyer is nothing short of magic. We'd all be lost without their assistants, Stephanie Sun and Shane King, who keep the important stuff signed and filed and sent. I believe film agent Jody Hotchkiss is as crazy about movies as I am, which is a good thing. Thank you all for falling in love with *Calling Me Home.*

Editors Hilary Rubin Teeman at St. Martin's Press and Jenny Geras at Pan Macmillan are full of wisdom and just the right amount of mercy. Because of your magnificent teamwork, *Calling Me Home* is deeper, wider, longer, and truer. Your enthusiasm, and that of the entire St. Martin's and Pan Macmillan teams, is a dream come true. To my foreign publishers and editors, I am thrilled and humbled and grateful to have so many readers around the world.

Kim Bullock, Pamela Hammonds, Elizabeth Lynd, Joan Mora, and Susan Poulos, what would I ever do without you? You have become more than my critique group and blog partners at What Women Write. You are my friends, my confidantes, and my writing compass. *Calling Me Home* would be a different book without you.

Others were instrumental in reading early versions and giving sage feedback or early endorsements: Carleen Brice, Diane Chamberlain, Gail Clark, Margaret Dilloway, Helen Dowdell, Heather Hood, Sarah Jio, Beverly McCaslin, Garry Oliver, Jerrie Oliver, Judy Oliver, Tom Oliver, and Emilie Pickop. Thank you all.

Here's to everyone at Book Pregnant, an invaluable cluster of debut authors, for helping me discern what to worry about and what to leave behind. I am honored to share the joys and trials of birthing books with all of you.

I'm continually amazed by the generosity of the multitude of other writers who have intersected my writing journey, including the folks at Backspace, The Seven Sisters, Barbara Samuel-O'Neal, Margie Lawson, and the Mount Hood retreaters, especially Therese Walsh, who introduced me not only to that group, but also to my agent.

I offer special thanks to a group of non-writer friends for encouragement and cheering along the way. May we one day find the eternally peaceful harbor for which we long, but in the meantime, as songwriter David Wilcox suggests, we'll let the wave say who we are. And speaking of David Wilcox, thanks for the wisdom of Rule Number One.

Without family, whether by blood, marriage, or honorary designation, none of this would be possible. My parents, siblings, and in-laws never doubted I would one day do this thing I love; it's how we live in this family. Gail and Jay Clark have loved and supported me longer than anyone I've known who is not blood related. I couldn't have survived without you, seriously. My children have taught me the meaning of true love from the moment they each came into my life. Heather, Ryan, Emilie, and Kristen, your hearts go with me wherever I go. And my husband, Todd, my best friend and true knight in shining armor, made it possible for me to rediscover and focus on my passions with his steady, unwavering support. How can I ever thank you for taking on, with gusto, this roller coaster of a ready-made family all those years ago?

Fannie Elizabeth Hayes, thank you for helping me conjure up Dorrie through more than a decade of sharing with me your courage, your compassion, and your corny sense of humor. May all your unique and biggest dreams come true.

To my grandmother, Velma Gertrude Brown Oliver, even though you are already wearing your celebration dress and might not hear me over the singing, thank you for the glimmer of a story that captured my heart and wouldn't let go. And thank you, Dad, for telling me.

Last, a note to my readers. Thank you for reading *Calling Me Home.* Any errors in historical facts or settings are mine alone. I hope you'll take this novel for what it is: a story I imagined about things that are true. If you live along the routes Dorrie and Isabelle travel, you know better than I do how far things have come and how far they still need to go. It's up to you to be the change.

ABOUT THE AUTHOR

Julie Kibler began writing *Calling Me Home* after learning a bit of family lore: as a young woman, her grandmother fell in love with a young black man in an era and locale that made the relationship impossible. When not writing, she enjoys travel, independent films, music, photography, and corralling her teenagers and rescue dogs. She lives in Arlington, Texas. *Calling Me Home* is her debut.

The employees of Thorndike Press hope you have enjoyed this Large Print book. All our Thorndike, Wheeler, and Kennebec Large Print titles are designed for easy reading, and all our books are made to last. Other Thorndike Press Large Print books are available at your library, through selected bookstores, or directly from us.

For information about titles, please call:
  (800) 223-1244

or visit our Web site at:
  http://gale.cengage.com/thorndike

To share your comments, please write:
Publisher
Thorndike Press
10 Water St., Suite 310
Waterville, ME 04901